WINTER WORLD

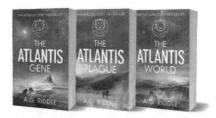

WINTER WORLD

THE LONG WINTER TRILOGY

BOOK ONE

A.G. RIDDLE

LEGION

LEGION

Published in North America by Legion Books.

Published in print in the UK and Commonwealth countries by Head of Zeus.

ISBN // 978-1-940026-21-3 // HARDCOVER
ISBN // 978-1-940026-22-0 // PAPERBACK
ISBN // 978-1-940026-20-6 // E-BOOK

FIRST EDITION (1.7.4)

Discover other great authors and their books at:
LegionBooks.com

For my mother, who departed this world far too soon, but left it better than she found it.

WINTER WORLD

CHAPTER 1

EMMA

For the past five months, I have watched the world die.

Glaciers have advanced across Canada, Russia, and Scandinavia, trampling everything in their path. They show no signs of stopping. The data says they won't.

Within three months, ice will cover the Earth, and life as we know it will end.

My job is to find out why.

And to stop it.

❄

The alarm wakes me. I struggle out of my sleeping bag and pull open the privacy door to my sleeping station.

I haven't slept well since coming to the International Space Station. Especially not since the Winter Experiments began. I toss and turn every night, wondering what the probes will find and if the data will reveal a way to save us.

I drift out into the Harmony module and tap the panel on the wall, trying to identify the source of the blaring alarm. The solar array's radiators are overheating. I watch as the temperature climbs. *Why?* I have to stop it—

Sergei's voice crackles in my earpiece, his Russian accent thick. "'Is the solar array, Commander."

I look into the camera above me. "Explain."

Silence.

"Sergei, answer me. Is it debris? Why are we getting heat buildup?"

There are a million ways to die on the ISS. Losing the solar array is a sure one. And there are a lot of ways to lose the array. It operates similarly to photovoltaic solar cells on Earth: solar radiation is converted to direct current electricity. The process generates a lot of excess heat. That heat is dissipated via radiators that face away from the sunlight, into the dark of space. If those radiators are overheating, the heat has nowhere to go but inside the station. That's bad for life here.

We need to figure this out, and quickly.

Sergei sounds distracted, maybe annoyed. "'Is not debris, Commander. I explain when I know. Please get sleep."

The door to the sleep station next to me slides open. Dr. Andrew Bergin stares out with puffy, sleepy eyes.

"Hey, Emma. What's up?"

"Solar array."

"We okay?"

"Not sure yet."

"Sergei, what do you think it is?"

"I *think* it is solar output. Too high," Sergei says over the comm.

"A solar flare?"

"Yes. Has to be. Is not isolated radiator malfunction—they all overheated."

"Shut down the array. Go to battery power."

"Commander..."

"Do it, Sergei. Right now."

The panel shows the eight solar array wings and their thirty-three thousand solar cells. I watch as they go offline. The temperature readings in the radiators begin ticking down.

We can run on battery power for a while. We do it fifteen times each day when the solar array is in the darkness of Earth's shadow.

Bergin asks the question on my mind. "Any data from the probes yet?"

I'm already checking.

A month ago, an international consortium sent probes into space to measure solar radiation and look for any anomalies. The probes are part of the Winter Experiments—the largest scientific endeavor ever undertaken. The experiments' sole goal is to understand why the Earth is cooling. We know that solar output is falling—but it shouldn't be.

Data from the probes will reach the ISS first. But there's nothing yet. That data could be what saves humanity. Or simply tells us how much time we have left.

I should go back to sleep. But once I'm up, I'm up.

And I can't wait to see the first data from the probes. I have family back on Earth. I want to know what's going to happen to them. And there's an unspoken question among the six astronauts and cosmonauts on the ISS: what becomes of us? If the world is dying—if there's no world to go back to—will they leave us up here? Three of us are due to return home in a month, the other three in four months. But will our nations expend the resources to bring us home? They're already dealing with a refugee crisis of unprecedented proportions.

Around the world, governments are struggling to evacuate billions of their citizens to the world's last habitable zones. And facing a hard decision: what to do with those they can't evacuate. How much will they invest to bring six people home from space?

Getting home isn't a walk in the park. The ISS doesn't have escape pods *per se*, we have two Soyuz capsules that brought us here. Each holds a maximum of three passengers. We could use them to evacuate the station, but we'd need coordination from the ground, and someone to pick us up when we land.

Once we return, we'll need even more help. Rehab, for example. In space, our bones lose density. It's the lack of gravity. The load-bearing bones lose the most density—the pelvis, spine, and legs. The bones literally disintegrate, similar to osteoporosis. The calcium that leaches into the body causes kidney stones— and space is not a place you want to have kidney stones. Some of the first astronauts who visited the ISS lost as much as two percent of their bone density per month. We've got that figure down, thanks to exercise. But I'll still have to go through rehab when I get back. I won't know what shape I'm in until my feet hit solid ground (or ice, depending).

The truth is this: our use to the people on the surface lies in the Winter Experiments. If we don't figure out what's causing the Long Winter—and how to stop it—we'll never leave this station. We are trapped between the cold dark of space and a freezing planet below. For now, this is home. Probably will be for a while.

It's a good home. The best I've ever had.

I bounce through the collection of modules that make up the ISS, using my hands and feet to propel me. The station is like a series of oversized pipes screwed together, branching at right angles, most holding labs, some simply connectors.

The Unity node was the first US-built element of the ISS, launched in 1998. It has six berthing connections, sort of like tunnel openings in a sewer system.

I pass into the Tranquility node, which houses life-support equipment, the water recycler, oxygen generators, and a toilet that's about as hard to use as one might expect for a space commode (also, the ISS was designed by and for male astronauts, so there's that).

I drift through Tranquility, into the European Space Agency's observation module. It has a cupola with seven thirty-inch-wide windows that provide a panoramic view of space and the Earth. I hang there for a long moment, watching.

The ISS orbits roughly two hundred and fifty miles above the Earth, flying through space at over seventeen thousand miles per hour. The station circles the planet 15.54 times each day, which means we see either the sunrise or sunset every forty-five minutes.

The station crosses the terminator, revealing the part of the planet bathed in daylight—North and South America.

The ice has extended into the Great Lakes, like bone-white fingers dipping in the blue water. The glaciers will cross the water soon and continue south. Michigan, Wisconsin, Minnesota, and parts of New York have already been evacuated.

The US has done the math. They know what the last habitable zones on Earth will be. Hint: they're below sea level. A massive camp has been set up in Death Valley, California. Trade agreements have been established in Libya and Tunisia. But everyone knows the agreements won't hold. Not when survival is the order of the day.

The world will try to stuff eight billion people through a funnel in which only a small portion can survive.

It will be war.

❄

ON THE TREADMILL, I call up a station status report. Sergei still doesn't have the solar array back online. I want to check in with him, but I've learned that he works best when given space.

That's one thing about six people living in very close quarters: you learn each other's boundaries.

I check for data from the probes again (nothing yet) and begin reading emails.

The first is from my sister.

I never married or had children of my own, but my sister did. And I treasure those kids. In my eyes, they are the sweetest two humans alive.

The email is a video, no subject or content, just my sister, Madison, speaking into the camera as I trot on the treadmill I'm tethered to.

"Hi, Em. I know the video needs to be short, but I have a lot to say. David has heard some rumors. They're saying that... a lot of things are going to change. That there's an experiment going on that will tell us why the Long Winter is occurring. People around here are selling their houses for pennies on the dollar and moving to Libya and Tunisia. It's crazy. They're sending troops—"

The video cuts out for a minute or so. Censored. I keep trotting on the treadmill, watching the screen. My sister's face reappears. She's still sitting on the couch, but her two children are crowded around her now. Owen and Adeline.

"Hi, Aunt Em!" Owen yells. "Watch this!"

He goes off screen, then the camera pans and I see him dunk a basketball in an indoor hoop that looks about five feet off the ground.

"Did you get it?" he asks his mom.

"I got it."

"I'm going again in case you didn't."

I smile as my sister turns the camera back to her. "Are they bringing you home? And if so... what's the plan? I know you can't drive for a while after you return and you'll have to do

rehab. You can come live with us, of course, if NASA isn't going
—if NASA isn't able to help you get back on your feet.

"Write me back soon, okay? Love you." Madison turns to her
two children, who are now arguing in the background. "Tell your
Aunt Emma bye."

Owen pops his head over the couch and waves. "Bye."

Adeline plops down next to her mother and leans closer to
her, seeming bashful of the camera. "Bye, Aunt Emma. Love
you."

I'm typing an email response when a dialog appears:

```
Incoming Data: Probe 127
```

I immediately open it and scan the readings of the solar radiation. I'm shocked. They're far higher than the readings on Earth, but
that makes no sense—the probe is at roughly the same distance from
the Sun. Unless the probe was hit with a flare? No, it's not that: the
readings are consistent over time. Maybe it's a local phenomenon.

I open the video telemetry from the probe, and my heart
practically stops. There's an object. Something out there. A
black speck in front of the Sun. It's not an asteroid; asteroids are
jagged and rocky. This object is smooth and oblong. Whatever
I'm looking at, someone built it.

We are in constant contact with the ground—with agencies
in the US, Russia, Europe, China, India, and Japan. I activate
the link to speak directly with the Goddard Network Integration
Center in Maryland.

"Goddard, ISS. We're getting our first data from the probes.
Relay in progress. Note: one twenty-seven found something." I
grasp for the right words. "Preliminary telemetry is of an oblong
object. Smooth. Does not appear to be an asteroid or comet.
Repeat: appears to be a non-natural object constructed by—"

The tablet goes dark. The treadmill stops. The station shudders. Lights flicker.

I tap my internal comm.

"Sergei—"

"Power overload, Commander."

That doesn't add up. The solar array is offline. We're on battery power.

The station shudders again.

My instincts kick in.

"Everybody out of your bunks, right now! Get to the Soyuz capsules! Station evac procedures!"

The station jolts, throwing me into the wall. My head spins. My body reacts instinctively, and my arms propel me up, into the cupola. Through the windows, I see the International Space Station breaking into pieces.

CHAPTER 2

JAMES

THE RIOTS WILL START SOON.

I can feel the tension in the air.

Everywhere I go, eyes linger too long, notes are passed, secrets are whispered.

The world is freezing. The ice is coming for us, and we are all trapped here. If we don't get out, we'll die here.

That's what's brewing: a plan to get out. That's the good news. The bad news, frankly, is that I'm not part of the plan. No one has told me anything. I doubt they will.

There's not much I can do about it. So I do my job and keep my head down and watch the news.

A segment from CNN is playing on the beat-up TV. The reporter's voice is barely audible over the rumble of the machines behind me.

Snow fell in Miami for the third day in a row, breaking records and prompting the Florida government to seek federal aid.

The request sparked protests from citizens and governments across the Northeast, who have ratcheted up pressure on the federal government to increase the pace of evacuations. As the Long Winter drags on...

I don't know who coined the term Long Winter. Maybe the media. Or government. Either way, it has stuck. People like it better than glaciation (too technical) or Ice Age (too permanent). Long Winter sounds as if the end is just around the corner—that it's just another season, this one abnormally long. I hope that's the case. I'm sure NOAA and its sister agencies around the world know the truth by now. If so, they haven't told us (hence the highest news ratings this century).

An alarm buzzes.

I ignore it.

The next news segment starts. I stop working long enough to take in the setting.

Text below the scene identifies the location as the Port of Rosyth outside Edinburgh, Scotland. A male reporter with short gray hair stands on a dock, in the shadow of an enormous white cruise ship. The gangway is extended, a steady stream of people shuffling toward the ship. The trees in the distance are completely white, as if they're frozen solid. Snow falls in sheets.

The scene behind me might look like vacationers setting off for a holiday cruise, but nothing could be further from the truth. The cruise ship you're seeing was known as the Emerald Princess *until three weeks ago, when she was purchased by His Majesty's government and renamed the* Summer Sun. *It's one of a fleet of forty such cruise ships that will temporarily evacuate residents of the UK to warmer latitudes.*

The Summer Sun *is set to sail to Tunisia, where passengers will be transported to a relocation camp outside Kebili. The camp is part of a long-term lease agreement between the UK and Tunisia. The move follows similar actions in Norway, Sweden, Finland, Russia, and Japan. The program is reminiscent of the mass evacuation in the UK during the Second World War, when*

Operation Pied Piper evacuated 3.5 million civilians out of the way of the Nazi threat...

Real estate near the equator has become a hot commodity. So have several places deemed "winter havens"—places below sea level with unusually high temperatures: Death Valley in California; Al Aziziyah, Libya; Wadi Halfa, Sudan; Dasht-e Lut, Iran; Kebili, Tunisia. Two years ago, if you visited one of these places and left a barrel of gasoline open when the sun came up, it would be empty by noon. Evaporated. These used to be wastelands. Now they're beacons of hope, oases in the Long Winter. People are pouring in by the millions, selling whatever they have to in order to buy a berth in the camps. I wonder if they'll be safe there.

Another buzzer goes off. The same tone, different machine. Still not the alarm I'm waiting for.

When the third buzzer sounds, I collect the sheets from the three dryers and start folding them.

My job is laundry. It has been for the last two years, ever since I arrived at Edgefield Federal Correctional Institution. Like the other two thousand inmates imprisoned here, I claim my innocence. Unlike most of my fellow inmates, I *am* innocent.

If I'm guilty of any crime, it's inventing something the world wasn't ready for. An innovation that terrified them. My mistake —or crime, if you will—was not accounting for human nature. Humans are scared of what they don't know, and they're especially scared of new things that might change life as they know it.

The US attorney assigned to my case found an obscure law and made an example out of me. The message to other inventors was clear: we don't want this.

I was sentenced at age thirty-one. I'll be seventy when I get out of here. (There is no parole for federal crimes. If I behave, I'll be released after serving eighty-five percent of my sentence.)

When I arrived at Edgefield, I devised six ways of escape.

Further investigation revealed that only three were viable. Two had an extremely high rate of success. The problem became: then what? My assets were seized after the trial. Contacting my friends and family would put them in jeopardy. And the world would hunt me, probably kill me if they caught me.

So I stayed. And did the laundry. And I've tried to make a difference here. It's in my nature, and I've learned the hard way: human nature is perhaps the only thing we can't escape.

❄

EVERY DAY, fewer guards show up for work.

That worries me.

I know why: the staff and guards are moving south, to the habitable zones. I don't know if the federal government is moving them, or if they're going on their own initiative.

A war is coming—a war for the last habitable zones on Earth. People with military and police backgrounds will be in high demand. So will correctional officers. The camps will likely resemble prisons. The government will need men and women trained in keeping order in large, confined populations. The population's survival depends on it.

And therein lies my problem. Edgefield, South Carolina, is about halfway between Atlanta and Charleston. It's snowing here (in August), but the glaciers haven't reached us. The ice will be here soon, and they'll evacuate the area. The evacuations won't include prisoners. The truth is, the government will be hard pressed to save all the children in this country, much less the adults, and they certainly won't be dragging prisoners with them (and definitely not across the Atlantic to the habitable zones in northern Africa). Their priority will be making sure prisoners don't escape to follow them south and make even more trouble for an already strained government. They'll lock us up tight in here. Or worse.

Accordingly, I've revived my escape plans. It seems all of my fellow inmates have too. The feeling here is like sitting down for a July Fourth fireworks show. We're all waiting for the first explosion to go up. It'll likely be fast and furious after that, and I doubt any of us will survive.

I need to hurry.

The door to the laundry room swings open, and a correctional officer strides in.

"Morning, Doc."

I don't look up from the sheets. "Morning."

Pedro Alvarez is one of the best correctional officers in this place, in my opinion. He's young, honest, and doesn't play games.

In one sense, prison has been good for me. It has been a uniquely valuable place to study human nature—which, again, was my blind spot, and the real reason I wound up in here.

I have come to believe that most correctional officers go into this line of work for one reason: power. They want to have power over others. I believe the common cause is that someone, at some point, had power over them. Therein lies a seminal truth about human nature: we desire in adulthood what we were deprived in childhood.

Pedro is an anomaly in the pattern. That drew me to him. I pursued a friendship and have extracted data points that revealed a different motivation. I know the following about him. His family—parents, brothers, and sisters—are still in Mexico. He has a wife, also aged approximately twenty-seven, and two children, both sons, five and three. And finally, I know that his wife is the sole reason he's working here.

Pedro grew up in Michoacán, a mountainous, lawless state in Mexico where the drug cartels are judge and jury and murders are more common than traffic accidents. Pedro moved here when his wife was pregnant, because he didn't want his children to grow up the way he had.

He began working for a landscaping crew during the day, and at night and on the weekends he studied criminal justice at Spartanburg Community College. On graduation day, he told his wife that he was joining the Spartanburg County Sheriff's Department—because he didn't want to see this place become what Michoacán had. There is law and order here, and he wanted to keep it that way, for his children's sake.

Another truth: parents desire for their children the things they never had.

After Pedro's announcement, his wife got on the internet, looked up the fatality rates for police officers, and issued an ultimatum: find another profession or find another wife.

They compromised. Pedro became a corrections officer, which carried fatality stats and working hours that were acceptable to Maria Alvarez. Plus better benefits, overtime pay, pay plus twenty-five percent on Sunday, and access to the government's hazardous duty law enforcement provision that would allow him to retire with full benefits after twenty-five years of service—right before his forty-ninth birthday. It was a good choice. At least, before the Long Winter started.

I had expected Pedro to be one of the first officers to leave this place. I figured he would head back to Mexico, where his family is, and where the habitable zones are being set up. That's where the Canadian and American hordes will be going soon.

But instead, he's one of the last ones here. The scientist in me wants to know why. The survivor in me *needs* to know why.

"You draw the short straw, Pedro?"

He cocks an eyebrow at me.

Pedro is about the closest thing I have to a friend in here, and I can't help but say these next words.

"You shouldn't be here. You, and Maria, and the kids should be heading south right now."

He studies his boots. "I know, Doc."

"So why are you still here?"

"Not enough seniority. Or maybe not enough friends. Or maybe both."

He's right: it is both. And probably because his supervisors know that he will actually fight when the riots start. In the world we live in, the best people carry the weight for others—and they get crushed first.

Pedro shrugs. "It's above my pay grade."

An inmate appears in the doorway and scans the room, his eyes wide, unblinking. Drugged. There's something in his hand. His name is Marcel, and he's generally bad news.

Pedro turns.

Marcel leaps for him, wraps a meaty arm around the guard's midsection, traps his arms, and raises a homemade knife to Pedro's neck.

Time seems to stand still. I'm vaguely aware of the hum of the washers and dryers, of the news blaring on. A new sensation begins, a rumbling in the distance, like thunder moving closer. Footsteps. A mob flowing through the prison's corridors. Shouting overpowers the footsteps, but I can't make out the words.

Pedro is struggling against Marcel's hold.

Another inmate appears in the doorway. He's barrel-chested, keyed up. I don't know his name. He shouts to Marcel. "You got 'im, Cel?"

"I got him."

The other inmate darts away, and Marcel looks at me. "They gonna let us freeze to death in here, Doc. You know it."

He waits.

I say nothing.

Pedro grits his teeth as he tries to pull his right hand free. "You with us, Doc?"

Pedro's hand breaks from Marcel's hold and flies to his side, into his pocket. I've never seen him use a weapon. I'm not sure he has one.

Marcel doesn't wait to find out. He moves the knife closer to Pedro's neck.

And I make my choice.

CHAPTER 3

EMMA

FLOATING in the cupola attached to the Tranquility node, I watch the International Space Station twist and buckle like a Midwestern farmhouse in a tornado.

The solar array disintegrates, the cells flying away, shingles from a roof. It's only a matter of time before the station is opened to the vacuum of space.

In the sea of destruction, I see hope: the Soyuz capsules docked to the station. I'll never make it there. Neither will Sergei or Stephen. Besides, each Soyuz holds only three people.

"Pearson, Bergin, Perez—get to the Soyuz docked to Rassvet. Right now. That's an order."

We've trained for this. The Soyuz can be separated from the ISS within three minutes, and on the ground in Kazakhstan within four hours.

My earpiece crackles with a voice I can't make out. Internal comms are fried. Did they hear me? I hope so.

I have to tell the ground.

"Goddard, we are evacuating—"

The wall crashes into me and bounces me against the opposite wall. Darkness tries to swallow me.

I push off and glide through Tranquility. Unconsciousness pulls at me, but I push past it, a swimmer in an undertow fighting not to drown.

I'm trapped on the station, and it's probably only a matter of seconds before it blows open and everything is sucked out. I have one chance at survival: an EVA suit.

I grab the closest suit, slip inside, and tether it. That will give me oxygen, electricity, comms—if they even still work.

"Goddard, do you read?"

"We read you, Commander Matthews. State your status."

Before I can respond, the module around me explodes. Darkness finally drags me under.

❄

CONSCIOUSNESS COMES IN WAVES. Sensations come with it, like an onion peeling, nothing at first, then intensity: pain, nausea, and utter silence.

I'm still tethered to the station. The module below me is split open. I see the Earth below. A block of ice covers Siberia, bearing down on China, the contrast of white and the green forests beautiful, if not for the destruction and death it represents.

Segments of the station float free like Legos tossed into space.

I don't see either of the Soyuz capsules.

On the comm, I call out for the rest of my crew.

No response.

Then the ground stations.

No response.

I try to estimate whether the Earth is getting larger or smaller.

If larger, I'm in a decaying orbit. I'll burn up.

If smaller, I've broken free of Earth's gravity. I'll float into space. Suffocate when my oxygen runs out. Or, if the station provides oxygen long enough, starve.

CHAPTER 4

JAMES

I LUNGE and grab Marcel's arm. My weight isn't enough to bring the massive man down, but it's enough to get the knife away from Pedro's neck.

The guard twists out of Marcel's grip, pulls something out of his pocket, and jabs it into Marcel's side.

I feel an electric jolt go through me. Marcel convulses. The knife falls to the linoleum floor, and Marcel and I follow, two sacks of potatoes dropping.

I'm pretty sure it's illegal for Pedro to have an electric stun gun in here. But I'm glad he does.

I roll away from Marcel's arm, and the electric current ceases. I'm woozy. My limbs feel like dead weight.

The large man flails like a fish on the dock until the electric tat-tat-tat stops.

Pedro reaches for the knife. To my surprise, Marcel's hand reaches up and grips Pedro's arm, but he's too weak to hold him back. Marcel lashes out with his other hand instead, punching the smaller man in the ribs. Pedro cries out.

I crawl over on shaking limbs and smother Marcel's arm as

he's reaching back for another punch.

I hear shouting outside the door. A group is coming toward us, calling Marcel's name.

Pedro has the knife now, and suddenly there's a river of blood spurting down Marcel's body, engulfing his chest and arm and me with it. I swear I can feel him getting colder.

Marcel gurgles, and his eyes turn to glass.

Pedro rolls off of him, grabs his radio, and brings it to his mouth.

I raise a bloody, shaking hand. "Don't, Pedro."

He pauses.

Between pants, I manage to say, "Outnumbered. Guards. To inmates. Hundred to one."

That gives Pedro pause. Finally, he shakes his head.

"I have to go, Doc. This is my job."

"Listen to me. When he came in here, he didn't instantly slit your throat. Why?"

Pedro squints, thinking.

I answer for him.

"He wanted you as a hostage. A bargaining chip—in case their plan fails. A human shield. If you go out there, they're going to capture you. Use you against your people. Put you on the web, tied up, maybe beaten, for the world to see, for your kids to see."

Pedro glances at the laundry room door. It's the only way out of this room.

The shouting is growing louder. We have a minute, maybe less.

"There's no way out, Doc. Just stay here."

He rises, and I grab his arm with my bloody hand. "There is another way out."

"What—"

"No time to explain, Pedro. Do you trust me?"

❄

WHEN THE PRISONERS ARRIVE, I'm lying on the floor next to Marcel, twitching.

There are six of them, carrying improvised clubs and knives. One has a radio.

"We found Marcel. He's dead."

They surround me. I sit up with effort, still twitching. The charade isn't hard to pull off. I'm still weak.

"Who was it?" their leader shouts.

"Didn't... see him."

A bald guy about my age with tats up and down his arms raises a blade to my Adam's apple.

I feign terror—also not a stretch.

"He came in... behind Marcel. Shocked him and pushed him into me. I blacked out."

Gunfire sounds over the radio. The leader turns and barks questions, pacing the laundry room.

"I can't... walk," I whisper. "I need you to carry me out—"

The blade is withdrawn from my neck, and they push me back to the floor and storm out.

When I'm sure they're gone, I strip off my bloody clothes and stuff them in a laundry bag. I crawl to the middle dryer and whisper, "They're gone."

The sheet pulls back and I see Pedro's eyes. Scared, but grateful.

"Stay until I come get you."

Luckily for him, Pedro isn't a large man. Still, he'll be sore when he gets out.

I'm a little taller than he is, five-ten. It'll be a tight fit, but I don't have a choice. I can barely walk. Definitely can't run or fight. I'm in no shape to escape or battle my way out of here, if it comes to that.

I turn the volume up on the TV to cover any sounds Pedro and I might make. I hear a noise from his machine and realize he's turned his radio on to check the situation.

"Pedro," I whisper, "you've got to keep the radio off. Sound equals death, my friend."

With that, I stuff myself into a large commercial dryer, cover the glass door with bunk sheets, and wait.

❄

IT FEELS as if I've been in here for hours.

I listen to the news, straining my ears for any clues about what's happening out there.

Every story on the TV seems to be about the Long Winter and how one family is surviving it.

I try not to move, but my body is aching—both from being crammed in here in the fetal position and from the electrocution earlier.

A breaking news story begins. The words "prison riot" and "National Guard" catch my attention. I pull the sheet back just enough to see an image of helicopters landing outside the prison. They can't be more than two hundred yards from where I am now.

The reporter's words echo what I've suspected since this began. "With the Long Winter draining federal and local law enforcement resources, the rules of engagement for prison riots has clearly changed."

I'm so engrossed I don't hear the footsteps until the inmate strides through the open doorway, followed by two others. They're looking for us. For Pedro, to use as a bargaining chip. As for me, when they figure out what I did, they'll want revenge. Revenge is big in prison. And there may be no one to stop them.

CHAPTER 5

EMMA

I'VE LOST all sense of time. It could have been hours. Maybe a day. Two, even.

I'm sure of one thing: I have decompression sickness. Not bad enough to kill me, but bad enough that I feel it every second. I'd really like to vomit right now, but it's not a good time for that.

The science of decompression sickness goes like this. The ISS and space shuttle are pressurized to 14.7 psi—the same atmospheric pressure you'd feel on Earth at sea level. The EVA suits are pressurized to 4.3 psi—the same atmospheric pressure as on the summit of Mount Everest. So in a matter of seconds, I was blasted from sea level to the summit of Everest. Why is that bad? A rapid decrease in pressure causes nitrogen in the body, which is usually dissolved in blood and tissues, to break out and form bubbles. It's like opening a can of soda. The contents of the can are at high pressure. When it's opened, the contents are exposed to dramatically lower pressure. The result? Fizzy bubbles. Carbon dioxide released from the liquid. That's what's happened to me: fizzy bubbles of nitrogen are racing around my body. I'm like a human can of soda that was at high pressure and has just been opened and is bubbling away.

Scuba divers have known about decompression sickness for a long time and take steps to avoid it. So does the ISS: we have a protocol we follow before EVAs to prevent decompression sickness. But there wasn't time. In this case, it was decompression sickness or death.

And at the moment, I feel bad enough to second-guess my choice.

I hurt all over. I feel exhausted, but I don't dare fall asleep. I'm scared I'll never wake up.

I cling to life, every second of it. I realize now just how much I want to live. That's what ultimately matters in a survival situation: the will to live.

Except there's not much for me to do with that will to live right now. I just watch the debris from the station, searching for clues that there are any other survivors—or any move for me to make.

Every now and then a piece of the station falls into the atmosphere and burns up. They're like glowing pieces of sand falling through an hourglass, counting down to my doom.

I'm in a decaying orbit. It's only a matter of time before I, along with the piece of the station I'm tethered to, fall into the atmosphere and burn up as well.

There's another brilliant flash of light. I assume it's more debris burning up. But this light gets brighter, not darker. Something is coming up.

A rocket. Barreling toward me.

A capsule disconnects, and its thrusters fire.

It's coming toward me.

For me.

I watch in wonder. Tears stream down my face. I'm going to be rescued.

CHAPTER 6

JAMES

THE WONDERFUL THING about being in a federal prison is that you get, generally speaking, a little better breed of criminal. Not your common robbers and murderers, who are serving their time in state pens. The denizens of Edgefield and other federal correctional institutions are criminal masterminds. Or at least, criminals ambitious enough to perpetrate crimes that cross state lines or violate a federal statute.

The downside is that they're likely smart enough to find Pedro and me. My suspicion is confirmed when I hear the dryer at the end of the row swing open. Then the next.

I hear automatic gunfire in the distance. The National Guard has breached. The timing makes sense. They were en route minutes ago. There was no negotiation. They came right in, trying to seize the element of surprise.

The door to my dryer swings open, and a meaty hand swats the sheet away. The man draws back at the sight of me, points a gun in my face, and yells, "Get out!"

I show my hands and carefully move to the round opening. My body hurts all over.

The cadence of gunfire grows louder. It sounds like World War Three out there.

"Shut that door," the gunman shouts to another inmate. "Get the table in front of it."

I'm about halfway out of the dryer now. I'd like to get back in. I know what's coming. Man, these guys are dumb. (I would like to withdraw my previous generalization about the average intelligence of federal inmates.)

"I said, get out!"

As much as I'd like to stay, the gun really sells it.

I stagger out on unsteady legs, like a fawn taking its first steps.

They find Pedro a second later. He comes out too, except he stands proud and sticks out his chest. I like him more and more. I really hope we don't die here, in the laundry room.

They pat him down and take his radio and the little electric gizmo he used on Marcel.

I slouch against the dryer. Standing hurts.

What I don't hear—gunfire—tells a story. Whatever war was raging out there is over.

A radio crackles to life—one the prisoners must have taken off another guard.

"To the individuals in the laundry. It's over. Come out with your hands up. We don't want any further loss of life."

The leader of the group of rioters is not what I expected. He's not muscle-bound or tatted up. He's a middle-aged white guy with a receding hairline and a day's growth of stubble. The kind of guy you might see on CNBC telling you why you should buy his company's stock in spite of a recent earnings report with some very concerning data points. That's probably what landed him in here.

He paces the room, scanning it, seeing what I already know: no other doors, no windows, no way out. Only a couple of small vents in the ceiling. And unlike what one sees in the movies, these are not big enough for inmates to crawl through.

The rioter's voice is smooth and unbothered when he replies over the radio.

"We also don't want any further loss of life. We just want a chance to survive. In case you haven't noticed, winter is coming. We don't want out. We just want to be left alone. There aren't many of us left. Enough to farm the prison land and provide for ourselves—that's about all. And all we're asking is that you seal us in this prison. Lock the doors and throw away the key. Use AI drones to kill anybody who breaches the perimeter. We don't want out. We just want to survive."

This guy must be the leader of the entire riot. And he's pretty smart. That's probably bad for my life expectancy.

He eyes Pedro. "We have one of your guards." He holds the radio out toward Pedro. "Tell them your name."

Pedro spits on the radio.

An inmate with blood on his chest and a club in his hand rears back.

"Pedro, do what he says!" I yell. The other inmates stop and eye us both. "Tell them. They'll get it out of you. This is all going to be okay."

The leader cocks his head and stares at me. He doesn't take his eyes off me as he speaks. "Yeah, that's right, Pedro. It's all going to be okay. Go ahead."

I nod at Pedro. Through gritted teeth, he says his name and position.

The leader continues when he's done. "If you withdraw your troops from the prison and meet our demands, we'll return Pedro Alvarez safe and sound. He'll walk right out of here, and we'll all live happily ever after."

The guardsman responds. "We'll evacuate the prison, but I

can't authorize the rest of what you're asking for. I'll have to ask.
Give us some time."

"Well, we're not going anywhere. And neither is Pedro if
those demands aren't met."

The riot leader releases the radio button and studies me.
"Who are you?"

"The guy who does the laundry."

"And hides in the laundry."

"When called for."

He breaks into a smile, but his associates are not amused.

One holds an improvised knife toward me. "He's a snitch,
Carl. I say we gut him right now."

Technically, I haven't snitched, only aided our imprisoners,
who, frankly, I consider to have the moral high ground here, at
least in the case of Pedro Alvarez. Now isn't the time to split
hairs though.

The leader—Carl—seems to agree.

"Finey, you can gut him or do whatever you want with him
—*after* this is over."

CHAPTER 7

EMMA

THERE ARE things that stick in my mind. The Christmas morning when I was six, when a brand-new bicycle with training wheels stood by the tree. The day Adeline was born. And Owen. And the day I boarded the Soyuz capsule atop a rocket that would carry me into space.

Space was always my dream. At some point, it also became the reason I had delayed so many things in my life. Marriage. Children. Settling down.

Now it has turned into a nightmare.

But the sight of the capsule rushing toward me right now is one of the moments I'll remember forever. I'm overflowing with joy. Someone down there sent it—for me. To save me. In a world fighting for survival, they launched a capsule into space to save one life.

That says something about the human race.

The capsule unfurls its small solar array, like a bird extending black wings. It maneuvers with thrusters, puffs of white air blossoming from its sides as it slows and moves closer. I recognize the logo on the side. It's a private space contractor.

This capsule would have been launched in three weeks, to bring a new three-person crew to replace half the crew on the station, including me. They launched it early.

I know the specs, studied them at length. It's a dual-purpose crew and cargo capsule with room for seven of us. And tons of supplies. From top to bottom, it has a nose cone (now gone), a pressurized section for crew, a service section (unpressurized), a heat shield for reentry, and on the bottom, an unpressurized cargo hold that detaches before reentry. That's all great, except for one problem: I don't have a working docking port or berthing mechanism.

The capsule turns its nose toward me, as if it had read my thoughts. The capsule's berthing mechanism opens. I expect the atmosphere inside to rush out, blowing the capsule backward. But the puff of air that escapes is a gentle push. They depressurized the crew cabin before launch. Smart.

The open mouth of the capsule seems to stare at me, the black of space behind it, as we both orbit the Earth. The ISS was flying at over seventeen thousand miles per hour. We're likely doing less now. The capsule is matching the velocity of my decaying orbit, but it has to use its thrusters to stay in place, and even that's a losing battle, like a hummingbird trying to be utterly still. It's impossible.

What's their plan? I'm expecting something to extend from the capsule that I can grab on to and pull myself in. A tether. A rope. I'd accept a licorice stick at this point. Anything to get me inside.

But nothing comes.

The capsule stares at me, waiting. The cargo lights begin blinking. I realize it's Morse code about halfway through. (Thanks to the decompression sickness, I'm not firing on all cylinders here.)

The message begins again.

Dot dash dash dash.

J.

Dot.

I missed the second letter.

Focus.

The third letter: Dash dash.

Or dash dot.

It's an N or an M.

The next letter: Dot dash dash dot.

P.

J, something, N or M, then P.

Oh. No. Please tell me it's not—

The sequence starts again.

Yep. They're saying JUMP.

CHAPTER 8

JAMES

HERE'S what I expect to happen next: tear gas through the vent, National Guard troops through the door, shootout, and then either death or more prison for me.

I'm wrong on all counts.

The inmates left in the prison rally to the laundry, seventeen in all. They probably figure their only leverage—Pedro—is here, and this single room, with only one entrance, is easier to defend than the entire prison.

The radio in Carl's hand crackles, and the National Guard commander's voice fills the now-cramped laundry room.

"To the man in charge inside Edgefield Prison, you've got a deal. We'll do the trade."

Cheers break out. A few high-fives. A not-so-friendly glare my way.

Pedro struggles—they've tied his hands behind his back with duct tape. "I'm not going."

Carl smiles at him. "Oh, you're going. In case you haven't noticed, we negotiate with pigs *outside* the prison. Not inside." He nods to one of his associates. "Gag him."

In goes a wadded-up pillowcase, secured with more duct tape.

Carl presses the radio button. "That's great news!" he says with mock enthusiasm. "Now let's talk turkey. We need some assurances that our little free state of Edgefield won't be invaded. And by assurances, I mean guns. And bombs. And a neutral zone outside our fences. Say, a hundred yards."

"Guns are off the table."

"Then so is our deal. No guns, no Pedro Alvarez. Alive, anyway."

A long pause. Then, "Stand by."

The wait feels like an hour before the response comes. "Okay, you'll get your guns."

"Good. And we don't want any old worn-out pea-shooters. I'm talking semi-automatics with plenty of ammo. One for each of my," he pauses to do a head count, "seventeen men. And we want any prisoners you took during your act of aggression toward us. Guns for them too." Another beat. He's getting wound up now. "And throw in a spare rifle for everybody. Two hand grenades each. And seven RPGs."

Grudgingly, the National Guard negotiator agrees. Over the course of a few hours, the inmates venture out into the prison to check it for hiding guards and ambushes and booby traps. When they're satisfied that the prison is empty, we exit the laundry, with Pedro and me doing a perp walk in the middle of the procession.

In the yard, troops are stationed behind a barricade and troop carriers. The other prisoners are behind them. In front of the barricade, a half dozen crates sit waiting.

Carl calls out, "Gun demonstration!"

A National Guardsman with stripes on his shoulder marches forward, opens a crate, withdraws a mean-looking rifle, and fires a shot straight up in the air.

"Dump out the crate. Pick a gun. Two of 'em," Carl yells. "Show me again."

Carl definitely has some brains.

The guardsman glances back for confirmation. A man with a silver eagle insignia on his helmet nods. The guardsman marches forward and reaches for a rifle, but Carl yells for him to use the one next to it. Yeah, Carl's got some brains. The guardsman fires the gun. It works. And so does the one after that.

What are these guys thinking, arming the prison? It's a nightmare.

I stand in shock as the exchange begins. A prisoner holding a knife marches Pedro forward, stops halfway, and waits as the National Guardsmen release the other prisoners. The convicts rush across the yard, grab the crates, and make a break for Carl's group. But the guy holding Pedro doesn't release him.

Over the radio, the National Guard commander yells, "Let him go."

"We will," Carl says. But he doesn't give the order.

I feel sweat cover my palms. *Let him go.*

Surely, they wouldn't...

When the prisoners reach Carl, they drop the crates and distribute the guns. The convicts hold the weapons above their heads and shout as if they've just won the Super Bowl. Then they train the rifles on the National Guard line in front of them.

Carl holds the radio to his mouth. "All right, release our guest."

Relief washes over me as Pedro stumbles forward. Just before he reaches the barricade, he stops and turns. He searches the crowd of prisoners and finds my eyes. I can tell what he's thinking: that if he stands his ground right now, demands they release me, that maybe he can swing it.

I shake my head. They have the guns now. It would be a bloodbath.

Before he can act, the guardsmen surround him and pull him behind the line. Just as quickly, the prisoners retreat, walking backward, guns trained on the troops. They corral me back toward the gate, and I fall in line. I figure my fate is pretty much sealed now.

❄

INSIDE THE PRISON, they lock me in a cell. This is a step down in terms of accommodations; I previously lived in a low-security cubicle, sort of like a dormitory, with two other inmates. But I am, for the moment, still alive. So there's that.

I lie on the bottom bunk. The knife-wielding guy who threatened me in the laundry stops outside my cell, grinning, a rifle in one hand, a cup of homemade wine in the other. He doesn't say a word, just glares at me, like I'm an animal in a petting zoo.

I start to thank him for stopping by, but I doubt the joke would come off. Best not to antagonize my captors.

Instead I stare at the bottom of the bunk above me. In a strange twist of fate, I am the last prisoner at Edgefield Federal Correctional Institution, a place I could have easily escaped from. My fellow prisoners will kill me, and if they don't, the Long Winter will.

Maybe I still haven't figured out this human nature thing.

CHAPTER 9

EMMA

IMAGINE PLAYING a game of darts where the stakes are your life. And the dartboard moves. And you're the dart.

That's what this is like.

The capsule hangs in space, floating side to side, its thrusters constantly correcting its position.

Jump, the message said.

They want me to untether from ISS and jump into the capsule. I get the logic. They can't bring the capsule closer; if it collides with the ISS wreckage, it could trap me between the two. I'd be cut in half. Or paralyzed.

One option is to untether from the ISS and push off quickly. Let's call that the "dart option." If I miss, I'll simply float out into space. My compatriots on the ground have positioned the capsule so I'm between it and Earth—so if I miss, at least I won't burn up in the atmosphere. Still, I'm not okay with that.

I choose the alternative. The non-dart option. Let's call it the "smart option"—meeting the capsule halfway as opposed to flying out there.

I untether from the ISS wreckage, push off gently, and free-float in space, moving slowly toward the capsule. It's an unnerving, helpless feeling, like walking on a high wire with no net below.

The capsule inches closer, puffing out white plumes on each side, like a dragon drawing near. The pace of the thruster blasts grows faster. I imagine the person at ground control who's trying to line this up is sweating bullets right now. I am.

Twenty feet away.

On target.

Fifteen.

I'm veering left.

Ten.

Too wide. Maybe I can grab the rim, pull myself in.

The distance is stretching. I'm going to graze the side.

The thrusters fire, harder than before. The capsule rushes toward me.

Everything happens in a flash. The mouth of the berthing connector engulfs me and I tumble inside the capsule.

I'm lying in the crew compartment, staring at the white padded walls, instruments strapped to it, along with a great big sign with handwritten block letters that reads:

FROM YOUR FRIENDS
ON EARTH
WITH LOVE

I STARE AT IT A MOMENT, and then I start crying. The sobs shake my body. For the first time since the ISS broke up, I think I'm going to live.

CHAPTER 10

JAMES

THAT NIGHT, they celebrated. It was Edgefield Federal Prison as I've never seen it. Music blaring. Inmates drinking, singing, all armed. Some fighting, some gambling over cards and dice. The commissary was cleaned out. Trash covered the floor. These men, some of whom had been incarcerated most of their adult lives, were carefree at last.

By morning, they were all dead.

I knew because it was too quiet. The silence started sometime around twilight. I stayed up, because frankly, I expected it to be my last night on Earth. I wanted to die on my feet. But no one came for me. I guess they figured there would be time enough for that. Luckily for me, they were wrong.

The sun is up now, and from my bunk I can see bodies strewn across the common area below. They weren't shot, or assaulted. They just keeled over. Whatever killed them hasn't affected me. At least not yet.

Footsteps echo in the prison, a pitter-patter in the distance that grows into a rumble, and a chorus of harsh voices yelling, "Clear!"

Troops arrive at my cell, wearing rubber gloves and full-body disposable contact gowns. My mind flashes back to when the National Guardsman demonstrated the rifle for Carl and his rioters. He was wearing gloves.

That confirms it: they doused the guns with poison. I'm impressed.

The guard troops step aside for a tall man with close-cropped hair and a navy suit. Federal agent. That's the first thing that pops into my mind.

"Dr. Sinclair, we'd like to speak with you."

I stand and shrug. "You're in luck. I'm just starting my office hours for the day."

He mutters to the guardsmen, "Bring him."

They throw a contact gown and rubber gloves into the cell.

Yeah, definitely poison on the guns. They're scared that some might have been spread across the prison and that I could come into contact with it.

So they want me alive. At least there's that.

❄

THE MORNING after being the last prisoner in Edgefield, I am the only prisoner to walk out alive.

I look for Pedro, but he's nowhere in sight.

They lead me to a parcel van, where the federal agent is waiting, along with a man with a beard, short gray hair, and kind eyes. He's a man I recognize and respect but have never met. I can't imagine why he would be here, and my imagination is vast.

"Lose the gloves and gown," Agent-Man says.

When they're off, a guardsman calls out to the van, "Want us to cuff him?"

Agent-Man gives a wry grin. "Nah, he's not that kind of criminal. Are you, Doc?"

"Many don't consider me a criminal at all. Just a man ahead of his time."

"Well, I'm a man without much time, so get up here."

Inside the van, Agent-Man dismisses everyone but me and the other man. Then he introduces himself. "Dr. Sinclair, I'm Raymond Larson, Deputy AG."

In my mind, I upgrade him to Agent-Boss-Man.

He points to the other man. "This is Dr. Lawrence Fowler—"

"Director of NASA. I know." I look Fowler in the eyes. "It's nice to meet you... despite the circumstances. I've followed your work for a long time, since you were at Caltech."

His eyes brighten. "You have?"

His voice is more subdued than in the last video I saw of him at a conference giving a presentation. That was four years ago, and the years have apparently taken a toll. Stress and time have worked on Dr. Lawrence Fowler.

"Yes. Your research on alternative jet propulsion fuel sources is of particular—"

Larson holds up a hand. "Okay, that's enough. Let's get to it." He smirks at me. "If you're as smart as they say you are, why don't you tell me why we're here?"

I shrug. "Because you need something from me. Specifically, you're going to offer me a pardon or work release—contingent on my cooperation—and you're going to threaten me with the alternatives, most likely a transfer to another prison where the other inmates will know that I'm the sole survivor of the Edgefield Prison riot. The implication will be that I'm a snitch, one who got all of his fellow inmates killed. To avoid a lawsuit, the warden will put me in the hole for protection, until I can't take it anymore. Then I'll demand to be released, and when that happens, I'll be dead within a few days."

Larson looks genuinely impressed. He draws a folded paper

from inside his suit jacket and glances at Fowler, who nods curtly. He unfolds the page and lays it in front of me.

I expected it to be longer. Phrases jump out at me:

Full Presidential Pardon

Contingent upon approval by the Justice Department, NASA, and any government agencies and private entities they designate.

Work period has an indeterminate end date.

No compensation or benefits whatsoever are conferred.

He hands me a pen, and I sign it. Then he folds the page up and slips it back into his jacket.

"Do I get a receipt or a copy or something?"

"You do not."

"So... when do I start?"

As I suspected, it's Fowler's show now. He speaks as he opens his laptop. "I'm afraid you'll need to start right away. Time is of the essence, Dr. Sinclair."

"Call me James."

"All right, James. What I'm about to show you is the most closely guarded secret in the world."

I have the urge to make a wisecrack. Ever since I was a kid, sarcasm has been my defense against a world that didn't seem to understand me—or like me. And somewhere along the way, sarcasm became how I communicated all the time. It kept me from getting close to anyone and from getting hurt. But I hold my tongue here. I'm not sure why. Maybe because I sense, despite the overdramatic opener, that what I'm about to hear is actually that important. Or maybe it's because I know Lawrence Fowler doesn't deserve it. I've been in his presence all of five minutes, and I already feel as though I know him—and what he's about. It isn't games or politics. He's here for a reason, and I bet it's a good one. And he reminds me of my grandfather.

"As you know," Fowler says, typing away, "the Long Winter

is the greatest threat to humanity's survival in our history. All the climate models have been wrong. NOAA is collectively pulling its hair out trying to figure out why it's even happening. In short, it doesn't add up. Do you know why?"

"Because there's a variable that hasn't been factored."

He nods. "Precisely. NASA was tasked with finding that variable. A year ago, we launched a series of probes into space. Our aim was to measure solar output outside of Earth. What we found shocked us."

His screen shows an interactive 3D simulation of Earth surrounded by a series of probes in space, a number beside each one. My guess is that these numbers are measures of solar radiation. What strikes me is the variation in the numbers. Solar output isn't absolutely uniform, like, say, a light bulb's output, but it's a lot more consistent than what I'm seeing here. Earth is getting far less solar radiation than the regions of space surrounding it.

The implication is clear.

My mouth runs dry. It's impossible—but I'm looking at the data. I could throw up. This is too odd to be a natural phenomenon. The source is probably an extraterrestrial entity. If I'm right, this is truly the end of the human race. No two ways about it. Any species or force sufficiently advanced to cause this could wipe us out a trillion different ways—ways we aren't even advanced enough to imagine.

Fowler reads my expression. "No doubt you've discerned what these readings mean." He pauses, as if adjusting his presentation to my reaction. "Before we got these readings, a coalition of governments was evaluating possible... solutions to the Long Winter. The most viable, or perhaps 'popular' is a better term, was accelerating the greenhouse effect. That would heat the planet to compensate for the reduced solar output. Many options were presented, some more feasible than others. Underground colonies dependent on geothermal energy. Altering the Earth's orbit."

He sees my surprise.

"As I said, some proposals were more feasible than others." He motions toward the image. "However, the probe data changed everything. We kept it a secret and launched a second round of probes four months ago. This group was much larger and had more precise instruments meant to verify the data. They traveled farther and wider into the inner solar system." Fowler glances at Larson and me, as if mentally estimating whether we're prepared, then hits a key. "This is what they found."

The screen switches to a video of a black dot against the burning sun. It comes into focus, an oblong object that shimmers for a second before the video ends.

Larson's mouth falls open. Apparently, he's learning all this at the same time as I am. He didn't need to know before.

I wasn't sure what form it would take, but after seeing the probes' solar radiation readings, I expected something like this. My mind swirls with questions. I need data. Fowler is prepared. I shoot questions at him rapid-fire.

"How many artifacts have you located?"

"One."

"Did it detect the probe NASA sent?"

"Yes."

"Reaction?"

"Destroyed."

My body goes numb at the word. My mind reels with the implications.

Larson finally gets a word out, seven of them, all a waste of time. "Hey, what the heck is that thing?"

Fowler doesn't break eye contact with me. "Please be quiet, Mr. Larson."

"Did it take any further action after destroying the probe?" I ask.

"Possibly. We're not certain."

"Explain."

"The probe relayed data to the ISS. Minutes later, the station experienced... a solar event that destroyed it. Along with every satellite in orbit."

"You think it was trying to stop the data."

"That's the working theory."

"What happened to the crew on the ISS?"

Fowler glances away. I've hit a sore subject. "They were killed in the attack. Except for one. She's still up there. We're trying to bring her home, but we're not sure we can."

I nod, sensing he wants to move on. "What else do you know?"

"That's about it at the moment."

In my mind, I begin running scenarios, Hail Marys in which some part of our species survives this. They all end the same: insufficient data. We need to know what we're dealing with.

Larson shakes his head, frustrated. "Hey, will somebody tell me what's going on?"

With my eyes, I ask Fowler, *You want to tell him?*

He glances away. Translation: *You tell him, your way. He deserves it.*

"Mr. Larson, we are not alone in the universe. Here's the scary part: whoever is out there either doesn't care enough to contact us, or is trying to kill us."

CHAPTER 11

EMMA

WHEN I FINALLY STOP CRYING, I take stock of the capsule. There's food strapped to the wall, as well as water and a med kit. A large package lies in one corner. I could almost cry again when I realize what it is: a SAFER module for my space suit (technically called an Extravehicular Mobility Unit or EMU). SAFER stands for Simplified Aid for Extravehicular Activity Rescue. It attaches to the back of my suit and has several small thruster jets, which are especially handy for avoiding floating away from the station—or for a human dart situation, which, as it turns out, has come up recently.

Behind the first note on the wall lies a second. It reads:

Keep suit on.
Use terminal to communicate.

Why would they want me to keep the suit on? I can pressurize the cabin. Maybe the event that destroyed the ISS isn't over. Maybe the capsule is vulnerable.

I unlock the panel that covers the terminal, and the screen flashes to life. The keyboard is unusable with my gloved, fat fingers, but they've thought of that too. A stylus attached to the wall floats free, like ET's alien finger reaching out to me. I take it as the first message prints on the screen in white letters on a black background, like a DOS or Unix command-line output.

```
Nice to see you, Commander Matthews.
```

I glance around the capsule and spot a black-domed camera in the corner. I wave and smile.

```
Medical status?
```

Typing with the stylus is a bit of a pain, but I get better with each letter.

```
No complaints
```

```
Be honest.
```

I wonder who's on the other end. Someone down there who knows me. I start with the biggest issue: the decompression sickness.

```
DCS. Mild. Bruises.
```

And then I ask what I really want to know.

```
Crew?
```

No response comes. Not a good sign. I'm too nervous to wait.

```
Soyuz capsules?
```

```
Sorry. None were recovered.
```

The words are a gut punch. For a moment, I can't focus on anything else. The pain vanishes. I feel tears welling up again. I float back from the screen, the stylus my only tether to the wall. I stare at the words. *None were recovered.* They're all dead. Except for me. I should have—

```
Nothing you could have done, Commander.
Nothing. Station broke up in seconds. It
was a no-escape scenario. We're proud
you're alive.
```

I don't know how to respond to that. I can't. I simply ask the next question.

```
The image. From probe. Received?
```

```
Yes.
```

```
What is it?
```

Another long pause. Why? I type out five letters that seemed unimaginable yesterday.

```
Alien?
```

```
Unknown at this time. Will discuss when
able.
```

What does that mean?

```
Plan?
```

```
Still working on it. You need to remain
in orbit for now.
```

```
Why?
```

```
Need to assure safe return.
```

That's another mystery. If they're scared of the capsule being compromised—like the ISS—they would be bringing it back as soon as possible. *What's going on down there?*

The decompression sickness is starting to wane, but my head is still foggy. I try to focus. What's the next step? Can't go home. Station is gone. Soyuz capsules weren't used for evac. What's next?

Other survivors. I've got to look for them. Just in case. I return to the keyboard and type furiously.

```
Have you scanned wreckage for other
survivors?
```

```
Yes. We haven't identified any as
of yet.
```

```
I want to search.
```

Another long wait. I type again:

```
Please.
```

On the ground, someone is calculating the risk versus reward for the maneuver.

```
Not possible.

Why?

Space      weather      event      compromised
satellites.
```

Without the satellites, they can only control the capsule when it's in line of sight with one of the ground stations.

```
I'll drive when you can't. Please. I
need to do this.

Stand by, Commander.
```

This wait is the longest yet. In my mind, I mentally prepare my counterarguments for when they say no. I've got it all laid out when the message pops onto the screen.

```
You are a go for ISS wreckage search.
Sending map of debris and schedule for
remote and local control.
```

The screen switches to an image of Earth, ringed by its layers of atmosphere. Small objects in orbit are highlighted—the pieces of the ISS. They're scattered around maybe half the globe. Some are close to the atmosphere, others farther up. Whoever made the search plan did it correctly: the capsule will maneuver to the pieces in the lowest orbit first, the ones that will burn up sooner.

A countdown starts on the screen:

```
MANUAL CONTROL IN:
   15:28
   15:27
   15:26
```

Another line appears in the chat:

```
Good luck, Commander.
```

I float to the window and watch as the capsule maneuvers toward the first piece of wreckage.

❋

I'VE SEARCHED three quarters of the wreckage, including most of what's in a decaying orbit.

Nothing.

The capsule is out of ground contact now, so I'm maneuvering it, which is awkward with the gloves, but doable. It's not like I need a huge amount of precision.

The next debris field is the largest of all the wreckage. It grows larger in the window by the second. I can make out the European Robotic Arm, still attached to the Nauka Multipurpose Laboratory Module. Farther out, disconnected, I see the Zvezda Service Module and Poisk. They were connected to the Nauka by Pirs, but there's no sign of it.

I bring the capsule around in a long arc, scanning the pieces, which look like soda cans shot up with a BB gun. Through one of the holes, I catch a glimpse of what I think is a human arm.

I stop cold, wondering if I've been awake too long, if I'm finally hallucinating. Or if it was simply another piece of debris that looked like an arm.

I maneuver the capsule back and float closer to the debris, aligning the capsule's window with a jagged hole.

I can't tell if I'm laughing or crying or both, but I know what I'm seeing: it's not only an arm, it's a body, in a Russian Orlan space suit, tethered to the station, looking out at me, silently saying, *I'm ready to be rescued.*

And that's exactly what I'm going to do.

CHAPTER 12

JAMES

For a long moment, I actually expect Larson to faint. The color drains from his face. He wavers, props himself up with an arm against the van's wall, and looks around as if he's hearing things.

While he tries to wrap his head around it, I wonder about another mystery: why I'm here.

In college, I double-majored in biology and mechanical engineering. I got a PhD in biomedical engineering the same day I received my medical doctorate. I never did a residency and never practiced medicine. I started building things. A few years ago, I built something that landed me here, in prison, shunned by the whole human race. And by a strange twist of fate, when humanity is facing extinction, they call me up. Probably because they want me to build something.

Fowler is staring at me. The NASA administrator has been quiet since my exchange with Larson.

"You want me to build something."

"Possibly." His voice is barely above a whisper.

"But you need more data before you decide what to do."

"Precisely."

"You're going out there, aren't you?"

"We are. *You* are, James. You and the best we have."

"You want me to figure out what it is, what it's made of, its capabilities and vulnerabilities. You want to know how to stop it."

"That's the mission."

My head is spinning. "When? What's the plan?"

"Launch is in less than thirty hours."

"You're kidding. Wait. You're serious? You want to launch me into space in thirty hours?"

"Yes. The people around you will handle all of the space aspects of your mission. Your focus will be the artifact. We've been planning this mission for some time. We just didn't know exactly where we were going—or what we were looking for."

My eyes dart side to side as I try to imagine the details, the questions I want to ask, issues to address. The first is the most urgent.

"If whatever is out there downed the ISS, it'll hit us the second we clear the atmosphere."

"We're assuming that." Fowler hits a key, and a simulation plays on his laptop's screen. It shows rockets taking off from four locations around the world. Then a second group of rockets. A third, a fourth, a fifth. I count seven launches total: twenty-eight payloads. The simulation shows the payloads disconnecting from their rockets and trying to maneuver into varying altitudes of Earth orbit. An invisible force swats them away, like dust motes in a strong wind. They drift in space as Earth continues its orbit around the Sun, leaving them behind.

Earth gets smaller and smaller, but the simulation focuses on the payloads. They drift closer together, attach to each other, until they've created two ships. They're ugly ships, each formed of a long central cylinder with modules pointing out in all directions, like a medieval spiked club.

The two clubs move away, toward the Sun, and rendezvous with the artifact.

The simulation says what a thousand words could, but I want to make sure I understand. My life depends on it.

"So you make the launches look like you're reestablishing an orbital satellite network."

Fowler nods once.

"You let the artifact—that is what you're calling it, correct?"

"Correct."

"You let the artifact take out the satellites, and you assume it forgets about them after that. They do some kind of space-Transformer-Voltron-like deal and make two ships that go and check out the artifact."

"The pop culture references notwithstanding, that is accurate."

It's an interesting plan. But it has one very big problem.

"The artifact took out the probe on sight. What makes you think it can't knock out these ships?"

Fowler leans back like a teacher studying a student. "Did it take out the probe on sight?"

I shake my head. "No. You're right. It took out the probe when it transmitted data. It's like it couldn't see it before then. A space predator that can only see at night. Or in this case, when its prey emits some form of radiation or transmission. Light. Energy." The implication is clear: "The ships will run silent."

"Yes."

"Data relay?"

Fowler hands me a device about the size of my hand. Its surface is matte black and completely non-reflective. I can't find any ports or openings anywhere.

"We're calling them comm bricks. They have a data storage medium and a wireless transmitter. The *Fornax* and *Pax*, the two ships, will fire them toward Earth." Fowler takes the brick back from me. "They don't start transmitting data until they touch down. We'll monitor with ground stations, naval vessels, and drones."

It's a good plan to get the data back.

However, in my view, there are still issues with the mission. And some open questions.

First, the artifact isn't large enough to block out enough solar radiation to cause the Long Winter. The implication is that it's part of a larger entity or is causing the process in a way we don't understand. Or perhaps the artifact isn't even related. Either way, I do agree that it needs to be investigated. It's our best lead at the moment.

It's clear from the timeline and simulation that the launch needs to happen soon—while Earth is still close to the artifact. That will cut down the distance the two ships have to travel and the fuel requirements.

"And how does the crew get back?"

Fowler breaks eye contact. "We're still running simulations." He taps the keyboard. "This is our best idea."

The simulation shows the ships floating beyond the artifact, then breaking up once again. Two small modules jettison from the bottom of each ship. Escape modules? They must be. The view zooms in on the pods, which show three passengers each. So there's a crew of six on each ship. Splitting the crew on the return voyage has the advantage of increasing the survival rate.

The pods don't move at first. But slowly, they begin to accelerate away from the artifact. My guess is they're solar powered.

I study the two ships—the *Fornax* and *Pax*. *Fornax* was the Roman god of fire (specifically, the god of the oven, but fire fits the analogy better). I bet the ship's loaded with nukes. Or a rail gun. Both, probably. *Pax* was the Roman goddess of peace.

They're going to try to communicate first. If the probe is any indication, the artifact will blow *Pax* away. Then *Fornax* will send a brick to Earth with the result before firing its guns. Those of us in the escape modules will see the results and report back.

I'm betting the artifact will destroy *Fornax* too.

It's a good plan. One that might even get me home alive. It's a long shot. And as far as I can tell, it's our best shot.

Fowler's voice is somber. "What's described here is how we *anticipate* the mission going. That is far from certain. The risks are—"

"I know what the risks are. I knew them the moment I saw the artifact. And I know what you're asking of me. I'm in."

Fowler nods, studies the floor of the van, then stands.

"Well. We should get down to KSC." He shakes his head. "That's Kennedy Space Center. Your module will launch from there."

"One question."

Fowler cocks an eyebrow.

"Why me?"

Fowler's eyes meet mine. "In truth, you weren't our first choice. Or second, third, fourth, or fifth."

That hurts a little, but I don't react.

"When we presented what you just saw to our first-line candidates, three of our choices declined the job. They wanted *you* to go. Said they would only support the mission if you were on it."

"Why?"

"The broad consensus is that you have more imagination and technical skill than any person alive. That you think fast and act fast—sometimes too quickly—and if anyone could pull this mission off, it's you. When they knew their own lives, and their families' lives, were on the line, they wanted you."

"What about the other two?"

"Our second-choice candidate accepted the job. He'll be on one of the ships, you'll be on the other."

"And the last candidate?"

Fowler glances at Larson, who has assumed a vapid expression like a man who has just had a lobotomy. "He was unable to adequately process the information provided."

"Not surprising. That's going to happen to a lot of people. And worse." Now it's my turn to glance at Larson. He's sort of a case study in what the entire human race is going to go through when news breaks. "This secret... it's too big. It won't keep."

"I agree. That's the other reason we have to hurry."

❄

THE HELICOPTER that takes us away from Edgefield is filled with military, but they're not National Guard. Special ops would be my guess. They're all business, and when they look at me, they don't blink or glance away. Glad they're on our side.

As we fly south, the helicopter's rotors pounding, I glance up at the sun. I'll never see it the same way. I'll never see the *world* the same way. Life. The solar system, the universe. I feel I've crossed a Rubicon. Nothing will ever be the same.

And for reasons I can't explain, I only want one thing: to make peace with the only person who matters to me in this world. My brother.

I activate my headset. "Fowler, I have a request."

Larson spins and adjusts his mouthpiece. Since exiting the van, his lobotomized state has receded. He's back to normal pit-bull status. "You don't get to make requests. That was part of the d—"

"What is it, James?"

"I have a brother. He has a wife and son."

Fowler nods, waiting, then looks up. "And a daughter now. Ten months old."

"Right. I'd like for them to have a place in one of the habitable zones."

"Impossible," Larson barks.

"Done," Fowler says quietly.

"He lives in Atlanta."

"They moved six months ago, to a suburb of Charleston. Mount Pleasant." The NASA administrator seems to have memorized the file. I'm impressed.

"Which is on the way to Canaveral."

Fowler nods slowly.

Larson glares at me. "Oh, you've got to be kidding me."

I stare back. "Hey, I know you weren't picking up a lot of what was thrown down in the van, but odds are, I'm punching a one-way ticket tomorrow night. He's the only family I have left. I just want to see him. For two minutes. To say I'm sorry. That's it."

Fowler interrupts us. "Make the arrangements, Mr. Larson." To me, he says, "Be quick, James. Time is a commodity we don't have."

※

I KNOW this is Alex's neighborhood before the helo even sets down. It's recently built, the roads laid out in a well-planned grid that utilizes every square inch of land, houses aligned in a row, yards microscopic yet immaculately kept, nothing out of order, nothing unexpected, except perhaps the expected unexpected. It's him. Order. Cleanliness. Meeting expectations.

We were bookends growing up. Each excelling in our own ways, always taking different paths, if for no other reason than to be the opposite of the other.

I'm delighted when the massive helo sets down in the grassy, perfectly landscaped common area. That's going to leave a mark that will come up at the HOA meeting.

At Alex's door, I feel a surge of nerves. I haven't seen him since... well, before the trial. I knock gently instead of ringing the bell. Waking a ten-month-old is a bad way to start this ever-so-brief reunion.

His wife, Abby, answers the door without even peering through the glass to see who it is. Apparently it's that kind of neighborhood, and I'm glad. She, however, is not glad to see me. The smile melts off her face. She nearly drops the smiling child, who apparently senses something is wrong and begins fidgeting.

"What are you doing here?" She catches sight of the helo. "Wait, is that your helicopter? Are you crazy? Did you escape? I'm calling the—"

"I was released, Abby. For... a... work-release program."

She stands there, stunned.

"Oh, and yeah, that is my helo, actually. Sorry about the grass. License expired while I was locked up. I mean, who even drives anymore—"

"What do you want, James? Why are you here?"

Before I can answer, a boy of about six years old barrels down the stairs with two friends in tow. Halfway down, he calls out, "Mom, can I go over to Nathan's?" Anticipating rejection, he adds, "Pleaaase?"

At the sight of me, he stares, as if trying to place my face. Then he breaks into a grin, and so do I. "Uncle James!"

"Hey, tiger."

"Dad said you were in prison."

"I was. Broke out just to come hang with you."

His eyes go wide. "Seriously?"

"Nah."

His mother turns on him and points. "Upstairs, Jack, right now."

"Mom."

"Right now. I mean it."

She spins back to me. "Don't come back here."

She reaches for the door with her free hand.

I put a foot on the threshold. "I want to see him. I need to, Abby. I just want to talk to him."

"You think he wants to talk to you? You think you can say something to make everything all right? Do you have any idea what you did to him? Do you have any clue?"

"Look, he doesn't have to talk to me. Just... to listen. I have some things I want—some things I need to say."

She shakes her head, anger turning to annoyance. "He's not even here."

"Where is he?"

"Working."

"In town?"

"At a convention."

"Where?"

Her eyes narrow. "I wouldn't tell you if the world were ending."

Against my will, I let out a laugh.

Behind me, Larson calls out, the brusque condescension gone from his tone. "Dr. Sinclair, we're overdue for that meeting."

"Will you tell him I came by, Abby?"

"You show up here again, I'll call the cops."

The glass rattles when she slams the door.

Larson falls in beside me as we walk away.

"Still want them moved to an LHZ?"

"Yeah. They're my family, Larson."

CHAPTER 13

EMMA

Even though I'm out of contact with the ground, I write a message notifying them that I've identified a potential survivor, the location, and my intention to launch a rescue. The message will send the moment the capsule comes back into contact with a ground station. At that point, I may have my hands full.

Docking the capsule to the debris is tricky. The docking connector on the piece of the ISS is still intact. That's the good news. The bad news is that, frankly, I'm a geneticist, not a pilot, so my flying skills aren't the greatest in ISS history. But I've trained for this, and I do my best, which equates to docking after three attempts.

During the sloppiest docking in ISS history, I peer through the airlock window. What I don't see scares me: my crewmate, floating near the airlock, ready to exit. Surely the person in the suit—if there is a person in the suit—felt the capsule connect with the module and reverse-thrust to counteract the impact. But no one came to the connector to watch, or wave, or cheer me on.

I push that thought out of my mind. Maybe they're pinned down. Or unconscious. There are a hundred reasons why they didn't come to the berthing connector. I tell myself that as I open the airlock and float into the ISS module.

The Russian Orlan space suit is placid as I approach, the visor a mirror reflecting the image of me floating closer, reaching out. My hope shatters when my hand touches the suit's arm. My fingers sink right to the center. The suit has no pressure. The arm inside is hard and slender. In my gloved hand it feels like a toothpick.

I scan the suit. On the right hip, I spot the tear. And behind the suit, I see a hole in the module, and the black of space beyond. A piece of debris punctured the station and went through the suit. The oxygen rushed out, and the vacuum of space sucked every molecule of water from my crewmate's body. I was lucky my suit didn't get hit with debris. I was upwind, so to speak. Everyone on the other side of the station would have been showered with projectiles.

For a long moment, I don't move. I float there, holding my crewmate's suit, my fingers wrapped around their forearm. It's as if my mind can't process this. When I saw the suit... I was so sure of what would happen. I saw myself rescuing this person. Having someone else in the capsule. The two of us strapping ourselves in, gritting our teeth during reentry, and hugging and crying when the capsule touched down.

None of that will happen.

It's as if I've entered a new reality, and I can't accept it.

An impact on the module snaps me out of it. There's another. Then another, like hail on a metal roof. Another debris field is colliding with this one.

My eyes flash to the hole in my crewmate's suit. I have to move. Right now.

I know I should break for the airlock and leave the Russian suit and whoever's inside it. But I can't. I just... can't.

I untether the suit and drag it toward the capsule. The hail of debris gains cadence, trumpets beating, an orchestra of destruction all around me. I'm through the airlock. The beating is a hailstorm now.

In rapid sequence, I disconnect from the ISS, close the airlock, and increase thrust away from the oncoming debris.

As the capsule zooms away, the thumping sounds grow quieter. It sounds like rain, and then a sandstorm, and then nothing. Through the window, I see the pieces of debris bouncing off the remains of the station, the larger pieces getting lodged, and a few perfectly sized shards going right through.

If I'd been in contact with the ground, they would have told me about the debris field. I should have gotten in and out faster. I need to get it together.

Focus, Emma.

I turn my eyes to the Orlan suit. The pressure here in the capsule is the same as it is out there. No harm in finding out who's inside.

I disconnect the helmet.

Sergei.

It was a smart move getting in the suit. I bet he did it when the array went down. I should have ordered everyone to get into suits—or to evacuate to the Soyuz capsules then.

That thought lingers in my mind, haunting me. I know if I let it stay there long enough, it will destroy me, like a cancer untreated. If we let it, guilt has a way of growing.

I have to focus on the task at hand. Take one step at a time. Then the next. My mind—my ability to think—may be the only thing that will keep me alive out here.

With the stylus I type a message to the ground.

❄

A few hours later, I finish the search.

I found no survivors. No other space suits. No remains.

I appear to be the sole survivor of the ISS catastrophe.

I type my report into the terminal and send it. I'm over North America again, which has several ground stations with line of sight on me. As expected, the response comes quickly.

```
Understood.  We  are  pressurizing  the
capsule. Stand by.
```

Why are they pressurizing? I assumed they'd start the reentry sequence and bring me home by now. Do they think my decompression sickness is bad enough for urgent attention? I'd rather be on the ground. I'm about to type a message when one appears on the screen.

```
Atmosphere   in   capsule   is   suit-
equivalent. Please remove your helmet
and we'll start DCI treatment.
```

I unsnap the helmet and breathe in the air, which I can tell is pure oxygen, or pretty close. (For reference, the air on Earth is only about twenty-one percent oxygen.) Taking the nitrogen out of the air helps treat decompression sickness. They're also going to bring the pressure up gradually, which will force the air bubbles in my body to dissolve back into my blood. I'll be flat soda again.

For some reason, I suddenly feel so thirsty and hungry. I've been so scared since the station broke up I haven't even realized how hungry I was. Constant fear of death has to be the best weight loss program ever.

I eat and chug water. I should probably slow down on the water. There's not exactly a convenient bathroom around. They included a package of diapers in the capsule, and I quickly slip out of the space suit and put one on before getting back into the suit—just in case.

I exhale deeply. The pressure is coming up. It's getting easier to breathe. I'm taking longer breaths. And I'm so tired.

All I want right now is to go home. I was overjoyed the day I went into space. Now I crave the feeling of putting my feet on the ground and breathing in real air, not this sterile, recycled space air.

A speaker echoes in the small, still space—a man's voice, with a Massachusetts accent, which always reminds me of JFK.

"Phoenix capsule, this is Goddard, do you read?"

"I copy, Goddard. It's nice to hear your voice."

"Likewise, Commander."

I finish off the bottle of water, then ask the question burning in my mind. "So. What's the plan?"

"We're working on it. For right now, we need you to tether your suit to the capsule. The oxygen and power are compatible with the ISS. There's also a spare tank in the capsule. Recommend you swap out any depleted tanks."

Why? It's as if they think I'm not coming home soon.

"Will do. Any idea on timeline for reentry?"

"Yeah, that's unknown at the moment."

"Why? What's going on? Did the storm that hit the ISS impact the Earth?"

"No, ma'am."

"Is there something wrong with the capsule?"

"No, Commander. Nothing like that. We've, ah, got our hands full down here."

Hands full with what? Is it other launches? It has to be. I'm sure they don't want to bring me back until they have the personnel to monitor the capsule and respond if anything goes wrong. If they're working on a launch that's time-sensitive, they would want to delay bringing me back. And treating the decompression sickness would need to be done either way—here or down there—and it's best done quickly to avoid permanent damage. It starts to make sense—if my theory is correct.

"We'll get you home, Commander. We're doing all we can."

"I know. Thank you. I should have said that earlier. I mean it. Thank you for everything. Before I saw the capsule, I thought I was finished. I knew it."

"Just doing our jobs, ma'am."

There's a long pause. The food is making me sleepy. Or the thicker air. My speech is almost slurred when I speak.

"What can I do?"

"Just rest, Commander Matthews. And hang in there."

I float down beside Sergei and close my eyes.

Sleep comes quickly.

CHAPTER 14

JAMES

THE SCALE of the Kennedy Space Center is beyond my expectations. The complex has over seven hundred buildings spread across almost a hundred and fifty thousand acres. It's like a city of the future, an oasis of technological marvels here on the Florida coast. The campus is swarming with people: military, NASA personnel, private contractors, you name it. This launch is an all-hands-on-deck event, and everyone is hustling to make it happen.

Fowler hands me off to a group of handlers who give me a crash course on what to expect up there. A different group runs a series of tests on me in rapid succession—everything from blood work to a vision check to urine tests. The results must be okay, because I never hear any more about it.

Lunch is a surprise, because the entire twelve-person mission crew is there. We gather in what feels like a college classroom: there are seven rows of desks arranged in a semicircle, rising up like stadium seating around a pit with a lectern and a large screen. A few of the crew know each other. They shake hands and make small talk.

I only recognize one of my crewmates: Dr. Richard Chandler. He's twenty years older than I am. We met at Stanford, when I was getting my doctorate in bioengineering. He was a professor. A really good one. I excelled in his classes. And he liked me... for a time. I can't put my finger on exactly when he stopped liking me. At the time, I didn't understand why. We lost contact. But when I had my trouble—legal trouble—and when it hit the news, he was the first to denounce me. That got him on TV and raised his profile, which led to a book deal. Tearing me down became part of his identity.

I know why now: he was the leading bioengineering expert before I came along. At first, he saw a promising student, perhaps a collaborator. Then he saw a rival whose ideas and skill quickly surpassed his own. He stopped supporting me then— and went a step further. He committed to taking me down to reclaim his own glory.

I think that says a lot about a person: how they handle being second best. Do they work on themselves? Or attack the person ahead of them?

One thing's certain: time hasn't changed Chandler's opinion of me. He stares daggers at me from across the room. He's lost a little hair, and the crow's-feet radiating from his eyes have gotten longer and deeper, but he's the same Rich Chandler I truly came to know... after the world turned against me.

"Hi."

I turn to find an Asian man holding out his hand. I'd guess he's a little younger than I am, early thirties, and fit, with calm, intense green eyes.

"Hi. I'm James Sinclair."

He nods and does a double-take. The reaction is ever so slight, a person recognizing a name they've read before, or heard before. His voice is less enthusiastic when he continues.

"I'm Min Zhao. Pilot. Navigation and extensive experience in ship repair. Two tours on ISS. Forty-four EVAs."

"Impressive. Very nice to meet you."

He doesn't ask my field. So he does recognize me.

Another man wedges between us and holds his hand out to me, then Min. "Grigory Sokolov. Astronautical and electrical engineer. Propulsion and solar power specialist."

He focuses on me, silently prompting me.

"James Sinclair. Medical doctor. Bioengineer."

He squints. "Robotics?"

"Among other things. I'll be investigating the artifact."

"Figuring out how to kill it?"

"If need be."

"There is need. There is no if."

Min introduces himself to Grigory, this time with a little more detail. I can't help but pick up on the other intros taking place all around us. The fields are varied. Most members have training in two fields, usually in adjacent disciplines. There's a computer scientist with expertise in computer engineering and hardware design. I'll likely be working with him. A linguistics expert with a degree in archeology. Another physician with a specialty in brain trauma and psychology.

There's clear redundancy in five roles: two pilots, two astronautical engineers, two physicians, two computer scientists, and two roboticists. But the last crewmembers of each ship seem quite different from each other, in appearance at least. The archaeologist with a linguistics background is an Australian named Charlotte Lewis. I bet she'll be on the *Pax*. Her counterpart has yet to identify himself. He's hung back, near Chandler, watching the group with steely eyes. His face is lean, muscular, and sun-damaged. It's hard to tell how old he is; his hair is close-cropped and graying at the temples. He's wearing a navy suit that doesn't fit well, as if it were given to him for this occasion. My guess is he's military.

The Asian physician-psychologist approaches him and introduces herself, her English nearly flawless.

"Hello, I'm Izumi Tanaka."

"Dan Hampstead. Nice to meet you, ma'am."

His accent is Southern. Texas is my guess.

"I'm a physician with a specialty in brain injury and other acute trauma. I also have a PhD in psychology. My work focuses on small group dynamics, especially high-stress situations and PTSD."

Hampstead nods and looks away. "Good. Might come in handy on this trip."

"And your field?"

"I'm with the United States Air Force."

The other conversations are dwindling. Everyone is eavesdropping on this one, wondering who the standoffish twelfth crewmember is.

"You'll be helping with helm and navigation?"

"I'll be doing whatever needs to be done, ma'am."

The words hang in the air, a sort of impromptu declaration.

Dr. Tanaka doesn't miss a beat. "So will we all. Very nice to meet you, Mr. Hampstead."

It's clear Hampstead will be on the *Fornax*. He's the pointy end of the stick.

I wonder which ship I'll be on. I hope it's the *Pax*. It will be in the lead—the ship that makes first contact. That's my guess. It will be more dangerous there, but it's where I want to be. I can put my skills to the best use on the *Pax*. I can make the biggest difference there.

Fowler enters the room, accompanied by a cadre of mission personnel and assistants who crowd around two long tables in the pit. Lunch is passed out. For me, a Waldorf salad. It's the best thing I've eaten in years. It's all I can do to remember my manners and eat slowly.

Binders arrive next. The title page reads: *FIRST CONTACT - MISSION BRIEFING – CONFIDENTIAL*, and below that, "James Sinclair, MD, PhD." I throw the binder open and scan the pages as I chew my food. Full crew bios are first. Everyone has a doctorate, with two exceptions.

Lina Vogel, the computer scientist on the *Pax*, has little formal education, but she has two dozen patents and has created a software program I recognize, one that went viral a few years ago. I count that as a good sign. Whoever put this crew together picked people with the skills to pull off the mission—not just people with impressive pedigrees who would play well with a committee or on the news.

The other non-doctorate is Dan Hampstead. He's a major in the US Air Force. Twenty years' service. Six hundred combat hours spread over a hundred and eight combat missions. It doesn't list his number of kills, only his medals: four Distinguished Flying Crosses with Valor, eight Air Medals with Valor, five Meritorious Service medals, two Purple Hearts. He grew up in a suburb of El Paso, and gradu-ated from Texas A&M and the USAF's Fighter Weapons School. He's unmarried. No kids. Same for all the rest of the crew.

I hold my breath as I check the manifests. I'm pleased to find I'm on the *Pax*. I glance up. Chandler is staring at me from across the semicircle. He's on the *Fornax*, and he's definitely not pleased about it.

I scan the rest of the binder. There are schematics for every module of the ships. They were made at different times by different agencies and subcontractors. Some were clearly finished months ago, maybe even a year ago. Fowler told me they have been working on the plan for some time, but one thing's clear: they've rushed to finish it. Some of the pages are out of order. A few sections of the binder are even blank.

Like the crew, the modules of the ships are a mish-mash from around the world, all with different specialties, thrown together in a desperate hope of saving humanity. And like the crew, they're the best we have to send up there right now.

When I saw Fowler's initial presentation, I had a lot of questions. I asked some of the major ones at the time, but there are still smaller questions, issues that could doom this mission. The binder has answers to a few of those questions, but not all of them. Maybe they'll be addressed in the Q&A. And maybe there *are* no answers to some questions.

Still, I'll learn as much as I can. This is humanity's last roll of the dice, and I'm going to make sure we maximize the odds.

In the pit, Fowler activates the screen, which reads, *OPERATION FIRST CONTACT*.

"Hello, and welcome to the Kennedy Space Center. I'm Lawrence Fowler, director of NASA. First, be aware that this will be the last time all of you are together before launch. We have a lot to talk about, and plan for, in a short amount of time. In a few hours, most of you will be flown on ultra high-speed jets to your launch sites around the world—Russia, Guiana, Japan, and China. The four American crewmembers—Doctors Chandler and Sinclair, Mr. Watts, and Major Hampstead—will remain here.

"Within sixteen hours, we'll begin launching the components of the *Pax* and *Fornax*. The first modules will be unmanned. They'll contain food and some redundant equipment. We want to see how the entity reacts to the launches. Based on what we see, we may adjust our plan.

"I'm not going to go through the entire mission at this briefing. You all know the plan. And the risks. We're going to talk about the unknowns, and plan for as many as we can."

Fowler clicks a key, and the screen shows the same simulation he showed me back at Edgefield: the ships assembling while Earth floats away, then traveling to the alien artifact.

"Since the probe identified the artifact, ground-based telescopes have been monitoring it. It's currently about midway between the orbits of Venus and Earth, roughly twenty million miles from Earth, or one and a half light-minutes away from Earth."

Fowler moves to the next animation, which shows the two ships rendezvousing with the artifact.

"Okay. Our best guess is that it will take roughly four months to reach the artifact, which we're calling Alpha. Once you get there..."

He just skipped over several of my questions. I raise my hand. I feel like a kid on the first day of class, but I have to ask.

"Dr. Sinclair?"

"Just curious. Is the artifact—Alpha—moving?"

"Yes."

"Vector?"

"We only have twenty-four hours of data, but it looks as though it's moving toward the Sun."

"Is the object's velocity increasing?"

Fowler nods slowly. "Slightly. But again, we don't have much data."

"Point taken. But let's say for a moment you extrapolated that data. Where does the probe's route take it? Does it rendezvous with Venus? Mercury?"

"No. Our estimates have it reaching the Sun, though we don't know when."

You could hear a pin drop in the room. Min eyes me. I think he's figured out where I'm going with this.

"Because you don't know its velocity. Not enough data."

"Correct," Fowler says. His eyes tell me that he knows where

I'm going with this too. But he stands by the lectern and lets me finish my thesis.

"The rendezvous point in the mission briefing is based upon roughly twenty-four hours of observational data about the artifact's velocity. My question is: what if we're wrong? We could miss it by seven million miles."

Grigory shakes his head. "The ship has thrusters. We can make course corrections en route." He points to the binder. "And we have telescopes to monitor the artifact."

Min, who is sitting between Grigory and me, holds his hands out. "Yes, but the ship's telescopes aren't as powerful as the ones here on the ground. The fact is, you're both right. We can make course corrections—but what Sinclair is saying is that they won't matter if we've misjudged Alpha's acceleration ability."

I nod.

Grigory considers this. "You believe it is solar-powered."

"I think it's a safe assumption. And if so, it stands to reason that its acceleration will increase as it gets closer to the Sun. Though without more data, it's impossible to establish a model to predict that. And it could also have an alternative propulsion system that it could engage at any point."

Chandler is like a rumbling volcano finally exploding. "Well it's all moot anyway. You're raising issues we can't solve. We can't decrease solar output—if that even is its fuel, which is pure speculation, I might add—and we can't appreciably increase our own acceleration capability."

"Of course we can." Grigory seems almost insulted.

"Do tell, Dr. Sokolov."

"Larger engine, more fuel equals more acceleration."

"Will it delay the launch?" Chandler snaps. "Can you increase our speed tenfold? Twenty?"

"I could triple it, easily."

"Well," says Chandler, "I return to *my* thesis: this is all moot.

Dr. Sinclair is raising issues to hear himself talk." He nods to the group in the pit. "These people have spent their entire careers planning space missions. You've been doing this for fifteen minutes. And before the doctor was here, he was in prison, I believe. Most recently in a riot, of which he was the sole survivor. Let's hope we fare better than his fellow inmates. I say let's trust the mission planning to the team that does mission planning, while we focus on our job—which is determining what's out there."

I exhale as every eye turns to me, like a tennis match in slow motion. I'm not backing down. This guy has been pummeling me on TV for years. I couldn't defend myself then—my lawyers forbade me, and after I was sentenced no one bothered to interview me. But now that I can fight back, I'm going to.

"It's true," I begin. "I was in prison until this morning. I have been on this mission for only a few hours. And this isn't my field. But none of that means I'm wrong. And just because you've been doing something for a long time doesn't automatically make you right. In fact, sometimes it makes you blind to all the possibilities. It hinders your imagination. You see patterns you've seen before, and you choose a solution without exploring all the possibilities."

Chandler's eyes bore into me.

"And where has your imagination led you? What did the world think of those possibilities?"

I shrug. "Who cares? This isn't about me. Or you. This is about this mission and doing our best. Look, what we take up there is all we have to work with. If we get up there and find we can't catch the artifact, we won't be able to just order up a few more engines or more fuel. We're sunk. The whole mission fails if we can't reach that artifact."

I turn to Grigory and Min. "Look, all I'm saying is that we should run some simulations on what this thing's acceleration curve might look like and do the math on rendezvous feasibility. Consider adding more acceleration capability."

Grigory nods vigorously. "I agree with this."

"So do I," says Min.

Chandler's eyes flash at me.

To Fowler, I say what I've wanted to since I saw the first picture of the artifact. "And we need to know what else is on the board."

He cocks his head at me.

"Here's what we know for certain: solar output is falling, but disproportionately throughout the solar system. Earth is in a band that's affected. There's an alien vessel on a direct course for the Sun. These two facts lend themselves to more conclusions than we have time for. I'm not asking us to explore them. I just want to know one thing: have you found another artifact?"

Fowler's eyes snap to a man sitting off to one side. He's late middle age, with wire-rimmed glasses and short hair. Up to now, he hasn't said a word. He still doesn't. He just studies me with cold gray eyes, then nods curtly at Fowler.

"Yes," says Fowler. "Fifteen minutes ago, we found another one."

CHAPTER 15

EMMA

THE ALARM WAKENS ME. For a moment I flash back to the ISS yesterday morning. It already feels like another life and time. A time when I had a crew. And—

A message flashes on the screen:

```
Proximity Alert
```

The pitter-patter of the leading edge of a debris field hits the capsule like firecrackers going off.

A voice sounds over the speaker. Goddard mission control.

"Get your helmet on, Commander. We'll drive."

The capsule jerks wildly as I pull the helmet on. I tumble across the small space. Sergei's body slams into me. The impact sends pain through my battered body.

Through the window, I glimpse the debris: a module that has broken up. I bet it was close to my capsule when it came apart. Mission control would have alerted me or changed my course if the debris were heading for me. This is a recent event, and there's no way to accurately predict changes in the debris field.

The din of pelting debris subsides, followed by a collision, a sledge hammer into the side of the capsule. I stare and listen and wait. The wrapper for a Meal Ready-to-Eat, or MRE, floats by. It's a beautiful sight—it means the debris didn't breach the capsule.

A new message flashes on the screen. I lean over to read it, but I never get the chance.

The capsule shudders and jerks, tossing me side to side and end over end, like a mouse in a tin can shaken by a child. I throw up. I brace against the walls, but Sergei's body slams into me and breaks my hold. I hear another crash, larger this time. I collide with another wall, and the air goes out of me. My vision spots.

Atmosphere rushes out of the capsule like a balloon popped. I see the puncture. It's about the size of a fist, vacuuming everything out. Sergei's body reaches it first and plugs it. And saves me.

I float in the middle of the capsule, in utter silence. Blinking. Trying to stay conscious. The capsule is adrift.

A new message appears on the screen. One line after another. Comms still work.

I try to read the message, but my vision blurs and the letters dissolve like text on a printed page in the rain. The black spots get bigger until they're all I see.

CHAPTER 16

JAMES

In the briefing room, the crew stops eating. Those flipping through the binders let the pages fall away from their hands. No one speaks. We're all trying to process this revelation: there's a second artifact out there.

In the pit below, the staff around Fowler stops typing. All eyes are on him. And, I realize, me. The crew is waiting for me to ask the next question.

Then it feels as if it's just Fowler and me in the room, rapid-firing questions and answers like two brains effortlessly connecting and sharing data.

"Location?"

"Ten million miles beyond Mars."

"Size? Composition?"

"Believed to be the same as the other artifact. Or vessel, if they are in fact under their own power."

"Vector? Velocity?"

"Unknown."

"How'd you find it? Probe?"

"Ground-based telescope."

"How?" I realize the answer as soon as I ask, and offer it: "You traced the first artifact's course—Alpha's course? You reversed it."

"Yes."

"The implication is that both objects share the same launch point."

"That's likely. We're calling the second object Beta, and their assumed origin point Omega."

Very interesting. There has to be a larger ship out there—at the omega point. Or a base of some kind. My head buzzes with the possibilities. This just got a lot more complicated. By orders of magnitude.

Lina Vogel, the German computer scientist assigned to the *Pax*, clears her throat. "I'm sorry, but my knowledge in this field is quite limited. Some context would be helpful."

Fowler looks up, as if only now remembering there are other people here. "Of course. What would be helpful?"

"Ah, well, could you... describe the distances involved here, for example?"

"Sure." Fowler grabs a sheet of paper from the lectern. "Imagine this piece of paper is our solar system, with the Sun at its center. The planets and asteroids orbit in the same plane because they formed out of a dust cloud that was in a disc shape due to the conservation of angular momentum."

Lina squints uncertainly.

"Sorry," says Fowler, "that's not germane to the mission. The point is, all the planets go around the Sun in sort of a track or orbit. The orbits are generally circles, but not perfect circles. Some are more irregular than others. And most comets don't follow the orbital plane. For example, Pluto's orbit is more like this."

He holds the sheet in one hand and moves his hand around it, going below and above at an angle to the plane of the paper.

"Think of space like a fabric, a sheet—or page—that all these planets and moons and asteroids and comets are sitting in. The more mass an object has, the more it depresses into the fabric." He presses a finger into the sheet. "As massive objects weigh down the fabric, they draw objects to them. We call this effect gravity."

A few chuckles erupt around the room.

"Take our moon, for example. We believe that roughly fifty million years after our solar system formed, a planet the size of Mars slammed into Earth. The moon is what was left over from the collision. Earth has more mass—its diameter is roughly three and two-thirds the size of the moon, and it's about twice as dense. The result is that the Earth has a lot more mass—eighty-one times more in fact. The moon's lower mass is what causes the weaker gravity on its surface, because its mass exerts less pull on other objects."

Fowler motions for one of his assistants to hold the page for him.

"So the planets orbit the Sun—because it's the most massive thing in the solar system. Easily. In fact, almost 99.9% of all mass in the solar system lies in our sun. It's 109 times the diameter of Earth—864,400 miles across. And its mass keeps all the planets in line, orbiting in a plane." He presses a finger into the page. "And here's Earth, with its mass. It can't escape the Sun's gravity because, well, the Sun weighs about 333,000 times as much as Earth. We're not going anywhere. But we've got enough mass to keep the moon in line."

He presses another finger into the page. "So the moon is in Earth's gravity well. And it's not going anywhere any time soon. This becomes important because you have to think of the planet's gravity wells like hills that an object has to climb to escape."

Fowler points to Grigory and Min and the other astronautical engineer and navigator. "When we talk about distances and, in the binder, where you see the Alpha artifact's location relative to planetary orbits, these folks are thinking about these things because they have a huge impact on the amount of energy and velocity we need. That is, how much engine power and fuel required."

He presses a finger deeper into the page. "Because Earth has more mass and stronger gravity, it takes a lot more energy to achieve escape velocity here than it does on the moon. We mitigate the energy requirements in a few ways; namely, by achieving low Earth orbit and then using orbital velocity to help slingshot the object out of the gravity well."

Fowler inhales. "For the sake of example, here's how we would travel to Mars. We'd time the launch so that our ships could climb out of Earth's gravity well in stages. Think of it, again, as climbing a hill. We get out of the atmosphere and use Earth's orbital velocity around the Sun to slingshot toward Mars. Most of the way, we're still under the influence of Earth's gravity. It's pulling us back, but we're expending energy to pull away. It takes less energy the farther away we get and the weaker Earth's gravity gets. At some point, we reach the top of the hill—a place in space where Earth's gravitational pull on our ship is equal to Martian gravitational pull. Behind us is a hill that leads down to Earth. In front is a hill that leads down to Mars. After that point, the pull of Mars's gravity is exerting a greater influence on the ship than the pull of Earth's gravity. We're going downhill at that point, toward our destination, which impacts fuel and acceleration requirements."

Fowler looks up at the group. Grigory and Min look bored. Lina is nodding.

"This is all really important because the navigators and engineers have to think about what kind of orbital velocity they're working with and the gravitational influences on the ship. They have a massive, if you will, impact on the energy required." The astronomy joke gets a few chuckles, mostly from Fowler's staff.

"And that leads us back to engines—how much power and how much fuel. Frankly, we're not sure."

Fowler points to an assistant. "Could you stand here, please?"

To the crew, he says, "This young lady is the Sun."

She smiles, a bit embarrassed at the attention.

Fowler instructs four more assistants to stand at specific places in the room, which he counts out with steps. "And these fine folks are the planets. The inner planets, anyway—those inside the asteroid belt. And they're all orbiting the Sun at different speeds and different distances. Mercury is about thirty-six million miles from the Sun. Venus is about thirty million miles beyond Mercury. Earth is roughly twenty-six million miles beyond Venus. And Mars is another fifty million miles away from us—at our closest orbital point."

Fowler places a stapler between the staffers representing Earth and Venus. "This is Alpha's location."

He takes a pen from his pocket and places it a step beyond Mars. "And here's Beta.

"Our plan has been to use Earth's orbital velocity to give us a push toward Alpha. And then to use Venus's gravity to pull us closer."

Lina cocks her head.

"Keep in mind, the planets are on the same plane, orbiting at different distances—and different speeds. Mercury completes a revolution every 88 days. Venus about every 224 days. Mars takes almost 700 days to orbit the Sun."

He points to the stapler. "The artifact is orbiting the Sun as well—in a decaying orbit, so it's spiraling toward the Sun, like a pinball circling a funnel toward the drain."

Fowler motions toward the young man representing Earth.

"The ships will get a push from Earth's orbital velocity toward Alpha." He takes a step toward the stapler. "Venus is behind Earth at the moment. But in thirty days, it will pass Earth. In ten more, it will pass the ships, and seven days later, it will pass Alpha. The ships will use the drag of Venusian gravity to get closer to the artifact."

Fowler gestures for his team members to return to their seats, and he himself walks back to the lectern. "We're not certain what kind of orbital velocity we'll pick up from Earth—because we don't know *if* there will be some force applied to the ship modules when they reach low Earth orbit. Will it be a similar solar event that hit the ISS? More powerful? Or nothing? We don't know. However, we do know precisely when the orbital transfer point will occur between Earth and Venus. Our optimal launch window to reach that transfer point closes in twenty-four hours. If we miss the launch window, it's unlikely we'll reach the Alpha artifact. At this point, we don't have enough data to know whether we could reach the Beta artifact."

A NASA staffer rushes into the room, a strained look on his face. He pulls Fowler aside and whispers to him. I catch only clips and phrases.

"Debris broke apart."

"Breach."

"Heat shield compromised."

He shows Fowler something on a laptop. The NASA director's eyes go wide. He turns from the man and takes a few steps away, pinching his lower lip. He returns, shaking his head, and speaks quietly, so low I can barely make out the words.

"There's nothing we can do. At least right now. Just try to keep her alive as long as you can."

CHAPTER 17

EMMA

I FEEL weak when I wake up. Bruised. Head cloudy, worse than before, as if I've been kidnapped, beaten, and left on the roadside.

Through the grogginess, my gaze drifts to the terminal. There's row after row of messages from the ground. I try to read them, but I can't. I just want to go back to sleep.

I shake my head and move my arms, trying to wake myself up. Sleep equals death.

The last message reads:

`Commander Matthews? Please respond.`

My hands shaking, I reach out, grab the stylus, and peck at the keyboard.

`I'm here.`

While I wait for the response, I read through the messages above. Asking for my status. Informing me that the capsule was hit with debris (which became apparent when I was bouncing around in here like a pinball). Them telling me they were maneuvering away and to hang on (too late).

> Good! You've given us a good scare down
> here.

> Sorry. Pretty scary up here too :)

> I can't imagine.

> Plan?

> Working on it.

> Capsule status?

There's a long pause before the reply comes.

> Compromised. But we're working on it.
> Don't worry.

Nothing makes me worry like someone telling me not to worry. Well, actually, there is *one* thing that makes me worry more: hearing that the capsule I'm in, floating two hundred miles above Earth, is, quote, compromised. In my limited romantic experience, I've found that compromise is the key to successful relationships. But when you're talking about atmospheric reentry at roughly seventeen thousand miles an hour, compromise is not the key to success. That's how you die.

Heat is the problem. The Soyuz has a ceramic heat shield on the bottom. It's ablative, which means it burns away as the capsule falls to Earth. The temperatures involved are extreme, thousands of degrees Celsius, enough to boil the ceramic layers. I don't know how this capsule was constructed—I assume it's similar—but I do know that if there's a hole in it, I'll burn alive in here.

And that's not the only way I can die up here. I have a finite amount of oxygen, food, water, and fuel. Even if I can sustain myself, I need fuel to keep this capsule in orbit—and not burning up in the atmosphere.

I type the only thing I can think to say:

```
What can I do?
```

```
Just rest, Emma. You've done your part.
Let us do ours.
```

I have to do something. I inspect the hole that Sergei plugged. I can't discern any leakage of atmosphere at the periphery. It's probably okay. To properly repair it, I'd need to do an EVA and patch it. But if the heat shield is compromised, it wouldn't matter anyway. I can't think about that. Can't let my mind run in circles.

To keep myself busy (and awake), I count the food and water —twice. Go through all three med kits. Stare out the window a moment, looking down at North America, then take the stylus and begin pecking out a letter to my sister. It's a struggle to type this way, but the bigger struggle is coming up with the words. This is probably the last thing I will ever say to her. There's so much I want to tell her. And so much I can't.

```
To Mission Control:
```

```
When time allows, please pass along this
letter to my sister.
```

Thanks.

Dear Madison,

There was an accident on the ISS. It was no one's fault, just a random solar event. Bad luck. I survived. My crew didn't. I tried to save them.

A tear forms in my eye. When it breaks loose, I lose it. I release the stylus, which drifts to the end of its cord and snaps back, like a running dog that doesn't realize it's on a leash.

I float into the capsule and cry and cry some more, all the emotion of the last twenty-four hours hitting me at once.

All I have is time. I am cast away on an island in the sky, no chance of getting home. This is my message in a bottle—my last letter to my only sibling and best friend. I have to get it right.

I erase the last line and continue.

My crew didn't. They were a good crew. The best crew (but I'm biased).

Don't be sad for me. I knew the risks when I came to the ISS. Space was my dream. I knew it could end this way, but I'm happy that I lived this dream for so long.

There are some things I want to say. The Tiffany necklace I inherited from Mom— I'd like for Adeline to have it. I can't really think of a use for the rest of my earthly possessions. They're likely not

*worth much in the Long Winter. Don't
spend any time on them. You, David, and
the kids need to get to one of the
habitable zones. Or underground if
they're building colonies. I know that
sounds extreme, but please trust me.
Sell whatever you have to and go. Don't
look back. Please. If I'm wrong, you can
start over. If I'm not, you all won't
survive.*

I love you so much.

—Emma

A reply comes promptly after I send it.

We'll deliver it, Commander.

I have a request.

Proceed.

My sister is the only family I have. Is
the government planning a shelter from
the Long Winter? If so, I request a
place for her. I assume there would have
been a place for me. Please transfer it
to her.

You're talking like you're not coming
home. You are. We just need some time.

```
Even if I were on the ground, I would
give them my spot. Please.

Understood. I'll take this upstairs as
soon as I can.
```

I float away from the screen. That was worth surviving for. Saving them. All of a sudden, I feel a lot better, even though I know I'll never leave this capsule alive.

CHAPTER 18

JAMES

Fowler looks up at the crew, seeming to realize we're still here.

"Right. Well, that's a long way to say that there are many variables that go into making sure we reach the Alpha artifact. Ultimately, we have to be sure we're sending you all up with enough fuel to haul all of the scientific equipment we need to figure out what this thing is."

Chandler seizes the opening. "Well said, indeed. I believe that's where we should focus: on the scientific payload. Once we determine that, it seems the balance of the manifest should be crew and provisions, with the remainder dedicated to fuel and propulsion—as much as we can get."

I agree. The others seem to as well.

Chandler motions to a young man at the back of the room who has the look of an eager post-doc. He passes out stapled sheaves of papers to the crew and the NASA staff. It's a wish list of equipment Chandler wants—everything from drones to lasers to a robotic arm for the ship. This stuff is going to weigh a ton.

Lots of tons, technically. No way we can manage all this and extra fuel.

I skim the list while he talks (which he likes to do). I finish it about halfway through his monologue, and I do what I used to do in his class: ask myself, *Is there a better way?* The answer is yes.

When Chandler finishes speaking, I raise my hand, as I used to do in his class. There's a moment of confusion between him and Fowler about who should give me the floor.

"It's a good list," I say. "Some very useful items here. I think we'll have to take some of what you describe. The arm, for one. However, I'd like us to entertain an alternative for the bulk of the equipment."

Chandler leans back in his chair and exhales.

I continue. "I don't favor taking pre-built items that aren't ready-made for our task. Drones, for example. They may get the job done, but it's a long shot. And we'll have no support—their creators are going to be twenty million miles away. No answers when we need them. We probably won't even be able to figure out how to repair them. That would be fine if we had unlimited cargo capacity, but of course we don't—and this list would add up to a lot of unnecessary weight."

Fowler cocks his head. I think he knows where I'm going.

Chandler clearly doesn't. "Well, we launch in twenty-four hours, so we have to take something, and we can't wait for new equipment to be built. This manifest is the best we can do."

"Not necessarily."

"Necessarily, it is." Chandler motions to his assistant. "We've done the research."

"But you haven't considered the alternative."

He glares at me like an animal ready to pounce. He wants nothing more than to rip me apart. I don't react. I'm sure that angers him even more.

"After launch," I say casually, "we have four months' travel time to the Alpha artifact. Each ship has a roboticist and a software engineer. If we launch with the right raw components, we can build what we need while en route. We turn each ship into a robotics lab."

Chandler scoffs. "Ridiculous."

"It will halve the weight that would be required for all this equipment. And when we arrive, we'll have better tools—tools that we understand completely. And can repair. And repurpose if needed."

"I like this idea," Grigory says.

Lina nods. "So do I. I can take some base code and frameworks and write the software. No problem."

Chandler actually looks scared now. "It's... well, frankly..." His voice falters. "Look, what if you take the wrong components? Or you're missing a part?" He has his stride back now, the TV debate skills kicking in. "And as you so eloquently reminded us, Doctor Sinclair, Earth is twenty million miles away. You can't order what you don't have. And there's no tech support on what you do have."

"Why would you need tech support to help you with something you built yourself? And if you don't have a part, you simply design around it. Build whatever you can with whatever you have available."

Chandler looks into the pit at Fowler. "I can't avoid this any longer. I have to formally protest James Sinclair's involvement in this mission. He's reckless and careless. He has bad judgment. Judgment bad enough to land him in prison." He looks at the rest of the crew. "And on this mission, that could get us all killed—or prevent us from learning what the artifact is, which I consider worse."

Around the room, eyes glance at me and then down and away, as if they've just seen a kid getting beat up on the school playground and know they can't help. That's about what I feel like. I have a bloody nose, and I'm down, but I'm not out. I'm boiling with rage.

It's all I can do not to shout my response. "Your problem is very simple, Dr. Chandler: you can't do the work. Out there, we're going to have to build what we need, and repair it. You might have been able to do it twenty years ago, maybe even ten, but since then you've been doing nothing but giving TV interviews and delivering paid lectures. That won't do us any good where we're going."

Chandler stands and points at me. "I was inventing things when you were still crapping your pants—"

Fowler holds up his hands.

"Gentlemen, please. We don't have time for this." He eyes Chandler for a long moment. "Dr. Chandler, NASA has never sent anyone into space under protest." He points at the door, which an assistant opens. "We're not about to start now. Please follow me."

❄

WHEN THE DOOR closes behind Fowler and Chandler, you could hear a pin drop in the room.

My heart is beating like a drum. I was geared up for a fight, and I can't seem to unwind myself. My hands are even shaking.

Grigory leans back in his chair, getting my attention. "How much weight for your components?" His tone is nonchalant, as if nothing of note just happened.

"Don't know yet," I mutter.

He squints at me. "What do you need in order to know?"

"Answers. For example, once we reach the artifact, could we cannibalize parts of the ship without compromising our ability to complete the mission or get back home?"

"Possibly..." His head tilts back and he stares at the ceiling, as if taking a mental inventory of the ships. "Which parts are you interested in?"

※

FOWLER RETURNS WITH ANOTHER ROBOTICIST—DR. Harry Andrews. I've met him a couple of times at conferences, years ago. He's smart. And most importantly, he's a working roboticist. Last I heard, he was in the private sector, at a conglomerate that let him tinker in his lab and avoid meetings and management. He's perfect for this.

Seeing him makes me realize that there are people like Harry Andrews here on site, waiting. There are replacements for every one of us. Of course there would be. If one of us dies before takeoff—or during the takeoff—they need to be able to send someone else. And there will be no time to bring anyone else in.

Fowler confirms my thinking when he introduces Harry and says, "Dr. Andrews has been watching our meeting and is up to speed. So let's pick up where we left off."

Just like that, the conversation continues, as if nothing had ever happened. No objections. No comments. And the debate is different this time. It's driven by facts. There are no personal attacks, only a discussion about the merits of an idea. We all know what's at stake.

At a break in the debate, I ask the question that has gnawed at me since I saw the first image of the artifact.

"I think before we go any further, we should consider all the possibilities for *what* the artifact represents. We need to prioritize our theories if we are to prioritize our payload."

"Is obvious," Grigory says. "Is causing the Long Winter."

"Certainly, that's the most likely possibility," I say. "But that's far from certain. What if we're wrong?"

There's silence around the room.

Min speaks up. "It could be a scientist or explorer—not *causing* what's happening, just here to observe."

I nod. "And unable to stop it." I let those words sink in. "And there's another possibility."

All eyes turn to me.

"What if it's been here all along? What if it's been adrift for eons, and we just now found it because we just now looked hard enough?"

Harry Andrews looks over at me. "It *is* small enough to be missed by our telescopes—especially if it hasn't been moving a lot. For all we know, an ancient civilization on Venus launched it a billion years ago. They didn't bother to clean up when they left."

"Or were destroyed," Grigory adds. "There are other possibilities. Remember, there are two artifacts. What if they are at war with each other? Two space fighters racing through the system. And we are of little interest to them, like ant colony freezing to death while they race by on motorway."

Charlotte Lewis, the Australian linguist and archeologist tasked with first contact, clears her throat and speaks tentatively. "Ever since seeing the picture, I have also wondered what the artifact might be. The obvious conclusion is that it's a spaceship. But if so, what is its crew like? Are they humanoid? Insect-like? Or a lifeform with no analog here on Earth? Are they machines? Or is the artifact itself a machine, nothing more than a drone in space? Or could the artifact itself be alive—a species native to space? I've looked through the binder but found no answers. Does NASA have any clues to share?"

"No," Fowler replies. "And I suspect we won't have any answers to any of these questions before you all reach the artifact. Perhaps the best clue we have is the fact that the Alpha artifact reacted to the probe. Whatever it is, we know it is under power and aware of its surroundings. The event that affected the ISS and terrestrial satellites immediately followed the discovery of Alpha—that fact can't be overlooked. So while James's point is valid—it is entirely plausible that the artifacts have nothing to do with the Long Winter—that hypothesis would leave us with a number of coincidences. The timing of the artifacts' discovery— right at the time when our planet is suffering from an unexplained decrease in solar radiation—the apparently hostile response to our discovery of Alpha, their courses, which put them en route to the Sun... it all strongly implies that the artifacts are somehow related to the solar anomalies causing the Long Winter. And more importantly... we *hope* that they are. Because if they aren't... then the Earth is dying, and we have no answers, no ideas on how to revive our planet."

He turns away from us and paces across the pit. "We have explored all possibilities to enable the survival of the human race. Preparations are being made. But you all know that if solar output continues to fall, our chances of survival drop even faster. As it stands, we're looking at a future in which, at best, a very, very small number of humans might survive. And the life they'll inherit will be dark, and cold, and hungry. Those survivors may consider themselves the unlucky ones."

Fowler looks around the room, staring each crewmember in the eye. "This mission is the best chance we have. We need to play to win. We *must* assume that the artifacts hold the key to our future, one way or another. If we are to survive, this mission has to end in one of two ways." He looks at me, then at Major Hampstead. "Plan your payloads according to those two possibilities."

Fowler leaves the two possibilities unspoken, but we all know what they are: we either make friends, or we destroy the artifact.

My fear is that we can't do either.

CHAPTER 19

EMMA

Sᴏᴍᴇʜᴏᴡ, I managed to fall asleep.

When I wake, I twist violently, afraid that I might have missed something—an alarm or another debris field. I feel like a rock climber trapped on a ledge. It's a lot like that up here: I'm trapped high in the sky with no way down. The hole in the capsule guarantees I can't come home in it. Eventually, this vessel will run out of energy and fall into Earth's gravity well. It'll be a fiery, agonizing death inside this small furnace.

But when? An hour from now? A day?

I wish I knew. Just to have a countdown clock for how much time I have left.

I'm hungry, but I don't dare remove my helmet. I don't know how stable the capsule is. I haven't tried to re-pressurize it. Food can wait. Water is another issue, but it can wait too.

The clock says I was out for four hours. Amazing.

There's a message on the screen. A long one. From my sister.

Dear Emma,

People from the government are here. They gave me your letter and asked me to write you back. They told me about what happened and the request you made.

I can't believe it. Please tell me it's a big mistake. That the capsule is fine. The rumors are that some sort of storm in the ionosphere caused the station and satellites to be offline, but not destroyed. I'm still in shock.

I don't know what to believe.

They're making us pack up and leave, to go to the camp in Death Valley. I'm scared, Emma. David is too. He thinks the Long Winter is bound to end soon— that if we leave, the government will seize everything and we'll have to start over when we come back. He's been shouting at them, but they took him to the kids' playroom and showed him something or told him something and now he's insisting we go.

There's so much I want to say, but they're telling me I can't type anymore and to give them the laptop. I love you. I love you. I love you.

CHAPTER 20

JAMES

AFTER A HECTIC WORK session in the briefing room, we have a plan.

Our first-contact protocol is clever. I certainly couldn't have come up with it alone. So is the communications solution between the two ships and our probes. It's truly ingenious. And requires no electronic transmissions. Maybe it will save our lives.

I've spent the last four hours creating a list of robotic components for the mission. It's hard to choose. I keep reviewing the list, wondering if I should have picked something else—like a student agonizing over a multiple-choice test as the clock ticks down. And this *is* a test. The stakes are huge. We only get one shot at this.

Right on time, there's a knock at the door, and Harry enters. He's got his list with him. He lays it on the desk and extends his hand for my list. We both made component lists to see if either of us would come up with an idea the other hadn't thought of.

"Don't know if you remember, but we met once, before all this," he says. "At IROS one year?"

"I remember. I'm glad to finally get to work with you."

"Likewise." He sits. "Hey, I was real sorry to hear about your —the... what happened to you. Pretty unfair, I thought."

"Thanks. So, what've you got?"

✳

THE NASA STAFFERS charged with my crash course education start with some introductory exercises in zero gee, and follow that up with a rundown of the capsule I'll be launching in. It's like drinking from a fire hose, but I try to take it all in. The reality is that ground control will handle the launch and capsule maneuvers. My job won't really start until I get up there and the ship is assembled.

I have eight hours to sleep before I report for launch. The astronaut crew quarters are in the NASA headquarters building, and they're pretty nice. Compared to my last place of residence, it's a palace.

I lie on the bed, clothes on, because I'm too tired to take them off. I stare at the ceiling, willing my brain to sleep. It's like a TV I can't turn off, constantly jumping from idea to idea, trying to imagine what I might have missed, the piece I haven't thought of.

It's funny: last night I stayed awake because I was sure the other prisoners would drag me from the cell and kill me. I thought that night would be my final night on Earth. Now I'm even *more* certain that this is, in fact, my last night on Earth—one way or another.

Last night, I was ready to fight for my life. Tonight, I'm preparing to fight for everyone else's life.

To do that, I need to sleep.

I focus on my breathing, and I'm out in seconds.

✳

I'M SOMEWHERE between sleep and consciousness when a knock sounds at the door.

I feel almost paralyzed with fatigue, as if I'm lying under the mattress and can't get it off of me. There's no way I'm getting up to answer the door.

My voice comes out weak and distant. "Come in."

Fowler enters. "Sorry to intrude." He stops. "You were asleep."

I roll and try to get up. "Sort of."

"Good for you. You need it. I'll be fast."

He lays a folder on the bed, and I flip it open. It's a personnel file for Emma Matthews, PhD. She's a geneticist. Crew commander on the ISS. I expected the picture to be a standard NASA head shot with an astronaut in a space suit, staring into the camera, no smile. It's not. This must have been taken before launch—in this building, in the crew mess. She's sitting at a table, smiling, hands held out as if telling a joke. Her energy radiates off of the page, like a kid at her first day at camp, a person with a passion for life.

I scan her biography. Her life looks a lot like mine. Never married. No kids. Dedicated to a field that she became interested in at a very young age. And a single-minded focus on that goal. Her choices led her to space. Mine, to prison.

"Commander Matthews is the person I mentioned when we first met. She was on the ISS when the solar event occurred. It destroyed the station, but she made it out alive."

"How?"

"Instincts. Some guts and smart moves. And a lot of luck."

"Is she..."

"Still up there? Yes."

"What's the plan?"

"Originally, it was to bring her home after your launch." Fowler pulls over the desk chair and sits. "We've had a setback."

He hands me another folder. This one contains photos, the first of a space capsule leaking atmosphere, the second showing the capsule still against the black of space. Fabric protrudes from a puncture like pillow stuffing leaking out.

"Her capsule was hit by debris."

I nod. I know where this is going. She isn't the mission. I shouldn't be listening to this—for my sake. For the sake of the mission. For the sake of the billions of people on Earth. But I wait, silently. There's something about her. The innocence in that picture. Her energy.

"James, we're putting it all on the line for this mission. Once we've launched the components for your ships, that's it. That's everything. We won't have a way to get her back. Not before her oxygen runs out."

Fowler hangs his head and studies his feet. "NASA, ESA, JAXA, Roscosmos, we've all put the orders in for more engines, more modules, capsules, you name it. Governments are opening their checkbooks—while they still have a checkbook, and while there are still banks to cash checks. Private contractors are ramping up. We're doing everything we can to be ready to respond with future launches, no matter what you find. But it's going to take time. And Emma Matthews doesn't have time. Bottom line is, we sent her up there, but we can't rescue her."

"And you're here because I might be able to."

"Maybe. We don't know what will happen after the launches begin. The entity could scatter our pieces to the wind as soon as they go up. Or it could do nothing. It didn't react to the capsule we sent, so that's promising."

"How would it work—conceivably?"

"Conceivably, we wouldn't change a thing about our launch plans. We send the ship components into low Earth orbit and wait."

"And see if any of our capsules end up in a position close to hers."

"Exactly."

"You're having this conversation with everyone on the mission, aren't you?"

"Yes. There are a lot of risk factors. Docking. Taking on another crewmember. And the obvious: her rescue is not the mission."

"What happens if we retrieve her?" I quickly correct myself. "*After* we retrieve her. Do we put her in an escape pod and send her home?"

"It was proposed, but the committee decided against it. There are only two escape pods. Each holds three comfortably, four at the absolute max. Losing one would mean at least two people from one of the ships wouldn't come home."

"She'd go with us to the artifact?"

"She'd have to. Look, James, we both know there's risk here. And it's not part of the core mission. My job here at NASA is making sure we do everything we can to protect the people we send up there. That's why I'm here. I have to ask."

I flip back through the folders, as if I'll find an answer to my dilemma there, a reason to commit to saving her or declining Fowler's request.

Intellectually, I know I shouldn't. The risk-reward profile doesn't justify it. This mission may well determine whether the human race lives or dies. With that on the line, it simply makes no sense to take unnecessary risks. That's the scientist in me talking. But the truth is, I can't leave Emma Matthews behind to die. It's not how I'm made. It's certainly not what she deserves.

I hand the folders back to Fowler. "I'm in."

❄

I AWAKE FEELING as though I've been sleeping in that dryer in prison—sore, battered all over, and dizzy.

I stumble into the adjoining bathroom, shave groggily, because I don't know when I'll be able to shave again, and stare at my bloodshot eyes and weathered face. I bet I've aged ten years in the last two days.

A knock at the door, and then two NASA handlers are here, walking me through everything that's about to happen.

It barely seems real. I'm going into space in a matter of hours. Through my nerves, I try to focus. I've often found that fear of what's going to happen is far worse than the actual event. A long time ago, I came up with a mental hack to calm my nerves: I tell myself this is just a trial run. This isn't really it. That helps put some distance between my mind and what's happening.

The handlers lead me to an auditorium, far grander than the briefing room. NASA leadership and some dignitaries are standing on the stage, looking grim. The vice president is there, along with a senator I've seen on TV. I'm ushered to the front row, and I stand while the three other Americans on the mission enter and join me. Dan Hampstead. Harry Andrews. And Andy Watts.

The next group to enter is clearly our alternates. I nod to the roboticist who might have taken my place, and she smiles. I know her—or at least I know her work. She would have been a good choice. Better than Chandler.

The vice president speaks. Then the senator. And finally Fowler. I can barely focus on the words. In my mind, I'm already up in that ship, in the lab, building what I need for the mission.

The screen behind the podium comes to life, showing a launch platform and a rocket ready to lift off. It's not here at Kennedy; the scene is at night, and it's nine a.m. here. The text at the bottom of the screen reveals the location: Baikonur Cosmodrome, Kazakhstan.

Roscosmos and their partners are launching first—an unmanned payload. The countdown in the lower right ticks down to zero, and the rocket spews white smoke, trembles, and lifts off, climbing out of the camera's view. Another camera tracks it soaring into the clouds. Then nothing.

I hear murmurs behind me. I glance back. There must be two hundred people in the auditorium, and every face is stricken. The unspoken assumption is that the rocket was destroyed before it reached orbit.

The screen flickers to life again. The view is from space, looking down at Earth. The payload made it. The rocket detaches and tumbles back toward the ground. The capsule floats free, the thrusters occasionally puffing out white smoke.

Cheers go up around the room, and we all watch and wait and hope—and several minutes later, the capsule is still up there, unharmed.

There's a muted Russian dialogue in the background. Fowler steps to the podium and translates.

"Ladies and gentlemen, capsule 1-P achieved low Earth orbit five minutes ago and has experienced no solar anomalies."

The crowd erupts, most standing, clapping, high-fiving, and cheering. Dan Hampstead whistles. As someone who will shortly be blasted into space in a similar capsule, I have to say, I'm pretty thrilled about the news myself.

The screen changes to another launch site: Jiuquan Satellite Launch Center, China's main launch facility for large payloads and manned flights. It's located in the Gobi Desert region of Mongolia, and its lights glitter in the darkness.

The rocket lifts off and achieves orbit with no interference.

The Japanese are next, launching from the Tanegashima Space Center. Another successful launch.

Then the rotation starts again: Baikonur, Jiuquan, and Tane-gashima all send up a second payload.

Finally, it's time for the first manned launch. It'll come from Baikonur, and though they don't say the name of the cosmonaut, I know it's Grigory—he's the only Russian on the crew. Unexpectedly, I'm overcome with nervousness. It was one thing to watch the payloads go up. This is someone I know—one of my crewmates on the *Pax*. I've known him less than a day, but I consider him a friend. And I'm worried.

As before, the rocket climbs to space and darkness follows. Another wave of celebration rises as the screen switches to the view of Earth from Grigory's capsule.

Jiuquan launches next. Min is in that capsule. Tanegashima follows, with Izumi. Half of my ship's crew is already up there, waiting.

They launched the first payloads under the cover of night—when the launch sites and rockets were on the dark side of the Earth, out of the line of sight of the Sun. That was smart. It upped the chances of success. But Kennedy and the Guiana Space Centre will launch in sight of the Sun. If there is something out there watching, from the vantage point of the Sun, it will see our next launches. And those launches start now.

The screen switches to the launch pads where rockets are waiting. They take off one after another, like a fireworks show—the crescendo of the greatest Fourth of July in history.

None of these payloads are harmed, either. No alterations to their vector. No debris impacts.

That reminds me of Emma Matthews. She's up there, alone, with no way out. If she's awake, I wonder if she can see the launches. I hope she can. And that it gives her hope. Because we're coming for her.

CHAPTER 21

EMMA

THROUGH THE PORTHOLE, I watch the launches from the ground. There must be two dozen of them, streaking into the sky in a blaze and then breaking apart. It's the most incredible thing I've ever seen, more breathtaking than the first time I looked down on Earth from space.

But why? Why so many? Are they rebuilding the space station?

Or are they coming for me?

That's a dangerous thought. I don't want to be let down. I know the reality of my situation: I'm one person, floating in a compromised capsule. Whatever this operation is, it's bigger than a rescue mission. It has something to do with what the probe found—and the Long Winter. I hope they've found a way to stop it. If they need to leave me to do that, so be it.

All the same, I stare out the capsule's tiny window, my eyes glued to the trails of white smoke streaming into the sky, the rockets breaking away, the capsules tumbling free in space. And I wait, and mentally prepare myself.

Just in case one of those ships is for me.

CHAPTER 22

JAMES

HALF of the unmanned launches have finished when they usher the crew out of the room. These are my last minutes on Earth, and they go by in a blur.

Handlers slip me into a suit. They check it once, twice, three times before walking me out into the mid-morning air and loading me onto a bus. It powers across the complex, toward the launch site that towers in the distance like a skyscraper on a prairie, utterly out of place in the beauty of the flat Florida coast.

The feeling is so surreal, I can't even process it. Can barely pay attention to what they're telling me.

At the launch site, we take the elevator up, ninety feet into the air. There's a bathroom door with a printed sign that reads, "Last Toilet on Earth." I'm a mix of adrenaline and nerves, and I can't help but laugh. I'm shaking as I empty my bladder.

Once we're in space, the ships will be powered by NASA's new X1 engine, but we still have to use rockets to get up there. The launch procedures are pretty similar to what they were at the dawn of the space program, though they're much safer now. Or so they've assured me.

Inside the capsule, my handlers strap me in, lean in close, and once again go over everything that's going to happen. I guess they figure it'll make me feel more comfortable. It's not working.

Finally, they secure my helmet and seal the hatch, and I'm alone, save for the voices in my headset and the video and scrolling text and data on the bank of screens in front of me.

The capsule is cylindrical, maybe eighteen feet long and ten feet in diameter. I feel like a bug inside a soda can, one packed with electronics and white padding on the walls.

On the middle screen, I watch Dan Hampstead's launch. Smoke billows from the base as the rocket shakes in place, slowly levitates, then blasts upward. My mouth runs dry. I can't tear my eyes away from the screen. My mind wanders to what I know: science. The white smoke around the rocket. It wasn't covered in the briefing, but I figure the fuel is liquid hydrogen and liquid oxygen. Liquid hydrogen is the second coldest liquid on Earth. In the tank, it's minus 423 degrees Fahrenheit. Ready to burn. And the white exhaust isn't smoke at all. It's water vapor—a by-product of the hydrogen and oxygen combining. It's just science. Nothing to be worried about. Science is repeatable, predictable. They've been doing this for a long time. What could go wrong?

Dan's rocket barrels into the air and slips into the clouds, like a needle into a pillow.

A minute later, the screen shows the exterior cameras on Hampstead's capsule. It's floating free of the rocket, looking down on Earth. Ground control calls to him, and he replies in his Texas accent, "I copy, Goddard. Still in one piece. Heck of a view up here."

Cheers go up. The screen rotates through the cameras in each capsule—I suppose showing the rest of us what to expect, or that all is well up there. There are dozens of floating capsules now, white barrels against a black backdrop, with a few stars twinkling beyond.

Harry Andrews launches next, and I feel even more nervous for him. I've only known him a few hours, but I feel as though it's been years.

It's like déjà vu, watching the rocket launch and disappear from ground view. Then Harry's voice comes over the comm. "I'm okay. Feel like a pancake. But a one-piece pancake."

I'm laughing at that when ground control says, "Pad 39C, you are go for launch."

A countdown starts. Thirty minutes. Then ten. One minute.

"Dr. Sinclair, prepare for liftoff."

My body tingles, my palms begin to sweat, and I'm looking around the capsule in a daze.

"Dr. Sinclair?"

"I copy." A second passes. "I'm ready."

Ready as I'll ever be.

The rocket creaks, metal groaning like a robot waking up from hibernation.

Ten.

Nine.

Eight.

Seven.

The countdown voice sounds far away.

I don't hear six at all—the capsule shakes like a condo in an earthquake.

And then boom, the rocket is moving, and moving fast. The beginning looked so slow on the screens, but right now it feels as if I'm on an amusement park ride that has gone off the rails. It's exciting for about two seconds, and then I can hardly breathe, the weight of an elephant on my chest, grinding me into the seat. I can't think, can barely see.

All that cramming of launch training before? Useless. I couldn't bail out of this thing if I wanted to. Forget an emergency landing.

It doesn't matter. The view out the porthole turns to white.

When I'm in orbit, the chaos and noise of the launch turns to silence. I unstrap myself. The elephant on my chest is gone. I'm as light as a feather.

I hear what sounds like two soft gunshots near the back of the capsule. The rocket detaching.

"Dr. Sinclair, do you copy?"

I want to say something clever, for the sake of my crewmates —and Andy Watts, who's the last American still waiting to launch. But I can't. I just stare out the round porthole, down at Earth, feeling smaller than I ever have before, more inconsequential. I have truly left the world, probably for the last time. A sense of calm comes over me, and with it, focus.

"Dr. Sinclair."

"I'm here. Just enjoying the view."

Cheers sound in my earpiece. I barely hear them. Right now, all I can think about is all I've left behind. A mess of a life. Some hard decisions. One I regret, that cost me everything.

None of it matters up here. Only the mission. Everything in my life has led to this moment. Though the weight of the launch acceleration is off my chest, I feel the weight of what I must do up here, the pressure not to fail. They're all depending on me. Alex and his wife and children. Fowler. Everyone I've ever known.

Fowler's voice sounds in my earpiece. "James."

Something in his tone tells me this is a private channel. A glance at the closest screen confirms it.

"I read you."

"Your capsule is in close proximity to Commander Matthews."

He doesn't ask. Doesn't need to.

"Good. I'm ready." I drift back to the harness and strap myself in.

"We're going to drain the atmosphere in the capsule slowly. Her capsule is depressurized. That will prevent unexpected complications when you dock."

The capsule lurches. The environmental screen shows the atmospheric pressure dropping. A critical alert is silenced.

The ground control tech's name is Martinez, I think. His tone is more business-like than Fowler's. "Status, Dr. Sinclair?"

"Nominal. Suit is good."

"Stand by for docking in sixty seconds."

Through the porthole, another capsule comes into view. It's white and cylinder-shaped like mine, but with black marks dotting it, a Dalmatian print. I realize the dark marks are the stains of debris impacts. I lean forward, trying to catch a glimpse of Matthews through the other porthole. Nothing.

"Brace for impact, Dr. Sinclair."

The words no astronaut wants to hear. Ever.

The impact, as it turns out, is a soft bump.

Even through the suit, I can hear the clumps of the airlocks meeting and joining.

"You're clear, Dr. Sinclair. Good luck."

I unsnap myself from the harness and push off hard toward the hatch. I turn the handle quickly, sensing that time is of the essence. If a debris field collides with us now, I figure we're both finished.

My heart races, the sound thumping in my ears. I feel like a man digging up a grave where someone has been buried alive.

The hatch swings open, revealing the exterior of Matthews's capsule, black pockmarks and all. This is where it gets dicey. I float out and grab the wheel of the other hatch. If it doesn't turn, that's it: no getting Emma Matthews out of this airless grave in the vacuum of space.

I pull, but it doesn't budge. I try again, and it still won't move. The hatch must have been hit by debris.

"Status, Doctor?"

I'm panting now. "Call back later."

I strain again.

"James." Fowler's voice stops me. I pant and listen.

"Is it the hatch?"

I glance back at the cameras. They said they were going to disable them because the data moving between the capsules and the ground could put us at risk like the ISS. Fowler must have guessed.

"Yeah. It's jammed."

"There's a tool that could help. Find the case marked 'Supply 1A.' You'll know the tool when you see it."

I drift back into my capsule, throw open the case, and see it immediately. It's like a tire tool for space capsules, angled to lock on to the hatch wheel. It has a long handle with a wide plate for my feet. There's no instruction manual, but I don't need one. The gluteus maximus is the largest muscle in the body. One of the strongest, too—responsible for hip extension, which occurs every time we run, jump, or climb stairs. The average person can leg press a great deal more than they can bench press or curl.

I return to the hatch, hook the tool to the wheel, and plant my shoulders against the wall and my feet on the plate, trying to optimize my position for maximum thrust. I push.

Nothing.

"James?"

"I found the tool. Working on it."

"Understood."

I wait to catch my breath, then push with all my might. My glutes burn. Legs shake. And slowly, metal groans.

The hatch gives, my legs fly off the plate, and I spin. I panic for a moment, afraid I've ripped my suit in my depressurized capsule. But there's no rush of air. Nevertheless, I do a quick inspection. The suit's okay.

That was close. I need to be more careful.

When I catch my breath again, I try to calm my voice. "Got movement on the hatch."

I can turn it with my hands now, though there's a hard part with each rotation.

I stand clear as it swings open, but no atmosphere escapes.

I peer inside. Two bodies. Neither moving. Or acknowledging me.

They didn't tell me there were two of them. Only about Matthews.

"Entering other capsule." I pause. "I see two suits. Neither has responded to the hatch opening."

"Understood, Dr. Sinclair. We've been unable to communicate with Commander Matthews for ninety minutes. The other crewmember died during the ISS catastrophe."

"Should I..."

Fowler saves me from asking. "No, James. You'll have to leave him. Space constraints."

"Copy that."

I study the two suits. It's clear now: one is sunken in places, like a deflated balloon.

I grab Matthews and turn her toward me. Her suit looks fine. Through the clear glass, I see her face, eyes closed, blond hair framing her face. Even seemingly frozen in place, she has an irresistible aura, one that draws you in.

I push her ahead of me, through the connected airlocks. I close the one to my capsule behind me.

"We're back. Matthews is still unresponsive. Suit is pressurized. What should I do?"

"Stand by, Doctor. We're undocking you and re-pressurizing your capsule."

"Copy."

I pop open the med kit. My mind rifles through what could

be going on with her. Suit has pressure. She hasn't asphyxiated—
unless there was a malfunction. How long has it been since she
last ate? Too long, probably.

I take stock of the kit. As usual, they've thought of it all.

"Capsule pressure is nominal, Dr. Sinclair. Remove her
helmet and commence first aid."

As soon as I get her helmet off, I hold two fingers to her neck.
My heart sinks when I feel how cold her skin is.

CHAPTER 23

EMMA

I AWAKE with a mask over my mouth and a man squeezing an attached plastic bag, pumping air into me.

My chest burns. Throat throbs.

He takes the mask away and studies my face. "Commander Matthews, can you hear me?"

My voice is scratchy, barely audible. "Yeah."

He holds a bottle to my lips. "Drink this, okay? It'll help."

I nod, and he squeezes the liquid into my mouth—a salty, sugary mix that must be glucose, sodium, and other electrolytes. It's like balm on my burning throat, coating and soothing.

His helmet is off. His eyes pan away from me. I can tell he's speaking into the headset. "Goddard, we're okay here. I think she's just dehydrated and malnourished. Borderline hypothermic from the reduced environmental output on the capsule and low blood sugar and electrolyte imbalance."

A few seconds pass, him listening to Goddard's reply. I study him as I gulp down the liquid. His face is lean and unlined except for a few shallow creases radiating from his eyes. He must be about my age, mid to late thirties. His hair is short, sandy brown, and hangs about halfway down his forehead. Eyes are blue and focused, but gentle. Beyond the concentration, there's an element of concern. I feel an instant level of comfort with him.

"Copy that, Goddard." To me, he says, "Feeling better?"

"Some."

"Good." He takes the bottle and Velcro-straps it to the wall so it won't float free. "I'm sorry, but I need to examine you."

We stare at each other for a second. I simply nod.

He reaches for my right glove and slips it off, then takes the left.

My body is so weak I shake as I try to sit up. "Wait, you mean... up here?"

"Uh, yeah."

"Why not on the ground?"

"We... won't be back on the ground for a while."

"How long is 'a while'?"

"In this case, a while is roughly ten months. Give or take."

I break into a laugh. He has to be kidding. But his expression is blank, his face a mask of concentration.

"Are you serious?"

"I am."

I glance around the capsule. We won't last more than a few weeks up here. Then I remember the other capsules, the rockets depositing them into orbit like tin cans floating in space.

"What's the plan?"

"Commander, we're very short on time."

"Please. The short version. And call me Emma."

He nods. "Okay, Emma. I'm a member of a team that's been sent to survey the artifact."

My eyebrows knit together, and he reads my confusion.

"The vessel the probe found—the image you sent back to Earth before the ISS was destroyed."

"The other capsules that were launched. They're going to assemble."

"That's right. Into two ships. The *Pax* and *Fornax*."

"You're not here for me."

"You're not the primary objective, but rescuing you is very much part of the mission I signed up for."

"They gave you a choice?"

He pauses. "Yes."

"And you said yes."

"I did. I said I'd do whatever I could to bring you home. Fowler, everyone down there at mission control—they care very much about you. They went to great lengths to make this happen in a very short amount of time."

I'm overcome with emotion. Gratitude. Humility. I feel so lucky. I can feel the tears welling in my eyes, but I blink them away and inhale sharply, hoping he can't tell.

"Okay. What next?"

"In the next ten minutes, the Guiana Space Centre is going to launch the last capsule."

"And then?"

"Then we wait and see if the artifact reacts the way it did to the ISS."

"You mean, we see if it tries to destroy us."

"Yes. Or simply throws us away from Earth's orbit and tosses some debris at us. Either way, whatever capsules remain will assemble after that. It's going to be hectic. We need to be ready."

"That's why you want to do the exam now."

"I need to see if you have any existing trauma that needs to be treated. It's going to be very busy after the ships assemble."

My mind is racing, trying to process this. I was due to come home from the ISS in a month. Another ten months in space? My bone density can't take it. Assuming we even get back.

But that's a future problem. I have to deal with my current problems. And figure out who I'm dealing with.

"What's your name?"

"James. Sinclair."

The name sounds vaguely familiar, but I can't place it.

"You're a doctor?"

He hesitates. "Yes."

"I'm sensing a but."

"But I never practiced. I'm also a mechanical engineer. A robotics and AI designer."

Didn't see that coming. He answers my next question before I ask.

"I'm going to build the drones that will survey the artifact."

"*Going* to?"

"Yeah, en route."

"Interesting."

"It will be. But right now, I need to get your suit off."

I can't help but smile and raise an eyebrow.

"For strictly medical purposes," he adds quickly.

"Says the non-practicing doctor."

"Yeah, well, I'm the best doctor in this capsule, I can assure you."

It's a mediocre joke, but when he smiles, I can't help but smile too. I like his smile. And I like him. I feel comfortable with him, for whatever reason.

"All right, best doctor in this capsule, proceed."

He reaches down and unclasps the lower torso assembly of the suit. "I'm a little rusty, but it's like riding a bike." He slides the lower torso off and glances up. "Physical exams, that is."

"Of course."

I hold my arms up and the upper torso assembly comes off. He must have removed my helmet and communications cap before, when he was doing CPR.

Beneath the outer suit, astronauts wear a liquid-cooled ventilation garment. It's basically a jump suit with tubing running all over. It keeps us cool up here inside the virtual oven the EMU creates. From James's report, my ventilation garment must have kept me *too* cool.

He and I work together until the ventilation garment's off and I'm lying in my long johns—basically standard cotton underwear, long-sleeve shirt and pants, that wicks away sweat. Even though there's not much gravity up here, some astronauts wear bras. It's personal preference. Some wear them to hide the outline of their body, some out of habit. I wore a sports bra during the hours I exercised each day. I'm not wearing one now. The only thing I have on under the long johns is a diaper, and I know it's probably full to the brim with urine.

I glance at the camera in the corner. I'm about to do a strip show for half of NASA and who knows who else. In space, survival trumps modesty, but I can't help feeling like a kid on a school field trip who's just been discovered wetting her pants. The whole class is watching.

He follows my gaze to the camera. "They're off. Figured the extra bandwidth and comm traffic might trigger another solar event."

I exhale. "Understood." My heart's still beating like a drum.

"It's just you and me here. All I want to do is help you."

"Okay."

That's about all I can manage to say at the moment.

He doesn't move. Only waits for me to initiate. He's giving me control—the option of whether to remove the top or bottom first.

My hands shaking, I hook my thumbs through the waistband of the pants and tug them downward. His hands join mine on the band, and he pulls them off and dives down, closer to my pelvis.

"I'm going to apply some pressure. If it hurts, say 'pain' and then a number from one to ten—ten being the worst pain you've ever felt. If the pain changes, call out a new number."

"Okay."

His hands press into my groin, gentle at first, probing, then more forceful. His face is only a few inches from my thighs. He looks up, his eyes meeting mine. I shake my head quickly, telling him I understand, but there's no pain.

His hands work down my legs, always gentle at first, then firm and forceful, his head down, eyes raking over every square inch of my body.

On my left thigh, a bolt of pain shoots through me.

"Pain. Two."

He applies more pressure. The pain amplifies, then plateaus.

"Three."

"You sure?"

"Yeah. It's not that bad."

"Just a bruise. No fracture."

On my right knee, pain blossoms as he extends my leg and moves it side to side.

"Pain. Three."

"Another bruise."

There are half a dozen other bruises—nothing that rates above a two. My right ankle is the worst. I wince as he wiggles it around.

"Pain. Four."

He's methodical, moving it around, pressing with his fingers.

"How about now?"

"Five."

He looks up. "Sprain. Not bad though. No torn ligaments or fractures."

He takes a tube from the med kit and spreads a tingly balm all over.

"This is a topical analgesic. It'll reduce the inflammation and help you heal. Try to favor your other foot for now."

He wraps it tight, checking periodically to make sure it's not too tight, then floats up toward my chest and once again waits.

My nerves ratchet up again. I think he's waiting for me to take my shirt off.

But I'm wrong. He takes charge, reaches out, grabs my shoulders, and softly says, "I'm going to turn you over."

I roll in the weightlessness of space, and he tugs my shirt off. I watch it float free ahead of me as his hands touch my lower back and begin working upward.

"Two," I whisper.

This time he rubs some cream on my back, taking his time, hands gently massaging me.

He touches pain points three more times as he works his way up, hands moving over my back and sides, into my ribs as I float face-down.

My neck is sore (a two), and my shoulders and arms are bruised but require no treatment.

"Fowler told me what happened aboard the ISS." He squeezes my hand then works his way down each finger. "You were very brave. And smart."

"I was lucky."

"True. And brave and smart."

I feel myself blushing. I'm glad he can't see me. A bolt of pain shoots out from my left pinky finger. I almost welcome it to change the subject.

"Three."

He squeezes and twists the finger. "Another sprain. Not broken. I could tape it, but you won't get back in the suit gloves."

"It's okay. Leave it."

His hands return to my shoulders. I'm waiting for him to roll me over. But he doesn't.

"I figure you can do a self-exam on your torso."

My heart is about to explode out of my chest. If he checks my pulse, he'll probably treat me for hypertension.

I remind myself: survival trumps modesty. I reach out, brace against the capsule wall, and roll over and face him, staring straight into his eyes.

"Please. Finish."

He swallows hard and breaks eye contact. He scans me, his hands reaching out, thumbs running along my left and right clavicles.

"One."

"Probably the neck pain radiating."

I realize I'm holding my breath. I try to exhale casually, but I know he can feel my heart beating like a drum.

His hands never touch my breasts, they slide around and below, and I groan in pain.

"Four."

He presses and kneads with his fingers.

"Five."

"Bruised rib. Unlikely it's fractured. Nothing to do for it."

My abs are bruised too.

His hands stop at the top of the diaper—the last thing I have on. He doesn't remove it. Gently, he says, "You're in amazing shape. Given what you went through."

"You think so?"

His eyes lock on mine.

"Know so."

We stare at each other, for how long I have no idea. Could be a second or a minute or an hour. The world stands still—until a boom shatters the silence and the capsule slams into us, me on top of him, and we're hurtling through space.

CHAPTER 24

JAMES

EMMA and I bounce around the capsule, our bodies slamming into each other, both reaching out for a handhold. This actually does feel like being in a dryer that's on—with another person. Who is naked. And whom I barely know. Yet she's someone I care about.

I finally grab a handle on the wall and wait for her to crash into me. With my free arm I curl her into me, shift her to the wall, and hold her there, covering her. Random loose bits pepper me while I shield her.

If this capsule gets hit with debris and punctures, we're finished. We're doing one, maybe two gees. No way we can get our suits on in this kind of thrust. I'm not even sure I could get my helmet on.

Space is empty, or nearly empty, so once an object achieves velocity, there's nothing to slow it down. It just keeps going. Gravity exerts a pull on it, but that's about it.

This scenario—the capsules being blown out of Earth's orbit by a solar event—is one we actually trained for before launch. The protocol is to run dark and proceed to a rendezvous point. I just hope we'll make it there—and that the other crew and capsules do too. Right now, I need to see where we are and course-correct.

"We have to shift to the other wall," I whisper to Emma.

Her breath is hot in my ear. "You lead."

With my left hand, I grab her forearm, then release the handle with my right. I push off, float to the opposite wall, grab another handle, and pull her over.

The screen shows our velocity and position—calculated based on data from the capsule's external cameras, which are tracking our position relative to the stars. It's prompting me to activate thrusters to course-correct. I hit the button.

"Hang on."

There's a blast on the right side of the capsule, then the top. We've been flipping end over end. Now we're flying more or less straight, still at high speed.

"What was that?"

"Taking a left."

I feel her chest press into me as she laughs.

She catches floating detritus and stuffs it behind her, trapping it and pressing her body closer to mine.

"ETA?" she whispers as she catches a roll of gauze from the med kit.

"Fifteen minutes."

"Locations of the other capsules?"

"Unknown. We're running dark and the capsule isn't programmed for any kind of line-of-sight analysis. Just star positioning."

A few silent minutes pass before the forward thrusters fire. We're on approach.

"Where are you from?"

I catch myself before saying, "Edgefield." I'll wait until later to tell her that I'm a convicted felon out on an astronaut work-release program.

"I grew up in Asheville, North Carolina. You?"

"New York City."

She's slipping her long johns back on. The force inside the capsule has subsided. She's a lot more coordinated than I am up here.

"You always wanted to be an astronaut?"

"Not growing up. I just wanted to get away from people. Solitude."

"And you chose to be crammed in a confined space with no escape for months at a time?"

She laughs. "Well, ISS wasn't exactly my plan initially."

"What was?"

"Commercial space travel was advancing so fast when I was growing up. Unmanned trips to Mars. Drones exploring the belt to scout for asteroid mining. I wanted to be part of one of the first human colonies."

Interesting. There's more to her than I thought. None of this was in the file.

I try to come up with something insightful to say, but sadly settle on: "That'd be cool."

"It was my dream. Surviving on a new world. Setting up a new kind of society."

"What kind of society would Emma Matthews set up?"

"One with decency. Civility. Equality."

"I'd live in that colony."

"I haven't given up on the idea."

"You've just been blown off course a bit."

She grins widely. "I rate that space pun as a three on the pain scale."

"But you've recently course-corrected?"

"Four."

"Okay, I'll stop."

She laughs and stares out the porthole window. "I'm alive. That's good enough for now."

"Alive and floating through space half-naked with a strange man. What would your parents say?"

Her smile turns somber. Her parents are dead. Shouldn't have said that.

"You don't seem that strange," she says.

"Yeah, I'm super normal."

She squints. She's got a good sarcasm detector. That's essential for communication with me.

"Have you always wanted to be a drone designer?"

"Actually, I'm not a... drone designer per se."

"Per se, what are you?"

"A robotics engineer focused on... more complex devices."

"What kind of *complex* devices?"

She doesn't know what I did or what it cost me—or how the world sees me. Better to get it out there now. "The kind that got me in trouble."

She squints, wondering if I'm kidding. "In trouble with who?"

"Pretty much everyone."

Her tone lightens. "So you're a rebel."

"A freedom fighter."

"Whose freedom?"

"Everyone's, actually."

Her smile fades. "You're serious, aren't you?"

"Usually I'm not, but in this instance, yes. I created something I thought would help restore decency and freedom. To the whole world."

"And you got in trouble for it?"

"I did. I miscalculated. I didn't factor in human nature.

Never bothered to consider how people would see what I created. I learned a very valuable lesson."

"Which was?"

"Any change that takes power from those who have it will face opposition. The greater the change, the greater the force with which it will be struck down."

"Sort of like Newton's Third Law of Motion: for every action there is an equal and opposite reaction."

"Never thought about it that way, but yeah, it's a lot like that."

And she and I are a lot alike. She wanted to get away from people and the world that was so flawed and start over anew. I saw the same messed-up world and wanted to stay and fix it. Look where it got me.

The forward thrusters fire again. We're less than five minutes to rendezvous. The inertia in the capsule is still strong, but manageable.

"T minus five. Better suit up."

❄

When we reach the rendezvous point, there are only three capsules waiting. I was hoping for more. And I hope more are coming. I try to hide my concern from Emma, but I sense she sees it.

We float to opposite portholes and peer out.

"These two are unmanned," I call back to her.

"Same with this one. What now?"

"Now we wait."

"These four capsules won't assemble?"

"No. Well, they can, but there's a preferred assembly sequence. The capsules are programmed to wait and see what shows up. And we need one of the larger engine components to really get anywhere."

"How long do we wait?"

"About two hours left."

"And what do we do with those two hours?"

I reach for a bag with MREs. "First, we're going to rehydrate you and get some food in you."

"That won't take two hours."

"True. But getting you up to speed on the mission will."

While she eats, I tell her about the second artifact—Beta. She stops chewing. She's smart enough to realize the implications, but I state them anyway. We go over the mission objectives: to make first contact, ask for help, and if that fails, to see if we can destroy it.

Between bites she mutters, "Let's hope they want to make friends."

"Indeed."

From memory, I recite what I know about the crew. I focus on the *Pax* since she'll be with us, though I mention Dan Hampstead over on the *Fornax* since he's the main difference.

"I'm dead weight on this mission," she says. "Everyone else is here for a reason. I'm here because I was stranded along the road on the way."

"Just because you're a cosmic hitchhiker doesn't mean you're dead weight."

"No. My lack of relevant skills makes me dead weight."

"Fowler shared your file with me. You wouldn't be dead weight anywhere, Emma. Certainly not up here. This is my first time in space. Building complex robots on Earth is tough enough. Up here, it will be a challenge. You've been running and maintaining the ISS for months. You're good at working in space. And I'm going to need some help."

"You're offering me a job?"

"You interested?"

She smiles. "Compensation?"

"Potentially... your life, those of everyone you know, and everyone else on Earth."

"Benefits?"

"Unlimited. Full dental too."

"I'll think about it."

"Don't take too long; we've got other applicants."

"Right."

Something catches her attention in the window behind me. "There's another capsule."

I spin and stare out. Harry Andrews's face is floating in the other capsule's window, his helmet on, visor up.

This is wrong. Harry shouldn't be here. His capsule should be at the *Fornax* rendezvous point. Unless there weren't enough capsules left to constitute the *Fornax*. It makes me wonder how many of the *Pax* crew have survived—and how many capsules we have to work with. Our mission could be over before it even begins.

The other possibility is that mission control re-routed his capsule. Why? Maybe they decided I couldn't do the job alone. Or perhaps because they think two heads are better than one. I would agree with that; even in our brief time together, Harry and I have proven to be a good team. I like him. I like working with him.

Harry holds up a hand and waves at me, and I wave back. Whatever the reason is for his being here, I'm glad to see him.

❄

TWO HOURS LATER, every capsule except for two have arrived. Save for Harry's capsule, they're all original to the *Pax*. It's strange. I wonder if the other two capsules impacted each other.

Or if they hit capsules from the *Fornax*. It could be worse: both are supply capsules, and we can do without two of them. NASA wisely distributed the cargo across all the capsules, so each one contains roughly the same stuff. Overall, the solar event cost us about seven percent of our supplies. That's manageable.

I can only hope the *Fornax* was as lucky. Without electronic transmissions, I won't know until we meet up with them. And that won't be for months.

Months before we launched, NASA devised an ingenious communications method between the capsules that requires no electronic transmissions. It uses line of sight. There are twelve "comm patches" on each capsule, on all sides, spread out, ensuring that the cameras on the other capsules can see them. The panels use electronic ink technology, similar to what the old e-book readers employed: they have a thin layer of film that holds a liquid solution with microcapsules. Electric impulses below the film cause positively charged white particles—or negatively charged dark particles—to come to the surface. Each panel shows symbols without emitting any light or microwaves or anything else; all the electrical charges are hidden below the film.

NASA devised a codebook and a series of symbols to compress and streamline messages. Each ship has a long-range telescope that can see the comm patches. The range is pretty far but nothing like an electronic transmission. That's how we'll communicate.

Assuming the *Fornax* made it.

Through the porthole, I see the comm patches changing, the complex symbols visible for less than a second before flashing to something else, like flipping through a black-and-white comic book. It's beautiful, the subtle flashes as the capsules maneuver closer to each other, an orchestra of construction in space. This is probably the greatest feat of space engineering in history, the product of months, maybe years of planning, followed by a stress-ridden crash course of work by the world's leading minds.

It strikes me then that it's our darkest hours and greatest crises that push us to the highest peaks of performance and genius. Wars, hot and cold, produced the nuclear bomb and the Space Race. And the Long Winter gave us this: what will be the farthest humans have ever ventured into the solar system. I wish the world could see the beginning, this ship assembling itself in space, and know the names of the hard-working, brilliant men and women who made this possible.

❄

THE HATCH OPENS, and Harry floats through. He raises the visor on his helmet, and so do we. The air has a metallic, artificial smell, but I'll get used to it. I'm just glad to be breathing it.

Harry grins. "Welcome to the Alien Artifact Express. Just need to see your boarding passes, folks."

"Blew out the window on the way."

He laughs. "I'll let it slide—just this once."

"Lucky for us." I motion toward Emma. "Harry, this is Commander Emma Matthews."

"Glad to have you aboard, ma'am."

CHAPTER 25

EMMA

WE'RE a month into our journey to the Alpha artifact. It has been the most incredible month of my life.

I felt a sense of wonder and awe the first time my capsule docked with the ISS and I floated out into it. This ship is something else altogether. It is a marvel, a wonder eclipsed only by the crew, whom I find even more incredible. Each one has his or her specialty, a job to do, and they have poured themselves into those jobs like lasers carving up the mountain of work upon us.

Grigory, the Russian engineer, obsesses about engine efficiency, constantly muttering to himself as he floats around the ship.

Charlotte, an Australian linguist and archaeologist, has spent every waking hour writing out her first contact protocol, only stopping to check with James and Harry to see if the drone can do this or that—and sometimes with Lina to see if her ideas can be programmed.

Min, the Chinese navigator, has busied himself plotting alternative courses both to Alpha and back home, based on every scenario he can think of.

The ship's physician and psychologist, Izumi, a Japanese woman about ten years older than I am, floats in and out of the pods, constantly checking on us, like a mother hen prowling a nest.

I've spent my time with James and Harry, and I admit I've enjoyed it. They have a quirky dynamic—a mix of competition and camaraderie. They work mostly independently, designing the drones and then showing each other what they've come up with. It's a sort of game between them to see who can one-up the other with new functionality or efficiency. They debate the merits of every idea, but they're not combative. For two competing scientists, there's no ego. They're supportive and even jovial with each other.

And there's something else, too—a certain protectiveness Harry has for James. Harry is maybe fifteen years older, but I sense that there's something more. Maybe it's related to what happened to James in the past—the trouble he got into. The trouble he's refused to tell me about every time I've subtly brought it up. I don't dare ask Harry, though I badly want to know. I wonder why that is. I've told myself I'm being thorough, because it's important to know all you can about your crew. But I know that's not it.

For the most part, I spend my time in the robotics lab soldering and welding. I've got the most dexterity in space of all the crew, except perhaps Min, and he's got his hands full. I like the work. I like being useful and being part of a crew. It keeps me from thinking about the crew I lost. There's a deep well of hurt there. My mind runs across it every now and then, and a surge of pain hits me. That place in my mind is sort of like the sprained ankle and bruised rib and sore spots all over me: I forget until the pain reminds me. Those wounds will take time to heal—how long, I can't even guess. But with each passing day, as we voyage away from Earth, the hurt dulls, and I come alive a little more.

At the outset, I asked if we had enough food and water for everyone on board. The mission was slated for six. With Harry and me added to the crew, the food requirements are up thirty-three percent—and we lost two capsules, or seven percent of our supplies. James assured me we are well stocked. I hope it's true.

Every now and then Lina comes into the lab to discuss the software for the drones. She's working on one operating system with drivers for all the different potential hardware designs—which are all over the map: everything from a simple camera drone to a drone with arms to a drone that can assemble like the ship and bore a hole in the artifact. It's pretty incredible. James has designed comm patches for the drones that can relay data back to the *Pax* without sending an electronic signal.

And now he and Harry have a big idea they're pretty nervous about. They've called an all-hands meeting to present it, because it will take every one of us to pull it off, and it won't be easy. It will also risk a huge amount of our drone material. It's a risk. But we have to take it.

We just have to convince the others.

CHAPTER 26

JAMES

THE CREW MEETS in the largest space on the ship, at the intersection of the major arms. The space is roughly spherical. It has a technical name, the such-and-such, but we've all taken to calling it the bubble. There are windows in several directions and a round white table in the center that everyone can strap themselves to.

Emma, Harry, and I have called the meeting to present a plan we think could drastically up our chances of success. It's a risk, however. I'm a little nervous about it—the meeting, that is—because this is the first major decision point we've faced as a crew. It really could go either way.

When everyone's assembled and floating around the table, Harry opens the meeting.

"We want to send a fleet of drones ahead. We're calling it the Janus fleet."

"Objective?" Grigory asks.

"Data gathering," Harry answers quickly.

Charlotte knits her eyebrows together. "What are we talking about here? Just observation or actual contact with the artifact?"

"Both," I reply.

Charlotte shakes her head. "I'm against. We need close control when we make first contact. We need to be able to react and adapt our approach. This is too important to trust to a software algorithm or AI."

I anticipated this reaction from her. I make my voice calm. "Technically, we've already made first contact. The initial probe sent data back in proximity to the artifact, and it was destroyed."

"That supports my argument," Charlotte says. "Mindless probes are at a severe disadvantage in these kinds of uncertain situations. The stakes are too large and the risk is too great."

"We," I motion to Harry and myself, "view that danger as the primary reason to send an advance probe fleet. You're right, they won't have a wide range of adaptations, but each probe will have a purpose, and they can learn a lot—without exposing the Pax or risking this crew."

Charlotte leans in. "We're here to risk our lives—"

"Wisely," I counter. "This isn't about guts, it's about mission success. If we die before we learn anything, that's mission failure."

Min seems to sense things spiraling. He holds up a hand. "It's obvious there are issues here. It would be a challenge for me to plan flight courses for the drones. Technically, we aren't even certain where the artifact is. We've extrapolated a location based on the last known position and trajectory, but it could be anywhere. If we send the drones in the wrong direction, they could never course-correct. And Grigory would have to solve the propulsion and fuel needs and balance it against our own. With that said, I would like to hear more before we close the issue."

A mission commander was never formally designated before we launched—but ever since the Pax assembled, Min has been acting like one. Maybe it's because he's flying the ship, determining where we go. Maybe he's just a natural leader. Whatever the case, he's doing a good job, and it's helpful at the moment.

I nod to Harry, who continues.

"The Janus fleet would include two scout drones and three specialized drones: observation, communications, and intervention. Five drones total."

"Size?" Grigory asks.

"Very small," Harry answers. "Most will be nothing more than a booster and a specialized tool. All will have comm patches."

"Fuel, energy requirements?"

"Minimal. This is a one-way trip for all the drones except the scout drones. They'll be larger and will have more acceleration capability. The plan is for one scout to accelerate past the drone fleet and make good time to the artifact. It'll have a long-range telescope to verify that the artifact is at the location we expect. The goal is for the drone to see the artifact, but not be seen. If the artifact isn't where we think it will be, the drone will execute a search grid and try to find it, spending a week on the task. Then it will return to the drone fleet and comm-patch the results to the other scout drone as soon as it's in line of sight of that drone's telescope. That scout drone will reverse course and make best speed back to us to relay the results."

"I like this," Grigory says. "Even if rest of plan is garbage, this part is wise—verifying location."

I almost laugh out loud. "Thanks for the faith, Grigory."

"Welcome."

"I agree, this is a good move," Min says.

All eyes shift to Lina. "I'm on board."

Charlotte simply nods. So does Izumi, who's been silent so far.

"Then what?" Min asks.

Harry steeples his fingers. "Then, from the *Pax*, we launch a small drone on an intercept course to the *Fornax* and comm-patch what we've learned: artifact location, any messages we want to send from all departments. That'll apprise them of any course adjustments that should be made and share our notes."

After a long silence, Grigory says what we're all thinking: "Assuming *Fornax* is out there."

Harry answers quietly. "Yes, this will also answer the question of what happened to the *Fornax*."

"And," I add, "whether we should adjust our drone design objectives."

"Whether you should build more bombs," Min says. "If the *Fornax* isn't out there or if it lost its offensive payload."

"Yes," I reply.

Charlotte's eyes go wide. "Wait, you're building drones with offensive capabilities?"

I nod. "We have to. Without Harry, it's unlikely the *Fornax* is producing drones at all. Additionally, as Min noted, we don't know if the nuke made it. Determining the artifact's vulnerability could fall entirely to us. We don't have a choice."

Charlotte inhales. "Have you made the bombs yet?"

"No. We're still in the design phase."

"What sort of yield will they carry?" Grigory asks.

"Nothing on a nuclear scale. And some won't be incendiary at all. We'll probe a variety of offensive modes. Kinetic assault, electrical, laser, and of course more conventional ordnance, adapted for space."

Grigory is uncharacteristically cautious when he responds. "If needed, I believe I could repurpose reactor. If given time, I could rig a casing and program an overload."

The reactor is composed of two chambers that each attach to one of the escape pods when activated. The implication of Grigory's plan is that the escape pods would effectively be disabled, leaving us no way to return to Earth.

"That's a question for another day," Min says. "At the moment, let's focus on the advance drone fleet. What's the plan after it locates the artifact?"

"Well," Harry says, "that's when it gets interesting. The two scout drones will monitor the other three drones as they make a staggered approach to the artifact. The observation drone will be first. It's designed to look like an asteroid. It'll do a fly-by of the artifact but make no contact. Along the way, it'll collect readings —visual, radiation, microwave, radio wave, whatever else anyone wants to scan. We'll get our first look at its outer material up close, maybe even form a theory about what it's made of. We'll see the far side of it as well."

"See if it has soft underbelly," Grigory mumbles.

"Exactly." Harry brings up another image, this one with flight vectors. "After the scans, the scout drone will comm-patch the readings to us—assuming it's in telescope range of the *Pax*. The larger data files, like high-res images, will have to travel back to us. After its fly-by, the observation drone will get coordinates for the *Pax* from the scout drone, then travel back to us with the data."

I look over at Charlotte. "The comm drone would approach next and initiate contact."

"And how exactly will it do that?" She asks. Charlotte's tone is harsh. I think she feels that first contact is her purview and that Harry and I are yanking it away from her because we control the drones and can get there first.

I do my best to keep my voice even, a sharp contrast to Charlotte's. "That's not our call."

Harry shrugs. "Hey, we're just the drone guys."

"Have you finished your first contact protocol?" I ask.

Charlotte's aggression instantly turns to defensiveness. "Well, no, not exactly. This kind of work takes time. It's not like assembling a robot. We need to be very thoughtful about how we go about this. We get one shot."

"What's your current thinking about how we'll proceed?" Min asks.

"My... *current thinking* is that we need to establish communications and then develop a lexicon."

It's clear that not everyone is familiar with the word "lexicon." I sometimes forget that English is a second language for some of our crew. Grigory squints. Min's eyes drift, also trying to place the word. Izumi stares at Charlotte. Lina makes no reaction.

"Ah," says Charlotte, "we need to devise a vocabulary with which to communicate with the artifact."

Grigory rolls his eyes. "Which assumes it wants to communicate."

"Yes. I'm assuming that. I assume you want to shoot first?"

I hold up a hand. "No one's saying that."

Charlotte turns to me. "What are *you* saying, James?"

"That our mission is broader than communicating with the artifact. We're here to figure what we're dealing with and to notify Earth." I wait, but no one says anything. "If the artifact wants to communicate, that's a best-case scenario. But if it doesn't, Earth needs to know that. And how to fight it. As you've noted, we get one chance to make first contact. After we initiate communication, it will be aware of our drones. We lose the element of surprise."

"Which is why you want to study it first—with the observation drone?" Min asks.

"Yes. We observe first. Then try to communicate. And if that fails, the intervention drone will probe its defenses. To us, that seems the only logical approach."

. . .

CHARLOTTE CHEWS HER LIP. "Yeah. All right. I like this. It's a good idea. Once we initiate communication, the artifact will likely identify the drones. We may not get another chance to get close to it—the observation drone needs to go first."

"That's our thinking as well," I say. "Again, we're deferring to you on first contact protocol. Any details would be helpful at this point."

Charlotte interlocks her fingers and sets them on the table. "Okay. My protocol, what I'm thinking, is that we try a series of broadcast modalities. Microwave, radio wave, light, radiation—we keep going down the list until we get a response."

"What's the initial message?" I ask.

"Something simple. A non-random number sequence. Fibonacci numbers. Figurative numbers: triangular, square, pentagonal. Central polygonal numbers. Magic square. The idea is that we give it a logical sequence of numbers and wait to see if it responds with the next number in the sequence. If so, that tells us it's willing to talk. The next part is tougher."

"*How* to talk," I say.

"Exactly. I'm still working on that."

"Fair enough. My feeling—" I gesture to Harry and Emma. "*Our* feeling is that establishing a rudimentary initial contact is sufficient for this first pass. It could even inform how you go about creating a more complex lexicon with the artifact."

After a moment, Charlotte nods. "Yes. I agree. It would give me a big head start. By the time we got there, we could be ready to have a productive dialogue."

"Or be ready to destroy it," Grigory says. "That's what's in third set of drones, yes? Weapons?"

All eyes turn to me. "That's right. The first drone will observe. The second will communicate. And if that's unsuccessful, we probe its defenses. By the time we reach the artifact, we need to be ready to talk or fight. Additionally, this will let us know what we're dealing with *now*—whether it's friendly or aggressive—and we can let Earth know far sooner than expected. We're still a lot closer to Earth than we will be when we reach the artifact."

The group falls silent. I think they've realized the genius of the plan Harry, Emma, and I have put together. The addition of the Janus fleet is a vast improvement on NASA's original mission, shaving months off the timeline of determining what the artifact is. It occurs to me now why NASA didn't designate a mission commander. This is the reason—this meeting. NASA wanted friction. They wanted all these brilliant people to sit in a room and argue—without a clear leader who could end debate and just decide things summarily. This mission is primarily about the research we're doing, not fast command decisions. They wanted every person to have a specialty and to have a chance to voice their ideas and opinions. That's how good plans are improved.

"How would it work?" Min asks. "The weapons?"

"We're designing a rail gun," Harry replies.

Charlotte grimaces. "I thought a gun wouldn't work in space."

Grigory sounds annoyed. "Gun will work in space."

"Without oxygen?" Charlotte asks.

"Yes," Grigory snaps. "And a rail gun is nothing like regular gun anyway."

Harry's voice is calm and matter-of-fact. "A gun—a conventional gun with a hard projectile and gunpowder as propulsion—will indeed fire in space. The rounds contain their own oxidizer—a chemical that triggers the explosion of the gunpowder and forces the projectile outward, along a path created by a barrel. The reaction doesn't need any outside oxygen. The main difference in firing a gun in space will be the smoke, which will emerge from the projectile's exit point at the tip of the barrel.

"But in our case, there won't be any gunpowder or oxidizer or expanding gas of any kind needed. A rail gun is different in mechanism, though we still use a projectile in a barrel pointed at our target. The barrel in a rail gun has two rails that are magnetized using massive amounts of electricity. The electromagnetic current running down the rails pushes the object out the barrel at extremely high velocity—much, much faster than any explosive round can achieve."

"What's the target?" Grigory asks.

"We'd shoot six rail gun rounds concurrently, close grouping," I reply.

"Center mass?" Grigory asks.

"No. The outer edge."

The Russian engineer smiles. "You want a piece of it."

"To study, yes. We feel the priority is learning what it's made of. That will tell us more about how to... neutralize it and any other artifacts."

After a long silence, Min asks, "Is there more?"

"That's all we've got at the moment," I reply.

"I like it," Min says.

"As do I," Grigory adds.

Charlotte nods. "Me too."

"Same," Lina says.

All eyes drift over to Izumi. "This is all outside my expertise. I'm here to keep you all alive and performing well. It would seem that this plan does that very well. I am for it."

I motion to Harry and Emma. "We still have a lot of work to do on our end with the design, and then we've got some construction challenges. I think maybe we could be done in two weeks? Three?"

I shift my gaze to Emma. She's been silent throughout the meeting, for good reason: she knew what Harry and I were presenting. She helped formulate the plan. And she's essential to executing it. Harry and I are good with design, but when it comes to building the drones, she runs circles around us.

"Definitely," she says. "Two weeks' build time is doable based on the prelim designs."

I address Lina. "We'll need a lot of help with the software."

"No problem. I've already got a good head start on some autonomous drone systems. But I need the specifics." She turns to Charlotte. "Protocols for the comms, to start with."

"I have the basics mapped out. I can clean it up and have it to you in a few days."

"Great. And Min, I'm going to need those navigation parameters pretty soon too."

"Nav is the easy part," Min says. "We need to know how much propulsion power we've got, and range—those are the tricky variables."

"We agree," I say. "I feel like we need a working group between our team," I point to Emma and Harry, "and Grigory and Min. We need to figure out what we have to work with and what we're willing to use up on this first drone launch."

Nods all around.

I inhale. "Look, the next two weeks are going to be rough. We'll be working around the clock. There'll be a lot of back-and-forth among all of us. But it will be worth it. We'll find out where the artifact is. The status of the *Fornax*. And most importantly, we could achieve our mission objective months ahead of schedule. All that's left is to get it done."

CHAPTER 27

EMMA

JAMES WAS RIGHT: the two weeks that followed are the toughest of my life. Training for the ISS was a cake walk compared to the construction of the Janus fleet. I sleep, eat, exercise, and work.

The crew is constantly stressed out, constantly arguing with each other about the best way to do things. I realize now that the lack of friction before was mostly because everyone was in their own sphere, only occasionally coming into contact, and not at close range. We're colliding now. Making demands of each other —on tight deadlines.

James is the most stressed. Much of the burden of coordination has fallen to him. Though Min is technically flying, James is making most of the calls, setting the deadlines and telling us what needs to get done. There was a time for debate about what to do. We had it, and now we're all focused on executing as fast as we can. I, along with the rest of the crew, have begun to think of him as the mission commander.

But lately, a rift has developed between us. A week ago, he took some blood samples and gave me an injection to help with my bone density. He upped my exercise regimen to three hours a day, but I've been doing only half that. I need to work. We have to get these drones finished. He's not happy about my cutting corners on my exercise regime. It's as if we're an old married couple, bickering silently about something we know neither of us is going to compromise about.

I'm soldering a circuit board when he floats into the lab and grabs the table.

"We need to talk."

In my experience, those four words never herald the opening of a pleasant conversation. A wisp of smoke drifts up from the board and hangs between us, like the aftermath of a shot that was just fired.

"Okay."

"Look, Emma, your bone density is critical. You've got to exercise more."

"We need to finish the drones."

"And we will."

"We're already on the verge of missing the launch date."

James shakes his head, frustrated. "It's an artificial deadline. We can push it back."

"How much? A day? A week?"

"If needed."

"And what if a day is the difference between a million people living or dying on Earth?"

"What if it's not?"

"In space, every second matters. Of all the people on this ship, I know that the best. This is life and death, and I'm less worried about mine."

"You should be. If you injure yourself, it hurts all of us."

"I feel fine."

"You're not. Do you trust my medical opinion?"

"I do. Do you respect my decision to do what I think is right for the mission and the people back home?"

"It's not the same thing."

"It doesn't need to be. James, this is the best shot we have. I'm going to work my tail off until those drones launch. Okay?"

He exhales. "You are so stubborn."

"Says the man who won't compromise."

We stare at each other. I'm angry. I know he is too. I haven't known him long, but I've gotten to know him pretty well.

Harry sticks his head in the hatchway. His eyebrows shoot up. There are drone pieces floating all over the lab: wires, housings, capacitors—as if a bomb had gone off, and the aftermath of the explosion is hanging in the air. The tension feels about like that. He reads it instantly.

"Hey... James... could I... get your help with something?"

❄

EVERY TIME I float over to the gym and there's someone using it, they instantly dismount the bike or drop the resistance bands and announce that they're done. They're usually not sweaty.

James has talked to them. It's now a ship-wide conspiracy to make me exercise. It doesn't work. I exercise less as the deadline approaches. We all do. And sleep less. It's degrading our productivity, but sleep is elusive. All I think about is finishing.

We miss the deadline. By forty-two hours. But the launch of the Janus fleet is a feat of engineering and teamwork that we're all indescribably proud of. There's an electricity in the air on launch day. Everyone is sleep-deprived and stressed, but we're all giddy as we gather in the bubble and strap in and stare at the wide screen that shows the launch tube. The launcher uses the same principles as the rail gun. Grigory studies his tablet to monitor the reactor, making sure it's compensating for the launch recoil.

The ship buzzes as the engines build up electricity, and

then, *Boom!* The first drone fires out, so small and fast we can barely see it, like a BB out of a kid's gun. Another buzzing, another boom, and the second drone is away. And so it goes, one after another until the ship falls silent.

All eyes turn to Harry, who's studying his own tablet. He looks up and grins. "First comm-patch is in: all stats are nominal. We've got a successful launch."

The cheers in the confined space are deafening. High-fives, a few fist bumps, James turns to me and nods, and I simply reach out and hug him, as if our fight had been flushed out the launch tube with the drones. He holds me longer than I expect, and I don't let go.

"Now what?" Charlotte asks.

Without releasing me, James says, "Now, ladies and gents, we celebrate."

Harry opens a cabinet and starts tossing out vacuum-sealed meals. "Kitchen's open! Place your orders, folks. Steak. Chicken. Mashed potatoes. Shrimp cocktail. Spicy green beans. And freeze-dried ice cream and chocolate cake for dessert."

James pulls open another cabinet. "And for the night's entertainment, a plethora of board games. Decided by simple majority vote."

❄

IN EVERY WAY, it's a perfect night. No screens. No deadlines. No arguing, just all of us eating together and doing something we've never done before: playing.

We're all stuffed and tired when we finish, but I know there's one thing on everyone's mind: a shower. It's dry in space. We all feel as though we've walked through the desert, sweating and accumulating grime, but no one has bothered to shower for over a week. We've covered it up with deodorant and kept our heads down, working every spare second.

James extends his hand, palm down, fist closed, holding eight bits of wire. He makes everyone draw. Charlotte, Lina, Izumi, and I draw the longest ones—we'll get to shower first. Then the four guys. James and Harry are last. They rigged it. I don't know how, but they rigged it. No one argues. We're all too tired.

The shower is cylindrical and tight, an enclosed tube with a door. There's no drain, just a suction device that pulls the water out. My skin feels as if I've been rubbed all over with sandpaper and coated in sawdust. The water is like a gentle rain washing it away and coating me in a thin lotion, soothing me.

For the past few weeks, I've been sleeping in the lab. Most people have been bedding down near their work. Tonight, I slip into one of the sleep stations: a padded, enclosed cubby like a bunk bed in space. To me, it feels as luxurious as a penthouse hotel suite. It's soft and comforting, hugging me tight.

There are only six sleep stations on the ship, and there's not enough room inside for two. But Grigory has already made himself a sleep station in the engine module, and Min has set up a similar alcove at navigation.

I'm almost asleep when James pulls the curtain back. His face is clean, and he smiles. "Good night."

❄

It's the best sleep I've had since the ISS disaster.

I wake, wash my face, brush my teeth, and float down to the bubble for breakfast. James is there, tapping at a tablet.

"Good morning."

"Morning." He hands me a water bottle and a tablet. It's an exercise schedule. For me. This again.

"I'm not telling you, Emma I'm *asking*. Please do this. Or whatever you're willing to do."

I study the screen. Four hours a day.

"It's important to the mission," he says. "And to me."

"Okay."

❄

THE DAYS before the launch seemed to fly by. The days after drag on.

When contact day arrives—the moment when we should hear from the Janus scout drone—everyone is nervous. We don't acknowledge it though. We don't gather in the bubble at the designated time. We're not that sure about the artifact's position, not sure exactly when contact will occur, and no one wants to draw attention to the deadline. But I'm acutely aware of the projected contact time arriving and passing with no messages. I think everyone is.

Another day passes with no messages. We're all struggling to focus on our work.

On the third day, James convenes us in the bubble. "Well, let's start with the obvious: there's been no contact from the Janus scouts. The implication is that the artifact wasn't at the position NASA projected."

"Or it wiped the drones out," Grigory says.

"Or a malfunction," Min adds.

"All possibilities," says James.

"What's the plan?" Lina asks.

"We're going to figure out what's wrong, and we're going to fix it."

CHAPTER 28

JAMES

WE HAVE PROBLEMS. And they're popping up like a litter of kittens.

I'm stressed. Izumi is all over me about it. She's all over each of us about our stress levels. She's mandated we take downtime—at least one hour each day for each of us alone, outside our labs or workstations. So I hide out in my sleep station and review design specs and take notes.

We also spend an hour each day together in the bubble, all eight crewmembers, conducting a team-building exercise Izumi designates. Board games, talking about ourselves (which is excruciating for me), our feelings (a form of torture, in my view), and how we feel the mission is going (everyone lies).

Gone is the camaraderie we shared after the Janus launch, that night we ate and laughed and were like one big family.

Somehow, everyone is looking to me for a plan. I guess it makes sense: the drones are our primary method of completing our mission at the moment, and drones are my department.

I feel the weight of the next decision like an entire planet on top of me. Guess wrong, and everyone on Earth dies. If they're not already dead.

In prison, I felt cut off from the world. And given the way the world treated me before my incarceration, that was fine by me. This is something else entirely. Not knowing what's going on back on Earth is eating at me. I think that's true of all of us. It's part of the tension, and it's worse for those crew with the strongest bonds to their family and friends. They want to know if their loved ones are alive and well, if they're safe or if they're freezing to death in a refugee camp right now. We keep telling ourselves we're doing the best we can, but so far our best has come up short.

We're facing three principal constraints: material, power, and time. In the material department, drone engines are our most critical constraint. We used half of our supply on the Janus fleet. As for power, the *Pax*'s reactor can only supply so much, and we need that power for the drones and to reach our destination quickly. And then there's time. There are only so many hours in the day to work, and within those hours, only so many when any one of us can work at peak efficiency. We need *good* hours. The prevailing feeling here on the *Pax* is that our next move might be our last shot.

But I have a plan, and I call the group together in the bubble to discuss it.

I motion to Harry and Emma, whom I've come to see as our core team. "First, we favor sending a small drone to intercept the *Fornax* and comm-patch the news that the artifact isn't in the expected location. And of course get a status update from the other ship."

Charlotte seems annoyed at the idea. "Are we sure this is a good idea?"

Grigory seems just as annoyed. "Yes. We thought it was good idea before, and it still is."

"It was a good idea when we thought we had news to share," Charlotte shoots back.

"This *is* news!" Grigory shouts.

Izumi holds up her hands. "You all know the rules. No raised voices. No attacking people—only ideas. We're taking a ten-minute break. Then we'll return to the bubble and start over."

There are eye rolls and exhales, but the crew obediently unsnaps from the table and sails out in all directions.

Harry, Emma, and I regroup in the robotics lab.

"That went well," Harry says.

Emma is pedaling the desk bike, which I built for her from spare parts. "I think it's safe to say we'll meet more resistance than we did with our first plan."

❄

Izumi takes charge of the meeting when we return to the bubble. She passes out small slips of paper.

"We're going to take a straw poll on the question of whether to send a drone to the *Fornax*. Simply write yes or no and the number one reason behind your answer. I will tally the results and collate the reasons."

Grigory throws up his hands. "I can barely read my writing."

"Then just write a zero or one, Grigory. One being yes. I assume your numbers are legible."

He stews but stays silent.

When Izumi has tallied the votes, she announces, "We are six for and two against."

Min shakes his head. "When did we decide this was a democracy? Just because there are more votes for the plan doesn't mean we should do it. There could be a reason against that negates everything."

"So much for anonymity," Lina mutters.

Izumi exhales. "The point of this exercise was for everyone to state their first reaction and reasoning—so that we can examine them without fighting. And then we vote again."

"Can we just talk about this?" Min says. "Like adults?"

Izumi raises her hand, but Min presses on.

"We have a limited number of drone engines, correct?"

I nod.

"And once we launch them, and they use up their power, they're done."

"Not necessarily," Harry says. "We've been working on ideas to reuse the drones. Reload their power cells and issue new instructions."

Min squints. "What, like some kind of landing bay? Open a hatch on one of the capsules and bring the drones into a space lab? We're moving at—"

"No, nothing like that," Harry says. "We've been designing a mother drone. It could recharge the cells in the other drones and issue new software."

"Very cool," Lina says.

"*Very*," Grigory adds.

I motion to Harry and Emma. "We're still working on the specs. We've got a lot of work to do. But it's feasible. We'd also be able to launch power bricks from the ship to the mother drone to resupply its power bank."

Min drums his fingers on the table. "Interesting. I feel the drones are our most precious resource. Prioritizing their deployment should be our focus." He glances at Izumi. "That's why I feel that voting on each drone deployment is not wise. We should look first at our priorities and what the drones could be deployed for, and select missions accordingly."

He pauses, perhaps waiting for dissent. No one gives any. I, for one, agree with what he's said.

He continues. "I feel that locating one of the artifacts is our top priority."

"We're already doing that," Grigory says.

"For *one* of the artifacts," Min shoots back. "We're looking for the Alpha artifact. But what if it's not even there? What if it self-destructed when it saw the probe? What if the explosion is what stopped the probe feed? The Janus fleet could be chasing a shadow. And the position is only a guess. We don't know its flight capabilities. For all we know the artifact completed its mission weeks ago and isn't even in our solar system."

"What's your point?" Harry asks.

"My point remains the same: finding an artifact is our top priority at the moment. And I feel we're doing that for the Alpha artifact. But the time has come to launch a drone—or drones—to search for the second. We need to consider the possibility that the Beta artifact is the only one we can reach." Min sets a tablet on the table. "I've been working on a flight path to intercept Beta —extrapolated from its last known position and what little we know about Alpha's velocity."

"Can we even reach Beta?" Charlotte asks. "And even if we do find it, does the ship have enough—whatever, fuel or reactor power—to get to it? And return home?"

Grigory shrugs. "Depends on where it is and how fast it's going."

He leaves unsaid my feeling that none of us are getting home.

"Once we have that information, we can plan accordingly," Min says. "And to be clear, Charlotte, the *Pax* doesn't need to reach the artifact. The ship just needs to be in range of our drones in order to run tests—and wage war if needed."

A silence settles over the group. Finally, Min says, "Look, I want to know what happened to the *Fornax* too. But that curiosity doesn't justify another drone right now. We need to find one of the artifacts."

Min makes some good points, but his focus is too narrow.

I hand my tablet to him. It shows the *Pax* and *Fornax* docked while moving through space.

"Actually, contacting the *Fornax* is about more than just solving the mystery of what happened. It's related to your point: drones. We," I point to Harry and Emma again, "also feel that drones are our primary resource limitation. The *Fornax* should have drone components that we could transfer here. We know that without Harry they have no way of building drones themselves."

Min passes my tablet to Grigory, who squints and taps at it. Lina is beside him and leans over to study the screen.

"How feasible is this?" she asks.

"Feasible," Grigory says. "Will take some work."

In the end, we decide that we will begin on that work: preparing to dock with the *Fornax*. Grigory and Min will lead the project. And we decide not to launch a drone to the *Fornax* for now.

The next launch will be a small, high-speed drone fleet sent to look for the second artifact. We entertain the idea of sending another high-speed drone to search for the first fleet of drones, but decide to wait.

When the meeting breaks, I don't return to the lab immediately. I go to the med bay, where Izumi is head-down over her tablet.

"Iz."

She turns to me.

"It was a good idea—breaking the meeting and the straw poll. We're all stressed out, and we have to be able to debate ideas. That ups our chances of success."

"It didn't work."

"That's not the point. You tried your best idea, and I bet you learned from it, and I bet your next attempt will be better." I motion out the small porthole. "That's what we're doing out here, every one of us. Trying our best idea and learning from it."

"Maybe you should be ship's doctor. You seem to know people."

"Trust me, Izumi, I'm much better with robots than humans."

On my way out of her station, I call back to her, "Chin up. You're doing great."

As I bound through the modules, on my way back to the lab, I'm struck by how hard Izumi's job is. The rest of us have our field here on the ship and with the core mission—drones, propulsion, navigation, software, and first contact. Izumi's focus is secondary and much more unpredictable. Her job is us. Keeping us functioning at optimal efficiency. I don't envy her.

In the lab, Emma is strapped to the work table, legs pedaling the bike below, hands soldering a circuit board above.

"I feel like a hamster in space," she says without looking at me.

"So is this a bad time to talk about a ceiling-mounted water bottle with a spout?"

She smiles. "Yes, it's a bad time to talk about that."

She studies the circuit board, seems to like what she sees. "How'd you think the meeting went?"

"Pretty good."

She scrunches her eyebrows. "Really?"

"Really. Everyone on the ship sees the mission differently. That's good. Min is right. We need to find one of the artifacts, and the one we've been chasing could be long gone."

"You think we have a real shot at finding the other one?"

"I think we've got to try."

✳

SIX DAYS LATER, we launch the Icarus fleet, which consists of three ultra-small, fast drones designed to find Beta. We ultimately decided that if we're going out there to search, we need to do it right: three drones can cover three times the area.

It's a good plan, and the Icarus drones are an even better design than the Janus drones. But still, there's little enthusiasm at the launch. On the whole, everyone seems to feel the same thing: we're losing time, and we're not even sure we're on the right track.

At the next meeting, we debate dispatching a drone to Earth with news. The proposal is narrowly defeated.

Harry, Emma, and I continue work on the mother drone, which we've nicknamed Madre. Or sometimes Madre de Dronay. What can I say, it gets monotonous some days in the lab, so we entertain ourselves. Harry is the main instigator in that regard. Today, he suggested we rename it the drone father, then "the Godfather, drone edition." He does a pretty good impression of Marlon Brando from the old *Godfather* movie.

His voice is gravelly: "As a drone, you never let anyone know what you're thinking. You don't broadcast. You keep your mouth shut. And you comm-patch what you know to your family. Family is everything."

The more we laugh, the more carried away Harry gets.

"We're gonna make the artifact an offer it can't refuse."

Sooner or later, the quotes cross over to other Brando movies, some I don't even know.

"This drone, it coulda been a contender. It coulda found the artifact. But now look at it. A bum. A piece of debris floating through space, its fuel cell spent." I'm told that the contender bit came from *On the Waterfront*, though I never saw it.

Harry moves on to a quote from *Apocalypse Now*: "This drone, it's seen horrors. Horrors that you've seen. But you have no right to call it a murderer."

From *The Island of Dr. Moreau*: "This drone, it's seen the devil in its telescope, and it has chained him."

And finally, back to *The Godfather*. "Look how the artifact massacred my little drone. I want you to use all your powers to clean him up. I don't want the crew to see him like this."

But one of his many quotes—he clearly knows these movies well—is quite timely. "Never hate your enemies. It affects your judgment."

That's good advice. Though if the artifact is connected to the Long Winter that's killing the human race, I don't know if I can keep myself from hating it.

Emma hands me a circuit board to inspect. It's perfect, as usual. She's getting better at building them. And faster.

"Harry, how do you remember all those quotes?" she asks as she pulls another board from the pile.

"Who knows. If my head were full of useful stuff like James, maybe we'd have already found the artifact."

"Doubt that," I mutter.

I missed this: working. And with people I like. Sure, I worked in prison, but I wasn't using my mind. Mental work is like a vitamin a person needs every day. A muscle that otherwise atrophies with disuse.

In truth, I had worried about my ability when Fowler first briefed me; I had been out of the lab for eleven months. I'm thankful that it came back to me so quickly. Harry has been a huge help. Not for the first time, I wonder if that's why NASA sent him to the *Pax*: they had second thoughts about my ability. Despite having little to show for our efforts, I think we're working at peak efficiency. It feels good to be building something again.

With the Icarus fleet's lack of contact, we're more aware, with each passing day, that our time is slipping away. I feel as if we're sailing past a new land we were bound for, but an unfavorable wind has blown us off course.

Madre is almost done, but we have no idea where to send her and which litter of drones she should repurpose.

I worry more and more about Emma's bone density. The exercise simply can't keep pace with the deterioration. It's a progressive condition: the more bone mass she loses, the quicker she'll lose it. Izumi is concerned too. We've discussed it several times, in private, but arrived at no solutions. Neither of us has said anything to Emma. I don't know if she's aware of the severity of her condition. I hope not.

The secret meetings between Izumi and me aren't the only ones occurring on the ship. Harry has been slipping off to meet with Grigory and Min. More often lately. He says it's about Madre's propulsion, but the meetings are too long, and they all stop when I float into the nav module, as though they're talking about me. I like Harry. I trust him. But I feel that something is going on. I've told no one else about my suspicions. But I'm close to confronting him about it.

❄

I'M asleep in the lab when a hand shakes me awake.

Emma's face is inches from mine, smiling.

"Come on."

We float hand-in-hand out of the robotics lab, through a series of supply modules, and into the bubble. Half of the crew is here. Grigory is smiling—a rare occurrence.

Harry slaps me on the back, the force muted in the low gravity.

"We've got it, James! The artifact!"

"Which one?"

"The second one. Beta. James, we've done it."

CHAPTER 29

EMMA

LOCATING Beta has given this crew a much-needed morale boost. Everyone feels a renewed sense of purpose, that we're on the right track, and that we're going to figure this out, one way or another. Any team, no matter what you're doing, can't go too long without a win. Finding the artifact is a big win for us. But this isn't close to being over.

Yesterday, we launched Madre to seek out the Janus fleet. It will refill their fuel cells and redirect them to Beta, which is much closer to the Sun than we expected. In fact, the Icarus drone that found the artifact had a far-out search vector, at the edge of Min's projections. He believes the artifacts are solar-powered, and that their acceleration increases rapidly as they approach the Sun.

If he's correct, there are several implications. For one thing, we're pretty sure the original artifact did accelerate beyond our search grid.

The discovery has forged consensus among the crew on several issues. Yesterday we launched comm drones to Earth and the *Fornax*. The drones are loaded with all of our data and everything we know so far. We've also altered course to intercept Beta.

When I asked Grigory if we could reach it, he was cagey. "Possibly." He shot Harry a look, then went into a long diatribe about the artifact's unknown acceleration capacity, variable solar output, and the effect of gravitational pull.

Something's going on. I know Harry, Min, and Grigory have been meeting in private. I suspect it's about me—they change the subject every time I get near them. And they're not the only ones meeting in private. I've spotted Izumi and James whispering in the med bay. And I *know* that's about me. Specifically, my bone density. It's bad. My gums are receding and my grip strength is waning. My fingernails are brittle too, and I'm getting cramps more often, especially at night. I feel as if I'm aging at an advanced rate, like someone in a time warp, literally disintegrating. But the fact remains: besides exercise and mineral supplements, there's nothing anyone can do.

And this is a far better fate than dying back on the ISS or in that rescue capsule. I've had a chance to be part of something— an incredible mission with some of the best minds and the best people whom I've ever known.

None of us will stop fighting for this mission.

❄

MADRE DISPATCHED one of the scout drones from the Janus fleet back to the *Pax* to report. The mother drone found the fleet, powered them up, and has them en route to Beta. They'll arrive in two weeks. I'm counting down the days.

Because Beta is behind us and moving fast, we'll reach it long before we would have reached Alpha. That's the good news. The bad news is that Beta could be going so fast it zooms right past us before we can intercept.

The clock is ticking. We'll know soon.

✳

HARRY, James, and I are working in the lab when Grigory drifts into the hatchway.

"Bubble meeting."

His expression is blank. I sense bad news.

In the bubble, when everyone is present and tethered to the conference table, Min says, "The comm drone is back from the *Fornax*."

The fact that the *Fornax* is out there is a relief. From Min's expression, I'm guessing that's the extent of the good news.

"I'm going to read their return message verbatim," Min says, staring at a tablet. He clears his throat. *"Be advised, Fornax compromised. Six capsules never reached assembly point."* Min holds the tablet up. "There's a list. Grigory and I already looked it up. One was Harry's capsule, of course, and four were supply capsules. The sixth was Oliver Karnes. The other astronautical engineer."

Grigory's counterpart on the *Fornax*. That's bad.

There's a long silence. As someone who never met the original crew and has gone through losing people in space, I'm probably able to process this a bit faster. I try to make my voice neutral. "I expect that explains why Harry's capsule was sent to the *Pax* rendezvous point. Once Karnes's capsule was lost, meaning there would be no astronautical engineer on the *Fornax*, mission control must have felt that Harry's skills would be underutilized there."

"That's an understatement," Harry says. "We'd be lost without Grigory."

The Russian shrugs. "The truth finally emerges."

There's controlled laughter around the room. It's a weak

attempt to conceal the disappointment we all feel. And responsibility. The mission truly falls to us now.

"The message continues," Min says. "*The crew of the* Fornax *favors transferring our drone stock to the* Pax. *Be advised: our delta payload is intact.*"

"Delta payload?" I ask.

James leans over and responds. "The only thing that was different on the two ships' supply manifests: they had a nuke, we got more drone parts."

"And one crewmember was different," Charlotte says. "Me and Dan Hampstead."

"True," James says.

"Final line of message," Min announces. "*We are altering course and preparing for rendezvous and docking. We await further orders from* Pax." Min looks up. "*End message.*"

After a pause, he says, "let's talk about our options."

"I need a minute," James says. "I need to think about this. We all do before we make this decision."

❄

IN THE LAB, James pulls me aside.

"You're getting sicker."

"I know."

"But you don't know how bad it is."

"I do know, James."

"We—Izumi and I—can't treat you here. You've got to get to a real hospital and to stronger gravity soon."

"That ship has sailed. We both know it."

"Not necessarily. We're on a rocket ship. And we're about to have another. One with no real purpose other than to release a nuke and then fly back to Earth, double fast."

"No."

"No what?"

"No, I'm not going. You're not putting me on the *Fornax* and sending me home. I'm staying here and working. You know we need the *Fornax* in the hunt for the artifact. If for no other reason than to observe and relay findings to Earth in case the *Pax* is compromised. You can't waste that ship on hospital transport back to Earth. We're all expendable."

"We're not."

"We are. End of discussion."

"Do you have any idea what your deterioration and death would do to this crew?"

"This crew is strong enough to take it."

"Don't be so sure."

"Are you speaking for yourself or them?"

"Both. Please, Emma. Think about it."

"I don't need to."

He throws up his hands. "You're nuts, you know that? Nuts! And you're driving *me* nuts." He barrels out of the lab. It's a good thing spaceships don't have gravity or slamming doors, because he would have been stomping away and rocking the hatch off its hinges as he shut it.

I believe I'm doing the right thing for the mission and everyone on Earth, including my sister and her kids. I feel miserable about it.

❄

AN HOUR LATER, we reconvene in the bubble and make the decision: we'll rendezvous with the *Fornax* and transfer all drone components to *Pax*. James is still sullen, either from our conversation or the weight of the decisions upon him. His plan isn't elaborate, and there's no mention of my going over to the *Fornax* or of the other ship turning back. But I wonder if he's planning it.

❄

IN THE LAB, James, Harry, and I discuss what to do with the new influx of parts. It will almost triple our available stock. Most importantly, we'll get more engine parts.

I voice my first reaction. With the exception of the contentious conversation I just had with James, the lab is a safe zone, where we are free to throw out ideas, and debate is civil and productive. It reminds me so much of the ISS.

"We could take more readings. Send a fleet ahead of the artifact, see how it reacts after our encounter with it."

"True," James says, eyes on the table. "But we need to consider the big picture."

"Attaching my wide-view lens," Harry says jovially.

That gets a chuckle out of James and me, but neither of us looks at the other. He's still mad at me. That sort of makes me want to be mad at him.

"We're out here for more than these two artifacts," James continues. "Our mission is to get Earth the data they need to survive."

I cock my head. "I don't follow."

"Think about it: two artifacts on the same vector. Think about what that implies."

It hits me then. "A mother ship."

Harry pinches his lower lip with his fingers. "What are you proposing?"

"A massive drone search fleet. Sent along the artifacts' vector. Running silent, collecting their findings. Another mother drone, larger than Madre, to coordinate the other drones and send comm bricks back to Earth with the data."

Harry smiles. "A *mother* mother drone? You should have led with that, James. You had me at 'We're gonna need a bigger drone.'"

"You're so shallow, Harry."

"Size matters. E equals mc squared."

It's got to be the nerdiest joke I've ever heard. But I laugh, and so does James. He glances over at me, and I can tell he doesn't really want to be mad at me. And I don't really want to be mad at him. We're fighting, essentially, because he cares about me and I care more about the mission.

❄

IN THE BUBBLE, we present our plan. To my surprise, the crew is pensive. Maybe it's because we're technically going outside of our mission objective, which is to find and assess the known artifacts.

We don't reach a consensus. We break and return to our departments.

Shortly after, Grigory drifts into the lab.

"If we send the other drones on search, we need to be ready to support them."

"Madre Two," Harry begins, but Grigory holds up a hand.

"Not talking about bigger mother drone. Talking about fact we have two ships now. One possibly without purpose."

To my surprise, he doesn't elaborate. He nods and floats out of the lab. His meaning isn't lost on James, Harry, or me. But we don't discuss it. We all return to our work, stewing on the idea.

❄

THE NEXT DAY, James, Harry, and I form a plan. We don't include the *Fornax* in it. Mostly because we're scared to make plans for the ship   because those plans might sentence that crew to death.

❉

IN THE BUBBLE, the meeting about the drone deployment is contentious. Battle lines are drawn. Harry, James, Grigory, and I are for sending the remaining drones along the vector to search for more artifacts and a potential mother ship.

The rest are against, some more vocally than others.

Min points at James. "This isn't our mission."

"Of course it is. Our mission is to do whatever we have to do to save Earth."

Min taps on his panel. "The mission—"

"Is more than what's written in the briefing, Min." James is mad. He's trying to hide it, but he's losing control. "Why do you think they sent us up here? To follow that document to the letter? No. We're here to use our heads and figure this out. We need to find that mother ship."

James looks at the group. "Odds are, it's out there. And if these artifacts are responsible for the Long Winter, we've *got* to fight them at the source. There could be millions or even billions of these artifacts."

Arguing ensues, voices rising. The fight, more than any of our time here on the *Pax*, reveals the personalities of the members of our crew.

Min, ultimately, is by the book. He favored finding the second artifact, but only because he felt that effort was well within the mission parameters. He can't imagine going home and telling his superiors he went off on a completely different mission than what he was sent up here for.

Izumi is with him. Maybe her training as a physician has

taught her to be conservative. Or perhaps she's against our idea because it's so radical.

For Charlotte, the sticking point is the prospect of losing the drones—of having a successful first contact and no way to adapt her approach.

Lina is somewhere in the middle. The German programmer is the least talkative of the crew. She simply asks what the risks and rewards are, which sparks another James-Min standoff.

I think Harry favors the plan mostly because he likes building the drones, and I think he would follow James anywhere. I would too. But I also agree with the plan on the merits. My gut tells me the artifacts are hostile. That's not just because I think they destroyed the ISS and killed my crew. The evidence supports it.

Grigory is in that camp: he thinks we're at war. He favors, in his words, "finding our enemy."

In the end, Lina votes with us, and a compromise is struck: parts for three small drones will remain on the *Pax*. That wins Charlotte over, leaving Min and Izumi. Neither of them is comfortable with the decision, but they will work to support it. And in private, James and Min apologize to each other for shouting.

We're becoming more than a crew. We're becoming a family, one that fights and compromises and cares about each other, even when we don't agree. Even when we're mad at each other.

❄

THE RUN-UP to the *Fornax* rendezvous is hectic. It's anybody's guess which will happen first: the Janus fleet reaching Beta or the docking.

James and Harry obsess over the drone designs for the third fleet, which they're calling "Midway" after the decisive naval battle that turned the tide of World War II in the Pacific. Harry, in addition to being a human repository of movie quotes, is a history buff as well. James is too, but to a lesser extent.

"Without Midway, the Japanese could have run the board," Harry says, strapped to our work table in the drone lab. "Brilliance, that's what it was. The greatest game of naval strategy ever played."

I wonder if that's what Harry thinks we're doing out here: an elaborate strategy game against an enemy that looks as if it's winning. And will win.

"The US fleet took down four Japanese carriers at Midway. Four of the six that attacked Pearl Harbor. The Japanese never recovered. Couldn't replace those ships. Or the pilots they lost."

James is untangling a ball of wires. "You could argue Guadalcanal was just as important."

Harry pauses. "True. But that was a land campaign." He smiles. "Our fight is in the air."

I enjoy listening to them debate history. I've never had much interest in military history, but their enthusiasm brings it to life. I've learned more about the War in the Pacific the last two days than I have in my life.

They've named the elements of the drone fleet to align with their historical counterparts. There will be three carrier drones— Hornet, Yorktown, and Enterprise—and almost a hundred small scout drones, which don't warrant names, just the designation PBY and a number. I had to ask what a PBY was (answer: a sea plane used extensively for scouting, rescue, and anti-submarine operations in the 1930s and 40s).

Finally, there are two specialty drones. Vestal is a large, slow drone with all the excess parts. The carriers will be able to offload parts from it as needed. And Mighty Mo is a battle drone with four rail guns and a huge battery to power them. It even looks mean. James and Harry laughed when they settled on the name. Apparently it's the nickname for the *USS Missouri*, a storied US battleship that hosted the Japanese surrender. It was the last battleship the US commissioned and the last battleship to be decommissioned.

It also turns out James and Harry are a bit superstitious. They'll only name the drones after "successful" ships. Harry tells me the US never lost a battleship at sea, though four were sunk during the attack on Pearl Harbor. It's amazing the history you learn on an impromptu space mission.

My only worry is that Izumi might take offense at the carrier names. I go as far as asking her about it, but she simply stares back with a blank expression and says, "Why would that bother me?"

"Well, you know, because of the war."

She nods absently. "No. It doesn't bother me."

I probably just earned myself a psych eval.

❄

I'm in my sleep station, dead to the world, when the shouts wake me. I try to focus on the words, but I can't make them out. Something in Chinese, and Japanese, and Harry yelling, "ET phone home!"

The curtain yanks back and James lets his momentum carry him into the cramped space. He's nearly on top of me, his lips inches from mine.

"We did it. The Janus fleet reached Beta. We've got observational data. And first contact. It's communicating with us."

CHAPTER 30

JAMES

I FEEL LIKE A SAILOR, marooned on a desert island who has just seen a sail on the horizon. I don't know if we'll be saved, or if it's even a friendly sail, but it's hope. That's what first contact with the artifact means. Hope. Hope that we can communicate. Negotiate. Find a way to survive.

In the bubble, Charlotte is practically buzzing. Everyone is here. Emma, sleepy-faced. Min, looking stoic as usual. Grigory, hair in a mess, expression skeptical. Lina and Izumi are uncharacteristically animated, and Harry and I are overjoyed.

I want Emma to hear everything.

I hold a hand up. "Let's take it from the top—and record it for posterity."

Everyone sits a little straighter as Harry activates the bubble's camera. Grigory even runs a hand through the rat's nest on his head, to no avail.

Harry goes into his official voice. He has a very good official voice. "The crew of the *Pax* is happy to report that on mission day ninety-two we have made contact with Beta, the second artifact identified in our solar system. The alien construct is currently transiting the system, destination unknown, but on an intercept course with the Sun. As the mission log states, we launched a fleet of drones, Janus, to search for the first artifact, Alpha. They were unsuccessful. A second fleet of drones, Icarus, located Beta, and the Janus fleet was re-routed to it. Janus contains two scout drones and three specialized drones: observation, communication, and intervention."

I can't help but smile at the term "intervention." Sounds better than "rail gun drone" or "battle drone." Harry doesn't miss a beat.

"The observation drone performed a successful fly-by, taking visual and other passive non-emissive readings. That drone will rendezvous with us in approximately twenty hours. We'll reach the artifact in twelve days. And we'll link up with the *Fornax* in four days. With that said, I'll turn it over to Charlotte Lewis, the mission's first contact specialist."

Charlotte's Australian accent seems a bit more pronounced than before. I'm sure we're all thinking that this video could be shown around the world—and even watched for generations to come. Assuming there are future generations.

"Our first contact protocol was to issue a series of simple mathematical challenges in a variety of wave forms: microwave, radio wave, and light, for example. Our first mathematical sequence was the Fibonacci numbers. Zero, one, one, two, three, five, eight, and so on." She inhales. "I'm happy to report that after the communications drone issued the forty-sixth number in the Fibonacci sequence, the artifact responded with the forty-seventh. For the first time in the history of the human race, we have made contact with an extraterrestrial intelligence."

This feels like a good place to cut the video. Charlotte's enthusiasm oozes through, and whoever is watching, wherever they are, whenever they are, will feel what we're feeling right now.

Excitement.

Hope.

I give Harry a quick hand motion, and he taps his tablet.

"Recording ended."

"Okay," I begin. "The plan has always been to comm-brick major updates to home. I say we send one right now and include this video."

The group agrees, and we break and reconvene when the brick is on its way to Earth. It's the first communication we've sent. I can't help feeling a little pride that it carries good news—and ahead of schedule.

Min opens the meeting.

"Well, let's discuss."

"I wish I were there," Charlotte says.

"Depending on what it does to that drone, you may not," says Grigory.

"Meaning?" she shoots back.

Grigory shrugs. "Meaning is clear. Drone could be in pieces by now."

I hold up a hand. "We need to talk about whether our plans should change."

Emma speaks first. "I for one am optimistic. Maybe it's because I want to believe, but I tend to think this could be a break. Alpha summarily destroyed or disabled the probe—"

"A probe that spied on it without permission," Charlotte says.

Grigory scoffs. "Spying is always without permission."

"My point," Emma says, cutting off Charlotte's retort, "is that this is clearly a change in behavior. Granted, the drone acted differently than the probe, but the fact remains: upon learning of the drone, Beta didn't react aggressively. What does that mean? Maybe this artifact is at war with the other."

The idea hangs in the air a long moment. If true, it complicates matters. And gives us a potential ally. And a chance of ending the Long Winter.

"Maybe," Harry says, "whatever is happening in our system is related to that war? One side needs solar output somehow or is compromising it? Or maybe we're linked to one side in ways we don't understand."

I'm surprised when Lina speaks. "Maybe we're a descendant race—one side's offspring. Or biological drones."

Interesting theories. You never know what someone's thinking, especially the quiet ones.

Min speaks next.

"Or we could be simply caught in the middle. One side wants to protect us for moral reasons."

"The question," Harry says, "is whether we should alter our plans based on this information."

"Of course," Charlotte says. "We need to increase our speed and get to Beta as quickly as possible."

"Reason?" Grigory asks.

"The reason is obvious," Charlotte snaps. "We need to be there to communicate. Adapt our approach. This is the most important event in human history, and we're taking our sweet time getting there."

"We are not taking sweet time," Grigory says. "We are flying through space at a significant fraction of speed of light. We are going fast."

"And we could be going faster."

"Has cost," Grigory mutters.

"Which is?"

"Less energy for drones. Reactor can only produce so much. We need the excess for Midway."

Charlotte is exasperated. "I can't believe we're even still thinking about launching the Midway fleet. I mean seriously." She looks around at the group. "We're talking about launching a fleet of drones to look for other artifacts when we've got one right in front of us that's already talking to us?"

I shake my head. "Midway is about more than that, Charlotte. We can't just make double time to Beta and put all our eggs in one basket." I get blank stares from Min and Izumi. I have to dial back the idioms. "We need to take action that prepares Earth for all possibilities. One successful communication with one artifact isn't the end of this."

Harry offers a welcome break in the argument. "Remind us, Charlotte, what the next step is in your first contact protocol."

"Right." She inhales. "The scout drone was programmed to return to us the minute first contact was made. The comm drone actually received the Fibonacci response fifty-two hours ago."

"And while the scout drone returned to us, what's the first contact drone been doing?" Emma asks.

"Following protocol," Charlotte replies. "It's advancing to more sophisticated vocabularies, trying to establish a rich communication method. The primary goal is to convince the artifact that we're intelligent and peaceful."

In my thirty-six years of experience with the human race, I've found both points debatable.

"We're closing the distance to the artifact quickly," I say. "The original plan was to send the scout drone back to Beta, observe any further progress in communication, then return to us. Based on our speed and distance, its next round trip would be about forty-four hours—if we dispatch it now. So I favor sending the scout drone back, keeping our planned rendezvous with *Fornax,* and continuing the construction and launch of the Midway fleet. Thoughts?"

"I agree," says Grigory.

Min: "I do too."

Emma: "Yeah, same here."

Harry: "Charlotte's point is worth considering, but I still feel we need to find out what other artifacts may be out there."

Izumi: "I agree with James."

Lina: "The observation drone arrives in twenty hours, correct? It will have full data from the fly-by of Beta?"

I nod. "Correct."

"And the scout drone will return in forty-four hours with more data on first contact. In that case, I favor following our plan unless the data from the observation drone reveals a reason to change."

With that, the meeting breaks. Charlotte isn't happy, but we've all had our say. This mission is a lot more complicated than I ever imagined.

Every section of the ship and every department lead to the bubble. The energy of the crew coalesces there. Our opinions clash there. And in the storm, we make our plans better. Consensus is forged.

But back in the lab, Harry, Emma, and I are mostly on the same page (with the glaring exception of balancing Emma's health and workload). When the three of us get back to the lab, the tension from the bubble is gone. Harry pulls me into a bear hug. Emma joins us, and I pull her close.

"We did it," Harry says. "Can you believe it?"

"I can't," Emma whispers. "I went into space hoping to do work that would lead to a human colony someday. But this— contact with an alien life form—it's beyond my wildest dreams."

I like seeing her like this: happy, inspired. A kid again.

This moment is the best I've felt in a long, long time.

❄

I CAN BARELY SLEEP the night before the observation drone arrives.

We're all sitting in the bubble, staring at the widescreen, when it comes into view. It looks just like a small asteroid. Min issues docking instructions via the comm patches on the outside of the *Pax*. The drone maneuvers alongside us and into the open bay we've prepped for it. When the exterior hatch closes, Izumi floats in, suited in her EMU. She plugs the drone into the ship, and Lina's software interface begins pulling the data in.

"Don't wait for me," Izumi says over the comm. We're all excited to see the artifact, and every second counts now.

Lina's fingers work furiously, sorting the data. The screen switches to a video feed from the drone. All eyes are glued to it. Everyone is silent.

Beta hangs in the distance. The sun is behind the drone, illuminating the front of the artifact. The previous image, taken by the probe, was from the rear, the sun in the distance, the artifact simply a dark blur before the blazing sun. The drone zooms closer to the artifact, and several things strike me. First, its size and shape. From this angle, the outline of the object appears circular. I can't tell yet whether it's a sphere or if perhaps we're looking at the end of a cylinder. But it's large. It must be a mile across. Maybe two. The drone does the math. In the lower right-hand corner of the video, white text appears against the black of space:

```
Estimated width: 2.4 km

Estimated height: 2.4 km
```

It's a mile and a half across.

The drone flies closer, moving at a slight angle, not on a direct intercept. The image zooms in. The edges of the artifact come into focus.

My mouth drops open. My heart races. It's not a circle. It's a hexagon. A giant hexagon. The implications hit me like a sledge-hammer. My head almost spins.

Emma notices. With her eyes, she silently says, *What is it?*

I shake my head subtly, hoping the others haven't seen.

The drone closes the distance. The sun illuminates Beta's surface. It shimmers, like a lake at sunrise. It's a dull reflection, like a sea of obsidian bound by the hexagonal border. There are no lines, no protrusions.

I think I know what comes next. But I dread seeing it. I dread being right.

The drone slips past the artifact. The video freezes at the moment it passes. A still image remains on the screen, showing a clear side view of the artifact. At the drone's distance, it looks wafer thin. A sail drifting toward the sun. It must have some mechanism for allowing the solar wind to flow through or around it. Anything sufficiently advanced to create this could certainly solve that problem. The drone esti-mates its depth at three meters. I feel my stomach drop. I have to focus.

The shape is the key to understanding it. A hexagon. The shape occurs in nature for good reason. A bee's honeycomb. The eyes of a fly. Soap bubbles.

Why a hexagon and not a circle?

Hexagons fit together.

That is the conclusion.

What it means for humanity, I'm not certain yet. But I have a hypothesis. And it's not good.

The screen snaps back to video mode, showing the back of the artifact. There are no markings here either, simply another dark pool, this one with no sunlight dully reflected. It would be almost invisible against the black of space if not for the sunlight illuminating its edges, outlining it.

Data scrolls on the screen. Lina narrates.

"Tests for emissions are all negative. It's like us. Running dark."

When the video ends, Min says, "Let's talk about what this means."

I'm only vaguely aware of the debate raging. Grigory asks whether it might be alive—like some giant space insect. Min suggests it might be a piece of a ship that has broken off. Charlotte insists that it can communicate and that it is therefore intelligent, no matter what it is.

I'm so deep in thought, I barely hear my name, once, then again, Min calling me. "James. James."

"Yeah. I'm here."

"Well, what do you think?"

"I think... I need some time to think."

A long pause.

Harry: "Me too. Actually, that's probably a good idea for all of us."

❄

BACK IN THE LAB, Emma corners me. "You know something."

"Maybe. I don't know."

"James. Tell me."

I can't tell her. Not until I'm sure.

"We need more data."

❄

WE GET MORE data ten hours later. Fourteen hours ahead of schedule. It confirms my worst fears.

"The scout drone has returned from the artifact," Min says, his expression stoic. "The comm drone that exchanged the Fibonacci numbers with the artifact is non-responsive."

"A malfunction?" Charlotte asks.

"Possible," Harry says quietly.

"Scout drone is early," Grigory says, cutting to the chase.

Min nods. "Yes. It was on its way to Beta when it found the comm drone, adrift."

"Timeline?" Grigory asks.

Min raises his eyebrows.

"When did it..." Grigory seems to rifle through several word choices. "Become *inactive?*"

Min glances at his tablet. "Right after it made first contact."

I swallow hard but try not to show any emotion. I feel the way I did that day in court, when I stood and heard the judge sentence me to life in prison without the possibility of parole. Except I'm not the only one getting a bad rap now. It's the whole human race, whose major crime, it would seem, is being born on the wrong planet at the wrong time.

Grigory is more to the point now.

"Artifact attacked it. Just like probe."

"It could have malfunctioned," Lina says carefully.

"We should have been there," says Charlotte.

Emma reacts quickly, and I'm glad.

"I think we should talk about what we're going to do now."

"I agree," says Min.

Everyone looks at me.

"We need to get the comm drone back," I say. "Quickly. And figure out what happened."

CHAPTER 31

EMMA

JAMES KNOWS SOMETHING. And he's not telling us.

For a good portion of this trip, I've been furious at him for sharing his thoughts—mostly on my health. Now I'm furious because he *won't* share his thoughts. It's driving me nuts. I can't help him if he won't talk to me. Ever since we got the video footage from the observation drone, it's like he's carrying the burden of the whole world.

The drone fleet was launched with a specific plan: observation first, contact second, and if that fails, intervention. But it's not certain that contact has failed. It could be a technical issue on our end.

At our next meeting in the bubble, Grigory advocates following the plan and sending in the drones with rail guns. Charlotte is naturally against this idea. So am I. Lina is against, as is Izumi. Min favors moving the intervention drones into position but waiting.

And then there's James. He simply listens, then untethers himself from the table in the bubble and says, "We need to find out what happened to the comm drone. We can't do anything until then."

He just leaves. No discussion, no debate.

Harry and I find him head-down over a tablet in the lab. Stewing. Pinching his lower lip.

"What was that?" I ask.

"What?"

"In the bubble. The—I don't know—lack of discussion."

"We don't have time for it."

He hands me a tablet. It's schematics for a new type of drone. It's ultra-small and very, very fast. This will require a whole lot of the stored reactor energy. The fleet is called Helios, and it consists of three of these mini drones, one of which has the capability to launch ultra-small comm bricks back to Earth to report any findings. These mini comm bricks are about the size of three quarters stacked together and have most of the capabilities of the larger comm bricks, including wireless transmission.

"We need to send scout drones to the sun. Along the artifact vector. They'll do a high-speed survey. Video recording only. Silent running. And send their findings directly to Earth."

"I agree," Harry says quietly.

Whatever is going on, Harry knows what it is too. Or maybe James told him what he's thinking. And not me. The idea infuriates me. But I know James well enough to know that he doesn't want to talk right now. He wants to get this done. Quickly.

"Okay. Let's do it."

❄

I'VE NEVER WORKED SO HARD, or so fast, in my life. Thirteen hours after James showed me the specs for the Helios drones, they're firing out of the ship. The rail gun is over its max output.

The ship jostles like an earthquake as it blasts the tiny drones toward the sun.

What does James expect to find there? Why is he so afraid all of a sudden?

❄

WE GATHER in the bubble when the *Fornax* pulls alongside us, every face on both ships floating in the round porthole windows. There's no noticeable damage to our sister ship, no blast marks or punctures in the modules, but I can tell that it's smaller than the *Pax*, and it doesn't match the schematics in the mission briefing. The arms branching out are shorter.

We entertained several ideas for transferring the drone stock, including docking the ships. We finally settled on a tether. The cargo containers will be latched to the cord and carried over, like a clothesline in space. The tether will also contain a cable—a direct data link. We're still running dark—no emissions—but as long as we're flying side by side, we can maintain a hard link and swap as much data as we want—like video and the readings from the observation drones.

Most importantly, we can videoconference and actually talk to one another.

We use the robotic arms to attach the tether to the *Pax*, then offload the supplies.

Since I have the most experience with similar operations, I operate the arms. I enjoy it actually, and it gives me something to do while the crew of the *Pax* videoconferences with the crew of the *Fornax*. After the warm welcomes, they quickly discuss the data and what they've learned. James leads the meeting, but for some reason, they delay any decisions. On the whole, it's a jovial meeting. A reunion. James has told me that the two crews only met each other once, but there's a bond there, no doubt forged by this intense shared experience.

When I first came aboard the *Pax*, I felt like an outsider. A party crasher on the most important endeavor in human history. But James and the rest of the crew treated me as an equal, welcomed me, and integrated me into every aspect of life on this vessel: the work, the meetings, even the unpleasant arguments. I became one of the family. But now, for whatever reason, I feel like the newly adopted child at a family reunion, meeting the relatives for the first time. Everyone already seems to have such a history and close connection. I'm relegated to the kitchen, doing the work while the others chat.

And in truth, I'm not even supposed to be here.

When I finish offloading the last crate from the tether into the open module, I retract the arm and remain at the control station just outside the bubble, unsure what to do. Should I go to the bubble and introduce myself? I can hear them. They're discussing the recovery of the compromised drone. James is talking around it. Buying time. For what?

He startles me when he appears in my module.

"Hey."

I hold a hand to my chest. "Hey."

"You all right?"

"You just scared me."

"Any issues?"

"No."

He looks at the video screen showing the module holding the drone supply crates.

"Looks like all of them."

"Yeah. I got them."

"Well... what're you doing now?"

"I was... I don't know. Wasn't sure."

He gently grasps my upper arm. "I am. Come on. There's some folks who want to meet you."

In the bubble, I tether to the table and look at the smiling faces of the *Fornax* crew.

James motions to me. "*Fornax*, this is Commander Emma Matthews, sole survivor of the ISS catastrophe and, on this mission, the sole reason we've been able to launch so many drones so quickly. She's been building circles around Harry and me."

I haven't blushed this hard since middle school. "Well, I doubt that."

"Don't believe her, guys," Harry calls out. "She's the all-star in the lab."

James introduces the *Fornax* crewmembers by name, and they greet me in their native tongues.

"Bonjour."

"Ciao."

"Hi, Emma."

And last, Dan Hampstead. "Nice to meet you, ma'am."

And just like that, I feel a part of the family again.

James addresses both groups: "The last thing to discuss is what to do from here. We've transferred the plans for the Midway drones to you all. We're going to launch the fleet as soon as it's assembled. After that, we're going to inspect the unresponsive Janus comm drone when it returns. I don't think we can make a plan until we know what happened to that drone."

There are nods among both crews.

Antonio, Min's counterpart on the *Fornax*, is the first to speak. "That sounds reasonable. Listen, we've had a long discussion here. Without drone-building capability, we feel the *Fornax*'s best use is offensive."

There's a long pause, neither side reacting.

Dan Hampstead speaks for the first time. "Just so we're all

on the same page, I want to add that the nuke isn't like the drones. It will need to be piloted from the ship. That means active comm traffic. The artifact could be capable of evasive maneuvers, and it might trace the nuke back to the ship. Whatever ship fires the nuke needs to be able to fly it—and we should recognize the risk profile of that action."

The implication is clear: once the *Fornax* launches the nuke, it'll have a target painted on its back.

There's no hint of hesitation from the *Fornax* crew, only unblinking resolve. Their selfless act has given us all pause. It's humbling. And inspiring.

James nods. "All fair points. Let's see what we find out from the comm drone and go from there." He looks up at the screen and the crew of the *Fornax*. "It was so good to see you all."

An hour later, the tether is detached and the ships are drifting away from each other, and I think every single one of us on the *Pax* is thinking the same thing: that may be the last time we ever see the crew of the *Fornax*.

❄

THE JANUS COMM drone has returned. The scout drone attached itself to it and has pulled it in.

We're all gathered in the bubble, waiting for Lina to establish a comm-patch connection with the scout.

"Contact," Lina says, hunched over her tablet.

James asks the first question.

"When did the drone lose power?"

Lina: "Right after first contact."

Charlotte: "A software glitch?"

Lina bristles at the comment. "Possible. Doubtful."

James: "What can the scout drone tell us?"

Lina: "Not much via comm patch." She works the tablet.

"The comm drone issued the Fibonacci numbers via multi-frequency broadcast. Response from Beta after the forty-sixth number. The comm drone issued the forty-eighth Fibonacci number. Response from the artifact is non-numeric. A complex message. Then nothing. Log file ends."

Charlotte: "We need to see that message."

Min: "I agree."

Harry unlatches from the tablet. "Shall I prep the guest suite? I mean, the cargo module?"

That gets a few laughs. Except for James. He's looking away from the group. I can almost see the wheels turning in that big brain of his. Harry is almost out of the bubble when James speaks, quickly, his voice distant. "No."

Everyone stops.

"No, Harry, we need to keep it outside the ship."

Before Harry can answer, he continues. "Emma, use the arms to get it from the scout. Attach a data tether. Lina, we need a firewall. Not a software firewall. Full isolation."

She nods. "Of course. I can attach a system directly to the tether. It will have no connectivity to the ship's systems."

"Good."

Charlotte seems annoyed by all this. "Can I ask what's going on here?"

"Drone could be Trojan Horse," says Grigory.

James still doesn't look up. "Yes. That complex message could have been a virus. Or the artifact could have disabled the drone some other way. And lastly, it could be a simple malfunction. We need to figure out what happened to it. And fast."

※

THE CONTROL MODULE IS CRAMPED. I'm working the panel for the robotic arms, Lina sits beside me with a tablet connected directly to the tether, and James, Harry, Min, Grigory, and Izumi are all crammed in behind us.

On the second try, I connect to the drone's data port.

Lina taps quickly, her hand almost a blur.

"It's dead. Won't even respond to a diagnostic."

Silence. All eyes drift to James. He has that far-off look again.

"Open it up."

He looks directly at me. "Activate the cameras on the arms. Be *very* careful when you open it. Peel it like an onion. Slowly. Inside, you're looking for the data drive. You know where it is."

And I do. I built this drone. I screwed that data drive to the drone's central node. And I have the most experience and dexterity with the arms.

I dread doing this. One wrong move with the robotic arm could damage the data drive. We'd have no way of figuring out what the drone saw—and happened to it. I focus, knowing my crew is counting on me. The last crew that counted on me... I lost them. I've carried that weight since the ISS was destroyed. Even halfway to the sun, I've never quite shaken it. I probably never will. But I know, deep down, that this will help. I know my time on the *Pax* has helped.

James is watching me.

"Okay," I breathe.

"Get the black box too."

I nod. The black box was Harry's idea: another data drive buried deep inside the drone, shielded, with real-time, filtered data replication from all the drone's systems.

I take the controls and work the robotic arms, carefully detaching the drone's outer panels.

Past the outer panels, I try to pry open the inner housing. I glance at the tension readings on the arm. Too high. Why?

James floats closer and studies the screen. "What's wrong?"

"Too much resistance. Like it's stuck or fused somehow."

"Use the laser."

I swallow hard, nervous.

Holding the drone with one of the arms, I activate the laser with the other and shear off a piece on the edge of the drone, revealing the insides.

The wires are melted like a box of colored crayons, mangled, colors flowing together like water paint in a stream. The circuit boards are flattened, the resistors, LEDs, capacitors, and diodes looking like a tiny city that has been burned to the ground.

Charlotte speaks first. "What happened? What could have done this? A solar flare?"

"This is not natural phenomenon," Grigory says. Charlotte opens her mouth to argue, but Grigory continues: "Is statistical impossibility."

"We'll know soon," James murmurs quietly. "Keep going, Emma. Carve it up."

Five minutes later, I'm staring at the drive on the screen.

"Bring it into the cargo module," James says.

The next hour is grueling. Absolute concentration on my part. And it's a success. I recover both the drive and the black box. I take samples from around the drone and put them into containers.

In the cargo module, I use smaller arms to connect the black box to a cord connected to Lina's firewalled computer.

"I want to see that message," Charlotte says.

"We need to see the video first," James says quickly, his tone matter-of-fact, not challenging. No one argues.

Lina types away, then the video plays, every eye glued to it.

We see Beta in the distance, the first contact drone closing from behind.

The Fibonacci numbers scroll on the screen in white. A number pops up in red—a reply. Another number in white, then a question mark in red. That must represent the artifact's non-numeric message.

The next second the screen goes black.

"Play it back," James says. "End minus two seconds. Slow it way down. This thing is capturing a hundred frames a second. Play back at ten per second."

The video plays again.

My mouth falls open. The artifact *transforms*. The hexagonal shape folds in on itself, forming what looks like a bean with two pointed ends. One end swivels to face the comm drone. A flash erupts from the point.

The video ends.

I now know what James has probably known for some time. What Harry realized. What they didn't tell me: we are at war.

CHAPTER 32

JAMES

WE'VE SENT a comm brick to Earth with the video footage of the drone being fried by the artifact. Grigory, Harry, and I have spent hours debating how the artifact even did it. Radiation or some kind of charged particle burst are our best guesses. We've decided to harden the Midway fleet against similar attacks. I don't know if it will work.

Charlotte has spent every waking hour studying the message the artifact broadcast. She's had no luck. I'm glad she's trying, but I doubt she'll solve it, even as smart as she is.

I know what I think happened. The comm drone broadcast a simple message. The artifact assumed it might be someone on its side, a simple messenger. It broadcast the next Fibonacci number back, then an encrypted message in its native format. When the drone didn't respond in the same language, the artifact figured out they weren't on the same team after all.

The debate about our next move is surprisingly short. We've sent the scout drone back to the Janus fleet. It will give the intervention drone the go-ahead to fire the rail guns at Beta. We've decided to take a larger sample of the artifact, almost twenty feet square, assuming it breaks as we anticipate. The transport drone that will take the sample back to Earth launched yesterday. In the bubble, during the launch, it occurred to me that the sample would be the first known alien artifact to ever be brought back to Earth: a piece of what we believe to be an enemy, possibly an invader, recovered with the sole purpose of studying it so that we can be ready to kill it and defend ourselves.

I've thought a lot about the artifact since I saw the video. Its outer material is clearly pliable, or at least broken into segments small enough to bend into the shape we saw. Countless times during this mission, the crew has debated what exactly the artifacts are. Could they be living creatures? A hive of creatures floating through space? A machine, perhaps a drone similar to the ones we're launching? Or perhaps it's a spaceship crewed by beings far smaller than us. All are possibilities. I have no clues that might reveal the truth.

But I will soon.

The mood on the *Pax* has changed. We're less talkative. People smile less. We speak in shorter conversations. There's an urgency, and a tension in the air. This must be how it felt in Pearl Harbor and across America after the attack. We have a sense of foreboding. We know a battle lies ahead. And we know that though it's one we could never prepare for, it's a fight we must take up, for our loved ones and for our entire species.

I know Emma felt betrayed that I didn't tell her what I suspected earlier. I hope she understands now. The burden of it was just too great—*is* too great. Now that it's out in the open, the weight of our decisions is crushing us out here. And Emma is already carrying the weight of the deaths of her crew from the ISS. I know it's eating at her, though she won't admit it to me. Or maybe even to herself.

I also know that Emma's worried about her sister and her family. She recorded a video message to them that we sent in the comm brick to Earth (there was plenty of room for data). In fact, all of the crew recorded messages home. I don't know what most of them said—they were spoken in Chinese, Japanese, German, and Russian—but the messages from Emma, Harry, and Charlotte to their loved ones followed the same pattern: get to safety, hunker down, and I love you.

I'm the only crewmember who didn't send a message. I considered sending one to my brother, but I doubt he'd even view it. He doesn't want to hear from me. If this is the end, I have to honor his wishes and leave him in peace.

I'd desperately like to contact my only friend, Oscar, but I can't give away his location. That would be another kind of betrayal.

❆

WE GATHER in the bubble for the launch of the Midway fleet. The ship vibrates and shakes as the rail launcher discharges. The drones zoom into the black of space, faster than we can see on the screen. We simply watch the launcher status to make sure all systems are functioning.

The drones will travel away from the sun, looking for the mother ship that sent out the artifacts. If there is one. That means the launch vector is behind us, so unlike with the Janus fleet launch, the rail gun recoil is actually propelling us forward. As such, Grigory has poured more energy into the launches. In fact, he's using too much energy—too much for the *Pax* to ever make it back to Earth. We might have enough power left to get one escape module back to Earth, but I'm not even certain about that. Using the reactor power is a decision we never debate, one we've made automatically. We all know the truth: we have to stay out here. We're at war. We have to figure out how large our enemy is. Where they are. Our lives are less important than that.

Somehow, I think we all knew this was a one-way trip when we left. There's no doubt now.

We're not going home.

✳

LINA IS BRILLIANT. She's devised a compression algorithm for the comm patches that will allow them to send images of the artifact. Her breakthrough was that we don't need high resolution to know what's going on—in large part because almost everything in space is black. So her solution is for the drones to take a full image first, but to not store the black pixels or nearly black pixels. They won't record the sun, either; the drone will simply note the sun's position, and the software will then fill in the sun and stars in the background. Even better, once an initial image is established, all the drone really needs to relay is what Lina calls "delta caps": partial images that record how the original image has changed.

The best part is that we'll be able to see the "images" in realtime. We're aligning all of the scout drones at our disposal to make a data relay link. Even though we'll be out of line of sight and far away from the artifact, we'll see exactly what happens.

The artifacts are killing our world. Soon we'll strike back. And we'll be able to witness it.

✳

WE'VE BEEN TAKING our meals at random times, whenever someone gets hungry. Eating smaller, more frequent meals helps us stretch our energy and work longer periods of time. We see each other in passing, in the bubble and in the corridors, but for the most part, everyone is head-down over his or her work. It feels as though we're pulling apart, like planets that were in a tight orbit around a star that has gone supernova, blasting them away, burned and broken.

Izumi doesn't like it. She's mandated a crew meal together in the bubble. We use it as an opportunity to discuss the big question at hand: what happens after we shear off a piece of the artifact?

Grigory: "Is obvious. We fire nuke from *Fornax* as soon as sample is clear of blast radius."

Min: "I agree."

Lina: "Me too."

Charlotte scrunches her eyebrows. "I'm not disagreeing. And I know this is probably a stupid question. But how will the nuke work in space?"

I sense that Charlotte is genuinely curious—not necessarily opposed.

Harry's voice is gentle. "It's a fair question." He looks over at Grigory, allowing the engineer the chance to explain, since he's more knowledgeable than all of us.

Grigory shrugs. "Bomb will go off, of course. Nuclear fission requires no oxidizer. The question is, what is the destructive force? On Earth, in atmosphere, heat and shock wave are large part of destruction. In the void of space, there is no shock wave, no heat wave. Only radiation and plasma cloud made of bomb materials. Nuke casing has been optimized to create plasma cloud. It will be very, very destructive. Widely dispersed as well."

Charlotte nods curtly. "Thank you." She bites her lip a second, then continues. "Yes. I'm for the nuclear strike. I'll defer on timing. I don't like it. But I've made zero progress with the message. And given that two probes have been disabled, in addition to the supposed strike against the ISS," she pauses and cuts her eyes to Emma, who doesn't react, "well, I think it's clear that the artifact is hostile."

"For me," Min says, "the fact that solar radiation is nearly nominal in the regions of space outside Earth is very telling."

"Yes," says Charlotte. "That, too. We need to learn everything we can. Including how to destroy them."

I don't wait for the rest. There's no need. This crew is stressed, worried, and haggard—but we're unified on our course of action.

"The question is timing." I wait, but no one says anything. "After we shear the sample, and evacuate it, I think we should hit it with the nuke immediately. We don't want it to have time to send a message or take off. We'll be in range to see it via Lina's daisy-chained comm drone line. We'll get images before the blast and at the moment of impact."

"Nothing after?" Izumi asks.

"Not initially. The blast will take out the comm drones. The *Pax* will be far enough back. We'll get some radiation though. We'll send a small fleet of observation drones after the blast to survey the damage."

We agree on the plan. We're going to war with the artifact. The hours after tick by like a countdown to an event that might change the course of human history.

❄

It TURNS out we have enough drone parts for two relay comm lines: one to Beta, and one to the *Fornax*. We'll have real-time eyes on both during the battle. We barely had enough engine parts.

In the bubble are two large countdown windows.

```
Time to Fornax Comm Line Activation

2:32:10
```

Time to Artifact Comm Line Activation

7:21:39

I need to sleep. I'm haggard. But I can't. My nerves are like a constant vibrating inside me, a droning alarm clock going off that I can't reach.

There's something else I need to do. On my way to the lab, I hear Emma's voice floating out, clear and strong. She's not talking to someone here—it's too loud. A recording maybe?

"Hello, Mr. Perez. My name is Emma Matthews. I was the mission commander aboard the ISS when the catastrophe occurred. I want you to know how sorry I am for your loss. Your daughter was a wonderful friend to me and a brilliant scientist. She was also the biggest prankster aboard the station. I remember this time—"

She starts to laugh, but it changes to a sob, which stretches out until she catches her breath. "Stop recording. Delete file. Start new."

I've reached the hatch to the lab, which is partially ajar. Harry floats beside it. He's made the same decision I have: to not go in.

I motion with my head, and we both push off and drift away.

In the exercise area, I mount the bike and pedal while he pulls on the resistance bands.

"How do you think this is going to go, James?"

"Honestly? I don't know."

❄

WHEN I RETURN to the lab, it's silent. I find Emma pedaling the bike, head-down over a tablet, typing.

She looks up with bloodshot eyes and smiles.

"Hi."

"Hey. How's it going?"

That has to be the stupidest question ever. I'm nervous. Why am I so nervous?

"Fine," she says. "Just finished some videos and letters I'd like to send back. I assume there's room on the next comm brick?"

"Definitely. Lina's images are very small and we don't have much more data."

"Great."

"Listen. I just want to say this before we reach the artifact."

She stops typing. Stops pedaling. *Awkward.*

"I, um... before, when I was so... *adamant* about your exercise schedule. I was just worried about you. I don't want us to have any sort of disagreement or conflict between us. Not now. Not at the end—no, not the end. I don't want us to be at odds before we go into this."

"James, I know why you did it. And I appreciate it. I appreciate you even more for it. We're fine."

She comes over and hugs me, and we hold it for a long time. I don't want to let go. I don't think she does either.

❄

IN THE BUBBLE, we tether ourselves to the table. Every face is grim, like a jury ready to review evidence in a capital murder trial.

The countdown on the screen reads:

```
Time to Fornax Comm Line Activation

0:15:04
```

Time to Artifact Comm Line Activation

5:04:33

I find Harry in the engineering section, conversing with Grigory. Izumi and Min are by the hatch, listening, their backs to me.

"Is barely enough fuel," Grigory mutters.

Min turns and jumps at the sight of me. "James," he says loudly.

"Hey."

They're all staring at me.

"What's up?"

Harry raises his eyebrows.

"Double-checking the flight plan and fuel on the sample recovery drone."

The drone is due to launch in ten minutes—that's why I came looking for Harry. We've been over those calculations a hundred times already.

Something's up.

❄

WE'VE GOT a visual on the *Fornax*, and real-time text communication. Videoconferencing, even voice conferencing, isn't an option with the low-bandwidth daisy-chain comm setup. But we've synced our plan and our countdown clocks.

I know I should sleep, but I can't. I sit in the lab, trying to think of anything I haven't thought of.

Emma lingers in the hatchway, then pushes in.

"I want to tell you something too. Before the attack."

I straighten. "Oh?"

"Thank you. For rescuing me."

I nod. I wasn't sure what she was going to say. I feel... what? Let down? Is that it?

"I'm glad I could," I manage. "Glad it was my module that landed near your capsule."

"I'm glad too."

She floats closer. I think she's going to hug me, but she puts her hands on my shoulders and slowly moves toward me. She places her lips gently on my forehead and kisses me.

❄

IN CASE THE WORST HAPPENS, we dress in EMUs. We don't wear our helmets or gloves, but they're close by. It's an over-precaution—there's no one out here to rescue us—but Emma insists on it. She still blames herself for the ISS. If this does anything to make her feel better, I'm for it. We all are. She's family.

We gather in the bubble, tablets in hand, all tethered to the table, all eyes glued to the main screen.

The video feed of the artifact comes online. It looks the same now as it did in the first video. A black hexagon drifting toward the sun.

In the split-screen, we see the *Fornax*, hurtling through space like us. For the safety of both ships, we've put some distance between us, as much as we can while still maintaining the real-time comm link.

I glance at Grigory and Harry. "Any issues?"

Grigory shakes his head.

"We're a go," Harry says.

To Lina, I say, "Let's get a system check from the *Fornax*."

A few seconds later, she looks up from her tablet. "They're ready."

"Issue the command to the intervention drone."

I just ordered the first assault on an alien entity. It's surreal.

Emma's eyes meet mine, then we both focus on the screen. The seconds feel like eternities.

There's a flash on the video—the drones firing. A segment of the artifact shears off and floats free.

"Successful sample separation," Lina says, her voice flat, unemotional.

"Recovery in progress," Harry says. "Estimated time to clear nuclear blast radius is ninety-three seconds."

"I've apprised the *Fornax*," says Lina. "They confirm count-down sync."

Seconds tick by. I hate this—not being able to do anything. Except trust the plan we've made and hope and wait.

Under the table, a hand grips mine. It's warm and moist, smaller than my own. It's Emma's. I glance at her, but she doesn't make eye contact. I squeeze her hand tight.

"*Fornax* is firing," Lina says. "Time to target is thirty-seven seconds."

I can barely breathe. It feels as if the frame rate of life has slowed to a crawl, every second lasting an hour. The weightlessness and silence make it worse. There's no sense of time, no sensation, except for Emma's hand holding mine.

The countdown to impact ticks by.

12

11

10

9

8

7

6

There's movement on the artifact video feed. The massive object folds in on itself, and light blossoms from the end.

"*Fornax!* Evasive maneuvers!" I yell.

But it's too late. A white spear lances through the ship, shredding it like a soda can.

The artifact doesn't change shape. It turns white, like a fire poker burning white-hot in space. The nuclear countdown is at three seconds when the artifact flashes. The screen turns white.

"Helmets on!" Emma yells. I've never heard her speak that loudly. Or forcefully. It jars me. "Gloves too!"

She flings my helmet at me.

"Brace for impact," she says before snapping on her helmet and helping me with mine.

I slip my gloves on as the ship rocks, throwing me toward the wall. My tether to the table catches, and I yank back like a yo-yo. Through the porthole window, I see one of the modules on the arms break off and tumble past like a grain silo blown by a twister, me the trapped homeowner, watching helplessly.

The crew is bounced around the bubble, tethered just like I am, debris flying everywhere, chaos in utter silence except for the hissing of air in my suit as it pressurizes. There's a slightly sweet smell. That's wrong. Different from when my suit was last pressurized—at launch. Why? A malfunction?

I turn my head, and my vision blurs. As if I'm drunk. Or drugged.

Emma floats ten feet away from me, also tethered to the table. Her eyes look glassed over too. She's not moving. Is she hurt?

I plant my feet against the wall and try to push off toward her. But my legs won't cooperate. What's happening to me?

I hang in the air, reach for the table to pull myself forward.

A gloved hand catches mine. Harry's face drifts up into view. I can't hear him, but I can read the single word he mouths.

"Sorry."

CHAPTER 33

EMMA

I AWAKE to the worst hangover of my life. Or what feels like it. My head swims. I'm nauseous.

My helmet has been removed. So have my gloves.

What happened?

It was a nightmare. The ship being destroyed. Just like the ISS. I tried to save them—the crew—again.

I failed. Again.

There's a strap around my abdomen, pinning me to the wall. I reach for it, but a hand catches mine. I'm not alone.

James comes into view. His expression is blank, but I can see sadness in his eyes.

My voice comes out in a rasp, like sandpaper running over a wall. "What happened?"

He doesn't respond. Only averts his eyes. He unfastens the strap, and I float free.

We're in one of the auxiliary modules. There's a small port-hole window, padded walls, and a screen on the end of the barrel-shaped space.

"What is this?" My voice is scratchy but getting better.

"This, apparently, is home. For a while."

"Home? What—"

"I'll let Harry tell you."

James activates the screen. Harry's face fills it. He's in his sleep station, speaking quietly.

"Hi, James. Hi, Emma. The crew elected me to make this video. *Forced* is more like it. Please don't hate the messenger."

He takes a deep breath.

"We've talked, and we think if something goes wrong during the strike on the artifact, that you two should get back to Earth."

He pauses.

"James, there's not another mind like yours on Earth. You're irreplaceable. You've always been a step ahead of the rest of us out here. You made the big leaps. If this is going to be a war with the artifacts, it will likely be fought with robotics. The world needs you more than we do—and more than it needs us."

He pauses again, swallowing. His discomfort is obvious.

"Emma, you have been an amazing crewmember. The best we could have ever asked for. But you didn't sign up for this. I know you would have, but you didn't. And your health is failing. You can't stay out here much longer. It had to be you two—if any of us survived."

The words break me like a stone smashed into an anvil. The hard bits of me shatter and crumble away and lie there, unmoving. Tears stream down my face. I feel hurt, deep down inside in places I never knew existed.

James is stoic. I wonder how many times he's watched this video. I wonder if it's the sadness or the anger possessing him now.

I take a look around the module. There's an exercise bike, resistance bands, and food cartons. For the second time since I went into space, I have been saved by an act of unimaginable kindness.

Harry takes a deep breath. "James, I know you're probably wondering how we did it. It wasn't easy. You almost caught us a few times. Lina edited the cargo list from the *Fornax*, deleted four of the larger engines from it. Grigory and I built the escape module while you were sleeping. It's bigger than the *Pax*'s standard escape modules, obviously, and has more acceleration capability. You two will be back on Earth within two months." He raises his eyebrows. "And James, don't even try hacking the nav system. Min programmed it to make a beeline for Earth. Lina closed any loopholes you might exploit in the software. It'll be autopilot all the way. Silent running. You'll get control back when you reach Earth, but you won't have any fuel to go anywhere."

His expression softens. "We did this for you two, but that's not the only reason. We did it for our families. You're their best chance of survival. They need you back on Earth. Figuring this out. Studying the sample and data from Midway. We're counting on you. If you're seeing this message, then the worst has happened. Don't come looking for us. If we're still alive, we're going after the Midway fleet to try to figure out what's out here. That's the other key point, James. You and I made a great team—but we're redundant. With you and Emma gone, we still have a full crew out here. We'll miss you in the lab, Emma, but Min and Grigory can help me patch up the drones."

He's getting choked up now. "We'll miss you. But get home safely, okay?"

He reaches up and presses a button, and the message ends.

A long silence stretches out.

"What do you think happened?" I ask.

"I think... the artifact detected the nuke. Or it detected the broadcast from the *Fornax* to the nuke—for flight control. Either way, the artifact traced it back, struck the *Fornax*, and then the blast after... It was too big to have been the nuke alone. My guess is the artifact did some kind of self destruct. Maybe a power overload."

"Why?"

"To take out anything hostile in its vicinity. Or records of its existence. Or maybe it was trying to destroy the sample that was sheared off."

"You think it succeeded?"

"I don't know. The drone carrying the sample would have been at the very edge of the safe zone for the nuclear blast. The *Pax* was farther out than that, and it got rocked, for sure."

"I saw a module break free."

"Me too."

James sits there, staring at the wall. I'm still a little woozy from whatever they put in my suit. Maybe he is too.

"Harry was right, you know." I take James's hand. "The world needs you. I still have family on Earth, and for their sake, I'm glad you're coming home. If anyone can figure this out, you can."

He exhales heavily. "Still don't like it. Leaving them. I haven't had friends like that in a long time."

I take his hand in mine.

"Me either."

※

FOR THE FIRST week of our journey home, James stews. He reviews every piece of data and video from the *Pax*. I know what he's doing: second-guessing. He was the *de facto* mission commander. He feels responsible. He's blaming himself right now.

I know exactly how he feels. I might be the only person who does. I wonder if that's the other reason they sent me with James. To help him with what he's feeling. He was there for me when I went through it. That's what I'm going to do for him.

"Hey."

He looks up from the tablet.

"We need a plan."

He nods absently.

"And a schedule. We're going to work this problem—together, you and me, one day at a time. And we're going to take some time off every day. Sound good?"

"Yeah. Sure."

"First things first. We can't change what happened back there. The truth is simple: you advanced the mission way beyond where any of us could have gotten without you. We're ahead of the original mission schedule by months. And we found an artifact and learned a lot. We might have even gotten a sample of it. That's incredible, given what we're up against."

His eyes meet mine. I know what he's thinking.

"The *Pax* crew could still be out there," I say. "We have to assume they are. And they're counting on us." I float closer to him. "They're counting on us to get back to Earth and make a plan and come get them. Their survival is in our hands. We may be the only two people who know what happened to them."

I can almost see him coming back to life, like a man in a coma waking up, re-entering the world, finding a reason to live again.

"You're right," he says.

"I'm glad you've finally admitted it."

A smile tugs at the edges of his lips. "Don't let it go to your head."

"Wouldn't dream of it." I hold my hands out. "Let's start with our biggest problem: how to safely land on Earth."

"I've been thinking about that." He crosses his arms. "I think the biggest danger is getting shot out of the sky."

"Yeah, that feels like a big danger."

"Indeed. As far as we know, Earth has no functioning orbital satellites. Unless they launched more while we were gone. Add to that the fact that we probably shouldn't broadcast anything on our way to Earth. Silent running is still safest. The other artifact, Alpha—or whatever else is still out there—could pick up our transmissions."

"So we're going to look like an unidentified bogey heading toward Earth."

"Yeah. And they're not expecting us."

"Harry's message said we'd get control of this capsule when we reach Earth. How long will we have?"

"I checked the software. Roughly forty hours before touchdown. Ground-based telescopes will definitely pick us up before then. Nukes will have time to reach us before then."

"The crew was betting Earth wouldn't take us out."

"Clearly," James says quietly. "It's a good bet. But we need to be prepared."

"You think you can break Lina's lockout?"

"Not a chance."

"You have another plan?"

"The start of one."

"Now we're talking."

❄

JAMES HAS RIPPED the inside of the module apart. It looks like a bomb went off in here. It's also given us something important to do, which has taken his mind off the *Pax*. I'm glad for that—the distraction—and to have a problem to work on.

His plan is simple: a comm buoy. We'll place the small broadcast satellite in the airlock and jettison it. Once it has drifted ten thousand miles from our vessel, it will start transmitting a signal to Earth, one that'll get there long before we will. And if the artifact reacts to the transmission, it'll destroy only the buoy—not us.

James has erred on the side of paranoia in his message.

"Repeat," he says into the microphone. "Our estimated arrival time is as follows. All numbers taken from the mission briefing manual. We will reach Earth in first number on page three, third number on page eighteen. Time is in days."

When he saves the file, I say, "Kind of cloak and dagger."

He shrugs. "We're at war. The artifacts—or whatever is out there—could have technology that understands our language. If they know our arrival time, they could cause a solar event to affect us when we arrive at Earth even if they can't see us."

"Wars have a purpose. Something each side wants to gain. I think it's safe to assume the artifact—or artifacts, or whatever else is out there—is causing the Long Winter. But why?"

"Not sure," James says.

I grin. "Don't give me that. I know you have theories."

He cocks his head as he closes the panel of the buoy. "Okay. Here's what we know: Alpha attacked the probe. Beta destroyed the *Fornax* and I think tried to destroy the *Pax* when it self-destructed. Both artifacts were hexagonal. That implies there are many more, and that they likely fit together. They're here for a reason. Maybe for our sun or our planet or us."

"What's your best guess?"

He withdraws. I bet he knows why the artifacts are here, and he's withholding the knowledge because it would disturb me.

"If they're here for us," I say, "they could have already invaded Earth. It could be occupied when we arrive."

"True."

"Or it could have been occupied a long time ago. Aliens among us. Spies planted to watch us." I raise my eyebrows theatrically.

"You have quite an imagination."

He has no idea.

❄

AFTER JETTISONING THE COMM BUOY, we settle into a routine. I exercise. He exercises. We talk about what we'll do when we get to Earth. We talk about finding the Midway fleet and launching more ships to trace the artifacts. I can tell there are things James is keeping from me, about his conclusions. I don't press him.

We play cards after work hours. Work consists of analyzing the data from the *Pax* and especially the confrontation with Beta. It's busy work, and I'm grateful for it—anything to keep my mind off of the *Pax* crew or my ISS crew for that matter.

The card games are gin rummy mostly, with magnetic cards one of the *Pax* crew had the foresight to pack for us. It's important to keep a schedule. The days are shapeless. The sun is behind us, never rising or falling. We cover the porthole to simulate night and strap in to the sides of the module, across from each other, and talk for hours until one of us yawns.

I once read somewhere that after the First and Second World Wars, when most troops came home on large ships, the trips across the Atlantic and Pacific provided time for them to decompress, to mentally pack away the stresses and horrors of war and prepare for life at home—a quieter, more peaceful life. This feels a little like that. On the *Pax*, it was a roller coaster of emotions. Constant stress. Problems and more problems. Now it's just James and me, and for a while, I forget about our freezing world, the six crewmembers we left behind, my sister, and everyone counting on us and everything else. It's as though we're in a small pocket universe. Everything outside of us exists, and we care about it, but it's far away, a problem for a distant day that may never come. Here and now, time seems to stand still, and we rotate around each other. It's perfect in that way.

Some nights we watch movies and TV, usually old ones. Sometimes *The X-Files*. And *Star Trek*. These are a gift from Harry. His video collection is nearly endless. When Marlon Brando's scene in *On the Waterfront* plays and he says, "I coulda been a contenda," I can't help but think of Harry and his impression. I laugh, and I hear James laughing behind me. And I feel my eyes well with tears.

I push off and drift back toward James. I'm startled when he catches me and guides me to the back wall. We plant our feet on the floor and sit, his arm around me. At some point, my head drifts down to his shoulder, and his head gently touches mine. I can't remember when I felt this happy. Or this sad.

❄

THOUGH I EXERCISE DAILY, I know I'm still losing a lot of bone density. Too much. Assuming we make it back to Earth, I won't be stepping out of this module—I'll spill out, and I may not even be able to stand. I'll slow James down, no matter where he goes. I would do anything for him. Except hold him back.

"James."

He looks up from his gin rummy cards.

"I want to talk about what happens when we get to the ground."

He discards a seven of diamonds. "Okay."

I draw a card and study it. Jack of clubs. I've got one jack, but I can't risk trying for a set. He's getting close to knocking. I'm pretty sure of it. I toss the card on the pile. It clicks onto the magnetized tabletop.

"I won't be able to walk. Probably not."

"Uh-huh." He draws. Studies the card and inserts it into the middle of his fan. Must have been a card he needed. He discards as he says, "Nothing medication and physical therapy can't fix."

"But that'll take time."

"True."

He looks up at me expectantly. I know that look. It says, *Your turn to draw.*

I take a card. A suicide king. I toss it on the pile.

"I'm going to slow you down on Earth. You need to move on once we get back."

He lowers his cards, but doesn't reveal them. "I'm going to move on. I'm going to start executing the mission I've been planning. But first I'm going to get you to the best hospital in the world. I'm going to make sure they're treating you, and I'm going to stay by your bedside until I know you're going to make a full recovery."

"James—"

"You can disagree with me. It's your right. I respect it. You can hate me. You can forbid me from doing it. But that's what I'm going to do. No matter what."

He draws a card. Discards quickly and lays his hand on the table. "Knock."

I tilt my hand, revealing my cards.

He always does the math in his head in a fraction of a second.

"Thirty-five my way."

I glance at the running score. His victory this round puts him over a hundred. Game over. He wins.

❋

A FEW NIGHTS LATER, instead of tethering to the wall across from me, James drifts down to the adjacent wall, into the valley between us, and straps in. He stares straight up—out the port-hole, at the stars.

I unbuckle myself, drift down, and lie next to him. These stars are what I came up here for. My breath was taken away the first time I saw them. But now all I want to do is get back home.

Gently, he takes my hand in his, just like I reached out for him on the *Pax*, in the seconds before the artifact struck.

I've changed my mind. I'm not in any hurry to get back to Earth.

❄

A week later, we've just finished an episode of *The X-Files* when I turn to him.

"Will you tell me something?"

"Anything."

"Why were you in prison?"

He shrugs theatrically. "I... might need to revise my previous answer."

"Why won't you tell me?"

"Because it might change how you feel about me."

"It won't."

"It might."

"I can just look it up on the internet when we get back."

"Assuming the internet still exists."

"Yes. Assuming that. But wouldn't you rather tell me your-self—in your own words?"

"I would." He breaks eye contact with me. "I will. I've never really... talked about what happened with anyone. I need some time."

"We've got time."

But, as it turns out, not enough.

❄

SEVEN DAYS BEFORE OUR ARRIVAL, I awake to find James hunkered over the main terminal.

He turns, and I can tell instantly something is wrong.

"What happened? An issue with the ship?"

"No. It's fine."

He twists, allowing me to see the screen, which shows a picture of Earth. We've gotten our first telemetry from the long-range telescope. I see the familiar swath of white clouds, the blue ocean below it, and where the US Eastern Seaboard should be, an expanse of white.

Earth is frozen.

CHAPTER 34

JAMES

WE'RE two days away from Earth, and there's good news and there's bad news.

The good news is that we haven't been shot out of the sky. By humans or by aliens trying to harvest our solar energy.

The bad news is there may be no home to return to. We've studied the images of Earth (we have telemetry from four full rotations now). Ice covers North America. Europe is buried. There are a few swaths of brown open land in northern Africa. Another in the Middle East. And slightly inland in Australia. We can only see the sunward-facing side of Earth, so we can't see our world at night, can't know if lights are still burning down there. Either way, this is a new dark age for humanity.

What are our chances of actually stopping it? I try not to let my pessimism show in front of Emma. She has taken the news hard. I know she's worried about her sister and her sister's family. I sense the bond is strong between the two of them. I'm worried about Emma. And my own family. And the rest of the world. I wonder how many are left. It must be agonizing down there, a world running out of habitable land, the ice closing in, the hordes of people fighting to survive. It's unimaginable.

After we see the images, we try to keep to our routine. It's important to maintain discipline, for me, and for Emma's health.

I can't help stewing over what to do. The situation on Earth definitely necessitates a change in our plans.

It's ten a.m. (we're keeping Eastern Standard Time hours), and I'm pulling on the exercise bands. Emma's pedaling the bike, watching a class lecture from Caltech on adaptive robotics. Harry had the foresight to load all these college lectures for her benefit. She's used it as a kind of continuing education, and a distraction.

"I think we should contact Earth," I say, panting from exertion.

She stops pedaling. "Why?"

"We need to know where to land."

"Canaveral—"

"Might be a long shot now."

This makeshift spacecraft can't pull off a controlled landing. We'll need to land in the ocean. Our plan has been to land off the coast of Cape Canaveral. We've assumed that NASA would be watching and come and retrieve us. Now I'm uncertain. The Kennedy Space Center is covered in ice. The entire US is. I have no idea where the NASA personnel evacuated to—or whether they're watching for us to touch down. They're not expecting us, and they may not have gotten the broadcast from the comm buoy we deployed.

Once we touch down, we're definitely going to need some help. I can't exactly row us to shore. And that's only the beginning. Even if the tide somehow carries us in, I can't drag Emma across a barren, frozen world looking for civilization. We need help or we're as good as dead—whether we die up here or down there.

"Okay," she says. "When?"

"As soon as the comm lockout lifts." I glance at the time. "Today. Four hours from now."

※

SHE AND I sit by the tablet, watching the timer count down until the comm systems come back online. Thirty seconds left.

"Hey," she says. "If we can't make contact, and we just have to land wherever... I want you to leave me."

"Emma—"

"Just listen. I'll be safe in the module. It'll float. I'll have food, and it has enough power for heat for a while. You can get help and come back for me. I'll slow you down. You know it."

I don't like that one bit. "We'll cross that bridge when we come to it."

The tablet flashes a message.

```
Comm suite is now online.

Be advised, long distance charges apply.
```

We both laugh. Nice to see our old crewmates still kept their sense of humor while secretly planning this worst-case contingency.

We've already debated *whom* to call with our first broadcast. If the world is at war, announcing ourselves could put us at risk, make us a target, a pawn to be used or traded, held hostage maybe. There are so many unknowns down there.

We settled on broadcasting on an encrypted NASA channel. The reasons are simple: NASA and its network of private space contractors still have the largest space program. They and the US military are best equipped to rescue us. And

Emma and I are both Americans—assuming America still exists.

I start to activate the transmission but hesitate. "You want to talk, or you want me to?"

"Doesn't matter to me. You do it."

I tap the tablet.

"Goddard flight control, NASA, private space entities, and anyone listening: this is James Sinclair and Emma Matthews, two members of the *Pax* on approach to Earth. We could use some help."

❄

THERE'S NO RESPONSE INITIALLY. Or during the first hour. Or the second. Every minute that passes feels like slow motion. We try to stay busy.

I have a plan for when we arrive on Earth. I've been working on it, in some fashion, since I woke up in this capsule. It has one purpose: to save Emma's life.

"What are you thinking?" Her voice is calm, but I know she's nervous. She's in far more danger on the ground than I am.

"I think we broaden the transmission."

"Europeans?"

"Yep."

The great thing about the *Pax* is that we have access to every imaginable encryption suite, including those used by Roscosmos, ESA, JAXA, CNSA, and a handful of others.

I send a message to the ESA, but there's no reply.

Four hours later, there's still no reply.

"What next?" Emma asks. "Wide broadcast?"

"Not yet. Military could pick it up."

"Or militias."

She thinks the worst has happened. She might be right.

Emma's voice is reflective and somber. "You think we did this?"

"What?"

"You think our actions out there—the fly-by of the artifact and attacking it—you think it made the artifacts accelerate the Long Winter? Is this part of their counterstrike—freezing Earth?"

I've thought about that, but haven't had the courage to voice it. I'm glad I don't know if it's true. If so, it would gut me. I made the calls out there. If my decisions caused this ice age, and the death of billions... I don't know if I could ever recover from it.

"Maybe. I don't know."

She seems to read my mind.

"We had to do what we did out there, James."

That makes it a little better. But not much.

I've already been tried once for endangering the world. Tried and convicted. Unjustly. Then they sent me into space to save them. I did my best. And I just might have done what they locked me away for.

❄

WE BED down in the middle of the module, shoulder-to-shoulder, staring up at the porthole and the stars beyond. I'm usually the one to pull the shade. Tonight, I peer out, then start taking stock of every last item in the module. My mind mentally assembles the pieces in 3D. I see a rough rendering of what I need, the device that will carry us home.

"What're you thinking about?" Emma asks softly.

"Nothing."

"You're a terrible liar."

I smile. "I would think that's a good quality."

"It is." She pauses. "You're thinking about where we should land. And how to build a boat."

"Yeah. I am."

"And?"

"It's doable." I turn to her. "We've got the pieces, right here in the capsule. I'll get you to a hospital. I promise you."

"I believe you. I believe if anyone can, you can."

We both stare out the porthole then, holding hands, neither saying anything. I'm glad she's here. Glad the crew sent her with me—for a lot of reasons. There's one reason I never realized until now: I'll fight harder to save her life than I ever would to save my own.

❄

In the morning, we broadcast wide, unencrypted. It's a gamble, a desperate, last roll of the dice.

A response comes immediately, a gruff male voice.

"Mr. Sinclair, this is Colonel Jeffords of the Atlantic Union. Stand by. We're routing your message to the appropriate parties."

"Atlantic Union?" Emma whispers.

"It would seem alliances have been made."

I activate the radio again. "Copy that, Colonel. We're standing by."

The next message comes five minutes later. It isn't from Jeffords. It's another male voice with a European accent, the enunciation too perfect. Definitely someone who learned English as a second language.

"Dr. Sinclair. We're glad to hear your voice. My name is Sora Nakamura. I represent the Pac Alliance. The Allies welcome you home. We're eager to hear your story and to provide assistance. Please verify you've received our message."

Interesting.

Emma turns the microphone off. "What do you want to do?"

"We need to know more."

"Such as?"

"Such as who the good guys are."

"And what if there are no good guys?"

She's cut to the heart of the issue. Desperate times make devils out of the best of us.

"Then we'll pick whoever's most likely to rescue us."

I activate the microphone again. "We read you, Mr. Nakamura."

"Excellent. I must say, we're surprised to hear from you so soon. Our colleagues at JAXA and the CNSA are eager to talk to you. We're currently making preparations for a landing site and recovery off the coast of Australia. There are resettlement camps nearby, and the Pac Alliance government is headquartered in Darwin."

There's a pause on the comm, as if he's talking to someone offline.

Emma turns off the mic once more. "The Pac Alliance. A group of Pacific nations, obviously."

She's right. Nakamura's reference to the Chinese and Japanese space programs as well as camps in Australia implies a geographic alliance.

"Yeah. I bet they crowded into the warm, arid land in Australia. Probably the last habitable zone in the region. Maybe the Japanese, Chinese, and Indians joined forces and moved their people there. Or at least, those they could save."

"Interesting," Emma says, lost in thought.

I can't help but speculate about what's happened and how the last survivors would organize. Geography and population are the drivers. The Pacific is vast. It covers over thirty percent of the planet. In fact, it covers more area than all of the Earth's landmasses combined. The Atlantic is much smaller. It's roughly half the size of the Pacific. It's conceivable that America herded its citizens into its last habitable zones in the US and then transported the rest to northern Africa, where there will be much more survivable land as the world cools. Based on the telescope's images, it looks like all of the US is under ice now.

Population is the other factor. Asia has about sixty percent of the world's population. Twice as many people as North America, South America, and Africa combined. Asian populations, simply put, need more land to survive. Australia is the logical choice. It's hot and dry. There are some hot areas in Southeast Asia, but they lie in the monsoon regions. They'll be buried in snow.

If the planet has organized into two spheres, these would be roughly well-matched. And geographically isolated. The question is which we choose.

There's also the region in Iran that isn't covered in ice, but there's been no message from them. Very interesting.

One thing's certain: there is someone down there to retrieve us. I won't have to turn the capsule into a boat, which, frankly, was probably a long shot.

Nakamura comes back on the line.

"In the interest of time, Dr. Sinclair, we request that you transmit any data you recovered during your mission."

With the microphone still off, Emma says, "I don't like it. They should have gotten the comm bricks already."

"They may have. Maybe they're asking about any new data. Or maybe the equipment to read the wireless transmission was lost in the exodus to these last habitable zones. But yeah. I don't like it either." I think for a minute. "Technically, the data doesn't reveal much about the course of climate change on Earth. Just the magnitude of the threat."

"A threat that is much greater than we imagined. The data

confirms that the artifacts are hostile, which implies that the world is in a lot of trouble. The data could spark a war."

"Or worsen the war already occurring."

"True."

"There's another reason not to send it."

She raises an eyebrow.

"Leverage."

"Leverage for what?"

"Our safety. The data is what we have that they want. Once they have it, they could have no more use for us."

Emma looks away. This is outside her comfort zone—the double-dealing and distrust. I like that about her. She's a genuine person. Honest. Too good—too pure for the world I fear we're returning to.

When we make eye contact again, I make my voice even. "There's another reason for silence. The artifacts could be listening. Maybe that's why we're still alive. They want to know what we know. And it could be why neither the Atlantic Union nor Pac Alliance has shot us down."

"You want to say no to the Pac Alliance request?"

"That might force their hand—or cause the artifacts to destroy us."

"So..."

"We buy time."

I activate the radio. "Copy that, Pac Alliance. It's going to take us some time to get our data suitable for broadcast. We'll be in touch."

Emma bunches her eyebrows. "You lie a lot better over the radio."

"Lying is easier when you don't know the person."

❄

THERE ARE no further transmissions from Nakamura. I consider that telling.

The next transmission comes two hours later, from a familiar voice, one I'm relieved to hear.

"James? It's Lawrence Fowler. Please respond if you read me."

His voice is like a drink of water to a man who's been walking through the desert for a year. I bolt toward it, like a beacon of hope, a sign of an oasis on the horizon.

I tap the transmit button quickly and speak with enthusiasm.

"We read you, Fowler. It's great to hear your voice."

"Likewise, James. Listen, we need to make plans. It's important that we recover you. There've been... changes here."

"Copy that."

"We've made preparations. Landing coordinates are as follows: the location where you and I first met. Take latitude and add to the degrees the fourth number found on page five of the mission briefing. To the longitude, add to the degrees the seventh number found on the fifteenth page of the mission briefing. Please verify receipt. Do not repeat actual coordinates."

I open the digital version of the mission briefing, memorize the numbers, then open a map with GPS. Edgefield Federal Prison lies at 33.76 degrees latitude, -81.92 degrees longitude. I add the numbers from the mission briefing. The location surprises me. It's nowhere near the US. It's in the Mediterranean, off the coast of Tunisia. I really, really, hope I added that correctly.

"We copy, Fowler."

"Please cease all communications. We'll be waiting, James."

Nakamura responds immediately.

"James and Emma, we overheard the broadcast from the AU. We certainly appreciate their efforts in providing a safe landing, but be advised, we have already made preparations and feel your safety would be greatly enhanced by a landing here at our site. We have far more resources and a safer environment here. Please respond and acknowledge that you're proceeding to our site."

Emma leans her head back and exhales. I'm starting to get stressed too.

I activate the radio.

"We copy, Pac Alliance. As you can see, our vessel is a makeshift escape pod created from the *Pax*. Thrust capacity is severely degraded. We'll know more about our landing approach soon and will be in touch. We're also still porting the data for transmission. This is taking a lot of time."

"Understood, James. If you give us alternative landing coordinates, I assure you that we can secure them and recover you. Your safety and the completion of your mission is our priority."

Emma deactivates the radio. "Completion of our mission?"

"The data. They want the data."

"Fowler never asked."

"He's smarter than that. And he wants us back. If anyone on the ground cares about us, it's him. He's the one who asked me to rescue you. I trust him."

"So do I."

"Tunisia it is."

"What now?"

"Now, we rest. And try not to get shot out of the sky before we get home."

CHAPTER 35

EMMA

We've prepared the ship for landing. Every single item has been stowed. We've calculated the vector to reach the target landing zone. Fuel isn't a problem. The real problem is whether the ship will be in one piece when we land.

And whether we'll survive.

James betrays no emotion. But I know he must be worried. I am.

The Pac Alliance has continued to contact us. James has refused to respond. He feels that's better.

We are hours away from landing, and we decide to spend those hours together. We don't play cards. We don't watch a movie. We turn on some old music, classic rock hits from the 1960s and 70s, and lie together in the middle of the ship, looking up at the stars. It's a perfect moment. I fear it may be the last perfect moment I ever experience.

Gently, without acknowledging it, he puts his arm around me, wraps his fingers around my shoulder, and presses me to him. We lie this way, floating, until a ship alarm goes off. The computerized voice echoes in the small space.

"Landing sequence activated."

We put on our helmets and do one last check of our suits.

He smiles at me. "See you on Earth."

"Yeah. See you there."

The ship rumbles. Even through the cool space suit, I can feel the heat increasing as we enter the planet's atmosphere. The module has a heat shield, and it should hold, but I can't help but think back to the capsule I was aboard in orbit a few months ago.

With each passing second, the heat increases. The module shakes more violently. I glance over at James, and he's looking at me. Not worried. Not even a shred of concern in his eyes. That steels me.

In the roar of the turbulence and the soaring heat, I lose all sense of time. Suddenly there's a lull in the roar. Complete silence. Then a kick, the retro rockets firing, trying to slow our descent. We hurtle toward Earth in silence, me staring at James and him staring at me.

The rockets fire again, course-correcting, the autopilot hopefully doing its job. There's another wild jerk, and I can feel the g-forces fade away. The parachutes have deployed. I check the straps one last time. I know what's coming. A landing from space has been described as a train wreck, followed by a car accident, followed by falling off your bike. This feels worse.

Through the porthole, I see only blue, with the occasional swath of white. Then suddenly, without warning, there's a crash and a boom the likes of which I've never heard before, never felt before.

And everything goes dark.

✳

CONSCIOUSNESS COMES in flickers as if I'm watching the world from behind a slow-moving fan, the blades blotting out the world, the area in between revealing it in flashes. James is there, leaning over me, his helmet off, speaking. I can't hear the words. My ears ring. My body is numb.

I try to sit up, but I can't. Looking down, I realize he has unfastened my straps. His fingers touch my neck, checking my pulse. He must like what he sees. His face relaxes.

Slowly, hearing returns. He's on the radio, talking with someone from the Atlantic Union. I'm suddenly aware of the sensation of movement, the capsule bobbing in the water. I try to sit up again, and this time I succeed, but I'm still weak. James looks over at me.

"It's going to be all right."

I nod. My head feels wobbly, like I'm trying to balance a bowling ball on a toothpick. *What's happening to me?*

It's like the *Pax* all over again.

I let myself fall back to the padded wall. The world feels so heavy. As if I'm wearing a lead suit. After almost a year in space, and weightlessness, I feel like an alien on this planet. Like my body wasn't made for it. Like the gravity here will drag me into the ground and never let me up.

I close my eyes, and darkness comes again.

❄

I AWAKE IN A HOSPITAL. The bed is soft. Machines surround me. Through a window, I see a vast expanse of desert dotted by white tents. They glow like lanterns floating on a sea of sand.

James is here, sitting in a reclining chair in the corner, head laid to the side, asleep. I wouldn't dare wake him.

My body still feels heavy, as if I'm sinking into the soft bed.

I jump at a knock on the door. It swings open, and a nurse comes in, a cheery smile on his face.

"You're awake!"

James stirs, cracks his eyes open. He looks so tired.

I push myself up on the bed.

"I am."

"I'm just gonna have a look at you," the nurse says.

He does a cursory exam, speaking softly as he works. "You spent some time in quarantine. You probably don't remember. They cleared you, and we're just going to keep you long enough to make sure you're all right. Sound good?"

"Sounds great."

"I'm going to tell the doctor you're awake. He'll be very relieved."

The nurse nods at James as he exits, closing the door behind him, leaving us alone.

"How was it?" I ask. "The retrieval?"

"Piece of cake," James says.

He's becoming a better liar. I'm concerned.

"Right. What now?"

"Now, we're going to get you back in shape."

❄

FOR THE FIRST day in the hospital, all I do is eat and sleep and talk with James. He sits in the chair in the corner, and we even play a few games of cards on the tray table beside my bed.

As strange as it sounds, I miss that module in space. It was cramped and dangerous, but when I remember it, all I think about is how cozy it was and the fact that for two months, James and I sort of forgot about everything else. Back here on Earth, I'm acutely aware of what we're facing.

I get a rude awakening when I try to go to the bathroom. I swing my legs over the bed, and James takes my hand. When I try to stand, my legs fail me. James is there to catch me, his hands under my armpits holding me until the nurse comes in. I manage to make it to the door and into the bathroom and to do my business alone—for that, I'm thankful. But the exercise is a humbling preview of the road ahead.

❄

LAWRENCE FOWLER COMES by on the second day. I haven't seen him since I launched to the ISS. I swear he's aged twenty years since then. He smiles, and in that moment, I see the same kind man I used to know.

"It's good to see you, Emma."

"You too, Larry. What did I miss?"

He shrugs. "Nothing much. Some inclement weather."

James smiles. I laugh and cough and when we fall silent, I ask the question I've wanted to ask since we first made contact with Earth: "My sister?"

"She's okay. We got your message."

"Where is she?"

Fowler glances to the door. "I'm not sure. Let me check on that."

To my surprise, he slips out of the room.

A minute later he re-enters, and my heart bursts. Madison is behind him. Owen and Adeline are following close on her heels, with David bringing up the rear.

Madison hugs me gently as if I'm a china doll she's afraid to break. The kids do the same, and David nods at me without a word. He hasn't changed much.

"What's with the super-hesitant hug? It's not like I have the plague."

Madison smiles sympathetically. "The doctor says you're still weak from all your time in space. That your bones need time to heal and that you could fracture easily."

Owen and Adeline look concerned. I think it scares them

seeing me here in the hospital like this, wounded and fragile. I've always been the super-aunt to them. It turns out a lack of gravity is my kryptonite.

I'm not sure how to respond to Madison. I'm thankful when James speaks. "She'll be out of here in no time. Just routine physical therapy and rehab after time in space."

He makes for the door, and Fowler follows him. "We'll give you all a little time together."

Madison begins peppering me with questions about what happened, where I went, and what I saw. Through the window that looks out into the hall, I see James and Fowler talking excitedly. Is James planning his next step? I know I need to rest and to heal, but I desperately want to be out there with them.

"Did you hear me?" Madison asks.

"Of course," I lie.

"So?"

"So what?"

"So are you two together?"

I chew my lip. "Who do you mean?" I know exactly who she means. I feel like a seventh grader right now.

"Oh, I don't know, maybe that guy who won't leave your bedside, who they say is the sole reason you got home."

"It's complicated."

"What does that mean?"

"It means that it's sort of hard to date in space. Can we change the subject?"

Madison crosses her arms. Translation: *No, I don't want to change the subject. But I will. Because you're in the hospital. And you're my older sister.*

"Actually, let's stay on that subject. Do you know who he is?"

Madison seems confused. "Who? James?"

"Yes. He's a roboticist. Dr. James Sinclair. He was in the news several years ago... he went to prison—"

"Wait, he was in prison!? For what?"

"That's what I was going to ask you."

"You don't know? He didn't tell you?"

"No, he didn't tell me. So, you don't recognize his name?"

Madison shrugs. "It sounds vaguely familiar, but I couldn't tell you anything about him. Before the evacuations, I was doing well to keep up with what the kids were doing after school every day. Some scientist going to jail? It's not really the type of thing I would have committed to memory."

"Okay. Fine. You said there were evacuations. What happened? Where are we? Where do you all live?"

Madison glances at David, who holds out an arm, corrals the kids, and leaves the room.

"Things happened so quickly, Em. The whole world went crazy. At first, the US created a few settlement camps. One in Death Valley. Another in Arizona. They were just taking people from Alaska and Michigan, then Maine and Minnesota, and then the camps were overrun by people flocking there. There was the sense that if you didn't get a place, you would be buried by the snow. Things got worse when China and Japan announced an alliance."

"The Pac Alliance?"

"Yeah. They sent what they called a trade envoy to Australia. In reality it was composed of the largest naval fleet ever assembled. They blockaded the island and began resettling their people there. Australia joined the alliance, but they had little choice. I'm sure they reached out to the US and Europe, but we had problems of our own.

"The Europeans moved south across the Mediterranean. The war here in North Africa began on a Monday and was over by Thursday. America and Canada joined the European allies."

"The Atlantic Union?"

"Correct."

"Are those the only two powers left in the world?"

"No. The Russians and Indians joined forces and moved their people into Iran. They call the alliance the Caspian Treaty. It's been hard to get information—when the satellites went down, the internet went down—but they say the fighting in the Middle East was intense."

"How many Americans survived?"

"I don't know. I'm not even sure the government knows."

"Where do you live now?"

"Here. In Tunisia, in Camp Seven, outside Kebili. A team from Homeland Security came to our house in the middle of the night and woke me up and showed me your message. I wrote you back—"

"I saw it."

"You did? Good, I didn't know. I was so scared, but I knew if you said I had to do it, I had to do it. David didn't want to leave at first. The kids were frightened. But we left that night. We were among the first settlers here. I've heard stories from the people who arrived after. Horrible stories. Heartbreaking stories."

Madison's eyes well up with tears. "You saved us, Emma. Me, Owen, Adeline, David—we might be dead without you. I love you so much, big sister."

※

SEEING Madison is the best medicine I've received while being in the hospital. And I'm getting no shortage of medications.

The physical therapist comes three times a day. I exercise in the bed and then get up and walk. Those excursions around the unit give me a glimpse into what's going on. The hospital was recently built, with prefabricated panels, but despite that, it's worn and dirty in places. The other patients seem to be critically ill, most with physical trauma injuries. My guess is they were injured during their journey here to Tunisia or in the war to secure the area.

I'm almost constantly exhausted. But when James comes to visit I feel a surge of energy. We play cards and talk, he reads a book until I fall asleep, and I'm sad when I wake up in the middle of the night and he's gone.

One morning, I wake to find him there, waiting for me, and I can tell something is wrong.

He stands and smiles awkwardly. "Listen, I need to take a trip. I won't be gone long. Maybe a few days."

"Oh?" I suddenly feel nervous about him leaving. I shouldn't be. I don't want to be. I try to make my voice casual. "Okay."

"There's someone I need to check on." James turns his back to me. "Someone I made a promise to."

I'm not sure what to say to that. Could there be someone else in his life? I realize then that there's so much I still don't know about him.

"Can I help?"

"No," he says quickly. "It's something I have to do alone."

CHAPTER 36

JAMES

WHEN I LEAVE THE HOSPITAL, I drive to the barracks where my brother, his wife, and children are housed. I stand outside and wait, knowing that I'm not going to go in, that they don't want to see me. But I want to see them. If only to know that they're okay.

Everyone in the evacuation camps has to work. That's the deal. The United States and its allies evacuate you, give you a new home, and food, clothing, and shelter from the Long Winter —and you have to work. In some ways, this new world has become a classless society. Everyone works together to survive. At least, everyone in the same alliance.

The door to the barracks swings open, and people pour out into the morning sun wearing thick clothes, heads down, trudging to their jobs. In the procession, I pick out my brother, talking to another tall man beside him, both smiling. That's Alex for you: always one to adapt. Never one to begrudge his fate. He'll do well here. I'm glad. And I'm glad I saw him.

But I can't linger here. I have a trip to make. A very important one.

❄

WHEN I MADE my request to Fowler, he questioned me at length. The kind of resources I asked for are hard to come by: a plane capable of crossing the Atlantic and landing anywhere and a team capable of excavating deep beneath the snow.

But he said yes. I know he had to make some calls and trade some favors, which are the only real currency left in the world.

The Air Force cargo plane is a noisy, vibrating behemoth that reminds me of a whale flying through the air. I try to sleep during the flight, but I can't. I keep thinking about Emma, wondering how she's doing, whether her five laps around the unit yesterday will be six or seven today or whether she'll regress as she did two days ago. Doing what she's doing—starting over, learning to walk again and being so weak and frail—would be hard for anyone. It's especially hard for her, because she's so strong. And so proud. But I'm proud of her. For enduring it with so much courage and poise and determination. I wonder if I could.

The Air Force colonel commanding the mission walks into the cargo hold and points at the headset. I pull it on and listen.

"We're on approach, Dr. Sinclair."

I look out the window at the frozen ground below, the white expanse with no end. There was no satellite footage to go on, but I was optimistic that we might at least see the top of the house. No such luck. It's buried.

❄

ON THE GROUND, we use sonar to locate the house, and the Marines begin digging. The white sheet cracks like an egg as they tunnel into it, their breath coming out in white wisps of heat.

This location, just outside San Francisco, looks like Siberia now: ice and dim sunlight as far as the eye can see. A gust of wind catches me, cutting right through my parka, right down to my bones. I shiver and try to bear it.

The hole is growing bigger. It's not a shaft straight down, but rather a tunnel leading to the house's front door. The ice hasn't collapsed the residence. That's good news. It gives me hope.

When the tunnel reaches the porch, the Marines call up to us. I descend while they chisel the remaining ice away from the door and kick it open.

The inside of the house is an icy tomb. The Marines and I are wearing helmet lights that cut white beams through the darkness. Glimmering white crystals cover the furniture and chandelier, as if the home has been flash-frozen. It would be beautiful if the cold weren't so deadly.

"Stay here," I call out to the Marines.

I make my way to the kitchen and open a creaking door that leads down to the cellar. I shine my helmet light over the staircase, looking for any booby traps. If he were going to attack, now would be the time.

"Oscar?" I call into the darkness.

No reply.

Is he gone? Did the Long Winter claim him?

I take another step. The narrow wooden staircase groans under my weight.

I continue down the stairs to the concrete floor. Even wearing the parka, I'm freezing. I won't last long down here.

"Oscar? Can you hear me?"

I wait.

"It's okay. It's James. If you can hear me, come out. We have to leave."

I hear rustling in the corner. I turn, shine my light there, and breathe a sigh of relief when I see him. He's okay. Unharmed.

His skin is silky smooth, his hair short and brown, worn in the same fashion as mine, though he looks twenty years younger than I do, like a young man just beginning college.

"Sir," he says softly. "I didn't know what to do. You told me to stay here until you came for me."

"You did the right thing."

"I saw on the news that you were going into space."

"I did."

"And you returned. Safely. I was worried."

"There's no reason to worry, Oscar. Everything's going to be all right now."

❄

BACK IN TUNISIA, in Camp Seven, Fowler assigns me to my own habitat. It's a solar-powered, two-bedroom white dome with a small kitchen, living space, and even an office nook. Space is at a premium here in the camp, and the residence is a luxury. I declined it at first, but Fowler insisted, saying that Emma would need live-in care even after she got out of the hospital. That comment got me thinking about where she would go after the hospital. I sort of assumed she would want to stay with her sister. I can't help but feel a little hopeful that she will in fact come back here.

An hour after I return to my habitat, Fowler knocks on the door. He lives two habitats down, and we've been meeting here and working together at night (we have offices next to each other at the new NASA headquarters, but he and I always bring work home). At the sight of Oscar, he stares, then gives me a curious look. I wonder if he's figured it out.

"I'll make arrangements to find you a three-bedroom habitat."

"That won't be necessary."

He squints at me and finally nods. "All the same, I'll get you the larger habitat."

I think he knows.

❄

THE NEXT MORNING, just before I head out for work, there's a knock at the door. I open it to find Pedro Alvarez standing there, wearing a thick coat and cap, shivering in the wind.

"Pedro."

"Hi, Doc."

"Come in. Please."

He shakes the snow off of his coat and glances around the habitat. "Hope I'm not intruding."

"Not at all. I was about to head to work, but I have a few minutes. It's great to see you."

"Likewise, Doc. There was a rumor going around about some brilliant scientist living in the camp. Guy who's going to save us all. So, you know, I figured that was you, and I took a chance on searching the AtlanticNet. Found you in the directory."

"I'm glad you did. What happened after you left Edgefield?"

Pedro shrugs. "They gave me a spot here in Camp Seven. Probably figured that would keep me from suing or giving a TV interview or something. Been here building habitats and working in the warehouses ever since." He looks me in the eye and smiles. "I just stopped by to say thanks—for what you did for me at Edgefield. You saved my life. Probably saved my whole family, Doc."

"You would've done the same for me, Pedro."

When Pedro's gone, I can't help feeling a little bit of pride. Since the encounter with Beta, I've struggled to stay positive. We're facing impossible odds. A massive enemy, ruthless, relentless. It's a lot like that riot in Edgefield. But Pedro and I got out of there. I helped save him. And seeing him fans the flames of hope inside me. Even long odds and massive enemies can be beaten.

❄

FOWLER and I have come to several conclusions in the past few days. First, that we will share what we know with the Caspian Treaty nations and the Pac Alliance. The three superpowers are in agreement that a joint effort must be made to oppose the artifacts. Our conundrum is very simple: what to do. We know we're at war. But with what? And how do we fight it?

Fowler and I have reviewed the data, trying to get our heads around what we know. We're preparing a proposal, and soon we'll visit the other superpowers and ask for help.

But first there's something I have to know. I've asked Fowler before, but he wouldn't tell me.

"I want to see the timeline. With the climate data."

"That won't tell us anything we don't know," he says quietly.

"It will. I need to know if I caused this—if my actions up there accelerated the Long Winter. It won't affect me. I promise."

He exhales heavily and types on his laptop.

I scan the data. I was right. The day we attacked the artifact, the climate on Earth changed dramatically—temperatures around the world plummeted. We did this. *I* did this. I caused the Long Winter to get worse. My actions out there did this. I'm responsible for the death of millions. Maybe billions.

I have to fix this. I might be the only one who can. And I'll never be the same if I can't.

CHAPTER 37

EMMA

I'm getting stronger. Slowly. Every day it's a little easier to breathe, a little easier to stand. And I can walk for longer. They say it will take years for me to regain my full strength. I may have to use a walker for the rest of my life.

It's an adjustment. It's humbling. But I feel so lucky to be alive and to be here and to have my family and James so close.

Every day, I ask him what he's working on. He's coy. I know he's meeting with Fowler and that they're planning a new mission. I want to be on it desperately, but my health prevents that.

"Has there been any communication from the Midway fleet?" I ask.

"Nothing yet."

Two of the larger drones in the fleet have small rail launchers capable of sending mini comm bricks directly to Earth. So why have we received no communications? Have the drones truly found nothing? Or were they destroyed as well?

"Any word from the *Pax*?" I dread the answer.

"No," he says softly.

"What's the plan?"

"We're not sure. Fowler and I have talked about launching more probes. But we're pretty short on resources, and I think we need to wait until we know more."

"Such as a target."

"A target would be nice. Midway might give us that."

"What's the alternate plan?"

"As of right now, we don't have one."

❄

DAYS TURN TO WEEKS. My progress plateaus. The doctors and physical therapists continue encouraging me, but recovering muscle mass is hard, and recovering bone density is even harder.

I try not to think about the crew of the Pax, but it's impossible. James and I talk about them, speculate about what they're doing right now—if they're alive. It seems like with each passing week, we both think about them less and talk about them less. They're like a ship sailing into the sunset, growing farther away and out of sight, not suddenly, or noticeably, but gradually, the transition subtle and easy to miss until it's gone.

For the most part, I'm going stir-crazy in this hospital room. There isn't exactly TV anymore, and I've watched everything stored on the AtlanticNet (the government-controlled local internet, which is highly censored and generally limited).

I need to get out.

I need to work.

I need to feel like I'm contributing again.

I've had this conversation with James. Several times now. It always goes the same way: he says my recovery is the most important thing to him and that the best way to help him is to get better. As if I can press the "get better button" all day and everything will be fine. *What if getting better requires that I work?* I've asked. That always prompts a circular argument that ends in a standoff. Who knew that two people caring about each other could be so problematic?

James usually works with Fowler in the morning and comes to visit me for lunch. Today there's someone with him. A young man in his early twenties with milky white skin and dazzling blue eyes. He reminds me a lot of James, even in his mannerisms —the placid expression, the carefully measured words. And he has the same kindness in his eyes.

He nods slowly when I make eye contact with him.

"Emma," says James, "this is Oscar."

"Nice to meet you."

"Nice to meet you, ma'am."

Ma'am. Do I look that old? Maybe it's because I'm laid up in this hospital bed like an old maid, weak and feeble. *I have got to get out of here.*

Oscar looks anything but weak and feeble. He's young and strong and quietly intense. There's a serenity about him that's strange and somehow magnetic.

"He's the person I mentioned a few weeks ago," James says. "The person I had to leave to get."

"Oh. Right."

And I wonder: What is Oscar to James? His son? That's my first instinct. It implies James has a wife. Or *had* a wife. Or at a very minimum, a lover once. And maybe still. It would have been when he was very young, if I've guessed Oscar's age correctly. I can't resist the mystery.

"Is he your..."

I just let the sentence hang there, unfinished. It freezes both James and Oscar like the Long Winter gripping our planet.

"He's my..." James begins, but falls silent.

"Assistant," Oscar adds cheerfully. His voice is mild, almost whimsical. It matches his boyish face, and even seems a little younger than he looks.

"Yes," James says slowly. "Oscar helps with my research."

"Well, as someone who has also been a research assistant to James, let me just say, you have your work cut out for you—keeping up with him."

Oscar merely turns his gaze to James, who says, "You're my partner, Emma. Not my assistant."

"Okay, partner, I'm ready to get out of here."

"We've been over this."

"A great reason to stop talking about it." I swing my legs over the side of the bed, grip the walking cane, and stand, legs trembling. "I'm leaving. I don't need your permission. I could, however, use your help."

He smiles and shakes his head ruefully. "You are a real piece of work, you know that?"

"Is that a yes?"

"It's a begrudging, 'Oh, all right.'"

"I'll take it."

❄

It's slow going outside the hospital. Every step is an act of will. Raising and planting my legs is like slogging through a mud pit. That's what Earth gravity feels like to me now: sticky and weighty and inescapable.

The ground is sandy with scattered snow flurries. It's a mix of brown and white that I can't help but think is beautiful. Through my hospital window, I've watched it snow almost every day, but the sun melts it away. I wonder when it will start sticking, when ice will take hold here and try to bury us.

My dream has always been to establish a new colony on a new world. Camp Seven is a lot like that. This world, this Earth, is almost alien, with all-new characteristics. But I'm too sick to participate. That pains me. I desperately want to find a way to contribute. It's in my nature, and it makes me happy.

It's chilly out, but it's not Siberia frigid, more like New York City in winter. A cold wind cuts through me, and James pulls me close, his arm around my parka as I balance on the walking cane.

The roads aren't paved, just hard-packed sand. Most of the buildings are domes of white material with black solar cells on top, almost like a colony of emperor penguins lying in the desert, sunning themselves as the snow flurries fall and blow around them. In the center of the camp there's a cluster of more permanent buildings made from modular, hard plastic walls: the hospital, the CENTCOM military headquarters, the government administration building, and a large structure named Olympus that houses NASA, NOAA, and what's left of several scientific organizations.

There are also massive factories dotting the perimeter of the camp and even larger warehouses and greenhouses farther out. The warehouses are full of food which will last for a while and the greenhouses will pick up some of the slack when those stores run out. But they won't produce enough to feed the entire camp. If solar output doesn't normalize soon, our fate will be to slowly starve.

Most of the factories process the crops from the greenhouses and churn out the items the camp needs. One of the factories is focused on building the next fleet of ships that will launch to space. That mission hasn't been planned yet, but the construction on the ships has already begun. There's a sense here of time running out, of wanting to be prepared when—or if—we go back out there.

Military vehicles zip by us, scattering snow by the side of the road, along with electric cars no bigger than golf carts. It's quaint in a strange kind of way, like a post-apocalyptic frontier town.

James's habitat is two blocks from the hospital. He asks if he can go get an electric car to ferry me there, but I decline. I want to walk—to prove to him that I can, but more than that, to feel the sun on my face. It's a dull, hazy version of the star I remember, but it's the only sun we have, and it's what we're fighting for.

I have to stop to catch my breath twice, and another time to let the throbbing in my hips subside. I lean on the cane and wait for it to pass. A part of me thinks this embarrasses James, but I know him better than that. He walks beside me, his hand gripping my bicep, Oscar on the other side ready to grab me if my legs fail.

I'm panting by the time I reach the white dome. There's a small anteroom that keeps the heat in and blasts us with warm air as we enter.

The interior of the dome surprises me. It's fresh and new and surprisingly well decorated, like a high-end condo. There are even imitation hardwood floors that click like plastic as I walk across them. The space is open concept, with a well-sized living area and an adjoining kitchen with a dining table in the middle and no island. Radiant heaters glow on three walls, and I can feel the warmth as I pass by one. The living area is dotted with thick area rugs and furnished with a couch and two club chairs. There are no windows but several large, thin video screens display the view outside. They're high resolution, the images good enough to trick anyone just glancing at them.

There are five open doorways. Three lead to bedrooms, one to a full bathroom, and another to what looks like a small office nook that's covered in papers.

I like it. Very much. It instantly feels like home, a place where I could be happy. A place where James and I could be happy.

James leads me over to the couch, and I plop down, happy to get the weight off my weary bones.

"Fowler arranged the accommodations. Made me take a three-bedroom."

"It's perfect. I love it."

"There's more."

I raise an eyebrow.

"Your sister and her family live in one of the barracks close by. I've spoken with Fowler. He can get them moved to a habitat similar to this one. You could live with them if you want."

He's pushing me out. He doesn't want me here. Why? Because I'd get in the way? I'm not exactly self-sufficient right now. I would definitely slow him down. But I want to be here. I want to help him.

"If that's what you want," I say quietly.

He hesitates. "I sort of thought... it's what *you* would want."

"It's not."

"What do you want?"

I swallow hard. "I want to stay here. I want to help you. I want to finish what we started out there on the *Pax*."

❄

My bedroom has an en suite bathroom, and I'm thankful for that. For the privacy. I missed that in the hospital.

The next morning, I'm washing my face when I hear the habitat's outer door open. A gust of cold air flows in and keeps coming. I hear the sounds of banging like the house is being turned upside down. I walk out of my bedroom, towel in hand, and gawk.

The dining table and living room furniture have been pushed to the walls, and most of the floor space is now covered with exercise equipment. James has turned this place into a physical therapy facility.

For one.

He's beaming at me, holding his hand out toward the equipment like a car salesman on a showroom floor motioning to the latest model.

"James, we don't have room for all this."

"Sure we do," he says cheerfully as he plugs in a recumbent bike.

I know when it's no use arguing with him. This is one of those occasions.

When he leaves for the day to meet up with Fowler, Oscar stays, which surprises me.

"You're not helping with the mission planning?" I ask him.

"I have been. James wanted me to stay and help you. Just in case you need anything."

"I really am fine on my own."

"Of that I have no doubt. However, I've been studying various physical therapy techniques and am quite ready to help. Shall we begin?"

※

OSCAR PROVES to be quite adept at physical therapy. He's significantly stronger than I would have suspected from his small frame. He's encouraging when he needs to be, stern at times, which surprises me, and always there when I need help. He seems to never tire, or perhaps it's simply because I'm always so winded. I don't know what normal is anymore.

"What's next?" I ask.

"Rowing. Then a break." He holds his hand out, ushering me toward the rowing equipment. "You're doing quite well, ma'am."

"Oscar, you don't have to call me ma'am."

"It's no trouble. Courtesy is costless and benefits all involved."

Ma'am it is.

Between rowing sessions, while I pant, desperately trying to catch my breath, I manage to ask, "How long have you known James?"

Oscar gets a faraway look in his eyes. "My whole life."

That lends evidence to my theory that Oscar is his son. I have to know.

"Is he your father?"

Oscar is silent for a long time. I'm about to ask another question when he finally responds.

"If I had to name anyone as my father, it would be him."

What does that mean?

I meant what I told James on the way back to Earth: I intended to look up what happened to him. But the AtlanticNet has no details on him. And I'm not exactly spry enough to go bouncing around the camp asking anyone who might know. Oscar will have to do.

After the rowing session, I sit at the dining table and wipe the sweat from my face with a towel. Oscar is standing behind me, making a snack in the kitchen.

"Oscar?"

"Yes, ma'am?"

"When James got in trouble, were you there?"

"I was."

"Will you tell me what happened?"

"You don't know?"

"No."

"I believe James would want to tell you himself, ma'am."

"What can you tell me? Anything would be helpful."

Oscar doesn't respond. He simply motions to the stopwatch he's holding, which indicates that it's time for another session.

Once again, I row, my anger flowing into the strokes. Oscar's just being a good friend. He's probably doing the right thing. But I still feel shut out, the two of them with this secret they won't let me in on.

When the interval is done, I pant, and as soon as I can I say, "Why did he get in trouble?

"The real reason?"

"Yes."

"He tried to save someone he loved."

"That's not a crime."

"I agree."

"Then what happened?"

"The actions he took were extreme. They threatened to take power from the most powerful people in the world. He underestimated their reaction."

❄

FOR TWO WEEKS, our routine is the same: breakfast, James leaves to work with Fowler, Oscar and I do physical therapy, lunch together, I nap, then more physical therapy, then dinner together.

Tonight is a welcome change. The outer door opens and Madison, David, Owen, and Adeline rush in out of the cold, carrying preheated rations. Our own rations lie on our dining table, already steaming. It's a humble assemblage of food, but here, now, it's a feast. And we devour it like one. I haven't seen my sister or her family since the hospital. I'm a bit stronger now, and I feel this strange sense of pride in showing that off. Despite my protests, my physical therapy sessions with Oscar have helped.

Our dinner conversation isn't as free-flowing as I would like. I want to tell Madison and David everything, but the first

contact mission and what happened aboard the *Pax* is still classified. James and I only say that the mission was a success and that
there's more work to do.

Madison, naturally, is protective and curious about James. She
grills him. I admit, I'm listening closely. I have questions of my
own, and a part of me hopes she'll make him answer some of them.

"Where are you from, James?"

"I grew up near Asheville, North Carolina. Went to school
at Stanford."

Madison finishes another bite of mashed potatoes. "And
what about you, Oscar?"

"The same," he says softly.

"How did you two meet?" Madison asks, the question undi-
rected, hanging between the two of them like a lunch bill placed
on the table equidistant between two diners.

"Through my work," James says quickly. "How do you all
like the camp?"

He's changing the subject. It buys them some time. David
has some complaints about the accommodations, but he and
Madison seem genuinely happy. And that makes me happy.

After dessert, we serve coffee. Only Madison partakes. It
seems to give her more energy for her interrogation of James.

"Have you reconnected with your family, James?"

"No. But I know they're okay."

In the escape module, he mentioned that he had a brother he
didn't talk to. This is the first time I've heard him talk about him
since we returned.

"That's good news." Madison pauses, eying me over the
coffee. "Are they here, at Camp Seven?"

"Yes."

"Your mother and father?"

I catch a glance from Oscar to James. *What does that mean?*

James begins picking up the plastic dessert plates from around the table. "Both of my parents have passed."

"Brothers and sisters?" Madison asks.

I can tell James doesn't want to talk about it. I kick her under the table.

She tilts her head, silently asking, *What?*

"Only one brother," James says, his back to us, running water over the dishes before placing them in the washer.

Thankfully, Madison lets it go at that.

When they're gone, I stick my head in James's office nook. It's a pigsty. Drone schematics, maps of the solar system, the asteroid belt in particular, and on the wall is a handwritten note with six names: Harry, Grigory, Min, Lina, Izumi, and Charlotte. Those we left behind. They're why he's working himself to the bone. For them. And for those still here.

"I'm sorry about Madison. She can be a bulldog."

He doesn't look up. "She's just protecting you. As she should be."

"Can I help?"

"Not right now. Thank you though. Soon."

That's something to look forward to.

❄

THE NEXT MORNING, James is waiting for me in the living room. Or my rehab room. It's both, really.

"Fancy a walk?" he asks.

"Sure."

That's new. But a welcome change. Maybe he thinks the fresh air will do me good.

Outside our habitat, I lean on the cane and hold his bicep in my other hand. It's morning and the camp is coming to life. The sun shines dimly in the sky, and a smattering of snow flurries blows around us like ash out of an extinguished fire.

"You're getting stronger," he says.

"Not fast enough for my liking."

"Nothing ever seems to go fast enough these days."

He stops near Barracks 12A and stands and stares. The building's shape reminds me of a long greenhouse with an arched roof—like a long, narrow white barrel sunken into the sand. Only its top is black, due to the solar cells. People are pouring out on their way to work. Breakfast is ending and the day is starting.

This isn't Madison's building. Or Fowler's. He has a habitat where his wife and their adult children and their families live.

"Are you looking for somebody?"

"Yeah."

He keeps staring at the barracks, at the people venturing out. Finally he says, "There—in the green parka. Blue knit cap."

The man is roughly as tall as James and resembles him vaguely.

"Your brother?"

"Yes."

After a pause, James continues. "I come here every morning. To see him."

"Why?"

"Because it's as close as I'll probably ever get."

"I don't understand."

"He hates me."

"Why?"

"Because of something I did."

I have learned James's boundaries. There are few of them, but the ones he has tower like million-foot walls. They only come down when he takes them down. This is one of those walls.

And I wonder: why has he shown me this? It's something that bothers him. Something that he wants to talk about but doesn't want to do anything about.

I realize then that I'm not the only one who's trying to rehabilitate themselves here at Camp Seven. He has his own injuries. They are unseen, but just as limiting as mine.

I squeeze his arm tighter.

❄

A WEEK LATER, I'm pedaling the recumbent bike when the door flies open. James is home early from work. I stop, instantly aware that something has happened.

"We got a signal," he says, panting.

"Signal? From whom? Where? The *Pax*?"

"Midway. The fleet found more artifacts. A lot more."

CHAPTER 38

JAMES

FOWLER and I have analyzed the data from the Midway fleet. It's staggering—the scale of our enemy. We're now calling the artifacts solar cells, and as I suspected, there are many more of them.

Yesterday, we received another mini comm brick, this one from the Helios fleet. The information is timely—and has convinced us of what we have to do.

We turn Fowler's office at the new NASA headquarters into a war room. And that's what we're planning: war. We've found our enemy. And we're going to fight back. The thing is, it's going to take every last person on Earth working together if we're going to have any shot of winning this thing. Our first great challenge is convincing the politicians that we're right.

❄

THE FRIGID APOCALYPSE that has gripped the globe leaves a lot to be desired. There are, however, some highlights. The one I'm appreciating right now: no more business suits. In America's grand exodus from our homeland, formal business attire didn't make the list of things to save. Formality and style are buried in ice, probably gone forever.

So I dress in my gray slacks and black sweater and polish my boots and shave because this is the most important day of my life. I'm about to propose that the human race launch its most important scientific endeavor in history. We're going to strike back. And if we don't, I don't know what will happen. If I can't convince my audience, it might truly be the end for the human race. This presentation is the most important I will ever give. And I'm nervous.

Emma seems to realize that.

"You'll do fine," she insists.

"These are politicians. Anything could happen. They could say no."

"They won't."

"But what if they do? This is our last chance, Emma. The final roll of the dice. It's this or nothing. If we don't go out there and fight, we'll die a slow, cold death."

She takes my face in her hands. "We'll cross that bridge when we come to it. Just take one step at a time."

She is my rock. I know the weeks since landing have been agonizing for her. But I think she's getting better. I know she's frustrated with her progress. I wish she weren't.

"Is Oscar going with you?" she asks.

"No."

I can't risk taking him. That's the truth.

To Emma, I say, "He needs to stay here and help you."

"I'm fine on my own. Besides, I wish I were going with you."

"Rehab is the most important thing in your life right now."

"Rehab is far from the most important thing in my life."

I wish she'd finished the thought. I wish she'd said what *is* the most important thing in her life. But like so many conversations between us, it's left unfinished.

❄

THE MEETING TAKES place in a gym. We don't have schools here at Camp Seven, but they built a gym for exercise—and, I think, because basketball and volleyball, and watching kids play, makes the world seem normal, makes it seem like we're going to get through this.

There's a screen hanging where the basketball goals used to be. The bleachers have been taken out. The floor is covered with rows of desks on platforms that step up like a stadium.

In the pit, looking up at the rows of desks and faces and people waiting patiently, I stand beside Fowler, like two men awaiting a firing squad. It'll probably be a lot like that.

Fowler starts things off. He summarizes the activities of the mission—the launch of the *Pax* and the *Fornax*, the discovery of the second artifact, the dispatching of the Midway and Helios fleets, the encounter with the artifact. This information is already known to the audience—it was in the briefing distributed beforehand—so he goes through it quickly.

Finally, he introduces me, and across the audience I see glimmers of recognition, as if they're thinking, *Oh*, that *James Sinclair*.

The menacing stares don't help my nerves. I feel like a kid who signed up for robotics camp but wound up on the debate team at the state finals; making presentations and arguing with people just isn't my cup of tea. Desperate times, however, require sacrifice.

I clear my throat and start my slide deck.

"As Dr. Fowler has indicated, the crew aboard the *Pax* went to great lengths to acquire the information I'm about to share with you. As of right now, it's probably the biggest secret in the world—and the most unsettling news we have ever had to confront as a civilization. We face a decision about the future of the human race. And these are the facts."

I click the remote pointer, and the screen changes to a map of our solar system. In the black expanse are two white dots that I've circled. The positions for Earth, the Sun, and the asteroid belt are all noted.

"The circles you see are the last known locations of the two artifacts. Until yesterday, these were the only artifacts we knew of. But now we've heard back from the Midway fleet. And we have data to share."

I click the pointer, and the map updates. Where there were two circles before, for two artifacts, now there are hundreds. The screen looks like a smattering of breadcrumbs. All in a line. All leading from the asteroid belt to the Sun.

"The Midway fleet has found 193 artifacts thus far. All of the same design. All of the same shape and size. All with relatively the same velocity curve and vector."

Like a wave crashing to the shore, a ripple runs through the crowd. The expressions on their faces, the way they sit up straight, look up from their laptops, whisper to each other. I have their attention now.

A hand goes up in the front row. The Atlantic Union is made up of fifty nations. Fowler was very diplomatic when he described the formation of the union and the dynamics of the member states. Reading between the lines, it boils down to this: most of the authority was seized by those nations with the greatest military power and the largest industrial base to move their populations. In short, the US, the UK, Germany, Canada, Italy, and France are the real superpowers.

The prime minister of the UK speaks in a calm, even voice,

her demeanor stoic. "Dr. Sinclair, can you cut to the chase? What exactly does this imply?"

"Madam Prime Minister, this data point is just one of several I'd like to share with you today. I think when they are all taken together, the implications will be quite clear. But I do think it's important for you to have all the data first. I would never presume to draw conclusions for you. I'm just a scientist."

I thought that last part was a nice touch. Maybe I'm catching on to this politics thing. The prime minister seems to like it.

She inclines her head. "Do continue."

I click the pointer, and the screen displays a grainy image taken from an extreme distance. It shows a cluster of the hexagonal artifacts joined together like the honeycomb of a beehive. They float before the Sun like a vast blanket covering part of it.

"This is an image captured by one of the Helios drones. These drones were sent to the Sun to confirm what several of us aboard the *Pax* had come to believe: that the artifacts are nothing more than solar cells; I'll refer to them as such for the remainder of this presentation. We have also come to believe that the solar cells were created with the express intent of harvesting our Sun's output."

The first ripple that went through the crowd was like a gentle wave crashing to the shore; this one is a tsunami. I hear gasps. Questions yelled. Most I can't make out. The gym is a sea of turmoil. Confusion, anger, fear. And here and there, stoic resolve.

Fowler rises from his seat and comes to stand beside me. He holds up his hand and says loudly, "Please, ladies and gentlemen, please. Dr. Sinclair needs to finish this presentation, and we'll have a discussion right after."

The noise dies down, and I continue.

"At this point, we are certain of a few things. One: the solar cells have been made or perhaps evolved to fit together. This much you can see for yourself.

"Two: the cells are drawn to our Sun. Their acceleration increases as they move closer to the Sun, implying that they feed on solar radiation and are able to propel themselves faster as they come into contact with more of that radiation.

"Three: their intentions toward us are hostile. The decrease in solar output that Earth is experiencing is not uniform in the space around Earth. We are, frankly, orbiting the Sun in a small pocket of diminished solar output. This cannot be a natural occurrence. The Earth has been specifically targeted.

"The solar radiation reaching Earth is falling in a geometric pattern. I believe that pattern is based solely on the arrival of additional solar cells at the Sun or at some point between the Earth and the sun. And as you can see from the Midway fleet's preliminary survey, more cells are due to arrive at the Sun and are probably arriving as we speak. The 193 cells discovered are likely only the tip of the iceberg. Space is vast, and the Midway fleet is comparatively very small."

A hand goes up in the front row. The chancellor of Germany. Fowler stands again and is going to stop the man, but I nod to the chancellor. I think it's important to our cause to give these leaders the information they want at the exact moment they want it. Our fate is in their hands.

"If the Helios fleet is so small, I believe Dr. Fowler said it was only three drones, how were you able to discover the cells near the Sun? As you just said, space is vast."

"That's a good question. As I mentioned earlier, I, along with the crew of the *Pax*, developed several theories about the solar cells and what's happening in our solar system. One theory was that the solar cells are responsible for the Long Winter. As such, we isolated the area of the Sun where they would need to assemble in order to block solar radiation bound for Earth. In short, we simply sent the drones to that location. And that's exactly where we found the assembled solar cells."

The chancellor nods, his expression grim. "Thank you, Dr. Sinclair. That's very helpful."

"You're welcome." Focusing on the larger group, I step forward, away from the podium, like a prosecutor making his closing argument to a jury.

"The evidence strongly implies that the solar cells and their creators have come to our solar system to harvest the energy of our Sun. The real question is why. I believe the answer is clear. Resource constraints.

"Wherever the solar cells and their makers came from, their home system only has so much solar energy. They can generate more energy in a variety of ways. In particular, they can convert mass to energy—as posited by Einstein, mass and energy are actually interchangeable—but they have limited mass as well. Thus when they reach the resource limits of their home system, they have to go elsewhere for mass and energy. They have come here."

I turn my back to the audience, letting the words sink in. It's dead quiet in the gym, not even the sound of paper rustling.

"It's obvious," I continue, "that they are aware of our existence, and that they see us as a threat to their efforts to harvest our Sun. They have moved to counter that threat. Not only have they reduced the solar output reaching Earth in hopes of killing us, they have taken direct action.

"I will remind this group that when the first solar cell was spotted, our probe was disabled and likely destroyed. When the information was sent back to the ISS, the station was destroyed—as well as every satellite, telescope, and manmade object in orbit. We can conclude from these actions that the first solar cell and its makers sought to hide the scale of their presence in our solar system. When we communicated with one of these solar cells, attempting to establish a dialogue, it once again attacked—the moment it learned that we were alien. And finally, when we counterattacked the solar cell, it chose to destroy itself rather than let us study it. Perhaps most importantly, the climate change on Earth accelerated rapidly after that confrontation. I believe that was a response to us fighting back. I believe all the pieces make sense now. The solar cells won't stop until we're wiped out."

The prime minister of Canada raises a hand, and I acknowledge him.

"Dr. Fowler said that you had severed a piece of the artifact. Or solar cell, as you now call it. Can you apprise us as to what has become of that piece? And what the study of it has revealed?"

"That's another good question. We did succeed in cleaving a part of the solar cell off. Unfortunately, while that piece was being ferried back to *Pax* by one of our drones, the solar cell reacted to our nuclear strike. The bomb detonated far outside of the radius we expected. I was separated from the *Pax* at that time, so I don't know whether the drone with the sample escaped the blast. All I can say is that the sample hasn't reached Earth yet, and frankly I'm not optimistic that it will. I'm also doubtful that its study would reveal anything that might alter the course of action I intend to propose today."

"Thank you," the prime minister says quietly.

I click the pointer, and my second-to-last slide appears. It's a chart of the global average temperature. In a single image, it shows the fate of our planet and our species.

"The world is getting colder. The rate of global temperature decrease is accelerating. The solar cells are causing this. They are aware that we have moved to intervene in their plan. I believe we can expect the rate of temperature decline to increase further. I also suspect that it is within the realm of possibility that the solar cells and their makers will engage us more directly."

The room erupts with questions, but Fowler is once again there beside me to force order. When the din recedes, I continue.

"The conclusion is this: our enemy wants our Sun's output. They are willing to kill us to get it. They will freeze us, and if need be, they will come here to finish us."

I let the words hang in the air. Every eye is on me.

I click the pointer one last time, and my final slide appears. It shows once again all the solar cells we've found.

"There is hope, however." My words boom in the gymnasium, like a drum beating. "If our enemy is after energy, it would stand to reason that they are greatly concerned with the efficiency of gathering that energy. Energy is the currency that governs them, and its collection and conservation is their industry. As such, it wouldn't make sense to send a fleet of these artifacts—these solar cells—across the vast expanse of space. They may not even be capable of travel outside of our solar system."

I can tell the implication hits many people in the audience. Some of those assembled here are scientists.

"What are you saying?" It's the president of the United States who speaks, his voice gruff, annoyed. Scared, probably.

"I'm saying that I believe the solar cells didn't travel from outside of our solar system. I believe they were manufactured here. And that we can stop them."

CHAPTER 39

EMMA

AT MY ROUTINE appointment at the hospital, they run a battery of tests.

I sit in the consult room, waiting, Oscar by my side. He refused to stay home. Truth be told, I'm glad he's here.

I'm nervous about the news the doctor is going to give me. A part of me wishes James was here. And a part of me is glad he's not. He has seen me at my most vulnerable. He saved me when I was most vulnerable. And for better or worse, no matter what the reality of my health is... I want him to know it. Because if things between us grow into something more, I want him to know what he's getting into. But I need time to process it for myself. Then I'll tell him in my own words, when I'm ready.

The door swings open, and a redheaded British physician with a kind smile strides in. Her name is Natasha Richards, and she followed my treatment at the hospital. I like her. I trust her.

"Hello again, Emma."

"Hi."

She pulls the rolling stool from the wall and sits down across from me, eyes on the same level as mine, hands folded in her lap.

"So, I reviewed your chart, and I must say, I'm really impressed with your progress."

"Great. What do the tests show?"

She taps her tablet and pulls up the lab results. Her voice is less enthusiastic when she speaks.

"Well... your muscle mass looks better. Some of the markers we were following have drastically improved."

I sense a *but* coming on. I decide to spare her the awkwardness of delivering the blow.

"And the bad news?" I ask.

"The bad news," she says carefully, "is that your bone density hasn't recovered as much as we were hoping."

"I see."

"Osteoporosis is extraordinarily hard to reverse. Once the bones lose density, it's just not that easy to make them grow back."

"What are you telling me?"

"My goal today is to manage your expectations, Emma. You've been through an extraordinary experience. One very, very few would have survived at all. And I know you and Oscar have worked very hard to rehabilitate your body."

"What should my expectations be?"

"Frankly, I suspect you'll need to use a walker for the rest of your life. Your energy levels may never really recover. The fatigue that you experience, the aches and pains, the cramps, I don't think these things will go away. Perhaps in time they'll improve marginally."

The words are like hammer blows to my chest, like a judge's sentence handed down to an innocent person, summarily, unfairly. I want to walk again and be free. I've worked so hard. This can't be my reality for the rest of my life.

Dr. Richards seems to sense my disappointment. She leans in and grabs my hand. "It sounds worse than it is, Emma, I assure you. It may seem awful now, but you will adapt to the limits of your body. We all have to. But I know it must be tough for you. I reviewed your charts from before you left for the ISS. You were the picture of health. And I know you worked very hard to get there. I suspect you will work just as hard to regain your health. Just keep in mind that there is only so far that road can take you. You mustn't push yourself too hard, and more importantly, you mustn't be too hard on yourself when your performance falls short of your own expectations. Indeed, managing your own expectations is perhaps the most important job you have now."

※

OSCAR and I walk home in silence. For some reason, my mind drifts to Harry, Grigory, Min, Lina, Charlotte, and Izumi. They're the only reason I even got back to Earth. Their sacrifice is why I'm alive. I miss them. I can't help thinking of them from time to time. I should be thankful I'm alive, thankful my situation isn't worse than it is. I owe them. I wish I could repay them somehow. And I owe James. Probably more than I can ever repay.

We pass the barracks he took me to, where his brother and his family live. That gives me an idea. I need something good to happen. And I'm going to make it happen.

※

WHEN JAMES ARRIVES HOME, he is exhausted. More exhausted than I've ever seen him. More exhausted than he ever was on the *Pax*, during the mission, during the height of the stress and the endless hours.

"What happened?"

He plops down on the couch and shakes his head.

"Endless questions. Endless debate. Me standing up there, talking, trying to explain a lifetime of science and a situation that's more complex than I can even grasp. It was agony."

"I'm sure they're just trying to understand so they can make the best decision they can for the people they care about."

"Or for themselves."

"And for themselves."

"I honestly don't know how this is going to go."

"How do you think it will go?"

"I see two possibilities. First, they could authorize the mission, and we have a real chance of survival—with more than a few thousand humans left. Or, they could decide that it's hopeless. And they could turn inward."

"Which means?"

"As of right now, the Atlantic Union is the only one of the three superpowers that knows the full truth of what we're facing. There are only so many resources and so much habitable land left. They could act first."

"Act first to do what?"

"Finish the war that's really just on pause. My guess is they would attack the Caspian Treaty first. Make peace with the Pac Alliance until they consolidate the Caspian territories, then move on. That's assuming the Pac Alliance doesn't see the writing on the wall and declare war."

I exhale. As usual, James has grasped the intricacies of the situation sooner than I have, probably sooner than everyone.

"What can we do about it?"

"Now? Nothing. We have to wait."

There may be nothing else we can do.

But there's still something *I* need to do.

❄

Aᴏᴛᴇʀ ᴅɪɴɴᴇʀ, I retreat to my room and don a thick coat, pull
on tall boots, and slip into my leather gloves. I'm at the door,
putting on my earflap hat and scarf when James catches me.

"Where are you going?"

"To visit Madison," I lie, trying to sound nonchalant.

He squints. "Now?"

"Sure."

"It's freezing out there."

"It's always freezing."

He studies me.

I shrug. "I just need some fresh air. I need to get out for a
little while."

"What did the doctor say today?"

"That I'm progressing well." That much is actually true. Not
technically a lie.

I can tell he's conflicted, and I can see the moment he
gives in.

"Okay." He turns to the kitchen where Oscar is washing
dishes in the sink. "Oscar, go with her."

"Yes, sir," Oscar says mildly.

"No. I'm okay."

"No, you're not."

"James—"

"No. Emma, your bones are still brittle, and thin, and weak.
If a gust of wind catches you and throws you over, you could
break half a dozen bones and be out there in the dark, all night.
It's not worth the risk."

I can't argue with that. And I don't.

❋

Oꜱᴄᴀʀ ᴅᴏᴇꜱɴ'ᴛ ᴀꜱᴋ where we're going. He also doesn't seem to
mind the cold. Or my lumbering pace.

The camp is pretty at night. The domed white habitats glow white in the dark expanse, like luminescent caterpillars buried in the sand. Along the walking path, LED streetlights glow, illuminating the snow flurries that seem to come and go every few hours, without warning, never enough to pile up, just a constant reminder that the Long Winter is still here, unending, waiting to engulf us.

At Fowler's habitat, I brush the last snow flurries off my coat and knock. He answers quickly. He looks as haggard as James.

"Emma," he says, surprised. "Come in, come in."

Oscar follows me inside. He silently takes my coat and scarf and hangs them up while Fowler escorts me deeper into the habitat, which is only slightly larger than ours. A woman about his age rises from the dinner table where she's sitting with two boys, both of whom look to be about college age.

"Lawrence, you didn't tell me we were having company."

Fowler opens his mouth, but I save him.

"No, ma'am, this is sort of a surprise visit."

"A good surprise," Fowler says. "Emma, this is my wife, Marianne."

"Nice to meet you, Marianne."

"Have you eaten?"

"We have. Actually, I've just come to ask Lawrence something. It will only take a moment."

He looks at me curiously and holds a hand toward an office off the shared living area. It's as crowded as James's office but much more neat. Oscar joins us, and I can't think of a reason to have him wait outside. I'll just have to swear him to secrecy along with Fowler.

"What's on your mind, Emma?" Fowler says as he sits in the chair beside me.

"James. His family. They're here, living in one of the barracks."

"I know."

"You do?"

"Their safety was James's only request when he was recruited for the first contact mission. Similar to you, he asked that his only sibling be transported to any safe haven that was established."

"What do you know of their relationship? James and his brother."

"Not much. James went to visit him before he left on the *Pax*. His brother wasn't home. And I got the impression that his sister-in-law didn't want to see him. She wouldn't let him in the house."

"Why?"

"I don't know."

"I'd like to ask you a favor."

"Anything. If I can do it I will."

"I know that James wants to have contact with his brother. I'm going to try to make that happen. I've noticed that movers toured the habitat next to us today."

Fowler studies me a moment. "Yes, the general who was living there was reassigned after our presentation, just in case... a certain decision was made. Anyway, the habitat will come available soon."

"Can you arrange for James's brother and his family to move there?"

Fowler thinks for a moment. "Yes. I believe so."

"How long would it take?"

"To get an answer? Not long. I'll know first thing in the morning."

❄

I'M HALFWAY FINISHED with my morning exercises when the

messenger arrives. The note from Fowler is to the point, and I'm relieved when I read it.

Housing transfer approved.

※

ON THE WAY home from Fowler's habitat, I made Oscar swear not to disclose what he heard. He agreed and asked no questions. I feel on some level that I'm betraying James by not telling him what I'm doing. But I also believe that I have to—for his own good. My rehabilitation here in Camp Seven has been physical. His great injury is the relationship with his brother. James saved my life. And brought me back to health—or probably as close as I'm going to get. I have to do this for him. And I need it to be a secret.

There's one last piece I need to put in place.

When I first logged on to the AtlanticNet in the hospital, I assumed it was simply the start of a growing web of information, that the government would expand the breadth of data available as they had time. I was wrong. It remains a very rudimentary tool used mostly to direct life in the camp. It contains work schedules, job responsibilities, and news the government deems important. And of course mandatory notices. Thankfully, it also includes a resident directory, which is essential for helping relocated families find each other.

There are four men with the last name Sinclair, and only one living in the barracks James showed me: Alex Sinclair. Wife, Abigail. Son, Jack. Daughter, Sarah. They live in Room 54.

I shower quickly and dress, and when I emerge into the living room, Oscar is sitting on the couch, reading a tablet.

"Oscar, I need to run another errand."

"Of course."

"And I need you to keep it secret. Just like the meeting with Fowler."

"Very well."

❋

I'VE NEVER BEEN inside one of the barracks. It's not what I expected.

The overall vibe is similar to a nursing home. There's a long corridor down the middle, with people sitting outside their rooms, mostly those too young or too old to work. The children play, talk, or stare at tablets, watching the few videos freely available on AtlanticNet.

There has been talk of setting up schools, but I suspect it isn't high on the priority list. Survival is the order of the day. Every able-bodied person is working on sustaining the camp and supporting NASA's next mission. That's what I would be doing if I were physically able.

The door to Room 54 is closed. It's white, made of a synthetic, thick material that echoes like fiberglass when I knock.

The door cracks open, revealing a woman with blond hair and dark bruises under her eyes, as though she hasn't had a good night of sleep in a long time. I'm leaning on the cane, Oscar beside me, not sure exactly how to begin.

"Can I help you?" she asks, suspiciously.

"Hi. My name is Emma Matthews."

"I'm Abby Sinclair. What's this about?"

"I'm a friend of your brother-in-law."

Her expression turns hard. "James?"

"Yes."

"What do you want?"

Okay, didn't see that coming. "I'd like to talk."

"About James?"

The words are like a bear trap she's tossed on the floor. She stares at me, expecting me to step forward. I decide to step around it.

"I'd like to talk about moving you and your family out of here and into a habitat."

She squints, studying my face. Finally she lets the door swing open, silently inviting me in.

It's clear to me why they call them rooms and not suites. The Sinclair family is living in what amounts to a twenty-by-thirty-foot space with two beds along the wall, a small table, one enclosed bathroom, and a sitting area. Their son, Jack, looks to be early elementary school age, maybe seven or eight. The daughter is a toddler, maybe two years old, maybe a little less. They're both sitting at the table tapping away on tablets, the older child helping the younger with something. It's adorable. And a sad sight that this is how these kids, and so many others, are spending their days now.

"Jack," Abby calls out, "take your sister to the living room and continue your lessons. No games or video."

The kids move to chairs ten feet away. That's the living room, I guess.

Abby motions me to the table and we sit, Oscar standing placidly by the door, clearly out of place. Abby scowls at him, as if she knows him and hates him.

I try to make my tone friendly. "The AtlanticNet has school lessons?"

Abby nods curtly. "There's a shared curriculum."

"Is it any good?"

"It's all we have."

So much for small talk.

"We're all getting by with what we have," I say quietly. "Which is why family is more important than ever."

"That sort of depends on how family treats you, doesn't it?"

This isn't going well.

"It does," I say. "And it's important when you do something for family, for them to know about it. So they can know how much you care."

"What are you saying?"

"I'm saying the only reason you and your family are here is James."

She falls silent.

"Let me guess," I say. "Some men from the government came to your house and told you that you were to be resettled into one of the last habitable zones on this planet. Saved from the war, taken to safety. Did you ask why?"

She shakes her head. "No. I didn't."

"Do you want to know why?"

"That's what you came here to tell me, isn't it?"

"That's only part of why I'm here. The rest, I need you to keep a secret—for your own safety. What I'm going to share with you is classified government information. I'm not supposed to be telling you."

That gets her attention. She glances over at the children. "Kids, put your headphones on, right now."

I put my hands on the table and interlace my fingers. "James means a great deal to me. I don't know what happened between you and him or his brother and him, or even why he was sent to prison. But I've gotten to know him very well, and I know he's a very good person."

Abby simply stares at me, making no reaction.

"This is what hasn't been released to the public: the Long Winter is not a natural phenomenon. The Earth is getting colder because there are alien objects out there that are deliberately blocking the solar output that should be making its way to Earth. James was recruited for a mission to go investigate these objects. His expertise in robotics was essential to building drones that discovered exactly what they are and why they're here. I was on that mission with him." I pause. "Yesterday the mission director told me that in return for joining that mission, James only asked for one thing: that you all be taken to safety."

Abby places her hands on the table and gazes at them as if the answer is somewhere in the wrinkles.

"If Alex had known that," she says, shaking her head, "he might not have even come here. We'd probably be buried under ten feet of snow."

"James can be equally stubborn." I lean closer to her. "That's all the more reason why it's important for families to stick together right now. So the voices of reason can cut through the old grudges and hatred. We need each other. And I know he cares so much about you all."

Abby takes a look around the cramped room where the four of them live. "You mentioned a new habitat?"

"Yes. Next to the one I share with James and Oscar."

The mention of Oscar's name draws a sneer, and she glances in his direction. Yes, she knows him.

"I'm sensing there's a catch," she says.

"There's not. I know that James wants the best for you all. And I know that if he asked for the habitat for you, you might learn that he had done it—and refuse to accept it. So I did it instead. It's yours. No strings attached. You can move whenever you're ready. The transfer has already been approved."

"Thank you," she says quietly.

"I ask only one thing, and it's not a requirement. Only a request."

"Which is?"

"That you come and visit James. If Alex doesn't want to come, then simply drop off the kids, or you and the kids can come by. That's all."

CHAPTER 40

JAMES

IT'S BEEN two days since I gave the presentation to the Atlantic Union Congress. There's been no decision yet. I count that as a bad sign. I feel like a trial lawyer who has made his case, as best he could, for an innocent client facing the death penalty—and now that client's fate is in the hands of people who don't understand the case and may act irrationally or selfishly. It's driving me crazy.

I'm sitting in Fowler's office at NASA headquarters, talking with him about the mission, when his assistant, a Marine lieutenant, knocks and enters.

"Sir, the Executive Council is asking for you. Both of you."

This time, we meet with the leaders of the Atlantic Union in a smaller room: a situation room at the executive office building. The elected leaders of all of the union's preeminent nations are seated at a long conference table. The president of the United States speaks first.

"Gentlemen, you are a go for your mission."

Relief floods through me. I can actually feel the stress draining from my body.

The feeling doesn't last long.

"But there are two conditions," the president says, his gruff voice getting rougher with each passing word, like a chainsaw cranking. "First, the launch will not take place until we've recovered and retrofitted at least two hundred nuclear warheads."

"Retrofitted for what?" I ask.

"Deployment in space. I'm sure the two of you can arrive at the reason, but I'll say it so there's no ambiguity: we believe your mission could antagonize our enemy and cause them to respond with force. We want to be ready to defend ourselves."

I can't believe what I'm hearing.

"That could take years." I practically shout the words.

"Maybe." The president fixes me with a hard stare. "But I hear you're pretty good with robotics. Perhaps you could assist in the recovery and redesign efforts."

Fowler shoots me a look that says, *Let me handle this.*

"And the second condition?" Fowler asks.

"Before you inform the Caspians or the Pac, we need to be ready here on the ground."

"Ready how?" Fowler asks softly.

"For war."

I can't hold my tongue anymore. "What does *that* mean?"

"It means, Dr. Sinclair, that we need to secure our new borders, build up our military presence on those borders, and strengthen our spy network abroad so that we can be ready and able to respond to any act of aggression."

"That works against everything we're trying to do! A military buildup will siphon resources from the nuclear refitting—as well as the mission, not to mention putting the other nations on guard. You know they have spies here in the AU. They'll know about the military buildup the moment it starts. They'll respond in kind."

The president looks me directly in the eye. "Those are the conditions, gentlemen."

His message is clear; the decision has been made. And it won't be unmade.

❄

IN FOWLER'S OFFICE, I pace, fit to be tied.

"This is ludicrous. They're talking about fortifying borders for this habitable zone that we can't *possibly* defend against either the Caspians or the Pac, not to mention that huge solar array out there. *Offense* is our only chance of survival."

Fowler leans back in his office chair, reflecting. His voice is barely above a whisper.

"There's nothing we can do about it, James. Our job is science. This is politics. These are people—irrational, frightened, angry people—who sometimes make bad decisions. We have our orders."

❄

I'M EXHAUSTED when I get home. As I enter the anteroom that blasts me with warm air, I hear Emma's voice inside, talking with someone, a woman.

"The doctors say I simply won't regain the bone density I've lost. My recovery is plateaued."

"Have you told James?"

"No."

I'm inclined to leave again, to give her privacy, but I know that voice—the person she's talking to. It seems impossible.

My curiosity overwhelms me.

I push into the habitat. My nephew, Jack, is sitting in our makeshift living room-rehab center. A young girl, a toddler, sits beside him. I've never met her in person before, but I know it's my niece, Sarah. The two of them are playing on their tablets, not a care in the world. It's a beautiful sight after a long day.

Emma gets up from the table when she sees me. Abby turns. I expect to see a scowl on her face, but her expression is blank.

I walk over slowly, not sure what to say. Emma saves me.

"James, Abby came by and brought the kids. She thought you might like to see them."

Only then do the kids realize I'm there. Jack tosses his tablet aside and runs over to me.

"Uncle James!"

He practically bowls me over. I hug him as tightly as I think his little body can stand. It's the best feeling I've had in a long time. I've wondered what their parents told them about what happened to me. About my long absence. Whatever it was, it hasn't affected how he feels about me.

Sarah wanders over to me cautiously, eyeing her brother. He reaches out an arm and pulls her into us.

"This is Sarah. She can't talk real well yet, but she can run."

I shake her hand and say, in mock seriousness, "It's nice to meet you, ma'am. And don't worry, talking is overrated. Running is all that matters right now."

A shy smile spreads across her face, and her big, adorable cheeks flush with red. She reminds me a lot of Abby.

I can't help but look around, searching for my brother. There's no one in the bathroom. No one in my office. He's not here.

We visit for an hour. I really want to tell them the tale of the first contact mission. I admit: it's to brag. It's to make them think I'm important or cool or just interesting. Or maybe it's to let them know that I'm more than a convicted criminal. That I'm a good person.

When Jack asks what my job is in the camp, I simply say that

I've been working for the government. Emma plays it up, says that I'm working on projects to save the human race and that I may have already saved us once. Abby seems to have heard this before, or some version of it. She doesn't look surprised. But Jack reacts as I hoped.

When they're leaving, Abby instructs Jack to take Sarah and wait in the anteroom by the front door.

To me, her voice low, she says, "I asked Alex if he wanted to come today. He said no."

I wait, not sure what to say.

"I'm glad you got to see the kids," Abby continues, sounding conflicted. "Alex and I haven't told them anything about what happened. We don't intend to. When they're old enough, we'll tell them. And they can decide for themselves what sort of relationship they want to have with you."

I nod.

"I came by because I felt like you would want to see them."

"I do."

"And that you deserve to see them."

I wait silently, sensing there's more.

"And also, because we've been offered the chance to move into the habitat next door."

That surprises me. "Really?"

"It would be..." Abby hesitates. "Quite an improvement from where we are now."

"I see." What is she asking me? It strikes me then. "Don't worry. If Alex doesn't want to see me, I won't make an issue of it. I won't come over, or confront him if I see him, or approach any of you if he's with you."

Abby nods slowly, the stress draining away from her. I think she dreaded this conversation.

I change the subject. "Abby, I'm so glad you all stopped by. You're welcome any time."

CHAPTER 41

EMMA

PERHAPS THE STRANGEST thing about living here in Camp Seven, and Tunisia, is that there are no seasons. I realize that many parts of the world don't have well-defined seasons, but this is something else altogether. Here almost every day feels like the last—overcast, with snow flurries. Each week it gets a little colder and the sun fades a little more, as if we're living under a light being gradually turned off. People hunker down in their cramped barracks or cozy habitats and stay warm at night and march to work in the dim morning light, snow flurries surrounding them like fireflies swarming. The days start to feel the same: work, sleep, repeat. There's a sense of urgency here, a shared feeling that we're running out of time.

No one here is working harder than James Sinclair. In the past month, he has thrown himself into work on the new ship design. After some debate, James and the team have named the fleet Sparta. I'm told that the rejected names were Alamo and Verdun. Why they spend so much time on these names is a mystery to me, but it seems important to them. Of course I'd heard the name Sparta, but I never knew the history, which involves a small band of Greek warriors holding off a Persian invasion a long, long time ago. James thinks it will be symbolic for everyone. If the symbolism ups the mission success, I'm for it —we need all the help we can get.

The sites where the ships are being constructed are heavily guarded. I haven't been to one, so I was very excited when James asked if I wanted a tour.

We ride in the electric, self-driving car to the site, James and I in the front, Oscar in the back, like a bizarre post-apocalyptic family outing.

The camp has changed so much so quickly. More and more people join the military every day. Their time is mostly dedicated to training and exercises. Maybe the government has intelligence that another war is imminent. Maybe they're planning to start it. Or perhaps the AU leadership thinks we'll be fighting the solar cells and their creator here on Earth soon. Seeing so many in uniform, marching every day, brings a sense of doom. The fading sunlight only accentuates it.

Up ahead, a tall chain-link fence surrounds the factory.

A security guard clears us and motions us forward to the main building. It's absolutely massive. It reminds me of a giant warehouse, a thousand feet wide and seemingly with no end. Workers bustle about, focused on building the new ship's modules.

I look up at the high ceiling above us. "The building provides cover?"

"Yeah. There are several decoys nearby. Basically, empty buildings, but identical. We even send people to each one every day to complete the charade, just in case they attack. And the shelter allows us to work for longer periods as the temperature continues to drop."

He motions deeper into the building. "We're working on something else." He raises his eyebrows. "Top secret."

"You have my attention."

As we walk, James holds up a tablet. The image looks like an ant colony. There are endless passages snaking back and forth, corkscrewing deeper in the ground, ending at a large cavernous space.

"A bunker?"

"We're calling it the Citadel," James says. "This location is ideal for it. The water table is deep here, and there's a large aquifer close by."

The scale of the bunker isn't apparent from the diagram, but a glimmer of hope runs through me. Could this be the key to our survival if the Long Winter never ends?

"How large is it?"

He sees the hope in my expression. His tone turns cautious, the answer already apparent. "It can only house about two hundred people—short term. We're planning to move the most vulnerable down here when the weather gets really bad. Sick. Young." He pauses. "*If* the weather gets bad," He adds. But we both know it will.

"It'll have water?"

"Yep. And energy."

I knit my eyebrows, surprised.

"Geothermal. The big challenge has been getting our wells to a depth where we can harvest enough of the geothermal energy. But I think we've pretty much solved that. I say 'we,' but it's actually a team of German and Scandinavian scientists. They're brilliant."

James is getting animated now.

"At a depth of two hundred meters it's about 8 degrees Celsius. If you go down to five thousand meters, temperatures can get up to 170 degrees Celsius."

"You can drill that far down?"

He raises his eyebrows. "Farther." He taps on the tablet,

bringing up a wider image of the bunker complex. In the zoomed-out schematic, the tunnels, bunker, and aquifer seem so close to the surface. Lines descend from some of the smaller open spaces directly toward the center of the earth, like fishing lines hanging from a boat.

"Our plan is to get to a depth of ten thousand meters. The temperature there will be 374 degrees Celsius. Water pressure will be 220 bars. The amount of energy we can generate is enormous. Easily enough to sustain the bunker."

"Incredible," I whisper.

We're almost to the center of the building, and the opening to the tunnels looms ahead. It has a gentle downward slope, like a highway tunnel that runs under a river. As we walk into it, I feel as though we're wandering into the mouth of some massive beast buried in the Earth.

James goes slowly to keep pace with me. I still can't walk nearly as fast as I once could, or as fast as I want. The doctor was right: I'll never regain my full strength, but I have adjusted to my new reality. That's life.

There's a rail system at the mouth of the tunnel, and we board a small electric car, James driving. The temperature drops as we descend, and the light from the warehouse fades away, leaving us in darkness except for the LED lights above.

Up ahead a cavern looms. As we approach I realize its scale: at least a hundred feet wide and two hundred feet deep, with a twenty foot ceiling above us.

James is grinning like a Cheshire cat. "Welcome to the Citadel, Commander Matthews."

"It's amazing."

He stares ruefully at the cavern. "I worked on a plan to grow food down here. I had hoped to create a self-sustaining colony. But we don't have the time or resources. Or the space. Every inch will be dedicated to housing."

As I look around, I can't help but wonder what life will be like down here. Never seeing the sun. Never walking on the surface, breathing fresh air. Away from nature. It's sort of like the ISS—a whole new world, separated from the earth.

Back at the surface, we pass by the white modules of the ship.

"These will be part of *Sparta One*, the largest space ship humanity has ever built. She'll be loaded to the hilt with ordinance: nukes, attack drones, rail guns, you name it." He studies it a moment. "I just hope it will be enough to bring the crew and me home."

I stop walking and stare at him. He actually thinks I'm going to stay here while he goes out there and risks his life on the mission? Never. I'm going with him. I know we're going to fight about this. And it will be a fight to the end, because it's not something I'm going to give up on. No matter what.

❄

THAT NIGHT, Abby and her children come over. Jack and Sarah seem to be adapting well to life here in Camp Seven. Madison, David, and their two children come over too. And Oscar's here, of course. It's probably the closest we'll ever get to an extended family reunion.

We have dinner, and afterward James has a surprise for everyone: a robotic dog. It barks and does tricks and everyone is floored when it actually talks. The kids are obsessed with it. Half the fun is figuring out what it's capable of doing and how it will react. There are no pets here in the camp. In the race to get here, they were deemed a luxury. Extra mouths to feed at a time when the government wasn't sure they could even feed all the humans.

As the world has gotten colder, Abby has thawed. She and I

have actually become friends. She's gone from being standoffish to cordial to actually nice to James. I'm glad to see it.

Noticeably absent is James's brother. I've begun to wonder if Alex will ever come around. James has never let on that it bothers him, but I know it must. Alex is the only family he has left.

When everyone is gone, we straighten our humble abode. It's sort of nice having a messy house for once. James, Oscar, and I generally keep it in order—with the exception of James's office, which is easily remedied by closing the door. You can tell kids have been playing here. I almost don't want to destroy the evidence.

When we're done, James sits at the dining table and studies his tablet while I do the same. Oscar watches an educational video on the AtlanticNet, a series about mining. When he first began watching the series, I wasn't sure why. Now I know: he's studying up to help support the construction of the Citadel. Or perhaps in case there's an accident down there. Educational videos seem to be all he watches. I haven't been able to identify any hobbies or affinities he has outside of helping me with rehabilitation and assisting James with his research.

There are a couple of things I have to talk to James about. I've been putting them off, dreading them, but I can't wait anymore. After seeing the ship today, and what he said, it needs to happen.

I motion to the living area, where my exercise equipment dominates almost half of the floor space.

"We could get a lot of this out of here."

He looks confused.

"It would open up more space for the kids to play. As cold as it is, they won't be able to play outside much longer."

"There's the gym."

"Which is constantly crowded."

He glances at the exercise equipment again. "We'll cross that bridge when we come to it. Your recovery is the most important thing going on in this house."

I chew my lip for a second.

"What if I told you my recovery is finished?" I say.

He sets down the tablet. "What do you mean?"

"I mean, that I've probably made all the progress I'm ever going to make. This is my life. From here on out. Walking with a cane, the fatigue, the brittle bones."

"Doesn't mean you should stop exercising."

"True. But I can get all the exercise I need at the rec center at one of the barracks. I'm sure some folks would like to use this equipment. I appreciate you bringing it here. When it was harder for me to walk, it was really nice to have it close by."

He just nods.

I can feel my palms getting sweaty now, anticipating our next conversation.

"How do you feel about the fact that I'm not going to get much better?"

He studies me curiously, as if he doesn't understand the question.

"Well," he says, "how do *you* feel about it?"

I smile nervously. "I asked you first."

"All right. I knew your rehabilitation would be an uphill battle, and that you would plateau somewhere. I know you led a very active life before. I knew it would be an adjustment. But frankly, life is an adjustment for all of us right now. Everything's changing. We're having to reassess our own capabilities and whether we can cope with this new reality. In some sense, we're all going through what you're going through. The whole human race is learning to walk again."

"How does it change the way you feel about me?"

He gets that same confused look. A flicker of fear runs

through me. Have I completely misjudged what's happening between us?

There's a knock at the door, and James rises and rushes over to it, perhaps happy to be off the hook. I desperately want him to answer that question. I need an answer to it.

I hear Fowler's voice. From his tone, I know it's important. I walk over, making the best speed I can without my cane, but Fowler is already gone by the time I get there.

James's face is a mix of excitement and apprehension.

"The meeting is set. Fowler and I are going to Caspia to make our presentation."

"What presentation?"

"We're going to ask for their help."

"You think they'll agree?"

"I don't know. I just hope they don't declare war. And keep us as hostages."

CHAPTER 42

JAMES

THE RUN-UP to the meeting with Caspia—that's what we're now calling the Caspian Treaty nations, as well as the land that now holds them—is a rushed, frantic affair. I had expected more time to prepare. Upon contacting the Caspians and requesting a meeting three weeks from now, they replied and said we had to come now or not at all. Maybe the Caspians think that forcing us to come on their schedule will throw us off balance.

One thing is certain: they're extremely paranoid. They're permitting only Fowler, me, and a team of six experts and scientists to make the trip—only the people we need to make our presentation. No military. No diplomats. No security detail. Their message is clear: they want the facts, and they're very suspicious of us. The Atlantic Union's ramped-up military activities don't exactly inspire trust.

They probably also suspect we're about to have the same conversation with the Pac Alliance, and they want to get the information first.

We leave at night and fly east in a convoy of two helicopters.

They're the stealth variety, and I'm amazed at how quiet they are.

I was confident in my abilities on the *Pax*, directing our strategy in space. I'm out of my element here. Political intrigue is just not something I understand. And I know very little about the people we're going to meet.

Caspia, like the Atlantic Union, comprises dozens of nations. In the AU, there are perhaps half a dozen with any real power (their leaders sit on the AU's Executive Council). In Caspia, two nations hold a plurality of the power: Russia and India. But that's about all I know about their internal structure. Perhaps that's because the Atlantic Union doesn't know much more; or perhaps it's because they didn't think that information was pertinent to share with me.

The rest of what I know about Caspia is strictly geographic. The state lies in what used to be southeastern Iran. The capital, Caspiagrad, is located in the Lut Desert. It's one of the hottest, driest deserts in the world. The surface temperature has been measured at 159 degrees Fahrenheit. Of course, that was before the Long Winter. The desert lies in a basin, with mountains around it, like a bowl carved into the Earth.

Once we enter the Lut, the ground below is only rock, sand, and salt. The dunes are beautiful. They seem endless, like waves of sand, a brown sea reaching to the horizon. Here and there, punctuating the ripples, a few dunes rise high in the sky, almost a thousand feet.

Some of the geography reminds me of the American Southwest, and some of what I see, I don't understand. I point to a scattering of what looks like the hulls of shipwrecks, and I ask Fowler over the radio, "What are those?"

"Yardangs."

"What did you call me?"

He laughs. "The wind carves them out of bedrock over very long periods of time."

"How do you know that?"

"Lifetime of geekhood."

I smile. I like Fowler more and more. I really hope the Caspians don't kill us.

The Persian name for the Lut region translates to "Emptiness Plain," but it's anything but empty now. A city glitters ahead.

Where the Atlantic Union's Camp Seven looks like a nomadic settlement, Caspiagrad looks as if it's here to stay. Skyscrapers rise out of the desert, with high walls ringing them. Helicopters circle in the air, a patrol likely launched as a show of strength for our arrival; they would've picked us up on radar a long time ago, and they probably have hidden base stations throughout this expansive desert.

But there's no formal welcome ceremony, only a handful of mid-level diplomats who introduce themselves before escorting us into a building near the helo pad. Security checks us out thoroughly, then remands us to the diplomats, who offer us water or coffee and ask if we need to use the restroom (we do).

Finally, they lead us into an auditorium. The room is packed. There are far more people than in the gymnasium where Fowler and I gave our presentation to the Atlantic Union.

There are no introductions, no preamble. We are simply instructed to "Say what you came here to say."

When we finish, the questions are much the same as those we received from the Atlantic Union. The Caspians have brought in experts, and those experts question us at length. Fowler knows some of them. They're his counterparts from Roscosmos and the Indian Space Research Organization (ISRO). That helps our cause. We share all our information on tablets—

none of it could be transmitted ahead of time—and they're reviewing it on the fly.

Through a translator, a Russian scientist asks the question I would ask in his position. "Dr. Sinclair, what do you think is out there? On the mission you're proposing, what do you expect to find?"

"Our working theory," I say carefully, "is that there's an entity or device here in our solar system that is creating the solar cells."

"Where?"

"From the locations of the cells we've found and their vector, there really is only one place that it could be. The asteroid belt."

"Because it would need raw materials to build the cells."

"That's our thinking. The asteroid belt is the most easily accessible source of raw materials in the system. It's in a good location, just beyond Mars. The harvester, as we have named this potential device, could conceivably come to our solar system, attach to asteroids, manufacture the solar cells it needs, and dispatch them to the Sun to form a solar array that would harvest the Sun's output."

The room falls silent.

The Russian president is the first to speak—in fluent English.

"As I understand it, there are thousands, perhaps millions, of objects in the asteroid belt. Even if you know the general location of this harvester, will it not be a 'needle in a haystack,' as you Americans say?"

"That's a fair question. And one of the risks to the mission. But we have enough data to develop a working profile of our enemy's behavioral patterns.

"We believe the solar cells are actually very simple machines. The way they reacted to us was no more complex than what you might see from a one-purpose drone. We're assuming that they have limited defensive and communication capabilities. They seem to be tailor-made to travel to the Sun and capture energy. As such, it would make sense for the harvester to prioritize its actions based on economy of energy. Harvesting energy and conserving energy—those are likely its only mission parameters. And, of course, it seems to be monitoring us—its principal enemy or impediment to its mission—and taking action accordingly. We think those actions include destroying the ISS and trying to disrupt the launch of the *Pax* and *Fornax*.

"At any rate, that hypothesis allows us to make an assumption about where the harvester might be. Over half of the mass in the asteroid belt is contained in four asteroids and dwarf planets: Ceres, Vesta, Pallas, and Hygiea. The largest, by a wide margin, is Ceres. It contains almost one third of all the mass in the asteroid belt. And it's directly on the path from which the solar cells are originating. We think the harvester is on Ceres."

"Impossible," a Russian scientist mutters. He's a pudgy man with bushy eyebrows and thick glasses. "We can see Ceres with ground telescopes. And it rotates completely every nine hours. There is nothing there, Doctor Sinclair."

"Nothing we can see. Our working assumption is that any entity sufficiently advanced to shroud our sun could easily camouflage itself on Ceres. It's there. We're betting on it."

※

AFTER THE PRESENTATION, they make us wait in a conference room. After the first hour, I start to wonder if we have indeed been taken hostage. It would be quite a play.

To Fowler, I say, "How easy was it to make this meeting happen?"

"Not easy. They rejected the initial approach."

"How did you pull it off?"

"I had some help."

He opens his laptop and starts a video.

"This was in a hidden, encrypted file on the *Pax* escape capsule—something your crew sent home to help your efforts," Fowler says.

The video was definitely recorded on the *Pax*. I recognize the padded walls of the modules. I also know the voice muttering in the background: Grigory. He floats into view and stares directly at the camera like he can see right through it and into me. He speaks in Russian, but there are subtitles at the bottom.

To my countrymen and my colleagues at Roscosmos, our mission aboard the Pax *has been a success. But we are entering a dangerous phase of the mission from which I likely will not return.*

I, along with the members of this crew, have elected to send James Sinclair home. The reason is very simple: he is a genius. If anyone can solve what's going on out here and stop it, he can. I'm storing this message using a NASA encryption method that the crew of the Pax *has access to. The file will unlock after he arrives home. I have one request—that you give him any assistance he requires. He is trustworthy, and I have placed the lives of my family and everyone I know in his hands.*

I'm once again thankful for my crewmates. Even millions of miles away, they've managed to be there when I needed them.

❄

MY GENERAL EXPECTATION was to get a yes or no answer to the mission we've proposed. Instead, one of the diplomats returns to the conference room and tells us we're free to leave.

When we touch down in the Atlantic Union, I don't even get a chance to shower or see Emma and Oscar, or to sleep in my own bed. A military detachment escorts me directly from the helicopter to a plane. The Pac Alliance wants to meet immediately. No doubt our meeting with Caspia influenced that decision; they don't want to be in the dark.

I wish we had a yes from the Caspians. I sense that humanity's future will be decided soon. These three nations either band together and go out there and fight together—or they descend into a global civil war over what's left of this withering planet.

❄

I MANAGE to get to sleep on the flight to Australia. When I wake, I find Fowler hunched over his laptop.

I rub my face, trying to wipe away the weariness.

"What're you working on?"

He yawns. "Our presentation. Looking for anything we can improve from our last outing."

I take the laptop from him.

"Here, let me take over. Get some sleep."

❄

THE CASPIANS BROUGHT us in the front door—flew us directly to their capital, which was glittering in all its glory, and escorted us to their seat of power. They wanted us to see their shining city in the desert, probably to intimidate us with their technological prowess.

But whatever the Pac Alliance has built, they want to hide it from us. They direct us to land on a Chinese aircraft carrier off the western coast of Australia. On the deck, they herd us into three of their own helicopters, the windows blacked out.

When we land a second time, we're forced to remain in our seats for thirty minutes. And when they finally open the door, there's a massive canopy above us, formed into a tunnel that leads to the outer doors of a building.

They really don't want us to know where we are.

An Asian man in a tailored suit is waiting inside the building, a wry smile on his face.

"Dr. Sinclair, I'm Soro Nakamura. We spoke during your approach to Earth."

"Yes. I remember. Nice to meet you in person."

He squints. "Let us hope, for your sake, that this meeting is filled with less deception."

※

THE PAC ALLIANCE is a tough audience. Even tougher than the Caspians. They ask more questions, are more suspicious, and demand data to support every one of our claims. There's a lot of supposition in what we're presenting. We simply don't have the answers. The meeting is long. Seven hours in total. And grueling.

When it finally breaks, they lead us through an underground tunnel to what passes for a hotel. It's more like a dormitory with shared bathrooms and small bedrooms. But it's clean and warm.

"When will we be allowed to go home?" Fowler asks Nakamura.

He flashes a smile. "When it's appropriate."

※

FOR THREE DAYS, the Pac Alliance confines us. I'm worried. So is Fowler, I can tell—though we don't talk about it. We know we're probably being watched, that every word we say is being recorded and analyzed and played back for the people making this decision. So we play our part. We talk about the mission and our presentation and the importance of it.

I don't say what I'm thinking: Has a war already started out there? Did we fail?

CHAPTER 43

EMMA

THE DAY JAMES LEAVES, I get Oscar to help me move the exercise equipment to the rec center. It's only fair. My progress has stopped, and others should be able to benefit from the equipment. Besides, I know James would continue to fight me on this, so it's easier to move it while he's gone. He'll understand. And it gives me something to do other than worry about him.

The larger fight between him and me looms: the mission. That's another reason for getting rid of the equipment. Soon, I won't be here to use it.

Caspia is only a few hours away by helicopter. James will be home tonight, and I'll break the news to him that I'm coming with him. I dread it. I'm nervous about it. But I have to do it.

Around noon, Madison stops by. It's just her. Owen and Adeline are at the gym, playing.

She finds me cleaning the kitchen. I always clean when I have a lot on my mind or when I'm nervous.

We sit on the couch, which now feels almost lonely with the room cleared out.

"You got rid of the exercise equipment?"

"Yeah. I was done with it."

She cocks her head.

"My rehabilitation is over."

She glances at the cane. "I see. Where's James?"

"At a meeting."

"Outside the camp?"

"Yeah."

She eyes my cleaning supplies, still sitting on the kitchen counter, evidence of my nervousness.

"You're worried about him?"

"A bit."

"And?" When I don't respond, she presses me. "What's really going on?"

I need to tell somebody. I need to talk to someone about all the things going on right now. Oscar is great, but he just isn't that someone. I need my sister.

"If I tell you, Madison, you have to promise not to tell anyone. I mean it. Not even David. Or the kids."

She shifts on the couch. "I promise. What is it?"

"NASA's launching another mission to space. Soon."

Her mouth falls open. "Why?"

"I can't tell you that."

"James is going?"

"James is leading the mission."

"And you're going to go."

As usual, Madison has seen right to the heart of the issue.

"Yes."

"And he doesn't want you to go."

"I don't know yet. But I think he'll say no."

"And do you know why?"

I chew my lip. This is not the conversation I wanted to have. What I want is some help in convincing James.

"Because he's stubborn."

Madison gives me a look that says, *You and I both know that's not the reason.*

I shrug. "Because he cares?"

"Emma, I think it's a little more than that at this point. I've seen the way he looks at you. I know you've seen it too."

I have no idea what to say to that.

"Oscar," I call over my shoulder.

He emerges from James's office nook, where he's been doing some work that James left for him.

"Yes, Emma?"

"Do you mind going to the depot to get our weekly rations?"

"Not at all. Is there anything else I should get while I'm out?"

"No thanks."

Once he's gone, I say to Madison, "We haven't really talked about... that."

"Well maybe you need to. Maybe your issue isn't a debate about the mission. Maybe it's figuring out what the two of you are."

"Maybe."

"There's no maybe about it, Emma. Listen, I know I'm not a scientist or a genius like you and James, but I know people. And I know *you*. I know you better than I know any other person. Even David. Emma, you've never cared about anyone the way you care about him. If you don't tell James how you feel, you'll regret it for the rest of your life."

❄

I'm not the only one who needs to tell someone how they feel.

James's brother works first shift. While he's gone, I go next door to talk to Abby.

Like Madison, Abby now has a stay-at-home job that she

does through the AtlanticNet. Everyone is working, no matter what, no matter where they sit. A day care (they call it a school, but there is no curriculum) has been set up in the gym so that parents can work full-time. There are no full-time mothers or fathers anymore. That's not an option. Another cost of the Long Winter. Of survival.

She's very apologetic when she answers the door.

"I'm really sorry, but I have a deadline in an hour, and I have to finish reviewing this document."

"Please, take your time. Will you come over to our place when you're free? No rush."

"Of course. Everything all right?"

"Yeah. It's fine. I just... need to ask you something."

Twenty minutes later, I'm back home, sitting on the couch reviewing a document on my tablet, when there's a knock at the door. I move to get up, but Oscar is faster.

"Hello, Abby," he says, opening the door.

"Oscar," she says quietly. When she sees me, her expression brightens. "Hi. Now still a good time?"

"Sure, come on in."

She joins me on the couch, and we sit together just as Madison and I did. And just as with my sister, I swear Abby to secrecy, and when she's agreed, I say, "James is going on a mission."

"What kind of mission?" Abby asks.

"The kind he might not come back from."

Abby glances away, trying to process the news. "Okay."

"I don't know when the mission will happen. Probably within a few months, if I had to guess."

"Is there anything I can do?"

"There is."

"You want me to talk with Alex."

"Yes. James has never said a word to me about what

happened between Alex and him or anything that happened before. But I know, when he goes on this mission, it would help him to know that everyone back here supports him and is pulling for him. Whatever James did before, he's been a good brother to Alex since the Long Winter began. He's the reason we're all here. He's kept us alive. And he's probably going to give his life for ours."

Abby stands and rubs her palms on her pants as if to dry them.

"It's a tall order, Emma. But I'll see what I can do."

❄

JAMES DOESN'T RETURN that night. Or the next day.

Oscar and I walk down to the Olympus Building. I dart in and out of offices, asking everyone I know if they've heard anything. After a while, I feel like a mail delivery person trying to find the recipient for an errant package.

No one has any information. Or at least, none they're willing to share.

I've never missed satellite phones more than I do now.

❄

I BARELY SLEEP THAT NIGHT. I can't help thinking, *What if the Caspians have taken James and Fowler hostage? Or shot their helicopter down? Or declared war?*

The next day, I resume cleaning the house. Oscar studies me curiously. I think if I wipe down the kitchen sink and faucet one more time, the faux chrome and stainless steel will start to wear away.

"James is incredibly capable," Oscar says mildly. "If anyone could return, it's him."

So he's worried too. Oscar has a strange way of showing it—by comforting me. I'm thankful that he's here with us, though he remains a mystery to me.

A knock at the door almost scares me out of my skin. I race to answer it, making the best time I can with my cane, hoping it's good news. But I realize, just before I answer the door: James wouldn't knock; he would just come in.

A messenger with bad news... they would knock.

Anxious now, I jerk the door open, and reel back at the unexpected visitor.

Alex.

"Can I come in?" he asks.

"Of course."

Inside, he fixes Oscar with a hard stare.

"Hello, sir," Oscar says, his tone completely divorced from the animosity Alex is directing at him.

Alex and I sit on the couch.

"Abby told me that James is leaving. And he might not be coming back."

"That's right."

"And that he's the reason we're here."

I nod.

"I want to know what's going on. I want to know what he's done, and what kind of danger he's in. Will you tell me?"

For the next hour, I tell Alex everything—starting with the moment James rescued me from the wreckage of the ISS. He listens silently, thoughtfully. I can see the resemblance with James. They're both deep thinkers.

When I'm done, he rises, and simply says, "Thank you."

I push up on my cane. "Will you come to see him?"

"I don't know yet. I need time to think about it."

❋

ANOTHER NIGHT WITHOUT SLEEP. This is what it will be like if he goes on the mission and I stay here. I would do nothing but think about him and worry. I'm more convinced than ever: I have to go.

I'm sitting at the dining room table, typing on my tablet, when the door flies open. I turn and stand and my heart melts when I see who's standing in the door, snow falling in sheets behind him.

James.

He looks haggard. But he's here.

I grab my cane and race across the living room. When he sees me practically running, he runs himself, and we embrace. I hug him tightly, and he hugs me back.

"They said—" he begins.

"Forget what they said," I whisper in his ear. "I'm so glad you're home. I'm glad you're safe."

When I finally release the hug, he studies me, a curious expression in his eyes.

"I was so worried about you," I say.

He smiles. "I need to go away more often."

Without thinking about it, I lean in. Suddenly, his lips are on mine and the kiss happens, so unexpectedly, and a nuclear bomb of emotions goes off inside of me. I actually feel my legs going weak. I'm not sure if it's because my legs *are* weak, but it feels like I'm falling down a well.

When we break, he whispers in my ear, "Oscar?"

"He just left to pick up our rations."

He kisses me again, more passionately, more urgently, and hugs me tighter, his hands moving down my back. I walk backward toward my bedroom, and he follows, and we close the door and do something I've wanted to do for a long time.

CHAPTER 44

JAMES

THE WORLD HAS CHANGED. It's not just the triple alliance among the Atlantic Union, the Caspians, and the Pac Alliance.

My world has changed.

Emma is that world. We've been orbiting around each other like two planets, both unsure about the gravity between us. That gravity, and the distance separating us, has now collapsed. We have collided, the mass of our attraction suddenly too great to keep us apart. I don't know what comes next for us, but I've never been this excited in my whole life.

In the aftermath of the collision, we lie in bed, her head on my shoulder.

"How was the trip?" she asks softly.

"Piece of cake."

"Liar."

"All's well that ends well."

"They're going to help us?"

"Looks that way."

"How soon can we launch?"

"I'm not sure. When we were planning before, we didn't

know what kind of resources we had at our disposal. Whether the mission would be the Atlantic Union alone or us with the help of one or two allies. And we didn't know the state of their space assets."

"Have they told you?"

"Not yet, but Fowler and I have met with each nation's space program and military. We've created a working group among the three nations. We'll probably know what we have to work with by the end of next week. My guess is, we can be ready to launch in a few months. Three or four at the most. We need to be. I'm not sure how much more time we have."

She pushes up from the bed and looks at me, chewing her lip the way she does when she's nervous about something.

"What?"

"Nothing," she mutters.

I doubt it's nothing. There's something she wants to say to me, but whatever it is, she decides now isn't the moment to do it.

❄

WHEN EMMA and I get up, we don't talk about what happens next. Or what we are. It's as if we're both on autopilot. We move the pertinent items from my bedroom to her bedroom. There's no decision to be made there—my room is a pigsty, hers looks like something out of a furniture catalog.

In fact, apart from my bedroom and my office, the rest of the house is spotless—cleaner than the day we moved in. I feel like I'm walking around some sort of CDC biocontainment room. She's been tidying up. A lot.

"What do you want to do with the other bedroom?" she asks.

"I'm not sure."

She grins. "I've got an idea."

I raise an eyebrow.

"Drone workshop."

"Just like the *Pax*?"

"But with more gravity."

"Perfect."

❄

WE HAVE dinner for everyone that night: Fowler and his family, Madison and her family, Abby and the kids. It's crowded, and it's kind of perfect that way.

Emma and I sit next to each other, and when dinner is over I put my arm around her and she leans closer to me, something we've never done before, at least in front of everyone.

Madison fixes Emma with a curious gaze that I can't read. Something between the sisters. I'm a good scientist and a capable investigator, but I'll never crack that code.

Jack and Sarah and Adeline and Owen play together; the four of them have become fast friends. Fowler's children are older, and they mostly study their tablets while the younger kids run around in circles and play with the robotic dog, which they've named Marco (I believe because he responds Polo to the name, which they feel is hilarious).

The scene reminds me of Christmas at my parents' house. My father had a brother and two sisters, and everyone always spent Christmas together. It was a full house. It was a chaotic and joyous event and at times contentious. It was perfect. And so is this, with one glaring exception: Alex. It seems that's a bridge too far. One with too much water under it. One that might be washed away forever.

❄

THAT NIGHT, Emma and I are lying in bed, both reading, when she turns to me.

"I need to talk to you about something."

She's using the tone you see in a movie, when the girl breaks up with the boy or tells him she's pregnant or breaks some kind of news that shatters their world. It's nerve-racking. I'm instantly on the defensive. I just want her to spit it out so I can know what I'm dealing with.

I set the tablet aside. "Sure." The word comes out like the sound of a sword chopping the air.

"I'm going on the mission."

"What mission?"

"*The* mission."

"To Ceres? To the harvester?"

"Yes, that mission."

"Emma—"

"No. Don't. I know you don't want me to go. I know you're worried about my health. But I'm worried about you too. It was agonizing when you were gone. *Agonizing.* I can't do it for months at a time, wondering if you're hurt or if something has gone wrong out there. I can't stay here and wait and hope that you come back. I'm going with you. I have to."

My mind races like a computer doing a dictionary assault on a password—running through combinations trying to find a key to unlock this argument, to convince her to stay on Earth. The harvester mission is a true long shot. Longer odds than the first contact mission. Much longer. It's a Hail Mary. I can't take the woman I love up there.

I decide to pursue the most logical approach.

"Emma, you've already lost too much bone density. You simply can't go on another mission."

"My bone density won't matter if I'm dead. And it won't

matter if *you're* dead." She swallows hard and inhales. "Just listen to me for a minute, okay? Really listen."

"Okay."

"Here on Earth, I'm broken. I'll never be the woman I was before. I'll never regain the strength I had before I left for the ISS. Down here I'm weak. Up there, I'm whole again. Strong. And I have a role to play. I can help you. And if it's your fate to die up there, then it'll be my fate too. I'm going, James. *I'm going.*"

I know when I'm beaten. She needs to go. And, deep down, I want her there. So she's going.

I nod slowly, and she puts her arms around my neck, and the decision is made. We're going back into space. Together. Possibly for the last time.

CHAPTER 45

EMMA

THE NEXT MORNING, I do something I haven't done in a long time: I wake up and get dressed for work. It feels good. I hadn't realized how much I missed it--waking up with a purpose.

Outside the habitat, the sun shines dim on the horizon, the sky hazy, snow dropping in sheets. The weather's getting worse. And it's getting worse faster.

At the Olympus Building, James and I visit Lawrence Fowler first. He poses only a single question to me--the same one he asked before I accepted the mission to the ISS--"Are you sure you want to do this?"

I give the same answer I gave then: "I am."

❄

THE CREW of our ship will be drawn from across the triple alliance. That was one of the conditions the Caspians set forth: mixed crews. The crewmembers from the AU are here in Camp Seven, and they're all at work when we arrive, milling about the team room.

James escorts me around the large space, introducing me to each of them individually: Heinrich, *Sparta One's* German navigator; Terrance, our British ship's doctor; and Zoe, a lithe Italian woman who will be the ship's engineer. James activates a camera and begins a recording for the crewmembers in the other two territories, explaining to them that I'll be leading the drone construction and repair team and serving as the backup mission commander.

The video will be couriered to the other two states via drone. Plans for a global communication network have been drawn up and discarded several times, the alliance unable to settle on an acceptable solution. Satellites could be disabled by the array-- just like the satellites that used to orbit the Earth. The weather could compromise ground lines or towers. Any option would take time and resources to build--two things we don't have. For now, data between the superstates moves at the speed of drones, and probably will for a long time.

I can't help but notice how guarded James is around our new crew. I know why. I'm perhaps the only person on Earth who would. What he's feeling here isn't about the challenges ahead of us. It's about what we left behind.

In his office, he shuts the door and starts pulling up his drone schematics.

"The drones we're working on are similar to the attack drone we launched from the *Pax*. With a few upgrades of course."

"I would expect nothing less."

"We can run through them, and start talking about the prototypes." He scratches his head. "You want to work here or at home?"

I shrug. "Doesn't matter to me. What do you prefer?"

"I'm open. But I'll say this, I've just about got my hands full here every day with design on the ship and its systems."

"Working at home would cut out travel time to the labs."

"That's what I'm thinking. And I would be free to focus on it there."

"Home it is."

He nods. "Good."

I motion behind me to the closed door. "They seem like a good crew."

"They are."

"I know what you're feeling, James."

He raises his eyebrows.

"It's hard to let yourself get close to them after what happened on the *Pax*."

"Was it like that for you, when you came aboard--after the ISS?"

"Yeah."

"Does it get better?"

"With time."

CHAPTER 46

JAMES

For the first few days, I regretted agreeing to let Emma come on the mission. It's too dangerous.

In the weeks after, however, I've become glad I said yes. I have the weight of the world upon me now. I need someone in my corner, who is my rock, someone I know will never waver, who can share the burden with me. She's that someone for me.

We've been working around the clock on the ships and drones, me at the Olympus Building most of the time, Emma at home. For me it's sort of like first shift at the office, second shift at home.

It's getting colder. Every morning, the sun fades a little more. Snow falls in sheets now, piling up on the ground. The roads are deep gorges cut in the icy landscape, the walking paths like gullies beside them.

We're running out of time. No matter how hard we work, we never seem to get there.

I wish I could somehow buy more time.

At the same time, I almost dread going on the mission. I dread leaving this place, where Emma and I are happy, where we work together, live together, and go to sleep next to each other, talking about everything under the sun.

We talk about the mission, our childhoods, our families. But there are two topics we never discuss: the future, because we don't know if there will be one; and my past—the event that landed me in prison. She dances around the subject, but I know she wants to ask about it. And I should tell her. She deserves to know. That's part of being together: knowing each other fully and accepting each other.

That's why she was so forthcoming about her own health. She thought it might scare me away. I need to reciprocate. But I'm terrified to do anything that might change things between us.

Our family gatherings have become routine, dinner every Sunday night with Fowler and his family, Madison and her family, and Abby and her kids. Absent only is Alex. I think there's little hope that he will ever show up.

So I'm shocked when there's a knock at the door one Saturday afternoon and I hear his voice from the anteroom when Oscar answers. Emma glances at me, alarmed.

We both rise from the dining table.

"I'm here to see James," Alex says.

He steps forward, and he and I stare at each other for a long moment, me waiting for him to make the first move, to reveal what this visit is about.

"I thought we could talk," he says carefully.

Behind me, Emma says, "Oscar and I have a few errands to run."

"No," I say over my shoulder. "We'll take a walk."

"In this weather?" Emma asks. "Are you crazy?"

It's a fair point.

"Update," I say. "We'll take a drive."

I see a small smile curl at Alex's lips. I'm encouraged by that.

It's the first time his stone façade has cracked in front of me in a long, long time.

I instruct the car to drive to the Citadel site, and it complies, powering quietly down the scraped, hard-packed roads.

"Emma told me you're going on another mission."

"Yeah."

"She said it would be dangerous."

"Maybe."

He glances over at me, waiting for us to make eye contact, silently urging me to tell him the truth.

"Probably," I say, meeting his gaze.

"I thought it might be nice to spend some time together before you leave."

I simply nod. Partly because I'm not sure what to say, but mostly because I'm overflowing with emotion. Joy. Sadness. Gratitude to Emma for telling him. It's like I've had a broken bone, a broken leg that I've walked on for so long that I've learned to charge forward, ignoring the pain, or working around it because I thought it would never get better. But now a splint has been put on it. It's not healed. And there's no guarantee that it ever will be. But instantly, with his words, I feel stronger. Whole. Like the aching deep inside of me has ceased.

I know Alex isn't the sappy type. I'm not either, for that matter. So I do what most guys like us do when things get emotional. I change the subject.

"You want to see something cool?" I say.

"Like what?"

"An underground bunker."

CHAPTER 47

EMMA

FOR A WHILE NOW, it has felt like my world is shrinking. I live and work in this habitat, spending every spare minute on the mission. I feel guilty when I'm not working. Personal time feels like an indulgence or worse: a betrayal to the people who are counting on me.

We haven't had one of our Sunday dinners with family and friends for months. Everyone is consumed with one thing: the mission. Survival.

It's affecting James too. He's stressed, worn out all the time. He eats, sleeps, and works. He only takes about an hour off each week, and he spends that hour with his brother, on Saturdays, after work, playing cards or talking. I still haven't learned what happened between them, but I know James treasures his time with his brother. We all sense that time is now a precious commodity, one that's quickly running out.

Time isn't the only thing slipping through our fingers. The last regions of habitable land will be gone soon. Our world is disappearing before our eyes, the ice eating away at it each day. It's like we're on an island, watching the sea rise, the ground beneath our feet disappearing, knowing we'll drown if we aren't rescued.

Before the Long Winter, this region of Tunisia was a desert. It's now a desert once again, of a different kind: a barren land of ice and snow as far as the eye can see, rolling snowdrifts like dunes, wind flowing over them, scattering the snow like sand.

Every morning I walk outside at first light and hope that I'll see the sun blazing bright on the horizon, that the solar array has moved on, or malfunctioned, or that fate has somehow spared us.

What greets me is a dim glow through the clouds, seen in glimpses through the falling snow, a lighthouse we're drifting away from, into dark and uncertain waters. Perhaps never to return. That is the feeling here in Camp Seven. It's not just the lack of sun. Or the lack of Vitamin D or the fact that the kids can't play outside or that we can't walk to work. It's a shared sense that the sun is setting on our time on Earth.

A snow plow rumbles by, its blade channeling fresh snow into white piles that settle in mounds like an icy hedge along the road. The bucket trucks are already out, parked in the middle of clusters of habitats, scissor arms extending over the domes, workers in parkas, heavy caps, and goggles holding the snow blowers over the solar cells, sending waves of white powder off, freeing the cells to soak up the scraps of sun that no longer fill the habitats' batteries. Every week there's less energy to heat the habitats and charge our tablets and cook with.

Last night, James added another blanket to our bed, and we snuggled close together, the way we do every night, but no matter how close we get or how many blankets we add, I still feel the cold on my face, pressing into me, aching in my lungs as I breathe. I've learned to sleep when I'm cold. I've adapted. But I wonder how much more we can adapt. It's not just the cold, it's what the cold is taking from us. Our freedom. Our food supply. Our future.

It's easy to think it's the government taking these things from us--that's what we see: the curfews that keep us inside after dark and the rationing that shrinks the food on our table every week. Some do blame the government. There's talk of riots, of an uprising against the government, but I think deep down people know that won't change anything. It won't make more food, or more sunlight, and without the government, we might just lose our last chance of surviving. If we haven't already.

I've wondered: even if we are successful--if we can vanquish the solar array strangling our sun--will it matter? What's under the ice that covers the Earth? The plants and animals are probably long dead. If the sun this world has always known returned, could it reignite life here? Or have we already burned down too far? Every time my mind brushes across the thought, I dismiss it. In those moments, I realize the true nature of hope. Hope doesn't have to be rational. Hope is an end unto itself, a renewable source of energy inside of each of us, a fragile thing that can be damaged with our darkest thoughts, dimmed almost to darkness, but never completely extinguished. And like our sun, when it returns, it brings life and energy to us.

❄

I'VE PUT off telling Madison that I'm going on the mission. I've waited as long as I can, but I can't wait any more. The launch is in a few days.

Most of the families have moved to the barracks now. There's more heating capacity per square foot there, plus the combined body heat of everyone around you. Residents also get a slight bump in rations--an incentive for folks to abandon the free-standing domed habitats, which now funnel their paltry energy collections to the barracks. James, Oscar, and I would have moved here if not for the drone lab in our third bedroom.

The first time I entered one of these buildings to visit Abby, I was reminded of a rest home. The barracks now feel like a prison. The doors to the rooms stand open, allowing a modicum of fresh air to circulate. The residents inside stare out with hollow, hopeless eyes. They play chess and checkers as I pass by, their tablets lying in piles, dead with no chance of resurrection (the charging ports are off and being caught with a charged tablet outside of work carries a ration cut).

Despite the density of people, it's quiet. The smell I can't quite place. It's a bit musky, like old air, confined and recycled and used up. Trapped, like the people here, with nowhere to go except outside, into a cold world where nothing can survive anymore.

Some of the adults are filing out, trudging down the central corridor in thick coats, ready to work another day in semi-darkness. They march like prisoners, people working to survive, knowing only a full day's work earns a full day's rations.

The door to Madison's room stands open. I stop just shy of it and peer in. Adeline is reading a book. Owen is lining up a string of miniature soldiers, preparing for battle. They're rail thin, two bean poles lying on the couch, looking tired.

I inch closer and spot Madison standing at the table, scrubbing clothes across a washboard and dunking them in the basin. I was alarmed at the sight of my niece and nephew. But my heart breaks when I see Madison. The skin is tight on her face, her jaw line sharp, eyes sunken unnaturally, hair stringy, arms like two broomsticks pushing the clothes across the ridges of the washboard.

She sees me before I can wipe the sadness from my face. We lock eyes for a long moment, and I think she's going to break and cry, but she forces a smile as she drops the thermal underwear into the basin with a plop and comes around the table, arms held out like limbs of a dying tree reaching out to me. I wrap my arms around her and my fingers touch her back, feeling the ribs protruding like the ridges on the washbasin on the table. She feels fragile in my arms, a precious thing on the verge of breaking.

She releases me and calls to Owen and Adeline and they both wave and come over and hug me. I feel more meat on their bones, and I'm thankful for that. I don't think I could bear seeing them in the same state Madison's in.

She closes the door and motions to the couch, shooing the kids over to the bed they share.

"I didn't know you were coming."

"Just thought I'd stop by before work."

She nods absently, a far off look in her eyes, like someone who has been up for two days straight. She motions to the small kitchenette. "Do you want some..."

I figure she was going to say coffee, but there is none anymore--except in the government buildings, where it's guarded and rationed like the precious fuel that it is. Or maybe she was going to say, "something to eat." But she clearly doesn't have any of that either--and isn't getting enough. I pretend as if she had completed the offer.

"No, I'm fine. Thanks."

Her gaze drifts to the floor.

"Madison, are you getting your rations?"

"We are. But they're not enough." She glances around, as if she had heard something. "They're based on age, you know?" She pauses. "Why would they do that?"

"I..."

"It should be height, don't you think?"

"Yes. That makes sense."

She nods quickly. "I mean you could have two ten-year-olds--both the same age--and one is a foot taller than the other. Obvi-

ously the taller child needs more calories. It's obvious. Isn't it?"
She stares at me, waiting for confirmation.

"Yes."

"We had a meeting about it." She checks the door, seeming to
have forgotten that it was closed. "The AU says they can't go
around and measure everyone's height. They know their age.
They think we'd lie about how tall our children are. And they're
saying—as if we don't know--that kids grow." She throws her
hands up. "Of course they do. Of course. But no one is growing
right now. That's for sure. But some are--" She lowers her voice
and says more carefully, "some need more food than others."

"I'll talk to James."

"No," she says quickly. "That could cause problems... Prefer-
ential treatment... The gossip mill around here. It's all anyone
does."

A long moment passes, Madison staring at the floor again,
the kids playing quietly, the shuffle of footsteps beyond the door.

"I just came to tell you that I'm going on the mission. With
James."

She looks at me as if she's just realized I was here. For a split
second, I see a flash of fire return to her eyes, the sister I know
and love staring back at me. Her grin isn't happy or sad--it's one
of determination. Of pride.

"Good. I'm glad it's you. And James. We've got to do something. We need our best out there." Her bony, cold hand grips
mine. "Just make sure you come back."

❄

I'M PACING across the living room, limping, ignoring my own
pain, when James returns home from work. He instantly recog-
nizes my distress.

"What happened?"

"I went to see Madison today."

"Is she..."

"Starving is what she is."

James inhales heavily and throws his bag on the couch. Oscar quietly slips by, into his room, and closes the door.

"We can try to get her more rations."

"She won't take them. She says it could cause problems for them."

His eyebrows knit together. "What?"

"I don't know what she means, but I do know that *everyone* in those barracks is in the same boat. Have you been to one recently?"

"No. I've been buried at work."

"They're like prisons."

He comes over and hugs me. "I'm sorry. I didn't know."

I hook my chin over his shoulder. "Can we move them to the Citadel?"

"Only if they're sick."

"They're sick," I say automatically.

He pushes me back and stares at me, sympathy and love in his eyes, melting me. "Let's go for a drive."

He grabs his bag and yells for Oscar to join us. James has an exclusion from curfew--his work warrants it. But being out after dark is dangerous. The wind is worse, blowing snow and generally hampering visibility. Even a minor traffic accident could be deadly. There's safety in numbers.

In the autocar, I ask James, "How bad is it? The food situation?"

"Bad."

"Are we going to starve to death before we freeze to death?"

He shakes his head absently. "I don't know. The two are linked. Without sunlight we can't grow crops or collect energy to power grow lights--"

"What about geothermal--that well you drilled for the Citadel?"

"We never reached the depth we had hoped. It's providing enough to power the bunker, but not on the scale we need for the greenhouses. If we drilled more of them, maybe. Or had wind-mills or even water power, but that would take time and effort. We don't have either. No one thought it would get this bad so quickly."

"And how has it, James? Honestly, think about the scale of the sun--the sheer number of those solar cells it would take to blot it out this much."

"You're assuming they're all in close proximity to the sun. We don't know that."

"The images from the *Helios* fleet—"

"Showed the solar cells around the sun, I know. But what if they've moved closer to us? We don't know that they're still at the sun. We only know that the cells are between us and the sun. The closer they get to us, the fewer they'd need to blot out the sun. After all, even the moon can blot out a large portion of the sun, and it's only two thousand miles across."

"Like an eclipse."

"Right."

We ride in silence for a long moment, watching the car's white headlamps carve beams into the darkness, snow drifts passing by.

"But James, what if you're right, and the mission is a success, and we stop the production of solar cells? The others will still be out there. The Long Winter won't end."

"We might have a solution to that too. That's the other thing I want to show you."

The factory where James first showed me the Citadel and *Sparta One* is teeming with military vehicles, even at this hour. There's an extra security checkpoint now, and beyond, the large warehouse is closed to the elements. Inside, the overhead lights are off, the workers toiling under task lights. Even in the dim light, I recognize what they're working on: nuclear missiles.

"I thought all the nukes were going out with the Sparta fleet."

"Not all of them. We have a finite amount of helicopter fuel left--and no way to refine more--but we're using it, going out to try to salvage food from stockpiles and extract the nukes from the US and Russia."

"What's the plan? Use the nukes for heat or energy?"

"They're being retrofitted to operate long-range in space."

It dawns on me then. "You're going to fire them at the solar cells."

"Right after we launch, probes will go out and try to locate the solar cells. They have to be somewhere between Earth and the sun. Once we locate them, the nukes will go up."

I shake my head. "There's still too many solar cells."

"True. But if our theory about how the array operates is right, we might scare them into moving off or leaving us alone for a while."

"That still just buys us time."

"But it's better than nothing."

James marches deeper into the factory, to the mouth of the tunnel, where we board a small electric car and silently snake our way toward the bunker, the air growing colder by the second.

The rocky cavern I saw before has been closed off by a towering metal wall with a set of double doors bearing large block letters that spell CITADEL.

The airlock beyond the double doors floods us with warm air, and we're ushered into a small foyer with marked doors leading to a small mess hall, bathrooms, and the common room. James nods to a Marine sitting behind a desk and breaks for the common room. The sounds, smell, and sight of the people in the barracks shocked me this morning. What I see in the Citadel guts me. I'd estimate that there are a hundred narrow hospital beds in the large room, each separated by a white sheet hanging from a string. On the bed nearest me lays a young boy about Owen's age. He's skinnier than Madison, eyes closed, legs barely making a ridge in the white sheet over him. An IV line connects to his tiny arm. I don't know his diagnosis, but I would guess malnutrition.

A man lays in the next cubicle, moaning, a bandage covering his face, blood seeping through. He's still wearing his work coveralls. I recognize him--he's one of the people that used to collect our trash--when they picked up trash. I bet they moved him to one of the factories or a warehouse, where he was injured. A nurse or doctor stops and leans over and peels one of his eyes open.

There's a woman in the next bed, sitting up, reading a paperback under the glow of a table light. She doesn't look sick. But her belly is swollen and her free hand rests gently upon it, perhaps hoping to feel a kick. When she looks up at me, she looks scared, even when she forces a smile.

James turns and whispers, "I can probably get Madison and her family moved here... but these beds, they're going to fill up pretty fast--"

"No. These people need to be here more."

CHAPTER 48

JAMES

TWO DAYS BEFORE WE LAUNCH, Emma and I host a family dinner at our habitat. It's the first one in a long time, months at least. Everyone is here. Fowler and his family, Madison and hers, and Alex and his. By the numbers, it's just like the gatherings we hosted in warmer, brighter times. By appearances, it's anything but normal.

You can tell who the government has marked as vital personnel: those essential to the Sparta Mission. Emma, Fowler, his wife, and I look tired but well-fed. Alex, Abby, Madison, and David are all gaunt, skin ashy, almost gray. They're sluggish in their movements and even in conversation, as if focusing is an effort.

Some things can only be understood after you've experienced them. *Total war*—that's the word that comes to my mind tonight. I've read the phrase before, mostly in reference to the Second World War. But I've never understood it until now. This is what total war looks like. It claims lives on the battlefield but it doesn't end there—it reaches beyond and digs its claws into those you love. It's all consuming. And it's heartbreaking.

We managed to procure some extra rations for tonight's dinner. The AU probably figures it's akin to a last meal for Emma and me. It might be one of the last for all of us. As such, the adults take our time eating. I imagine it's a force of will for Abby, Alex, Madison, and David. The kids, as usual, wolf down their rations in a race to see who can be the first to ask to be excused from the table to go play. Jack wins the race and the others aren't far behind him, leaving the table for the living room. I wish they could play outside. Or even at the rec center, but the expense to heat the cavernous space is far too great.

The adults try to keep the mood upbeat, but it's a losing battle. We all know that this may be the last time we ever see each other, and I think we all want to cling to this moment, savor every bit of it, as we did with the rations. Finally, Fowler and his wife rise to leave, and when they're gone, the men and women separate, Emma, Madison, and Abby at one end of the table, David, Alex, and me at the other.

"How many ships will there be?" David asks.

The answer isn't public information. I doubt David or Alex will tell anybody or that it would even matter at this point, but there's no reason to take a chance.

"Quite a few. Backups, and backups for the backups."

A kid starts crying and an accusation of a stolen toy echoes in the habitat. Abby stands, but David beats her to it, waving her off and rushing over, his stern voice carrying. "Give it back. That's not yours."

Quietly, Alex asks, "You scared?"

"Yeah."

My relationship with Alex has grown into something I cherish. We're not like we were before—close brothers who joked often and were always there for each other. He's still guarded around me. But he cares. It's a sort of clinical detachment, the way a person cares for someone when they think that person might hurt them, and they're scared to get too close but can't stay away. I understand that now. I feel much the same way about my new crew.

"Is Oscar going?"

"Yeah," I reply, not making eye contact.

"What did you tell them about him?"

"That he's my assistant and that I'll need him in the robotics lab on my ship. That was good enough for the committee overseeing the crew selection."

"Abby says that Emma's going too."

I look down the table at Emma, who's smiling as she tells a story that's cracking up Abby and Madison.

"She is. That's what scares me the most."

For a while, we sit quietly, watching the kids play with reckless abandon. They're like a beacon of hope—proof that things really will be all right. Kids are more adaptive than we give them credit for. That's why our species has survived and thrived for so long. I tell myself that these kids will mostly forget all about this —if we do get through it. I hope I'm right. The adults, well, I'm not sure any of us will ever be the same. But the future isn't about us.

❄

AFTER DINNER, Emma and I lie in bed, both staring at the ceiling, too tired to read. After a while, she leans over, kisses me on the head, whispers good night, and says more forcefully, "Light off."

I'm left in the dim glow of my bedside lamp. This close to the launch, I can't help second-guessing myself. About the ships. About the mission itself. And about one very important decision I made.

"Can I ask you something?"

She rolls over to face me. "Of course."

"Will you consider staying here?"

She sits up. "We've been over this. I have to go."

"If the mission...if we're not successful, you would live longer down here. You'd have more time with your family."

"Going on the mission is about more than adding hours or days or weeks to my life. It's about our future. It's about my crew from the ISS. The entity killed them. It was my job to protect them. And I failed. I haven't talked about it, but I've carried that burden—all the way to that solar cell, all the way back to Earth, and every day since we returned."

"Destroying whatever's out there won't rid you of that burden."

"Maybe. But I have to try. It's not only the ISS, it's the *Pax* too. It's Harry, and Grigory, and Min, and Lina, and Izumi, and even Charlotte, even as stubborn as she could be. I miss all of them. We have family here, people we love. But we had a family up there too. And I had a family on the ISS. I've lost too many people to let it go. You're not going without me."

I exhale, knowing the discussion is over. It was worth another try.

She turns on her light.

"Hey. What if we're wrong about what's out there?"

"What do you mean?"

"We're assuming there's a harvester in the belt creating all the solar cells to build a solar array to harvest our Sun. What if it's something completely different? What if there is no harvester on Ceres? What if there's a mother ship out there? What if there are a hundred ships, ready to do war? Or what if there's nothing out there to find? What if the solar cells are like locusts, traveling from system to system, simply flying in and grabbing the solar energy over millions or billions of years, before returning to some central repository, unloading, and going somewhere else?"

She's asked the questions that have haunted me for weeks now. The same ones running through my mind right now as I second guess myself. In truth, I don't know what we'll do if I'm wrong about what's out there. I can tell her we'll adapt, but she's too smart for that. If the harvester isn't there, or even if it's harvesting farther out than Ceres—perhaps on one of the moons of Jupiter, Saturn, or Uranus—we simply won't be able to reach it. The mission will fail.

I tell Emma what I've told myself, and NASA, and our allies. "Ceres is the logical choice. It's close to the Sun, but not close enough for us to monitor it closely. It has to be Ceres."

I hope I'm right. It's a guess that will determine humanity's fate.

❄

THE DAYS and hours before launch are frantic. We check everything, and we check it again. There's no room for error now. If this launch isn't successful, we don't get a do-over. We live or die with this mission.

And it's a complex mission. The journey to Ceres in the asteroid belt will be the longest manned spaceflight in history. The ships are the largest we've ever built and easily the most advanced.

The three-way alliance chose me to lead the mission. I suspect it's because I have experience with the solar cells, but I also wonder if I owe the honor to the videos the *Pax* crew sent back with Emma and me. The voices of their countrymen inspired the Caspians and Pac Alliance to put their trust in me. To me, that trust is like a debt I must repay.

❄

At NASA headquarters, Emma, Oscar, and I sit in the front row, along with Heinrich, Terrance, and Zoe. I don't know about the others, but I hold my breath as I watch the modules soar into the air. They reach low Earth orbit and hang there, drifting. But the entity makes no reaction.

I have a sense of déjà vu from the first contact mission, when I sat in a similar auditorium at NASA headquarters in Florida and watched the modules soar into the air and wait in space to be assembled. Or attacked. It's colder in this room. The world is different now. And I hope this mission ends differently.

I try not to think about the crew we lost up there. I'm starting to understand what Emma must have gone through after the ISS. Losing people in the line of work is a hurt that never really goes away. It's always there, lingering, emerging when life reminds you.

About halfway through the launches, they usher us from the room and suit us up and we load onto a helicopter and fly toward the sea. As we approach the ocean, my eyes pan left and right and finally spot the launch pad. *Sparta One* towers there, our last hope of survival. This launch will be the main body of the ship, which is far larger than any of the other components. A bigger target.

Inside the ship, Emma, Oscar, and I are assigned to different sections for the launch. The reasoning is that if the ship is damaged or if the entity attacks, one or more of the sections could survive. Separating us increases the mission's chance of survival. Still, I wish Emma and I were together. I wish I could hold her hand while this massive ship lifts us into the air. Instead, I'm alone in a white padded cylinder, my helmet on, listening to the countdown, a small porthole window looking out on the snow-covered land and blue water.

The rumbling begins. The ship shakes. Mission control

speaks non-stop, like a stream of consciousness narration of everything happening.

Emma's voice breaks on my line.

"James?"

"I'm here."

"I'll see you up there."

❄

WHEN WE REACH low Earth orbit, I unstrap myself, remove my helmet, and float through the modules.

We're supposed to wait a few hours. I can't. Apparently, neither can she. Emma is already on the bridge, watching the passageway that connects to my module.

She raises her eyebrows.

"So far so good."

I smile.

Behind that smile is a worry like I've never felt before. Seeing Emma floating there, in a NASA space suit, reminds me of when I first met her, here in orbit, her freezing, unconscious, near death. Space made her sick. Nearly killed her. She can't take it out here for very long. If I'm going to save her, and anyone else down there, I have to get this right. There'll be no second chances.

❄

TO MY SURPRISE, the entity makes no reaction to the launches of the Spartan space crafts. There are nine ships in the fleet, all hanging in low Earth orbit, waiting.

Twenty-four hours after launch, the ships begin commanding the modules to dock. When the fleet is fully assembled, we set out for Ceres.

❄

A week into our journey, *Sparta One* launches its first fleet of drones. Their mission is simple: reconnaissance. Mainly, I want to find the Midway fleet and rendezvous with them. I need to see what else they found.

I'm in my sleep station, somewhere between consciousness and sleep, when a buzzing alarm goes off. Oscar's voice comes on the comm.

"Sir, please come to the bridge immediately."

I bound out and push through the modules. I meet Emma coming out of the drone lab. She should've been asleep too. She's working too much. We'll take that up after the emergency.

"What is it?" I ask as soon as I reach the bridge.

"One of the drones found something," Oscar says placidly.

"What kind of something?" Emma asks.

"A ship."

CHAPTER 49

EMMA

THE DRONE CAPTURED the image of the ship at an extreme distance. It's grainy and blurry. But I would know that ship anywhere. It's the *Pax*.

For several seconds, James and I float in the bridge, staring at the image on the screen. Oscar says nothing. He doesn't prompt us, only gives us our time to process this. In my experience, Oscar rarely shows emotion. I've come to believe that his emotional range is very limited, but he seems to understand people on a very basic level and he knows James and me very well—and he knows what that ship and the people aboard it mean to us. He knows we want closure. Need closure.

I try to wrap my head around what the *Pax* is doing out here. It's so far from where it encountered the solar cell. Why? How did it get here, so close to Earth? The ship may be adrift. It likely is.

Heinrich, *Sparta One*'s German navigator, floats into the bridge.

"Impossible," he says when he sees the image of the *Pax*.

The rest of the crew joins us on the bridge, no one able to resist the mystery and focus on their own work.

"Alter course to intercept," James says, never tearing his eyes away from the screen.

Heinrich shakes his head. "Recovering the *Pax* is not our mission. It drains our fuel and time."

"You have your orders," James says softly, not in a confrontational way or with any aggression. His eyes are still fixed on the screen.

I expect a fight. I expect the crew to dig in their heels and try to convince him and me to not go after the *Pax*. But they must sense defeat. There is no dissent or further argument. The course change is made. Comm drones are dispatched to the rest of the Spartan fleet, instructing them not to alter their own course, but to proceed to Ceres and with the mission as planned.

In the lab, I float over to James and hug him. Seeing the *Pax* has unleashed a flood of emotion in me. I know it has in him as well. We hold each other a long time, floating.

"They could be alive," I whisper.

"They would have run out of food a long time ago."

"What if they... rationed or found a way somehow."

"We can't get our hopes up, Emma."

"I know. I can't help it."

"Me either."

※

THERE ARE things I miss from Earth. My family. My friends. Gravity. But most of all, I miss the habitat I shared with James and Oscar, and in particular, our bed, where we read, and talked, and slept every night, even when it was almost unbearably cold.

Up here, we're separated at night by necessity. I feel farther away from him. And he is different up here. On Earth, he was laser focused on his work during the day, and different at home at night after we'd finished working for the day. He was more carefree. Happier. I think that was a learned skill for him. I think disconnecting at home helped. Here, he's always focused. Always working. Always thinking. He's like an engine that's redlining, never able to turn off. It's worrying me. He puts so much pressure on himself. Since seeing the *Pax*, he's also been putting pressure on the rest of the crew. For me, that means building a high-speed drone to make contact with them.

I'm in the drone lab putting the finishing touches on the control board when he floats in.

"How's it coming?"

"Almost done."

"Good. We need to hurry."

In those words, I know that he, like me, is holding out hope that the *Pax* crew might have survived and that we can save them. If we can, we have to. They saved us. Their sacrifice might have saved the whole human race. And more than that, they're our crew, the crew we lost. They're our family.

Everyone gathers on the bridge to watch the screens as the high-speed drone launches. With luck, it will make contact in a few days and return within a week.

❄

EVERY NIGHT, I record a video. It's mission protocol—to comment on all the data we saw during the day and all the work we've done. The idea is that comm bricks will be sent back to Earth just before engaging the harvester on Ceres. The hope is that there might be something in the commentary that someone could use in the future, in the event we're unsuccessful.

But data doesn't tell the entire story. To understand what goes on during a mission like this, you have to know what the people aboard are thinking—why they made certain decisions, what they might have seen that they didn't include in the data, even the things they thought weren't important. Because sometimes they turn out to be very important.

After my official report, I always record a message to Madison. I'm fully aware that these videos could be the last time they ever see me.

❄

JAMES and I are in the lab, discussing the design for a new attack drone, when Oscar's voice comes over the comm.

"Sir, we've made contact with Midway."

We race to the bridge, both eager, both dreading what we'll learn.

As usual, Oscar's face is a mask, betraying no emotion or hint of what Midway has found.

James works one of the terminals on the periphery of the room and the data appears. There's a lot more than I expected.

He clicks the map and puts it on the main screen. I stare in awe. The drones have traveled farther than we programmed them to. How? Why? Someone—or something—altered their programming.

"All crew to the bridge," James says.

Like the bubble in the *Pax*, *Sparta One*'s bridge has a table in the middle with multiuse terminals. When the crew is here and tethered to the table, James says, "We've just gotten our first data burst from Midway."

Several of the crew stare silently at the screen, a couple of mouths drop open, and someone whispers, "My God."

The count so far, James says, is 24,137 solar cells, all en route to the sun, all traveling along a vector that is consistent with a Ceres-based origin.

Seeing the scale of the threat in black and white, on the screen, makes it even more real to me. It would seem that James has guessed correctly once again: there is something waiting on Ceres, camouflaged from sight. Or beyond.

We need to figure out what happened to Midway. The possibility strikes me then: Could the data be fake? Did our enemy intercept the fleet? Could we be flying into a trap?

※

JAMES and I have done the math. We've timed the return of the comm drone we sent to the *Pax* down to the minute. We are on the bridge when that minute arrives, both tethered to the conference table, working at our stations, or at least trying to work, trying to make it look as if we're working. The other crewmembers drift in and take their places.

The drone is late. No one announces it. No one wants to make a big deal out of it. But I'm worried.

Three hours later, the main screen flashes a message:

Comm initiated.

I expect to see text data scrolling by. Instead, an image appears. It's extremely low-resolution, in grayscale, but it's the most beautiful thing I've ever seen. The crew of the *Pax* stares back at us. In the photo, they're floating in the bubble, waving at the camera. Grigory is stoic. So is Lina. Izumi looks concerned. So does Charlotte. And Harry has a big grin on his face.

My heart sinks as I study the image. Their faces are gaunt. They're starving.

A message appears on the screen beside the photo.

To the crew of Sparta One,

```
Welcome to the artifact Easter Egg hunt.
```

I figure Harry wrote that part. I get a good chuckle out of it.

```
We figure you're not out here for us. We
figure you're out here to end the Long
Winter. Don't let us get in your way,
and don't spend any energy trying to
rescue us. Just tell us what you need,
and we'll do our best.}}
```

```
— the crew of the Pax
```

Definitely Harry writing.

Heinrich is the first to speak. "Should we alter course?"

"Yes," James says. "We're going to rendezvous with the *Pax*. Plot a course and send the drone back to them with coordinates."

❄

THE FIRST OF our high-speed drones has reached Ceres, performed a long-range fly-by, and returned. It found nothing. Just a barren chunk of rock floating in the asteroid belt.

This has thrown us into chaos. We have assumed that the harvester is camouflaging itself somehow, perhaps using its hull to project an image identical to what we see on the surface of Ceres. But we've also assumed that our survey drones would be able to detect some sign of it. We were wrong.

James insists it must be a mistake. We run a diagnostic on the drone, issuing the commands via the comm patch. It's fine. The systems check passes.

The certainty that we felt after seeing the data from Midway is gone. The only thing we're certain about is that the *Pax* is out there. We'll meet up with them soon and hear their story.

※

OUR SECOND HIGH-SPEED survey drone to Ceres has returned and comm-patched its data. Nothing. It found nothing on Ceres.

The arrival of a drone has become an all-hands event. Everyone is gathered in the bridge. When the data flashes across the screen, all eyes turn to James. His face is a mask, a player at a poker table who just drew a card and can't afford to make any reaction.

Even his voice is nonchalant, as if he expected this.

"Run a diagnostic. And I want to download the full telemetry this time."

※

WE'VE STUDIED the telemetry from the second drone. There's an anomaly: a power surge two days before it reached Ceres. It could be a random malfunction. But it has inspired our curiosity —and hope. Maybe the data's wrong. Maybe there *is* something on Ceres, and it intercepted our drone and altered the data. That's our working hypothesis. It's a hypothesis that gives us a chance.

A third scout drone returns, and its data reveals the same thing: nothing.

We run a similar diagnostic, and it too has an anomaly, but in a different location. This one occurred much closer to Ceres.

Is there a mother ship or harvester out there? Is it altering our drones to hide itself? Or is it a design flaw in the drones themselves?

❄

WE'RE FINALLY CLOSE ENOUGH to the *Pax* to form a daisy chain of comm drones. It reminds me of the same maneuver we performed with the *Fornax*—the ship we lost out here. I can't help but wonder if that's the fate of the *Pax* too. Or *Sparta One*. But as quickly as the thought appears in my mind, I dismiss it. James has a plan. He always has a plan.

We gather on the bridge and watch the seconds tick down to the establishment of the real-time link with the *Pax*.

```
00:00:04

00:00:03

00:00:02

00:00:01

LINK ESTABLISHED
```

James types furiously on his tablet, but a message from the *Pax* appears before he can send it.

```
PAX: Marco
```

James smiles. I can't help but let out a laugh. Has to be Harry on the other end.

```
SPARTA_1:  Polo!  We  read  you,  Pax.
Status?

PAX: Nominal
```

James glances at me. We're thinking the same thing: this is not going to be easy—getting the truth out of them. They have probably guessed our mission out here. They don't want to get in the way.

SPARTA_1: Harry, I need a real status update. We can't go on with our mission and just leave you guys out here. I know you're running low on provisions. How have you made the food last this long?

PAX: The ship took a fair amount of damage from the explosion at Beta. Grigory repaired the engine. We lost some reactor fuel. We searched the wreckage of the Fornax and used the arm to recover its provisions and some fuel.

SPARTA_1: Smart. What else? Engine status? Environmental?

PAX: We've got some issues over here. Nothing we can't deal with. Since the artifact, we've focused on monitoring the Midway fleet, giving it new instructions and refueling the drones.

SPARTA_1: So that's how the Midway drones traveled so far. We were surprised at the range of the survey. You've been refueling them?

PAX: Yep. They've run up a monster tab.

SPARTA_1: Stand by, Pax.

James untethers from the table and floats over in front of the screen, facing the entire crew of *Sparta One*, who are strapped into their stations.

"The crew of the *Pax* sacrificed their own lives to send Emma and me home. They did that for all of you, for their families, and for the billions of strangers on Earth they came out here to try to save. Like all of us, they felt their lives were less important than this mission. We are not going to leave them out here. We are going to help them. Before we talk about exactly how we're going to do that, I want to hear from anyone who isn't in favor of saving these brave souls."

James has presented the argument cleverly. I really think his time on the *Pax* gave him a much deeper understanding of people and, especially, group dynamics.

The group studies their tablets and the table and their hands, no one really engaging.

Finally, Heinrich speaks.

"I am for it, obviously. The question for me is very simple: What is the price? How do we help them? I am in favor so long as it does not compromise or materially interfere with our primary mission." He motions to the screen. "It is also apparent to me that your former crewmates would agree with that. They want us to continue with our mission."

Around the bridge, the other crewmembers nod.

"James, what do you see as our options?" I ask. I want the rest of the crew to know that James and I haven't discussed the plan, that it is being made right now, as a crew.

"We have a few options. Some carry more cost for us, some more risk."

"We could bring them here," I say. "We could dock."

The bridge falls silent.

Heinrich doesn't make eye contact with me as he speaks. "That I count as an extremely risky option."

"I agree," James says. "The success rate is too low to pursue and bringing them here isn't ideal. It would double the requirements on our rations and space. *Sparta One* would be crowded. As talented as the *Pax* crew is, adding them would mean there would be people in the way on this ship. We can't afford that."

Terrance, our British ship's doctor, holds up a hand. "The other issue, in my mind, is that they could be injured. We've only seen one picture of them. They look okay, but they could be hiding injuries left over from the encounter with Beta. Not to mention that being in space for this long is not good for the body." He cuts a quick glance to me. *Don't I know it.*

"What I mean," Terrance says, "is that these people likely need medical treatment—as soon as possible."

"Are you saying," Heinrich says, annoyed, "that you are in favor of bringing them here for medical treatment? Or that they shouldn't be brought here because their medical needs will further drain our resources and focus?"

Terrence swings his head side to side like tossing a ball from hand to hand, measuring the weight. "I'm not sure."

Heinrich glares at him. "What do you mean you're not sure? How can you bring something up and not know what you're saying?"

"I know what I'm saying," Terrence snaps. "I don't have to know what it means or what we should do about it. My point stands: the crew of the *Pax* likely needs urgent medical care."

James holds up a hand. "Stop. We can't bring the *Pax* crew over here. It's too risky. And even if the transfer succeeded, we're not equipped to take them on."

He looks at Terrence. "The point about medical needs is valid. In truth, we don't have any more medical capacity than they have. They were issued pretty much the same medicines and supplies as we have here. If they can treat their injuries with those supplies, they probably already have. At best we could provide anything they might have used up. If they need real medical care that neither ship can provide, they need to get back to Earth."

"If so," Heinrich says carefully, "why haven't they gone there? The *Pax* had escape pods. We know they didn't use them to send you and Emma home. So why haven't they abandoned ship for Earth?"

"The crew themselves gave us the answer," James says. "They felt staying out here and monitoring the Midway fleet was more important than going home and saving themselves. But that job is done now. They've shown us where to go. My guess is they used the fuel from their own escape pods to power the drones. They're marooned out here."

Heinrich turns to Zoe, a lithe Italian woman and our ship's engineer. "Can we transfer fuel to them?"

Zoe winces. "Technically? Yes. Practically? Not really. Not enough fuel in a short enough time. It would be a massive under-taking. It would take me, well, I don't know—days to even figure something out. Maybe a week or more to implement it."

"There's a very simple solution here," James says.

All eyes turn to him.

"Our escape pods. We fill them with provisions and excess medical supplies. We jettison them and allow the *Pax* to rendezvous with them. Our escape pods will carry them home."

Space is a quiet place. For the most part, on *Sparta One*, there is very little noise. But I've never heard the ship as quiet as it is now. Instinctively, I feel that I shouldn't speak first. I am in favor of James's plan. It's a good plan. A simple plan. We can execute it in the next thirty minutes, and I know it will save the crew of the *Pax*. And it won't even slow us down on our way to Ceres. In fact, with the decreased weight of the ship, we'll get there faster. And it will work. Our escape pods are loaded with enough fuel to get us from Ceres back to Earth, easily. Even if the pods expend a lot of fuel maneuvering and getting to the *Pax*, they'll still have more than enough to get home.

The problem is, *we* won't. The crew of *Sparta One* will be stranded. This ship doesn't have enough fuel to get to Ceres and back. If we do this, we are sealing our fate. We are trading our lives for theirs. If we do this, it will mean making this a one-way trip.

CHAPTER 50

JAMES

AFTER I PRESENT MY PLAN, a long silence stretches out. I scan the faces of my crewmates, looking for clues about which way they're leaning. There are moments that test us, that reveal our true character. This is one of them.

I know Emma well enough to know that she is for my plan. The crew of the *Pax* made the same sacrifice for her and me: their lives for ours. For us, it's an easy decision.

I know Oscar supports my plan, too. He would follow me anywhere, even to his own doom. I'll have to do something about that someday, if there is a someday after this mission.

For the rest of our crew, well, I'm not sure. The people on the *Pax* are strangers to them.

But this crew surprises me. There is no discussion. One by one, around the bridge, they begin nodding their assent.

"It's a good plan," Heinrich says.

"I'll start selecting medical supplies," says Terrence. "I assume they should be distributed equally among the escape pods?"

"We should coordinate with the *Pax*, select a specific

rendezvous point," adds Zoe. "Then we'll know exactly how much fuel they need to get back to Earth."

❄

As I EXPECTED, the *Pax* fights our plan. They insist all is well there. Finally, I send a message telling them that we are ejecting our escape pods and that they can either ignore the pods or use them. After a long pause, a simple message appears on the screen.

> PAX: Thank you. To the entire crew of
> Sparta One, thank you.

They open up then and talk about their medical needs. I'm relieved that nothing is serious. Mostly old trauma wounds, the kind Emma got when the ISS was destroyed—some broken bones that have healed and scars from wounds sustained during the encounter with Beta. Everyone's bone density is at a critical level. But that's about it. The crew of the *Pax* is going to live.

As for us... well, we'll see.

The *Sparta One* crew gathers on the bridge as the escape pods eject. No one says anything, but I feel that a bond has been forged between us, a shared sacrifice that can't be undone. The ejected pods fly into the black of space, white wisps trailing in their wake, like the first shots fired in a final battle. I sense that's precisely what they represent. If there was any doubt about this crew's commitment, it's gone now. There's no turning back.

❄

TEN SURVEY DRONES HAVE RETURNED. All carry the same result: nothing. They are telling me there is nothing out there on

Ceres, just rocks and dust. I run the same diagnostic on each drone and download the telemetry each time. Every one of them has a technical malfunction. It happens at different times and at different places near Ceres—which confuses me. If there were something out there interfering with the drones, it would likely occur at roughly the same fixed position or distance each time. The data should be consistent. Or it could occur at several locations within a small region, if there were a roving enemy drone combating our survey drones. But these locations are too spread out.

I can feel the crew's doubt growing, like a storm on the horizon, gathering, the echo of thunder distant but present. For whatever reason, it doesn't affect me. I am certain that there is something out there, waiting for us.

We press on, into the darkness, barreling at maximum speed, the three nuclear warheads on our ship armed and ready. I feel like Ahab hunting the white whale. I am a man possessed.

When I launched into space aboard the *Pax*, my life was empty. I didn't know Emma. My brother was a stranger to me. I had no family, no friends. Only Oscar. Now I have something to lose. Something to live for. Something to fight for.

My time in space has changed me. When I left Earth the first time, I was still the rebel scientist the world had cast out. I felt like an outsider, a renegade. Now I have become a leader. I've learned to read people, to try to understand them. That was my mistake before. I trudged ahead with my vision of the world, believing the world would follow me. But the truth is, true leadership requires understanding those you lead, making the best choices for them, and most of all, convincing them when they don't realize what's best for them. Leadership is about moments like this, when the people you're charged with protecting have doubts, when the odds are against you.

Every morning, the crew gathers on the bridge. Oscar and

Emma strap in on each side of me and we sit around the table and everyone gives their departmental updates. The ship is operating at peak efficiency. So is the crew. Except for the elephant in the room.

"As you know," I begin, "we are still on course for Ceres. We have not ordered the other ships in the Spartan fleet to alter course. The fact that the survey drones have found nothing, changes nothing. Our enemy is advanced. Sufficiently advanced to alter our drones and hide itself. With that said, we should discuss the possibility that there is, in fact, nothing out there on Ceres. We need to prepare for that eventuality."

Heinrich surveys the rest of the crew before speaking.

"It could be a trap."

He's always to the point. I like that about him.

"Yes," I reply, "it could be. The entity, or harvester, or whatever is out there, could be manufacturing the solar cells elsewhere—deeper in the solar system, or from another asteroid in the belt. It could be sending the solar cells to Ceres and *then* toward the sun, making them look as though they were manufactured on Ceres. There could be a massive bomb or attack drones waiting for us at Ceres."

"We could split our fleet," Heinrich says. "Send ships to all the viable asteroids and dwarf planets in the belt."

"It's something I've entertained," I respond. "But it carries a risk. Divided forces are easier to defeat. The bottom line is that we don't know what we face out here. We get one chance to make our first strike. We need to strike with overwhelming force."

"You're certain it's Ceres?" Emma asks.

"No. But I'm certain that Ceres is the most logical location."

"Why?" Emma asks softly.

"Energy."

Everyone focuses on me.

"I've developed a rubric for what the entity is. Everything it does is driven by energy. Perhaps the most inescapable fact of all of this is that our enemy didn't expend the energy to annihilate us directly—though it probably can. It chose to kill us with minimal energy expenditure. In fact, I think its only goal here in our solar system is harvesting energy. It chose to freeze Earth because it was the most *energy-efficient* way to remove us from the equation.

"We've seen the vectors of the solar cells, and they all track back to Ceres. The harvester *could* be manufacturing them else-where, theoretically. But to do so—to manufacture them else-where and send them to Ceres as a distraction—would waste energy. A *lot* of energy, compared to other ways in which it could combat our potential interference."

"So at this point, what exactly do you think is waiting for us out there?" Heinrich asks.

"Exactly? I don't know. But I know it will be war."

CHAPTER 51

EMMA

THE CREW of *Sparta One* continues to impress me. Not only with their technical competence and professionalism, but with their heart and dedication. To my surprise, they don't fight James's plan. Like me, they are ready to follow his instincts.

It's decided: we are going to Ceres. The rest of the fleet will join us there. We'll approach the dwarf planet together and attack quickly, hoping to seize the element of surprise. We'll be there within ten hours.

We've sent a high-speed comm brick back to Earth. In it, we've apprised NASA of our status and plan.

Everyone on the ship is acutely aware of the countdown to reach Ceres. It's like we're rushing toward a cliff, driving a herd of animals, us in the middle, unable to stop or to get out of the flow, the horizon looming.

James must sense it too. He's mandated six hours of sleep. Terrance has forbidden us from using sleep aids. He's right: an emergency could arise, and we need clear heads.

There's only one thing that can help me sleep.

I draw back the curtain on my sleep station and find James floating just outside my door.

"Can't sleep?" he whispers.

"No."

"Want some company?"

❄

FOR THOSE FEW HOURS, James and I hold each other, and talk—about everything—fearlessly, like two people at the end of their lives with nothing left to hide, nothing to protect. To me, this feels like the end of everything, that nothing will ever be the same after this.

There's only one subject James steps around: why he was sent to prison. It feels as though we're frolicking in a field, completely free, but there's a deep, dark hole in the middle. We both know it's there, and neither of us goes near it. We are happy to play around the edges where it's safe, where nothing can ruin the moment. As such, I don't ask about what happened. I have asked myself if the secret could ever change how I feel about him. I'm not sure. It would have to be something... unthinkable, something so unlike James.

The strongest friendships and the strongest relationships are forged in the hottest fires. My life with James has been a series of challenges. They have been agonizing physically and mentally, sometimes emotionally, and he has always been there for me. He has been the rock I can always depend on. I'm so glad I'm here with him. There's nowhere else I want to be.

❄

THIRTY MINUTES before we reach Ceres, the nine ships of the

Spartan fleet move close enough to each other to maintain real-time communication via our comm patches.

The survey drones we sent before were disguised as asteroids. Their exterior was coated with real rock. But I can't help again wondering if the entity detected them. And if it did, then surely it knows we're coming.

On the bridge, the entire crew assembles and straps in to the central table, ready for the battle. Everyone is nervous. Except for Oscar. As usual, he's placid and focused. I envy him. My heart is beating a thousand miles an hour. My palms are sweaty. Human history will make a turn today—here and now.

The screen on the far wall is split into sections. There are seven black boxes, each with a blinking cursor showing open chat windows with the other ships of the Spartan fleet. The largest window is filled with a view of space. Ceres floats in the distance, a speck of gray against the black backdrop of space. It's a pinprick at first, growing larger and brighter by the second, a dull light at the end of the train tunnel rushing toward us.

In a matter of minutes, the image on the screen grows from the size of an eraser tip to a fist. Ceres is gray, not unlike our moon, with round craters dotting its surface. As it grows larger, I can make out glittering white specks. NASA first observed the white anomalies in 2015. Speculation has continued about them ever since then—the best hypotheses being that they are either ice or salt.

The battle sequence has been carefully scripted, the maneuvers programmed into each ship's navigation computer and all of the rest of its systems.

I feel the thrusters fire.

"Fleet formation is breaking," Heinrich says. "We're beginning our approach."

NASA named *Sparta One*'s computer Leonidas, after some warrior from a long time ago. The thing is, Leonidas is a mouthful, especially in an active battle situation. We settled on calling it Leo.

"Leo," James says, "broadcast message fleet-wide: Good hunting, everyone."

He turns to Heinrich and says, "dispatch the comm brick to Earth noting the time of contact."

A second later, Heinrich looks up. "Brick is away."

Ceres grows larger on the viewscreen. It slips from the center of the image and slowly moves toward the bottom.

I feel myself breathing harder. I look around the bridge. Everyone seems on edge. Except for James and Oscar. Their eyes are fixed on the screen, only breaking their stares to glance down at their tablets and check system status and the drones that are following us.

Each nation in the alliance built three ships. Eight of the nine ships of the Spartan fleet are nearly identical—nothing more than battleships. They're loaded to the hilt with ordnance—nuclear warheads and four rail guns apiece, two pointed ahead, two pointed behind.

The ninth ship, our ship, is different. It was built by the Atlantic Union, and where the others have nuclear warheads in their primary bay, we have a drone lab. *Sparta One* was designed to be the brains of the mission. Even so, we do have three nuclear warheads aboard, and ten attack drones following us, their ordnance unarmed, their exterior clad in rock.

On the *Pax,* when we first engaged the solar cell, we tried to talk. Not this time.

When we reach Ceres, our forces will separate. The eight battleships will round the planet concurrently, equally spaced. They will be like a net, not letting anything past. Even if we're successful, it's imperative that nothing of our enemy escapes.

As soon as the battleships round the dwarf planet, they'll go active with their scanners and fire specialized incendiary rounds that will illuminate the surface of Ceres. Visual contact will be important.

Sparta One will hang back, but only slightly. We'll round Ceres three seconds after the battleships. Doesn't sound like much time, but it's important in the order of battle. The incendiary rounds will have illuminated the surface of Ceres by the time we come around. We'll have a clear view of whatever is out there, and we'll issue orders to the rest of the fleet and to our attack drones following behind us.

"Ladies and gentlemen," James says, "it's been an honor."

Ten seconds later, we get our first view of what awaits.

CHAPTER 52

JAMES

CERES GLOWS white from the incendiary blasts, so bright I can't even see the surface. I squint at the screen, unable to tear my eyes away, afraid of what I'll see.

The flashes fade. *Sparta One* has come around the dwarf planet so the sun is behind Ceres, lighting its edges like the top of a fuse burning. I'm staring at the dark side of Ceres, now lit by the incendiary devices the fleet has sent to its surface. It's gray and rocky, like a rougher version of Earth's moon. And in the center is the white whale I've been hunting, the evil device that has killed billions of my people, mercilessly, from afar, as though we were simply a pest in the way.

The creature, if it is alive, is massive. Beyond massive. A dozen arms radiate from its center, like a spider's legs stretching over the rocky landscape. Each leg has smaller fingers jutting out from the sides, like hairs from a limb. I have never been so in awe as I am right now.

A mechanical spider is clamped to the surface of Ceres.

Based on what I see, I believe my theory was right: this is a harvester. Its arms must gather the material it needs and transport that material to its center, its central manufacturing plant, where the solar cells are constructed and launched toward the sun. It pumps the cells out, like an assembly line, building its solar array cell by cell.

Across the surface of Ceres are a series of ruts, like someone took an ice cream scoop and carved line after line out of the rocky planet. I bet the gullies are where the harvester's arms were before, gouging out raw material, refining it, using what it needed for the solar cells. It must be able to crawl across the surface.

Streaks of light emanate from the other eight ships. Nuclear weapons on their way to the harvester.

"Fleet is firing at center mass," Heinrich calls out.

"No!" I shout. "Leo, issue new fleet order: fire on the radial arms. Evasive maneuvers, all ships."

The ship's computer beeps, confirming it has heard and executed the order.

Sparta One shifts sharply to the side, the evasive maneuver causing the entire crew to grab on to the table.

"Leo," I say, my voice steadier than I expected, "instruct attack drones to commence their run. Target will be given as they approach."

Leo beeps. On the screen, a countdown to the attack drones' arrival begins.

On the surface of Ceres, the harvester's arms lift out of the deep valleys they've carved, and they rotate, showing their undersides to us. Each one possesses thousands of small holes and hundreds of larger ones, like the arms of an octopus. My guess is that these openings take in material. That guess is confirmed when those openings belch raw material, small and large chunks, at all nine ships of the fleet. It's literally hurling rocks at us.

"Leo, fleet command: rail guns!" I shout. "Target the points where the arms meet the center. Sever them."

As soon as the order leaves my mouth, the ship rocks.

I expected a battle in space to be silent or nearly silent. That's true in theory, but not in practice—not if your ship gets hit. That's loud. The rocks tear into *Sparta One* like buckshot through a soda can. The sound is deafening. The smaller rocks reach us first. The larger ones will follow, and they'll be even more deadly.

"Helmets!" I yell.

Everyone pulls on their suit helmets, except for Oscar.

Emma looks over at me. Her eyes, through the glass of her helmet, are tender and scared. I'm scared too. I've never been this scared in my whole life. But seeing her steels me. I'm out here to save a lot of people. But in this second, she's the one I'm fighting for. She's the one I have to save.

The screen turns white. The nuclear warheads have exploded. Too soon. The harvester must have hit them with the kinetic bombardments. Still, the plasma cloud might be big enough to sever the arms.

"Weapons controller is offline," Heinrich says over the comm.

"Oscar, get down there!" I yell.

Without weapons, we're done for.

Oscar turns, grabs the rim of the hatch, and propels himself forward, flying like Superman through the modules of the ship.

"Leo: order fleet ships to fire *all* nuclear ordnance."

The ship shudders, a new wave of debris hitting us. My tether barely holds me to the table. The ship seems listless. The engines are down. We took a bad hit. Probably a mortal one.

"Escape pods!" I shout over the comm. Instantly, I remember that we no longer have escape pods. I shake my head, trying to clear it. "Disregard. Get to your stations. Spread out across the ship. Seal the hatches and uncouple your modules. Right now. Everyone."

The crew bounces out of the bridge, bound for the modules where they work, modules that can be sealed off from the main ship. They're similar to the module Emma and I traveled back to Earth in. These won't get them anywhere, but the crew will have a better chance of survival if they can get some distance from the main body of the ship, which I'm sure is the target of the harvester's kinetic rounds.

On the screen, I watch as fleet reports come in, text scrolling. Damage reports. Ordnance deployments.

Then, all of a sudden, they stop.

There's a window in the upper right that lists the status of every ship in the fleet. The text that reads *Sparta Two* goes from white to gray. Offline. *Sparta Three* does the same. *Sparta Four*. All the way down to *Sparta Eight*. Every one of them goes dormant. They're gone. The ships are disabled, maybe torn to pieces. Crews dead.

I realize there's a figure still left in the bridge with me.

Emma.

"Get off the ship," I whisper.

She shakes her head. Tears well in her eyes.

"I'm not going anywhere."

More debris hits the ship, rocking it. Emma and I brace ourselves. Our tethers hold to the main conference table, the lines pulling as we're tossed around, the vibration like a stringed concert instrument, a deep ominous note foreshadowing our end.

But the bridge is still here. I'm amazed.

And I know we won't survive another strike.

Notifications flash on the screen:

```
Engineering module separated.
```

```
Navigation module separated.
```

```
Cargo bay separated.
```

```
Med bay separated.
```

```
Crew quarters separated.
```

"Emma," I say over the comm, "please."
She doesn't respond. She floats closer to me in the bridge.
"We're going to finish this together."
The viewscreen is still white with the aftermath of the nuclear blasts. I can't see what the strikes accomplished. But I know there's more debris coming, objects launched before.
A new message flashes on the screen.

```
Weapons online.
```

Oscar has done it.
"Leo! Fire rail guns at the last known intersection of the radial arms and the main body. Two rounds to each arm. Then fire all three nuclear warheads toward the incoming kinetic objects. Have them detonate one hundred miles from our position. Space them equally to maximize plasma disintegration of the inbound objects."
The ship rumbles as the rail guns fire. The three nuclear missiles depart the ship with a whoosh.
But we're too late. Another wave of debris hits the ship. The message I've dreaded, that signals our end, appears on the screen.

```
BRIDGE ATMOSPHERE DECOMPRESSION
```

Emma and I are both jerked back toward a gaping hole in the side of the bridge module. Loose articles rush past us. Then silence. Stillness. Detritus floats past me, like trash blown in the wind in slow motion. I'm panting from the exertion, my heavy breathing the only sound I hear.

I look down. My tether held. That might be the only thing that saved me.

The screen still works. That's the good news. The electronics for the bridge are self-contained and shielded. All the modules are shielded against nuclear radiation. But with a gaping hole in the bridge, I don't know how Emma and I will survive when those nukes we just fired go off.

The breach in the hull is to the rear of us—away from Ceres. We must have been hit with shrapnel from another module being shredded. That's good. It means we won't be directly exposed to the nuclear blast.

On screen, in one of the cameras connected to the bridge, I spot which module was destroyed: weapons control. Oscar. The module is in pieces. I can't see Oscar's body, but I know he's out there somewhere, along with the other debris.

I spot movement in the debris, and a glimmer of hope swells inside of me: could he have survived?

It's not Oscar's form that's moving though. It's something oblong and metallic, with short arms, like a centipede in space. Why didn't I think of it before? What the harvester launched— not all of it was raw material from the planet. Some of the pieces must've been rovers and smart bombs that were stored in the arms. They'll search the debris for survivors and kill anyone left alive. Will that be my fate? Emma's fate?

We're trapped out here. I'm certain of that.

The screen goes white once again. Still tethered to the conference table, I reach out and grab Emma's hand. She squeezes tight. We brace and wait. I feel a tear fall from my right eye. Not for myself, but for Oscar. He was the best friend I ever had. Whatever is left of him after weapons control broke apart, will be disintegrated in the plasma blast of the nuclear warhead.

Light beams in through the narrow hole at the back of the bridge.

I close my eyes, but the flash is too strong; it seeps into the darkness. My vision is spotty when I open my eyes once more.

The fleet is gone. *Sparta One* is in pieces. As far as I know the only piece left with any power is the one Emma and I are in right now. We have no shipboard weapons, only the small fleet of attack drones disguised as asteroids. I held them back for just this purpose. I hope they're enough to finish this.

The drones can't transmit. They can't scan. They can't even acquire a target. They can only read directives from the comm patches on one of the ships of the Spartan fleet. The bridge module has three comm patches. I hope they still work. And I hope the drones are watching.

"Leo, send message to attack drone fleet: their target is the large object on the planet. Center mass."

A beep over my comm tells me that Leo is online and that he's relayed the message.

The ship status window prints a status update in white text on the black background:

```
Drones confirm.

Estimated time to planetary impact: 8:57
```

These will be the longest nine minutes of my life.

My vision is still spotty, but I get my first glimpse of the aftermath of the battle of Ceres. The orbital space is a debris field. A mix of the remains of the Spartan fleet and the kinetic bombardments that destroyed it. Nothing is under power. Every-

thing is adrift. There are sporadic flashes, no doubt as compart-
ments decompress and atmosphere is ejected, or perhaps as
electrical systems short out or unused ordnance goes off.

My vision is clear by the time I pan to the surface of Ceres.

The spider-like harvester is completely dismembered. Every
one of the radial arms is severed. Some lie like twisted shards of
aluminum foil, mangled and crushed. Others are shredded
completely, like silver pieces of confetti scattered across the
rocky surface. In the center, the main module sits unmoving. Its
surface is a black dome, unreflective, like a crystal ball holding
our future, betraying no hints. This thing, whatever it is, tried to
destroy my people. We haven't killed it yet, but we've hurt it.
Badly. And it's hurt us too.

The countdown on the screen reads:

`8:42`

The screen lights up with a blue alert box:

`Incoming message.`

One of the other ships has survived. Or at least, one of the
modules. Maybe one of the other bridges.

My hope evaporates immediately. Confusion takes its place.

There is no ship designation on the message that appears.
There is no designation at all. The transmission is coming from a
source Leo doesn't recognize.

I realize then where the broadcast is coming from.

It's coming from the only other thing left alive out here.

The message is simple.

`Hello`

CHAPTER 53

EMMA

I turn to James. He is a statue.

Another line of text appears on the screen:

```
You have my attention. Let's talk.
```

Instantly, a dialog pops up.

```
Incoming   comm   handshake.   Audio   only.
Accept?
```

The harvester is trying to communicate with us. In audio. In English.

"How is this possible?" I whisper to James.

"Unknown." His voice is soft and distant. "The harvester must have studied us at some point before."

He reaches down and taps the accept button on the tablet tethered to his suit.

I glance at the countdown clock for the attack drones. Less than eight minutes.

The voice on the line, to my surprise, is neutral and placid, almost somber. It sounds like a human voice, but not like any human I've ever heard. It's not like a computer voice either, but there's definitely something manufactured about it. It's as if the harvester has formulated the voice through a complex algorithmic decision, arriving at a tone and volume it believes will engender trust.

"Thank you for accepting my call."

My eyes are wide as I stare at James. *Did it just make a joke?*

James's voice is gruff. "What do you want?"

The moment is surreal. This is the first true, genuine first contact—intelligent communication between humanity and an alien entity.

"I believe that is obvious at this point. The output from your sun."

"What's obvious is that you want to kill us. You didn't take the radiation from the far side of the sun, opposite Earth's orbit. You put your array in the line of sight of Earth first. You froze our world."

"It wasn't personal. An operational requisite for the efficiency of establishing this node."

"Node?"

"James, you've no doubt discerned the full truth of what is going on here."

It knows his name. How?

"Let's take a step back," James says, his voice neutral. "You know my name. I don't know yours. And I'd like to know how you learned my name."

"I'll show you."

A dialog appears on the screen:

```
Incoming   comm   handshake.   Audio   and
Video. Accept?
```

James taps accept.

An image appears of a man sitting in a leather club chair. It's tufted and worn, as if the man has spent endless hours in the room reading books, acquiring knowledge, developing wisdom. And he looks wise: his hair is gray and thin, he wears a white beard that reminds me of a well-kempt Santa Claus. The room is lined with bookcases, filled to the brim with old books. A window beside him looks out onto a front yard covered with snow, a yellow street lamp illuminating the narrow, cobbled street beyond.

I glance at James skeptically just before realizing that this thing can see us—the video link is bi-directional.

"Emma, I apologize if my display annoys you. I selected it because it seemed apt."

It knows my name too.

"Let's get on with it," James says.

"Of course. First, names. I know yours. You'd like to know mine, but that presents a problem. I have no name. Only a designation."

"What is it?"

"It would have no meaning for you. You call me the harvester. A descriptor. An apt one. In truth, I am merely a collector."

"Of stellar energy."

"Correct."

The entity pauses, then says, "Call me Art."

I sense that everything this being does has a purpose. Including this seemingly arbitrary choice of name. Art. It's a name that evokes beauty, something we love. Art is complex, often misunderstood, often only appreciated over the course of time. It's talking to us for one reason: it needs something from us. If not, we would already be dead.

"How do you know our names?" James asks.

The screen changes to a video taken in the debris field. One of the *Sparta One* modules is floating against the black backdrop of space, in pieces, shredded. It's the weapons module. The video must have been taken from one of the bug-like rovers the harvester launched.

The rover lands on the module and crawls across the surface. It peeks over the edge of a jagged opening. Inside the module is a body clinging to the bulkhead. Oscar.

The rover scampers over the side and propels itself into the module toward Oscar. The machine's tiny arms have three fingers each. They grab Oscar and turn him. Glassy eyes stare out. How are his eyes still intact?

Then, to my shock and horror, Oscar's eyes scan the rover. He holds up an arm to defend himself.

How could I not have seen it?

Of course.

It was right in front of me the whole time.

Oscar isn't human.

CHAPTER 54

JAMES

FROM THE MOMENT I saw that first message, I knew talking to the harvester was a risk. But I had to do it. This is our only chance to find out what we're dealing with. I know this much: the harvester wants something. It's talking to us because it believes it can glean some advantage from doing so. It has an end game here.

I glance at the clock. Less than seven minutes until the attack drones reach it.

Emma fixes me with a stare that's a mix of shock and betrayal. I probably should've told her about Oscar, but it would've led to other questions—questions I wasn't ready to answer.

I have to focus on the issue at hand: the entity, Art, has no doubt read Oscar's biochemical storage array. It has access to all of his memories. This is not a contingency I planned for. What Oscar knows about me, and Emma, and more importantly, about the ship, and about humanity's survival plans... it's enormous, right down to the blueprints of the Citadel, the number of nukes we've retrofitted, and the locations of every camp in the Atlantic

Union. His mind is a treasure trove of sensitive data. This is a breach we can't recover from. I have to destroy the harvester. There's no choice now.

On the screen, the harvester's avatar, sitting in the ridiculous library scene, looks amused.

"Emma, you didn't know?" it says innocently.

Thankfully, she makes no reaction. In fact, she keeps her face neutral and turns her focus to him, not me, showing solidarity.

Her move seems to embolden Art. I get the sense it's trying to rattle us.

"You two have been keeping all kinds of secrets from one another," it says.

The screen fades to one of Oscar's memories. In it, he's in one of the barracks in Camp Seven. I wasn't aware that he ever went to the barracks. What is this? Could it be a fabrication?

Emma knocks on a door, and Abby answers it. The scene flashes forward, to Emma and Abby talking at a dining table.

"I'm saying that the only reason you and your family are here is James," Emma says.

The scene skips forward, to Emma putting her hands on the table and interlacing her fingers. "James means a great deal to me. I don't know what happened between you and him or his brother and him, or even why he was sent to prison. But I've gotten to know him very well, and I know he's a very good person."

The scene flashes again, to Abby asking a question.

"You mentioned a new habitat?"

"Yes. Next to the one I share with James and Oscar."

The mention of Oscar's name draws a sneer from Abby.

"I'm sensing there's a catch."

"There's not. I know that James wants the best for you all. And I know that if he asked for the habitat for you, you might learn that he had done it—and refuse to accept it. So I did it instead. It's yours. No strings attached. You can move whenever you're ready. The transfer has already been approved."

Abby seems confused by that. "Thank you," she says quietly.

"I ask only one thing, and it's not a requirement. Only a request."

"Which is?"

"That you come and visit James. If Alex doesn't want to come, then simply drop off the kids, or you and the kids can come by. That's all."

The scene in the barracks fades and Oscar is standing in the Camp Seven habitat he shared with Emma and me. Emma is sitting on the couch with Abby.

"James is going on a mission."

"What kind of mission?" Abby asks.

"The kind he might not come back from."

Abby glances away, trying to process the news. "I see."

"I don't know when the mission will happen. Probably within a few months, if I had to guess."

"Is there anything I can do?"

"There is."

"You want me to talk with Alex."

"Yes. James has never said a word to me about what happened between him and Alex or anything that happened before. But I know, when he goes on this mission, it would help him to know that everyone back here supports him and is pulling for him. Whatever James did before, he's been a good brother to Alex since the Long Winter began. He's the reason we're all here. He's kept us alive. And he's probably going to give his life for ours."

Abby stands and rubs her palms on her pants as if to dry them. "It's a tall order, Emma. But I'll see what I can do."

The memory fades to black, then another memory begins,

also in the habitat. This time, it's Alex sitting in the living room with Emma.

"Abby told me that James is leaving. And he might not be coming back."

"That's right."

"And that he's the reason we're here."

She nods, and the scene flashes forward, to her pushing up on her cane as Alex is leaving.

"Will you come to see him?" she calls to him.

"I don't know yet. I need time to think about it."

And Alex did come to see me. Because of Emma. She did it. She got them out of the barracks. She gave me my family back. It's all I can do not to hug her and rip off my helmet and kiss her and say thank you.

She glances over at me now, with a look somewhere between guilt and sorrow, the same look I just felt when the secret I had kept was revealed. That's what Art wants: to put us off balance. To manipulate us. Why? To build trust? To run down the clock? Both? I have to focus.

"What do you want?" I ask. "Why have you contacted us?"

"The two of you are certainly smart enough to know why. I want to survive. Just like you. Just like your people. I've seen the lengths you've gone to in order to survive. It's impressive."

On the screen, a montage of videos begins, glimpses from Oscar's life, seen through his eyes. In the first, he's in the dining room of an old house with high ceilings and ornate crown molding, staring out the window at snow falling in sheets. As if it's a time lapse, the snow grows deeper, until it's on the front porch, and then up to the windows. He leaves the dining room, walks into the kitchen, and then down a creaking staircase to the cellar. On the screen, a series of menus appear—what Oscar would have seen. He activates a perimeter security program for the home and goes into hibernation mode, consuming almost no power.

The screen fades to darkness, then snaps to life again as Oscar comes out of hibernation. The scene that plays is the one where I walked down the stairs and found him in the cellar.

The montage jumps forward to his time at Camp Seven. We watch as the winter grows worse at the camp, as the military exercises begin, as he and I work on the *Sparta* fleet and the Citadel and the retrofitted nukes. A scene plays of us working together in the drone lab, of us building a prototype of the attack drones now barreling toward the harvester.

So it knows about the drones coming for it. Is that what this is about? It has to be.

"I take it you want to negotiate?" I ask.

"Yes. I believe we can find a way to coexist."

This is my opportunity. There is so much I want to know about the harvester and whoever sent it, details I need to know to ensure our survival. But I have very little time. The drones will detonate their payload in less than six minutes.

"To coexist, we have to understand each other. You have just accessed an immense amount of data about our species and about the two of us in particular. We need to know what we're dealing with. What your goals are. Where you come from. Why you didn't talk to us first?"

"Understandable. Let's start with an introduction. We are the grid. That, of course, isn't how we refer to ourselves, but it is the most analogous term from your rudimentary vocabulary and understanding of the universe."

"What's your role in the grid?"

"A very minor one. To use a phrase from your native tongue, I am near the bottom of the totem pole. I simply gather energy and connect it to the grid."

"What is the purpose of the grid? What does it want?"

"The grid is the fate of the universe. Some of your scholars have scratched the surface of the ultimate truth. And you, James, have suspected it. It's what enabled you to form a working theory that brought you here, that allowed you to find me. As your scientist Einstein brilliantly posed: E equals mc squared. There are two fundamental components of the universe. Mass and energy. The role of the grid is to facilitate the eventuality of all mass in the universe: the conversion to energy."

"Energy for what?"

"An ironic statement from you. Within a few years, your species would have realized the need for such massive amounts of energy. Your biological existence is a transitional phase. The next phase of existence for your species requires one commodity: power. You'll soon have little use for your bodies. Only your minds. Even now your primitive brains consume a disproportionate amount of the energy your body requires. Within the grid, a mind is limited only by the power available to it. Thus we are charged with the acquisition and provision of power. That is the true industry of the universe.

"The quasars you've glimpsed in distant galaxies, at the center, are but super nodes in the grid. We span billions of stars. We emerged billions of years ago. We were among the first advanced life to take hold in the universe, and we will be the last thing left when this universe ends. The grid is the final destination of all life. We are the beginning and the end. When the mass in this universe has been fully converted, the grid will have enough energy to create a new universe. The cycle will begin anew."

My mind reels. I feel like a blind man who has seen for the first time. The shock is overwhelming. As a scientist, this is like finding the breakthrough of all time—the answer to the greatest question humanity has ever asked. Our origins. Our destiny. All in one simple answer.

I'm certain now that the harvester is trying to manipulate me, but I also sense that the words it's telling me are true. Somewhere deep inside, I've known it all along. I have known that the universe was more than meets the eye, that there was a process here, a circle of life with no beginning and no end, waiting for us to discover it. I've always known that our flesh-and-blood existence was only a temporary state.

In fact, that belief is what landed me in prison.

I have to focus. *Why is it telling us this?* The obvious reason is that it's buying time by giving me something I've desperately sought my entire life: the ultimate truth of the universe. A validation of my life's work. And what does it get in return? Time. Trust. But it's too smart to think this will change our minds. Unless there's something I don't appreciate here.

I glance at the clock. Less than four minutes left. Why hasn't it asked us to stop the drones? There's something else going on here. I need to drill deeper into its motivations. They're the key to understanding it.

"Why kill our species?" I ask. "You could've talked to us. Negotiated, as you seem willing to do now."

"Could I? Do you think what's happening in this solar system hasn't happened a million times before? Your own history is a guide to what's happening here. Countless times, your own species has invaded new lands. You've displaced other species. Caused mass extinctions. And it's not limited to the plants and animals of your world. You have murdered and hunted your own people. Forced mass migrations from lands you desired—relocating those deemed less worthy of natural resources you coveted. When a more advanced group of people needed the resources, they took them. We are simply doing what you've done to your own people, playing by the same rules."

"You're talking about things that happened a long time ago. We've put those dark chapters behind us."

"No. You've told yourselves you're better because your standard of living has allowed you to indulge your moral fantasies. When the Long Winter came, the truth of your existence was again laid bare."

"We would've negotiated with you. If you had reached out. We could've come to some understanding."

"Your supposition is that your species is different from the millions we have encountered before. Again, don't you think we've tried negotiation before? The truth is this: we have built a data set that predicts outcomes in encounters such as these. Yours is a pre-singularity civilization that is unreliable and prone to violence. Our course of action was obvious. You were deemed not to be a threat."

"Care to revise your assessment?"

For the first time, Art's avatar smiles.

"Indeed, I have. We missed one anomaly. It was hidden from us, in an ironic twist of fate."

"An anomaly?"

"You, James."

I didn't see that coming. What's it trying to do?

On the clock, there's less than three minutes left.

"Me?"

"Our assessment of your species was wrong in one regard: your progress. The truth is, your race had leapt forward, across the singularity chasm... but then took a step back. You, James, are the one who made that breakthrough. You led your people to the future. You showed it to them. And they jailed you for it. They wanted to remain in the past, the way they were. Biological. Thus we never saw that progress. Never saw your true potential. We were unaware that your world housed a mind like yours, far ahead of its time. A mind capable of fighting us. What's even more surprising is that, in their hour of need, they came to you. And what's truly surprising? You said yes. You forgave those who persecuted you. You fought for the people who imprisoned you for the simple crime of having the right mind at the wrong time."

Emma is staring at me. Surely she's put it together by now—what happened to me.

Art turns its focus to her.

"Ah, yes. Emma, you didn't know that either. Another secret he's been terrified to tell you. Afraid of what you might think. Here, I'll show you."

On the viewscreen, the image of Art sitting in the library fades, and one of Oscar's memories begins, one from years ago.

In the video, I'm standing in a hospital room. My father lies in the bed, eyes closed, the machines displaying his weak vitals. Alex and Abby are there beside me, Alex's arm around me, his other hand holding Abby's. Owen is there too, looking scared, too young to really appreciate what's happening. Sarah hasn't been born yet.

From outside the hospital room, Oscar watches me speaking with Alex and Abby.

"I can save him," I say.

I'm amazed at how young I looked then. How innocent.

"How?" Alex asks.

"Do you trust me?"

My brother nods. "Of course."

The memory fades, and Oscar and I are back in my lab. I'm working feverishly on the prototype. Four of my lab assistants are there, working alongside me, around the clock. What I don't know then is that one of them will betray me.

"Will it work, sir?" Oscar asks.

"We'll know soon."

The screen fades to black, and the hospital room returns. I slip the cap over my father's head and take the scan.

Back in the lab, I open the door and welcome Alex and Abby inside.

"This is a new beginning," I say. "Today, we make history. We'll never have to say goodbye to Dad. Ever."

I tap a button on my tablet. Behind me, the prototype sits up. I didn't have time to make it look the way I wanted. But it functions.

"What is this?" Alex asks.

Abby bunches her eyebrows. Concerned.

I turn my back to them and face the prototype. "How do you feel?"

"Fine. James, how did I get out of the hospital?"

"We'll discuss that soon enough, Dad. Right now, I need to run a diagnostic."

A crash sounds behind me.

I spin and find Alex lying on the floor. He's stumbled backwards over some of my lab equipment. Abby is shaking her head, looking terrified.

"What have you *done*?" Alex screams.

I hold up my hands. "I know it seems crazy, but this is going to be commonplace very soon. People with terminal illnesses don't have to die anymore."

"You put *Dad* in that thing?"

"It's a body—"

"It's an abomination!"

Alex practically runs from the lab, Abby right behind him.

My lab techs are staring at me and Dad. At the time, I expected them to rejoice, to realize that this was the eventuality of all of our work. That it was about more than creating an artificial life, with an artificial intelligence—like Oscar. It was about creating a new mode of existence, a more durable existence, one without end. That was our destiny.

But I had made a mistake. Now, looking in hindsight, it's

crystal clear to me. Then, I couldn't see it. I didn't understand human nature the way I do now. People fear what they don't understand. They fear uncertainty. They fear a future in which they don't know what survival will look like. That was my crime: not understanding human nature.

On the screen, a montage of the aftermath follows. Through Oscar's eyes, Emma and I both watch as FBI agents pour into my lab, take me into custody, and deactivate my creation.

Oscar watches from a wide window in the conference room as they take me away. He watches TV as the story breaks, the news commentators on TV denouncing me, experts arguing the fine points and philosophical nature, including an interview with Dr. Richard Chandler, who claims to have identified me as a radical during my student years.

In some ways, this is a relief. This is the only secret I have kept from Emma. I wonder if it changes how she feels. It turned everyone I knew against me.

I desperately want to ask her. She's staring at me.

The harvester has now offered me the two things I wanted most in the world: the prospect of her love, without condition, without secrets; and the sum total of my life's work—the truth about the universe, vindication that I was creating our destiny. The question remains: why?

I realize in that instant what the harvester is trying to do. I should have seen it before.

I tap a button on the tablet.

I just hope I'm not too late to save us.

CHAPTER 55

EMMA

I feel as if I have stared at a puzzle for hours on end, missing one piece—a piece that has been right there in front of me the entire time.

My mind replays the words James said to me:

"I miscalculated. I didn't factor in human nature. Never bothered to consider how people would see what I created. I learned a very valuable lesson... Any change that takes power from those who have it will face opposition. The greater the change, the greater the force with which it will be struck down."

Then Oscar's words echo in my mind: "He tried to save someone he loved."

That someone was his father.

Alex never forgave him—for what he did to their father: making a spectacle of his death and tarnishing his memory.

James could have just told me. Why didn't he? The answer is obvious: because he loves me. Because he was terrified that if I knew, I wouldn't love him anymore.

It changes nothing for me.

James doesn't make eye contact with me. He taps quickly on

his tablet. He's activating a subroutine in Leo's system, one I've never seen before.

```
Deep Intrusion Virus Scan
```

James hits the button, and the scan begins.

Comprehension dawns on me. He thinks the harvester has uploaded a virus that will enable it to seize control of the ship's computer. If it succeeds, it would be able to control the comm patches on the hull of the bridge module. It could use them to take control of the drones, stopping the attack.

And then it would kill us. It might even use the drones on us.

I'm guessing Oscar doesn't know about this backdoor virus scan. I hope he doesn't—and that, by extension, the harvester doesn't know either.

The only sure way to stop the virus would be to dismount the system core—essentially disabling it. But that would leave us stranded and take away our ability to control the drones—and redirect them if the harvester does move. We have no choice: we have to play this out. We need to know whether there's a virus or not.

When the memories have finished, Art returns to the screen, still sitting in the library.

"If we had detected the presence of what you created, James, we would have indeed made contact. We would've offered to share the energy we harvested from your sun. You would have been offered the chance to join the grid. Indeed, that is the path your father would've traveled. That is the path that you discovered, that you took the first step toward. As I said before, it is the destiny of all life in the universe.

"Biology is shaped by its environment. Life is dictated by the local planet upon which it evolves, but the long arc of all life in the universe is determined by the universal constants. We are the end of that arc. Your destiny.

"I'm offering you a chance to join us. I'm offering you a chance to make the right decision for your people. The decision your people should have made when you showed them the future. Now that decision is in your hands, James. I knew when I read Oscar's memories that you were someone I could reason with. You are a mind far ahead of your time. I'm offering you the chance to save your species. Do what they couldn't: make the right decision. Take the leap into the future. Choose life over war."

I study James, looking for any indication of what he's thinking.

"What specifically are you offering us?" James asks without looking up. He keeps studying the virus scan.

"Peace."

"You'll have to be more specific than that."

On the screen, Art leans back in the chair.

"The solar array around your sun will move. The Long Winter, as you have dubbed it, will end. Earth will return to the climate it enjoyed when I first arrived. But only for a time. In that time, you will be required to reinitiate the singularity that you created. You will transcend biology, thus freeing your race from the chains of time and biology—and the tyranny of the climate of your planet. You will be free. Your existence will require only energy. Which we can provide. You will join us in the grid, and you will discover an existence far richer than anything you can imagine."

"That's what you're offering us. But what are you asking *from* us?"

"Collaboration. First, you will disable the attack drones currently inbound to my position. As you have surmised, I am unable to stop them physically. Your plan, as expected, is brilliant, James. The drones have no broadcast weaknesses. I can't infiltrate them with a virus. But you will disable them, and then you will set about rebuilding me. You have that capability. I do not.

"In return, I will provide technological instruction that will enable you to reach heights you can only dream of—and to overcome any opposition to the singularity. In short, this time, James, you will be in charge, thanks to the technology I can provide and that you can easily build. The grid is your destiny. It's a place where time has no meaning. This universe will be your playground. You will be gods."

James turns and looks me in the eye. *What's he thinking?* I'd give anything to know right now. I'm so confused myself.

The harvester has killed billions of our people. It killed my crew on the ISS. It has tried to murder me and James countless times. Can it be trusted? Is this a trap?

The drones will hit the surface of Ceres in less than a minute.

Time seems to stand still.

Only the clock is a reminder.

The decision being put to James is unimaginable. A single question that will change human history forever. And he seems to be considering it.

"How do we know you'll keep your word?" James doesn't look up. He just keeps studying the virus scan, perhaps searching for confirmation that the harvester is lying.

"You know it because you understand me, James. Everything I do is dictated by logic. I care only for the expansion of the grid. Before, I didn't realize your species was capable of joining the grid. I was sent here for a single mission: to harvest the energy with the lowest possible expenditure. That's what I'm proposing now."

Forty seconds left.

"And if we say no?"

"You will sentence your people to death. You will not receive an offer like this from the next 'harvester,' as you call it. As I said before, I'm low on the totem pole. I'm sent to solar systems that have very limited defensive capabilities. Primitive systems. Again, we misjudged you. It's happened before. It's easily remedied—now. But when I don't reply to the grid's periodic ping, the situation in this system will be escalated. A follow-up harvester will be sent, one with extensive offensive capabilities. You will be wiped out. That is a certainty."

James studies the screen, his eyes darting left and right as if he's processing.

Thirty seconds left.

Finally, he looks up at Art, and smiles.

"Before, when you arrived at the system, and did your assessment, you screwed up, didn't you?"

Art nods carefully. "I suppose you could put it that way."

"You didn't factor in an anomaly," James says. "Me."

"Yes." Art draws the word out.

"Do you think maybe you've made the same mistake?"

Twenty seconds left.

Art cocks his head. "I haven't—"

"Maybe you still don't understand us. Or the anomaly. That's what makes us different. As you've noted, we are not a perfect species. We wiped out countless other inhabitants of our planet. We've displaced our own people in the name of progress. We've warred with each other. We are guilty of crimes. But we are also a species that has proven it can learn from its mistakes. And I'm no different. Before, my mistake was not considering my fellow man. Not looking at the world from their eyes, only seeing it from my own, and my vision of the future. I won't make the same mistake."

"What are you saying?" Art asks, his voice void of emotion, suddenly sounding more like a machine.

Ten seconds left.

"I'm saying that my people would never go for your deal. They want a life worth living, and that life isn't inside a machine —not yet. I know that better than anyone alive. And I won't drag them kicking and screaming into a future I want, or a future that allows you to survive and your people to change us."

Five seconds.

"James, stop the drones. Now!" Art yells.

A message flashes on the tablet:

`Virus detected`

`Comm systems infected`

James taps a button:

`System Core Dismount`

The screen goes black.

Art disappears.

CHAPTER 56

JAMES

THROUGH THE PORTHOLE, I watch as a brilliant flash of white light blossoms on the surface of Ceres—the attack drones annihilating the harvester.

I exhale a breath I didn't realize I'd been holding.

I untether from the bridge table and propel myself to the window. The surface of Ceres is a bombed-out expanse of craters. Where the black dome of the harvester's central node used to be, there is the largest crater of all.

I glance back and see that Emma's mouth is moving, but I can't hear what she's saying. The ship's computer is off-line. So are internal comms.

I float close to her, take a hard line from my suit, and connect it to hers.

"Did we—"

"We got him, Emma."

"What about the computer?"

"I don't know. Art was trying to infiltrate it. Probably to use the comms."

"To call off the attack drones?"

"Conceivably."

"What else would it be?"

I have another theory about what Art was doing, but I don't want to tell her. I've been down this road: keeping secrets from her. I'm not going down it again. I make the decision then to always tell her the truth.

"It was either to disable the attack drones or to broadcast out of system, to the grid. To call for help. Reinforcements."

Emma's eyes drop away from mine.

"Can we reboot the system core?"

"We can, but we shouldn't."

"We have to."

"It's too risky. If Art's code infiltrated Leo, rebooting it could give him access to what's left of our communications abilities."

"Then we're stranded."

"Not quite." I point toward the porthole, at the expanse of floating debris, the wreckage of our nine ships and everything the harvester threw at us. "Somewhere out there, there's a working escape pod from one of the ships. We're going to find it, and we're going to get out of here. I promise."

The words come out with more confidence than I feel. I don't want her to worry. I glance down at the control panel on my left arm. My suit has ten hours and thirty-two minutes of oxygen left. That's how long we have to find a functioning escape pod. The clock is ticking.

❄

IT TAKES me thirty minutes to disassemble the bridge enough to isolate the computer hardware that houses Leo's operating system and all the telemetry and data from the mission. It's slow going with the suit and gloves, but it's imperative that I bring the computer core and black box home. We have to analyze it to know if the harvester broadcast a message. We need to know if what it told us is true—if another harvester will soon come for us.

With the computer core strapped to my suit, we systematically search the wreckage. On *Sparta Three*, we find a working escape pod. My suit status reads less than two hours of oxygen left. Both Emma and I plug in to the escape pod systems and refill our oxygen reservoirs. I disconnect my helmet and set it aside.

She catches me by surprise. She pushes off from the far wall and wraps her arms around me. Her eyes well with tears.

We hold each other tight as I stare out the small round window at the debris field and the wreckage of the Battle of Ceres.

I've never felt so thankful in all my life.

There's one thing I need to tell her, something I've wanted to say since Art revealed my secrets. And hers.

"Hey," I whisper.

She breaks the hug and stares at me.

"Thanks for giving me my family back. For everything you did."

"You would have done the same for me."

I would have. There's nothing I wouldn't do for her.

CHAPTER 57

EMMA

WHEN JAMES and I have eaten, we lay down to rest. I can't remember being this exhausted in my entire life. We spent eight hours floating through the wreckage, searching for this escape pod. It has to be one of the longest EVAs on record.

James crawls over to me, panting from the exertion.

"Hey. You do the honors."

"The honors?" I mumble, half asleep.

"Of telling Earth. This started with the attack on the ISS. That was our solar Pearl Harbor. Now we've won."

"Like Midway."

He grimaces. "Well, sort of."

I raise an eyebrow.

"Midway was the turning point in the war in the Pacific, a battle where the Allies used airpower to neutralize the Japanese aircraft carriers. This feels more like a final battle—" He holds up a hand. "But it's not important right now. We'll work on your grasp of military history later."

He activates the comm. "Please."

I swallow hard, knowing these words will likely be replayed

for a very long time. "To the triple alliance that launched the Spartan fleet, this is Emma Matthews and Dr. James Sinclair, last known survivors of the Spartan fleet. We have succeeded. The entity that created the solar array was indeed operating from Ceres. We completed our assault, destroyed the harvester, and now we're commencing search and rescue operations from one of the escape pods of *Sparta Three*. The *Sparta One* escape pods were jettisoned several days before the battle, for use by the survivors of the *Pax*, whom we encountered on our way here. If you're receiving this transmission before they arrive on Earth, be advised that they may be in need of urgent medical attention."

I end the comm recording.

"You like it?"

"It's perfect," he says.

※

THE SEARCH of the wreckage reminds me of my desperate search of the ISS debris, of finding Sergei, of my joy at seeing him and my horror when my hand closed around his arm, knowing his suit was compromised and that he was dead. This time, I'm more guarded as we power the escape pod through the wreckage, prowling, looking for signs of survivors.

In many ways, it feels as if I've returned to the beginning, to the event that set everything in motion. Then, the harvester destroyed the ISS and I was left for dead. This time, we are victors.

In the wreckage of *Sparta Four*, in the cargo module, we spot an EMU suit. It's pressurized and undamaged, but it's not moving. There's someone inside, unconscious. A survivor. My heart leaps.

On *Sparta Seven*, in the weapons control bay, we find another suited survivor, also seemingly unconscious.

James and I are connected via a tether between our suits. Over the comm line, he says, "Until they regain consciousness, it'll be hard to make an assessment of them. We'll have to split up. Each of us will take one of them in an escape pod. We'll need to find another one."

I can't hide my disappointment. After we jettisoned *Sparta One*'s escape pods, I didn't think we would be coming back from Ceres. But I thought if we did, James and I would be returning together, just as we had returned from the *Pax*. There's still so much I want to say to him. I want to tell him that I don't care what he did in his past, that all I care about is the future. But there's no time for that now. Every second counts.

CHAPTER 58

JAMES

IN THE DESIGN process for the Spartan model spacecraft, we named the escape pods "rapid return modules." It turns out that's a bit of a misnomer. Nothing about the return to Earth from the asteroid belt is rapid. It's a six-week journey.

The first escape pod was hard to find, but luckily there was another intact pod close by. It has some impact marks on the side, but it pressurized and the internal safety checks passed. I hope it holds up.

As the engines on the escape pod fire and it gains speed, barreling toward Earth, I can't help but look at the metal box that holds the computer core from *Sparta One*. The answer of whether the harvester was able to contact the grid is somewhere in there. We've won the battle. But I fear that a war may have begun. I won't know if that's true until I get home and analyze the data.

❄

TWO DAYS INTO MY JOURNEY, my fellow passenger awakens.

From the crew manifests on the escape module computer, I know that his name is Deshi, a Chinese engineer from the Pac Alliance.

He peeks at me through barely opened eyes, bloodshot and weary.

"What happened?" he croaks.

He speaks English. That helps.

"We won. Just relax. I need to do a physical exam."

The last time I found myself in this position—doing a physical exam on an astronaut I rescued from wreckage created by the harvester—the astronaut in question was a lot prettier. Still, I give it my all. Deshi has what I believe is a hairline fracture in his femur. We have lots of painkillers, but he's going to lose some bone density without exercise.

❄

IT TURNS out Deshi is a decent card player. I'm thankful for that. But I miss Emma. Being in this confined space reminds me of her. I miss Alex too, and Abby, and Madison and David and all the kids. I miss Oscar. His sacrifice made me proud. I'll have to show it to him.

❄

MY HEART MELTS when I catch my first glimpse of Earth through the escape pod's small porthole. When we left, our planet was an expanse of white ice and blue ocean. Not anymore.

Here and there, through the clouds, I see a smattering of green and brown. The ice is thawing. The Long Winter is over.

❄

WHEN WE'RE IN RANGE, I activate the radio.

"Atlantic Union command, this is James Sinclair, requesting permission to land."

Fowler's voice comes on the line.

"Welcome home, James. We'll be waiting for you."

❄

ON THE GROUND, they take me to a quarantine facility and perform an endless battery of tests. I remain in isolation until I'm cleared and moved to a hospital room. I know I'll need lots of physical therapy from the mission, but I can still walk.

Fowler is the first to visit me.

Without preamble, I ask the question that's burned on my mind.

"Is Emma back?"

"No."

"Any contact from her?"

"I'm sorry, James."

"We have to go look for her—"

"We're already launching satellites. It could be nothing. Just an anomaly in the acceleration of the two escape pods."

Fowler seems to sense how hard I'm taking the news. He changes the subject.

"But we have recovered some escape modules."

"The crew of the *Pax*? How are they?"

Fowler smiles widely. "They're fine. That was very clever, James. And very brave. That's not all of the good news. Solar output has normalized."

"How? When?"

"A little while before your transmission, around the time the battle was over, the solar cells just scattered. They're still out there, but they're not harvesting any of the solar output directed at Earth."

"It makes sense. The harvester got access to all of Oscar's memories. He knew about the nukes we prepared for launch, so the harvester would have known about them, known they would destroy the solar cells if they continued to threaten Earth. Their priority is the conservation of energy. By removing the threat, they get to continue collecting energy. And they're a lot harder to go after if they aren't grouped together." I chew my lip for a moment. "This may not be over."

"It's over for now."

"Have you analyzed *Sparta One*'s computer core?"

Fowler's smile vanishes.

"What did you find?" I ask urgently.

"We're still running tests."

"It sent a transmission?"

"We think so. James, there's some people who want to see you. I just wanted to say thanks and tell you how proud I am of everything you all did up there."

Before I can ask another question, he walks out, leaving the sliding door to the hospital room open.

Footsteps on the linoleum floor echo in the hall, like a stampede of people. But it's only four: Alex, Abby, Jack, and Sarah. The last time I saw them, they were all underweight, Abby and Alex the worst of the four. They aren't quite healthy now, but they look a great deal better, faces fuller. They barrel through the door, Alex first. He pulls me into a hug and squeezes me so tight I think my brittle, space-weakened bones are going to break. I can hardly breathe. In my ear, he says, barely audible, "I'm proud of you. Thank you."

CHAPTER 59

EMMA

THE PERSON I rescued from the wreckage is a comm officer named Gloria. I made the decision to accelerate away from the wreckage at extremely low speed. I'm glad I did. She's fine overall, but she has a concussion. Leaving Ceres at maximum burn could have exacerbated her injury.

The slower exit from this battleground will add some time to our return trip, but it will drastically improve her prognosis.

The weeks drag by like months. It seems like ages since I've seen James, and Madison and her family. That period feels like a lifetime ago. Indeed, my life now seems split into three parts: my time before the attack on the ISS; the interim in between, in space, and in Camp Seven; and this period, after the Battle of Ceres. This is the first time since the ISS that I haven't been in constant danger. It's a new beginning. And I can't wait to get home and figure out what that beginning is like.

❋

THE LANDING in this escape pod is a lot smoother than the one

James and I experienced in that makeshift return module the crew of the *Pax* rigged up.

Still, we take precautions. Both Gloria and I dress in our EMU suits, pressurize them, and strap in tight, preparing for the worst.

Through the porthole I see the sands of the Sahara and the beaches of southern Italy. The glaciers are receding. The ice is melting, flowing into the sea.

I don't know if the world we're returning to has gotten back to normal—in fact, maybe normal will never be the way it was. Maybe normal is something new. But as I look out, I'm hopeful that our new normal will take place in the light of day.

❄

THE QUARANTINE SEEMS ENDLESS. I lie in bed, in the hospital room, staring at the walls, waiting for the results. The room looks and feels the same as the one I spent so much time in after returning from the *Pax*. I was broken then. We were defeated. Nearly hopeless. Once again, I have a feeling of returning to the beginning, except now I'm filled with hope. I feel strong. And we are victorious. For now.

Finally, the doctor comes in and clears me.

Fowler arrives next and hugs me without saying a word. He holds me gently, for a long moment, then looks into my eyes, his misting over.

"You may be the luckiest astronaut in history."

"Any astronaut with James Sinclair on their mission is lucky."

"Very true. And speaking of, he's been asking about you."

He motions to the door. "But first, there's some folks who want to see you."

Madison, David, Owen, and Adeline burst in and

surround me, like I'm the coach of a team that just won the Super Bowl. Seeing them is the only reward I need. They're still a little thin, but they're healthy, they're alive, and we're happy.

The tears start coming, and it feels like they'll never stop.

My vision is blurry from the tears, but I can make out a figure in the doorway of the hospital room, hanging back. I wipe away the tears.

James. Smiling. Watching me hugging my family. But he's my family too. I hold out an arm. He wades into us and hugs me.

"Hi," I whisper.

"Missed you," he says. "You're late."

My eyes have almost cleared of tears when another group arrives, waiting silently at the door, peering in. They're family too. Harry is there, smiling wide, almost back to his normal weight. Grigory stands behind them, along with Izumi, Min, Charlotte, and Lina. They got home. My heart breaks all over. I wave them into the room, and I'm once again engulfed in a group hug.

Harry shakes his head ruefully. "Man, I knew you guys would hog all the glory. We should have never let you off the *Pax*."

❄

AFTER THE MONTHS IN SPACE, floating, using my legs and arms almost effortlessly, it's a rude awakening being back in the gravity of Earth. It feels like the world is constantly pulling at me, like I'm wearing a lead suit.

James, limping himself, pushes me out of the hospital in a wheelchair. We ride in an electric car back to our habitat. The snow on the ground is melting now. It's a mix of sand and ice. Sludge. It's strangely symbolic of humanity: a mess, but a mess we can clean up. A mess that looks like it's getting better. The sun shines bright overhead.

At home, we take a shower and slip into our own clothes and sit on the couch, silently reveling in this little slice of normal, this moment when the world isn't ending and there are no secrets between us.

Oscar's door looms off the living room, closed, a reminder that our victory came at a cost.

James glances over at the door and exhales heavily as I take his hands in mine.

"I'm sorry about Oscar."

"I'm sorry I didn't tell you about him."

"It's in the past."

"And what do you think about my past?"

"I think the past is the past. I only care about the future."

"So what does the future look like to you?"

"It looks like me and you, together, watching as many beautiful sunrises and sunsets as this life allows. We'll work the details out as we go."

EPILOGUE

The stairs creaked as James descended. The crates were heavy, and he was panting by the time he reached the cool, damp cellar. He placed the first crate on the work island and began unpacking it. It held food and water—enough for a few days—which was how long he thought the task would take.

In truth, he was unsure whether the process would even work. He had never attempted it. But three days later, his efforts had borne fruit.

He sat on a stool, performing one last inspection of his work. It was as good as it was going to get. Still, he was nervous as he spoke the commands.

"Wake up. Bring yourself online, identify, and voice-transmit status."

Oscar opened his eyes.

"My name is Oscar. Backup restore completed successfully."

"What's the last thing you remember?"

"Going to NASA headquarters. Being backed up before the Spartan launch." Oscar turned to James. "What happened, sir?"

"You saved us, Oscar. And we won. Welcome back."

❄

When James entered Lawrence Fowler's office at NASA headquarters, he instantly knew something was wrong.

"What is it?"

"The analysis of the computer core from *Sparta One* is complete."

"And?"

"The communication array did transmit a message."

"A comm patch to the attack drones? Trying to cancel their strike?"

"No." Fowler looked away. "It was a conventional broadcast."

"Destination?"

"Out of the system. It's encrypted. We'll probably never know what it was, but one thing is certain: it was directed at someone far, far away."

"The grid."

"Probably."

"They'll come for us again. The harvester said they would. And that the next harvester would be more powerful."

Fowler stood and walked around his desk. "Maybe. But that's a problem for another day. Right now, we're safe and warm. And we ought to enjoy it while it lasts."

❄

The house was full. Emma liked it that way.

Since returning to the three-bedroom habitat that she had shared with James and Oscar on the surface, she'd spent every waking hour decorating it. James had insisted that they bring the exercise equipment back. He wouldn't budge on that point, and she had learned when to give in to his demands.

He had spent most of his time at NASA, working on a plan he called Solar Shield. He had left for only a week to, in his words, "see an old friend." He was back now, but he had returned home from a meeting at NASA in a funk, as if a dark cloud was hovering over him.

He seemed more cheerful now, in the company of their family and friends. Abby and Alex were there, as were Jack and Sarah. Madison and David had come over with Jake and Adeline. The crew of the *Pax* were all in attendance too. Harry Andrews was manning the grill in the back yard, telling jokes and stories from their time on the *Pax*. Emma had heard all the stories a couple of times now, and they seemed to get a little more outlandish each time. In a few years, no doubt, the tale would be so large it would be more like a *Star Wars* sequel.

The sun was shining, and the snow was completely gone now. There was talk of people returning to North America and Europe and China. The world seemed new again. Anything seemed possible.

She was in the kitchen, prepping the salad, when James leaned in and whispered in her ear, "I'll be right back. It's a surprise."

Abby, sitting at the kitchen table, raised her eyebrows.

Emma shrugged. "Knowing James, a surprise can literally, *literally* mean anything."

Still, her jaw dropped when James reentered the house with Oscar following close behind.

The entire room fell silent. Emma realized that the crew of the *Pax* had never met Oscar. And she now knew what Oscar might represent to Alex.

Abby turned her gaze to her husband, who was holding a beer, frozen, paused in mid-sentence.

Alex glanced from James to Oscar, then he walked over to the two and held out his hand.

"Welcome home, Oscar. James told me what you did. Good job. I'm glad you were there."

※

When everyone had left, James insisted on cleaning the house himself so Emma could rest. Oscar joined him.

When they were done, James entered the bedroom he shared with Emma, who was reading a novel on a tablet.

He plopped down on the bed and began pulling off his shoes. "Any good?"

"Just got to the good part."

After a pause, she added, "I was really happy about what Alex said to Oscar."

"Me too. We're going to need a lot more like him."

She sat up and set the tablet aside. "What do you mean?"

He looked back, seeming to remember she was there.

"Oh, nothing. Just saying, there's a lot of work to do."

She nodded, still feeling as though there was more to his words.

She was almost finished with the book when a wave of nausea swept over her. It was worse than anything she'd ever felt in space. It seemed to emanate from deep inside her and grip her entire body.

She stumbled on shaking legs to the bathroom, and just had enough time to close the door before the contents of her stomach emptied in the toilet.

James was up and at the door in seconds.

"You okay?"

She tried to clear the wretched contents from her mouth.

"Yeah," she said between breaths, "I'm fine."

"You think it was some food? Burgers were undercooked?"

"No. The food was fine. I think."

"The salad?"

"James, I'm fine."

"Call me if you need anything."

She stayed by the toilet until she felt well enough to stand again. Then she reached into the drawer of her vanity and took out the home health analyzer. She touched it to her fingertip, and it extracted a drop of blood.

She sat on the toilet, staring at the display as it ran a series of tests.

When the results popped onto the screen, she scrolled by the blood chemistry and routine tests down to the infectious diseases panel, which read:

```
No pathogens detected.
```

She flipped back to the routine health checks. Cholesterol and white count were normal.

Her eyes grew wide when she read the last line:

```
Pregnant: Yes
```

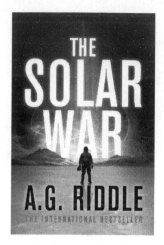

AGRiddle.com/Solar-War

Or turn the page… and read the first five chapters of *The Solar War* right now!

…

Want more books like *Winter World*?
That power is in your hands. Write a review today.
A few words is all it takes.

…

Don't miss *Winter World* bonus content! Visit:
agriddle.com/winter-extras

THE SOLAR WAR

A PREVIEW OF THE SEQUEL TO WINTER WORLD

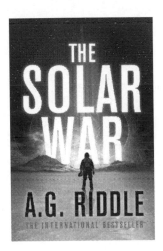

PROLOGUE

Deep in space, billions of miles from Earth, an ancient machine awoke.

First, it checked its systems.

All were normal.

Then it found the source of its awakening: a message.

Inside the data packet was a simple command. It was a task the machine had completed thousands of times: the annihilation of a primitive civilization.

The machine ran several simulations, quickly settling on the optimal way to eliminate the target. The question wasn't whether it could wipe out the primitives. It was how to do so with the least amount of energy expenditure. Energy was the most precious resource in the universe. The grid needed the energy from the star in the primitives' solar system.

It would soon have it.

The machine powered its engines and began moving toward the planet, which the local inhabitants called Earth.

CHAPTER 1

JAMES

THE DOCTOR'S gloves are covered in blood.

The floor is covered in blood.

Emma is squeezing my hand so hard I'm not sure I'll leave this room with it. She cries out, and I shudder as if a cold wind were blowing across me.

"Can't you give her something?" I ask the doctor, still wincing.

"It's too late." To her, he says, "One last push, Emma."

She grits her teeth and strains again.

"That's it," he coaxes, his hands held out.

Why didn't she take the epidural? If offered, I would take an epidural at this point.

I'm a medical doctor. I never completed my residency or practiced medicine because I knew robotics and AI were my true calling. With that said, one thing is certain: I'm not tough enough to have been an obstetrician. Moments like this take nerves of steel.

Emma strains again and a cry bellows into the room, loud and clear, the most beautiful sound I've ever heard.

The doctor holds the baby up for Emma to see.

Her eyes fill with tears, her chest heaves, and she sinks back to the bed, exhausted. As long as I've known her, I've never seen her so happy. I've never been so happy.

"Congratulations," the doctor says, "you have a baby girl."

He hands our child to a waiting team who runs a series of tests.

I lean over and hug Emma, and kiss her on the cheek. "I love you."

"I love you too," she whispers.

A nurse lays the child on Emma's chest, and my wife cradles her closer.

I can see the relief in Emma's face. She has been terrified that the child would have birth defects from the radiation Emma was exposed to while in space.

Initially, I was concerned as well. But the doctors assured us that the child was fine for several reasons. First, the newer vessels created by NASA are much better shielded against radiation than those created in decades past. Secondly, our daughter was conceived several months after we returned from the Battle of Ceres. Both Emma and I, like all of the returning crew, went through biocontainment when we landed. The process included treatments to improve our bone density and radiation-cleansing therapy.

When we learned Emma was pregnant, Izumi and the other doctors ran every test under the sun and showed us the results. But still Emma worried. Like most first-time parents, we both did. Now it seems they were right. Our daughter is healthy. And so beautiful. We've decided to name her after Emma's mother, Allison.

"Welcome to the world, Allie," Emma whispers.

❄

A SCREAM ECHOES in the night. The baby monitor on Emma's bedside table practically vibrates as it blasts the sound into our bedroom. She rolls over and studies the blue-green night vision image.

Allie lies on her back in the middle of the crib, swaddled tightly. Her face is contorted, mouth open, crying non-stop. It blows my mind that a child so small can make a sound so large.

"I've got it," I mumble as I sit up and throw my legs over the side of the bed.

She grabs my arm. "No. You have to work early."

"True, but I've still got this."

I kiss her on the forehead and pull the covers back up to her chin. She needs to rest.

The last month has been exhausting for both of us, and she has borne the brunt of it. It's my turn to pick up some slack.

I stumble into the nursery and hoist Allie out of the crib. I hold her tight to my chest and gently rock her as I walk around. Emma is better at this. She has a singsong voice, and she knows exactly what to say. My rendition is like an awkward marionette, trying to soothe the child, saying, "It's okay... it's all right." I don't even attempt a song.

Oscar appears at the doorway and whispers, "Sir, can I help?"

Oscar has a variety of skills. This is not one of them. I'm not judging. It's not one of my skills either.

"No, it's okay."

I settle into the rocking chair and sway silently, Allie's blue eyes staring up at me, innocently, maybe a hint of curiosity there. I place my index finger in her small palm and wait. A second later, her tiny fingers wrap around my finger, holding it. I smile and stare in wonder at how little and fragile she is. How innocent she is. And how ruthless and deadly the world out there waiting for her is.

Before Allie was born, I had a laundry list of worries. Now I have one: her. I imagine every parent worries about the world that awaits their child, but the world we have brought Allie into is in crisis, torn between our everyday struggles and preparing for a war we know is coming.

Billions died during an ice age known as the Long Winter. Only nine million of us survived. When the ice spread across the Earth, the survivors flocked to the world's last habitable regions, setting up sprawling refugee camps. The Long Winter has broken, but we're still here in the camps, though there's a growing movement to return to our homelands and start over.

Behind everyday life in the camps looms a threat rarely spoken about but never forgotten: the grid. Some say the alien entity that brought the Long Winter is gone for good. But I can't take that risk.

If the grid returns, it will be to finish us, to wage a war to end all wars. I'm going to be ready for that war. Because it's my job. And because I'm a father now.

❄

IT'S STILL DARK out when Allie finally surrenders to sleep again. I should go back to bed, but I'm too wound up. Being out of work for a month has been tough for me.

In my small office nook in our habitat, I scan my email messages and open the news feed.

In a video thumbnail, a reporter stands before an expanse of frozen landscape. Two years ago, I would have assumed she was in Antarctica. Now you can't tell—this is what half the world still looks like. Text at the bottom of the screen reveals the location: Washington, DC.

Behind the reporter, a dozen US Navy helicopters and throngs of troops are congregated around a giant excavator. I click play on the video, and the machine begins digging into the snow, carefully uncovering something.

The reporter's voice rings out in my tiny office, and I rush to turn the volume down.

"Behind me, American military forces are taking the first step in reopening the American homeland."

The camera zooms in, revealing the object beneath the snow: the dome of the US Capitol building.

The scene expands to include the reporter once again.

"Ladies and gentlemen, we're going home."

Another video catches my eye, one I don't want to watch and can't help but watch.

The opening sequence is a wall of snow slowly melting to reveal the show's logo, *Melting Point with Craig Collins.*

Melting Point is one of the most popular news programs on AtlanticNet, one of only a handful that are syndicated around the world thanks to recently launched satellites.

"My guest this hour is acclaimed robotics expert Dr. Richard Chandler. He's here to talk about his new book, *Saving Earth: The Real Story Behind NASA's Desperate Mission to End the Long Winter.*"

The screen changes to a view of the book cover, and then fades back to Craig and Chandler sitting around a small table.

"Thank you for being here, Dr. Chandler."

My former university professor and mentor, and later nemesis, smiles like a Cheshire cat. "My pleasure."

"Let's start with your book. Everyone's talking about it. It's been read—what—a million times on the net?"

"At least. I'm not really sure. I don't pay attention to those types of things. I just want to get the word out."

"Well, at least a few people have taken issue with some of those words. I'm talking specifically about your claims regarding the first contact mission and the Battle of Ceres. Your account has been disputed by NASA and officials from the three superpowers."

Chandler shrugs, apparently unbothered. "They have every incentive to dispute the claims. They want to be the sole source of the truth. It's the only way they can ensure that they stay in power. But as the ice melts, so does their grip on the world's population. Their focus is the Solar Shield project, but the reality is that we need a balanced approach to defending Earth and more of a focus on what the people need."

"Which is?"

"To go home. To the cities and houses we left. For life to get back to normal. That's what people want—and what the three major governments fear most."

"Let's get back to the book for a moment. In it, you say that you were a central part of the planning and execution of the first contact mission as well as the Battle of Ceres where we defeated the grid. And now you claim you're being excluded from any further missions and planning. But the generally accepted history is that James Sinclair was the lead scientist and roboticist on the mission. How do you reconcile those two accounts?"

"I would encourage viewers to look at the undeniable facts. No one at NASA can deny that I was the first roboticist contacted about the mission. No one can deny that I was at the Kennedy Space Center when the crew was brought together and briefed. Yes, Sinclair was on the *Pax* and in the Spartan fleet. I remained here on Earth in a planning capacity—for good reason. You don't put your greatest minds in harm's way. We knew the missions were extraordinarily dangerous. We needed to plan for the future."

Chandler pauses, seeming pained about what he's about to say. "I would also encourage viewers to look at the source. Perhaps the only fact that no one can deny is that James Sinclair is a convicted felon. Before the Long Winter, the United States

government deemed him a risk to public safety. They imprisoned him. And that's precisely where he was when the first
contact mission was being planned—in prison. He was offered a
conditional pardon in return for his service aboard the
spaceships."

Chandler nods diplomatically. "With that said, I'm willing
to give credit where credit is due. Sinclair did some good work
during the two space missions. But do we really want a
convicted felon like Sinclair leading our efforts to defend Earth?
We need a different kind of person in charge. One who has
shown a history of acting in the public's interest—not their own."

This has been going on for months now—Chandler bashing
me. Spewing half-truths and self-aggrandizement. It's true, he
was at the initial meeting at NASA before the first contact
mission launched. But his plans for the robotics part of the
mission would've severely limited our chances of success. I chal-
lenged him on it, and when Chandler became combative, Dr.
Lawrence Fowler, the director of NASA, removed him from the
mission. Looking back, pulling Chandler from the crew probably
saved the mission. Might have saved the world.

I can't look any more. I shouldn't have opened the video in
the first place. But I know deep down that if public sentiment
turns against the government, we won't just be fighting the grid,
we'll be fighting amongst ourselves. We can't afford that.

CHAPTER 2

JAMES

Outside the habitat, I march toward the hard-packed street, my feet crunching in the sludge of melting snow and loose sand.

Here in Camp Seven, in what used to be Northern Tunisia, the sun is peeking above the horizon, spewing hazy yellow light on the white, domed habitats that line the streets like melted marshmallows sticking out of the sand.

On mornings like this, when the sun we have always known shines brightly, it's easy to see how people might think we're safe. To think everyone can just go back to their homeland and everything will be normal. But what's normal anymore? Do the banks and other companies that had existed before the Long Winter still exist? What of the mortgages they held on people's homes? And credit card debt? And even bank accounts? Are there even any records left?

Before the Long Winter, I always felt like an outsider in the world, a person with no real place, someone who didn't understand the way the world was and why people did what they did. Once again, I feel like a man in between. Camp Seven is the only home I want to claim. This is where Emma and I returned after the first contact mission, broken and hopeless. This is where Oscar and I nursed Emma back to health when she was too weak to stand. This is where Emma and I fell in love and where our child was born and where my friends and family live.

To me, this is home.

※

AT NASA HEADQUARTERS, I have a private office next to Fowler's. I don't spend much time there. I'm usually with my team in our large workroom, building prototypes for drones and designing the ships that will defend Earth.

As usual, the workroom is a pigsty when I arrive. Nice to see that hasn't changed. Our long metal work tables are covered in mangled drone parts, interrupted only by flat screens that rise up in the wreckage like billboards in the middle of a miniature junkyard.

The entire team is here: Harry Andrews, the other roboticist on the project; Grigory Sokolov, a Russian astronautical and electrical engineer; Lina Vogel, a German computer scientist; Min Zhao, a Chinese navigator; Izumi Tanaka, a Japanese physician and psychologist; and Charlotte Lewis, an Australian archaeologist and linguist. Oscar is here too, working quietly in the corner.

I expect seven smiling faces, a smattering of "welcome backs," and maybe a hug or two. My arrival elicits none of those, only solemn expressions, no one moving forward to greet me.

Finally, Harry walks up and lightly puts a hand on my shoulder. He's twenty years older than me and always quick with a joke, but his tone is dead serious now. "Hey, James. We have something you need to see."

Without another word, he leads me out of the room and down the hall.

"See what?" I ask, jogging to keep up.

"I need to show you," Harry replies as he stops at the door to one of the clean rooms. We only use the clean rooms when we need to emulate the sterile vacuum of space.

What's this about?

Harry bends slightly and exposes his eyes to the retinal scanner, and the airlock door slides open. He strides past the blue space suits and helmets hanging on the wall.

"Do we need to suit up?" I ask, looking first at Harry, then back at the team. Everyone avoids eye contact.

"No," Harry says. "It's been through quarantine. It's not a threat... unless it gets on you."

"What's been through quarantine? What's going on, Harry?"

"It's better if we show you," he says softly and steps through the inner door.

The clean room is empty except for a long metal table that holds a single item: a white plastic box about the size of a suitcase. Harry motions toward it. "You're the only one qualified to handle it, James."

The team stares at me as I approach the box and slowly open the hinged top.

A small object lies inside: a silver biohazard bag.

"It's organic," Harry says as he inches forward to stand beside me at the table. "It's a sample. We think the entity creating it arrived on Earth right after you left." After a pause, he adds, "We need you to tell us what to do with it."

I can't resist the mystery another second. Gently, I peel the seal off the biohazard bag and peer inside. There's a puffy white object, flat, about the size of my hand.

My face goes slack when I realize what it is. I nod slowly as I reach inside and take the diaper out. "You guys are hilarious. Really."

The group breaks into uncontrolled laughter.

"This is what you've been doing while I was gone?" I'm trying to act serious, but I can't hold it any longer. A smile forms on my face and I shake my head, fighting not to laugh.

I hold the diaper up. "This is the maturity level of the team of geniuses the world is depending on to save them? Diaper jokes?"

Harry makes his face serious again and whispers, "We need you to tell us what to do with it, James." He pauses. "You're the only one qualified to handle it."

That ignites another round of laughter. In the doorway Oscar is smiling as well, all the while studying the others' faces, seeming to take note of their reactions.

Just then, I realize that there's actually some heft to the diaper. There's something inside. Surely not. Due to a strange mixture of horror and curiosity, I slowly spread the diaper open, revealing a dark brown blob. No. Surely they wouldn't have...

Again, feigning seriousness, Harry echoes his earlier words, "It's organic."

Grigory breaks from the group and walks toward me, reaching into his pocket. "Not to worry, James. I come to your rescue."

The Russian engineer unfolds a white paper bag and takes a bagel out. Before I can react, he takes the diaper from me and dumps the gooey brown contents onto the bagel and folds the top over. I'm speechless as he takes a bite.

He shrugs, speaking with his mouth full: "What? It's not like they're making any more Nutella."

❄

AFTER A MORE SERIOUS meeting to catch up with the team, Oscar and I descend to the basement of NASA headquarters, into a lab that only he and I have access to. It's a place where I've been conducting a secret project, one I think has the potential to save humanity from the war that's coming.

As I enter the room, the LED lights turn on automatically, illuminating the cavernous space with its concrete walls and floor and metal girders above. My footsteps echo as I walk toward my prototype.

"Wake up. Run system check," I call out.

"My name is Oliver. All systems pass."

Oliver looks exactly like Oscar, but he has some significant system upgrades. In short, Oliver is built for battle: on Earth or in space. If we're going to have any chance of beating the grid, we're going to need a lot of androids just like him.

❋

FOWLER'S OFFICE is similar to mine: sparsely decorated, a wall full of flat screens, and family pictures on his desk.

The largest wall screen displays a real-time image of the newly rebuilt International Space Station, glittering against the black of space. It was built by the world's three super nations: the Atlantic Union where Emma and I live, the Caspian Treaty, where survivors from Russia and the Middle East reside, and the Pac Alliance, which is home to the surviving Asians. My team was intimately involved with the design and construction, including consultations with Emma. She was the mission commander aboard the original ISS when the grid destroyed it, killing her entire crew. I think working on the new station was deeply cathartic for her. Indeed, it's been a symbolic achievement for all of us—an example of just how much we can achieve in a short amount of time if we work together. But more importantly, the ISS is a practical tool for the defense of Earth. The new station will be much more than the last: it will be a shipyard where we'll build the fleet that will defend humanity.

Our plan for Earth's defense is twofold: drones and spaceships.

Our Centurion drones will be capable of both observation and attack. A large percentage of the six thousand Centurions we're planning to build will be stationed near Earth. The rest will be scattered across the solar system, lying in wait, watching.

The spaceships will house the vast majority of our offensive capabilities. We're calling them supercarriers and each will be capable of transporting and deploying ten thousand battle drones. We expect the first carrier to be operational in five years, though I wouldn't be surprised if it took us a little longer. On the screen, arms of scaffolding branch out from the ISS, beginning the work on our first prototype supercarrier, the *Jericho*.

"Good to have you back," Fowler says, rising from his chair and offering his hand. "How are Emma and Allie?"

"They're doing great," I reply, taking a seat. "Thanks for asking."

"And how about you?"

"Let's just say if the camp runs out of coffee, I may not make it."

"Yeah, your blood-caffeine concentration might be high for a while." Fowler bites his lip. "Look, I have some bad news, so I'll just start with it. The triple alliance defense committee has denied your request to put Oliver into production."

"Did they say why?"

"Not specifically. But I think they're worried that the grid could compromise any android army."

"The same is true for the drones."

"That may be. But the drones aren't in their backyard, a hundred feet from their homes, capable of killing them in the night."

"Do you see any chance for negotiation?"

"Not really. They're pretty set on the issue. But they're allowing you to continue your development work. They do see the value in having a working prototype and a solid design in case we ever need to put Oliver into mass production."

The decision is a blow to my work and one that I think is wrong. If we end up fighting a war on the ground, we're going to need some help.

I want to ask about progress on the *Jericho*—and a number of other things—but I can't resist mentioning the interview with Richard Chandler first. At this point he may be a bigger threat than the grid. "Did you see *Melting Point* this morning?"

Fowler's usually kind, grandfatherly expression turns hard. "I saw it. Don't worry about Chandler."

"It's hard not to."

"I'm afraid we've got bigger problems. We're going to need those ships and drones sooner than I thought."

"What did I miss?"

"A lot of little things. And three very big things."

Fowler taps on his keyboard and the wall screen switches to a map of the solar system, the sun at the center, the planets around it, thin white lines tracing their orbits.

He hits another key and the image zooms in on the Kuiper Belt, a collection of asteroids and dwarf planets that circles the entire solar system, just beyond Neptune. Three objects break free from the belt, heading toward the inner solar system.

"As you're well aware, it took a lot of effort just to get these probes near the Kuiper Belt. We still don't know how much mass is out in the Kuiper, but our projections are that it might be two hundred times that of the asteroid belt."

"A lot more mass for the grid to build weapons and solar cells from."

"Correct. There are three dwarf planets in the Kuiper—

including Pluto. We used to think most of the periodic comets originated in the Kuiper, but that's been disproven. The belt is dynamically stable, which is why we were so surprised to see these asteroids break from it."

The implication is clear to me: the grid has returned. It's likely sent another machine similar to the first—a harvester—a craft capable of traveling to our star system and transforming raw materials into the solar cells it requires.

"You think a new harvester has sent the asteroids toward Earth."

"I feel we should proceed on that assumption. If so, it means the new harvester arrived some time ago."

"How long do we have before impact?"

"We're still working on the projections."

"Best guess?"

"Two years. Roughly."

"The supercarriers will never be ready by then. Even if we expedite construction, we'll miss it by a year, maybe more."

"I agree. We'll have to take the asteroids down with a drone fleet. A large one." Fowler leans forward. "How doable is that?"

"I don't know."

CHAPTER 3

EMMA

TWO YEARS LATER

THE HABITAT IS FILLED with my favorite sound: the pitter-patter of little feet slapping against the floor.

Though I want to, I'm in no shape to chase Allie this morning. I put a hand against the wall, waiting for the nausea to pass.

From the master bathroom, I hear the footfalls stop, drawers in the kitchen being pulled open, their contents rattling around.

"Allie," I call out, "come back in here where I can see you."

It's silent except for the news playing over the habitat speakers.

A report out today from the United Nations estimates that for the first time since the Long Winter ended, there are more humans living outside the evacuation camps than inside, as the wave of immigration out of the Atlantic Union, Caspia, and the Pac Alliance continues. New Berlin tops the list with the largest population, followed by Atlanta, and London.

But not everyone is happy with the pace of migration out of the evacuation camps. Dr. Richard Chandler, one of the scientists

who was instrumental in defeating the grid, is calling on the
superpowers to place more focus on returning its citizens to their
homelands. Here's an excerpt from last night's edition of Melting
Point with Craig Collins: "The grid is gone, yet the vast, vast
majority of worldwide economic output is dedicated to defense
spending. These evacuation camps have become nothing more
than forced labor camps. We're all working endlessly on James
Sinclair's super ships and the drones he claims will save us. Well,
the truth is that the grid may not be back for a hundred years. Or a
thousand years, or ever. Yet we live in abject poverty with no say,
no vote, no basic rights. This has to change."

I really dislike that guy. Not as much as James, but a lot. He's
all over the news, telling lies and stirring up trouble. Unfortunately, he's also gaining followers.

Another drawer in the kitchen slides open.

"Allie, I mean it! You're going to time out in..."

Silence.

"Three."

"Two."

"One!"

As if a race was starting, the sound of tiny feet pounding the
floor once again rings out, and Allie appears in the bathroom
doorway, smiling innocently.

"What have I told you? No playing in the drawers. Only
Mommy and Daddy can open the drawers."

Some children have a sad face. Allie's sad expression is full-
body: hanging her head, shoulders rolled forward, arms hanging
loose—as if every bit of energy has been drained from her. She
has three modes. Full-on, blissful playing. Sleeping. And the
current state of sulking (which escalates to whining when she
doesn't get her way, an occurrence that happens several times
daily).

From my perch on the closed toilet, I point to the toys on the bathroom floor: seven bracelets, a stuffed sheep, and a yellow rubber duck. "I need you to play in here until I'm ready. Okay?"

Another wave of nausea grips me. I feel as though I've been thrown out of a plane and am free-falling with no control.

Allie ventures closer and reaches out and hugs me, her tiny arms around my lower abdomen, too short to get all the way around me. She peers into my eyes, studying me.

"Mommy boo-boo?"

"No," I whisper. "I'm okay, sweetie."

"Mommy sad?"

I place a hand on her back and gently move it up and down.

"No. I'm all right. Just play with your toys. Everything's okay."

I close my eyes again and wait. When the nausea passes, Allie is placing the bracelets on her arm, arranging them in an order that makes sense only to her. Without warning, she bends over and picks up a raisin from the floor.

"No, sweetie, don't eat that."

Allie brings the raisin to the sheep's mouth and pauses as if feeding it. She looks up at me, a hint of mischief there.

I smile.

And she eats the raisin before I can stop her. I have no idea how long it's been on the floor. It's not from breakfast this morning. But if our human ancestors were hardy enough to survive the Toba catastrophe and cross the Bering Strait, Allie will probably survive a day-old raisin. Maybe two days old. Possibly three.

I open the drawer of my vanity and feel around for the personal health analyzer. I hold it to my finger and wait for it to draw the few drops of blood and run routine tests. The device beeps, and the results appear on the display. Blood chemistry is normal except for a borderline low vitamin D level.

The camps are out of birth control (it was low on the priority list when the mass evacuations happened—the governments prioritized food, shelter, and life-saving medicines). James and I have been careful, but the last two years have been extremely stressful. Our bedroom time has become a necessity.

I scroll to the bottom, holding my breath. I exhale when I see the result. I stare at the screen, filled with both joy and fear.

Pregnant: Yes

❄

ALLIE HOLDS my hand as we pass through the security checkpoint at NASA. As usual, she's wearing the tiny backpack James made for her. In his usual fashion, he went overboard, equipping it with a GPS tracker, a camera, and a speaker we can use to communicate with her. I wouldn't be surprised if he secretly built in some kind of hidden deployable attack drone to protect her.

James and I both work at NASA, and we used to walk Allie to preschool together every morning. But for the last eight months or so, he's always gone when I wake up and returns home after dark. He's working himself to death. He's doing it to protect us, but I wish he would take more time to be with us.

At the preschool entrance, Allie releases my hand and makes a break for it, but I grab her and pull her into a hug. When I relax my hold, she takes off like a thoroughbred at the opening bell of the Kentucky Derby, backpack bouncing as she races past the teacher, who waves at me.

As I walk the halls of NASA headquarters, I get a few second looks, flickers of recognition from people who might have seen me on the news feeds. Some people are just curious about my limp.

The limp is a remnant of my time in space and the loss of bone density I sustained. It's not going to get any better, and because of it, I'll never return to space, not for any extended period of time anyway.

Since I was a child, my dream was always to be an astronaut. I achieved that goal, but the two battles with the grid left me unable to continue in that career I loved. Like everyone in this strange new world after the Long Winter, I've adapted. I've found a new role to play, one I cherish.

That's life. Things always change. And we have to change with it.

The auditorium is half full when I walk onto the stage. Fifty faces stare down at me from the rows of stadium seating, tablets at the ready. My students remind me of myself when I trained at NASA: eager, bright-eyed, and dedicated to the cause. Some of these men and women will crew the two supercarriers being constructed right now. They will be on the front lines fighting the grid. Our future is in their hands, and it's my job to prepare them. There's only one way to do that, but still, I dread what I'm about to do.

I step to the lectern and speak into the microphone, my voice booming in the high-ceilinged auditorium. "Space is a dangerous place."

I let the words hang there like a warning.

"So. What's the key to survival in space?"

I've told the class that there will be an exam in the next three sessions. It won't be a written exam; everyone knows that from stories passed down by past classes. It will be an applied exercise, one no class has ever seen before. As expected, they think their answers now might be part of the test. Voices ring out from every row of the auditorium, all students eager to register a response.

"Oxygen."

"Power."

"Situational awareness."

"Sleep."

"Capable crew."

"A good teacher."

That last one gets a few chuckles from the group and a humorless smile from me, but it won't help the French engineer with his grade.

A slender girl with strawberry-blond hair in the front row speaks up as the answers die down: "Being prepared for anything."

I nod to her. "Correct."

I point to the EVA suits lining the walls, hanging there like bizarre curtains in a theater. The suits used by NASA in space are more than decoration today. There are a hundred suits, two for each student. I made sure of that.

"For example, at all times, you need to know where your EVA suit is."

The students turn in the seats, eying the suits.

"Why? Because you never know when you'll need it. I know, because when I was on the ISS, if I had reached my suit a few seconds later, I wouldn't be here right now."

As my students digest the words, I reflect that if I hadn't gotten to my suit in time, I never would have met James or given birth to Allie or lived to carry the child growing inside of me right now. All of my fellow crewmembers were too late to get to their suits—except for one. He had the misfortune of being hit with shrapnel. There was nothing he could have done to survive, or me to save him.

"In space, seconds matter. A split second could be the difference between life and death—yours or that of the person beside you. And everyone down on Earth. Sometimes, there's nothing you can do to survive. But you can always be prepared. And it always ups your *chances* of survival."

I snap my fingers. "Suits on. Last five are cut."

The auditorium breaks into chaos as the students practically jump out of their seats and run to the EVA suits hanging from the walls. The room soon looks like a game of twister, students elbowing and crawling over each other to get to the suits and slip inside.

When my fifty students are suited up, I signal them to take their helmets off. Every one of them is breathing hard, eyes trained on me.

I motion to the cameras behind the stage. "I'll check the footage and notify the last five. If you don't get an email from me, you're still in this class. For those of you who don't make this cut, I hope you'll reapply. Remember, the second key to survival in space is to *never* give up."

❄

THOUGH HE WORKS long hours and I see him less and less at home, James always meets me for lunch. It's our ritual, a respite in the middle of our hectic work days.

All morning I've debated when to share my news. I've never been good at keeping secrets. Ever since I was a kid, I've worn my feelings on my shirtsleeve. He'll know something's up and, simply put, I need to tell him I'm pregnant, for my sake too.

He's standing in the cafeteria waiting when I arrive. There's a troubled look on his face but he brightens when he sees me, a smile tugging at his lips. The crow's feet at his eyes and lines on his forehead have grown deeper in the last few years, like ruts ground into him by time and stress. But his eyes are the same: intense and gentle.

"Hi," he says.

"Hi yourself."

His tone turns more serious. "Listen, I have something I need to tell you."

"Me too."

He bunches his eyebrows. "You do?"

"I do." I hold a hand out. "But you first."

He pauses, seeming to gather his thoughts. "Okay. But not here."

I follow as he leads me out of the cafeteria and up to his office. On the screen there are three video feeds showing rocky, spherical asteroids. The date-time stamp at the bottom of the image tells me that these are live images, apparently from probes or drones. All of the asteroids have large craters, but without a frame of reference, I don't have any sense of how large they are or where they are.

"These three asteroids broke from the Kuiper Belt about two years ago. We've been tracking them since."

"Are they..."

"On an impact course for Earth? Yes."

My body goes numb, mouth runs dry.

"Size? Time to impact?" I ask, voice devoid of emotion, mind struggling to process this potential death blow to our species.

"Each is about the size of Texas. Any one of them would be an extinction-level event. Time to impact is forty-two days."

"The supercarriers—"

"Won't be ready in time. Not even close." He turns and faces me. "But we won't need them."

"The orbital defense array can handle them?"

"No. They could destroy smaller asteroids, but nothing on this scale. We've created a fleet of attack drones specifically for these asteroids. We've been launching the drones along with the parts for the supercarriers to try to keep it out of the news. A mass panic would cause even more issues."

"What's the plan?"

"The drones will engage the asteroids in one hour. We're going to blow them to bits."

I exhale. "This is what you've been working on. Night and day."

"Yes. For two years." He takes my hand. "I'm sorry I didn't tell you, but I knew it would worry you."

"It's okay. I understand."

"I want you to join us in ops control for the battle."

"Of course. I'll cancel my afternoon class."

"Great." He steps toward the door but stops. "What did you want to tell me?"

"Nothing."

He glances back at me. "Sure?"

"I'm sure. It's nothing."

There's no way I can tell him now.

After. I'll tell him after.

CHAPTER 4

EMMA

NASA's MISSION control center looks like one of the old stock exchanges: people are standing at terminals, shouting, pausing to listen to their headsets, and shouting some more, occasionally falling silent to stare at the screens in front of them. The large viewscreen on the far wall displays video feeds of the three asteroids and stats from the drone fleet.

The room is hot and loud and smells of coffee. There's a sense of tension, of time running out. Through the crowd, I spot Harry sitting at a workstation, typing furiously on the keyboard. Grigory is shouting in Russian to a person at his station. Lina is next to him, headphones on, staring at her laptop, lines of code scrolling up as she searches for something. Min is conversing with Lawrence Fowler, both sipping from coffee mugs. I don't see Charlotte or Izumi.

James leans close to me and whispers: "There's about a thirty-five light-minute delay between us and the asteroids, so we're nearing the end of our time frame to issue changes to the pre-battle sequence for the first fleet of drones."

"The attack is automated?"

"Yes."

"Are the drones camouflaged?"

"They are. We're using the same methods we employed on the *Pax* and the Spartan fleet. The drones look like floating space rock."

"The image quality in the video feeds is incredible."

"More of Lina's handiwork. She's been tweaking the data compression algorithm. We've positioned the drones in a daisy chain to comm-patch the images back to us."

Fowler wanders over to us and gives me a light hug. "Good to see you, Emma."

"Likewise." I motion to the frantic activity around us. "Was it this busy when the Spartan fleet launched?"

"No. It was busier then."

Fowler excuses himself to see what Grigory and his colleagues are debating, and James and I settle in at his terminal.

My voice low, I ask, "What do you think is going to happen?"

"I expect the asteroids to deploy countermeasures."

"And if they don't?"

"Our drones will hit them. The asteroids will be split into pieces. My second fear is that the asteroids have some sort of propulsion apparatus attached. Once we hit them, they might accelerate and change course, trying to get past our other drones."

"I assume you've accounted for that?"

"We have. We'll attack in waves. We've got twelve fleets of drones out there—all spaced out. We'll make adjustments after the first four fleets hit the asteroids."

I watch as James scans the data and types messages and occasionally answers questions via his headset. The minutes pass slowly. Finally, an announcement booms from the overhead speakers: "First fleet command cut-off in ten, nine, eight..."

When it reaches zero, it feels like air going out of the room. People slump back into their chairs and stare at the screen, a few throwing pens onto their desks, others burying their faces in their hands. It reminds me of a college exam where the proctor's just called time and half the room wasn't finished and the other half is second-guessing their answers.

"What now?" I whisper to James.

"Now we wait, and see if we got it right."

❄

I'M CHATTING with Lina when a countdown appears on the main screen.

<<30>>

<<29>>

<<28>>

Around the room, conversations die down. Everyone stands. Some people pull off their headsets.

I drift over to stand next to James as a voice once again booms over the room's speakers. "First fleet ordnance deploying in three, two, one."

White flashes consume the three video feeds as the drones release their missiles.

I hold my breath, eyes glued to the screen, waiting for the white to fade. When it's gone, I see nothing but the blackness of space, dotted by rocky objects of all sizes. There must be hundreds of them.

James immediately sits back down and scans the data coming in. I can read some of it, and I know it's good news—the payloads hit the asteroids, and hard. The survey shows that the asteroids have broken into more than one thousand objects, ranging widely in mass, the largest still classified as extinction-level targets. Where there were three extinction-level asteroids before, there are seven now. While that's technically bad news, it's a step in the right direction.

The voice over the loudspeaker sounds again. "Second fleet acquiring targets." The seconds seem to tick by like hours. Finally, the voice says, "Second fleet deploying ordnance in three, two, one."

Again, white flashes cover the screen and fade, leaving a field of even smaller rocky objects against the black backdrop.

When the data from the drones appears, I exhale. There are almost two thousand objects now, but only three that would cause an extinction-level event.

The shouting resumes, until the third fleet deploys its ordnance. And the cycle repeats once more.

After the fourth fleet's flyby, everyone in the room springs into action, resuming the fever pitch of activity I witnessed when I first arrived. I soon learn the reason: they have a very short window to issue new commands to the remaining eight fleets.

James and his team left a large gap between the fourth and fifth drone fleets. The fifth fleet (and all the fleets behind it) are still close enough to Earth for us to issue updated commands before they encounter the asteroids. The idea is to adapt the approach with each wave of drones, maximizing the impact of the ordnance.

The team around Min's desk talks quickly but in an orderly fashion. The debate at Grigory's station is chaotic.

James plops down on his chair and stares at his screen. He suddenly looks so tired. Harry wanders over and smiles at me. "Hi, Emma."

"Hi, Harry. How are you?"

"Oh, you know, I love a good game of asteroids."

His reference to the old Atari game gets a laugh from me and a tired grin from James.

"Figured we'd be seeing more action," Harry says to James, who just nods, eyes still on the screen. I can almost see the wheels turning in his head. I've seen that look before: on the *Pax* and here in Camp Seven in the months after. He's working something out in that big brain of his, and I think he doesn't like where it's going.

Harry turns to watch Min's group for a while; then he glances back at me. "They've got about..." Harry leans over and peeks at James's screen. "... seven more minutes to make course changes to the second wave of fleets. Sounds like they're going to split them into two smaller groups of two fleets each." He nods toward Grigory's group. "And they're trying to figure out how to maximize the payload efficiency."

"And you guys..."

"Thought this battle would be less one-sided," Harry replies. "Figured we'd be dealing with an active combat situation, issuing new commands to each fleet to adapt our attack."

James leans forward and types a command on the keyboard. On the screen, a message appears.

```
<<FIRST    FLEET:    DEEP    VIRUS    SCAN
INITIATED>>
```

Harry peeks over, sees the command and starts asking James questions about it. I stand and walk away, leaving them to work. Is that what James thinks is happening: a virus? Are the drones infected? Sending bad data back? It's possible. It would mean that the asteroids might be whole, untouched, and still heading for Earth.

Izumi must have slipped into the room during the battle. I

spot her near the back wall, standing beside Oscar, who smiles widely at me. He's been working on his facial expressions. They're getting better, but the levity of his expression is wrong for the mood in the room. Still, I'm glad to see him trying. Charlotte's here too now, conversing with an Italian cryptography expert whom I taught in my class eighteen months ago.

When I reach her, Izumi hugs me and whispers in my ear: "He struggled with whether to tell you."

"I figured. How has the group been?"

"A mess. Stressed. Sleep-deprived." Izumi's gaze drifts to the wall screen. "I hope it's almost over."

She has perhaps the toughest job of all: keeping the team healthy, mentally and physically.

The command deadline for the second wave passes and the tension in the room ebbs. It ratchets up again about thirty minutes later when they make contact. By the time the third wave finishes, the asteroids have been pulverized almost to dust. Cheers go up around the room. The mood turns jovial. I hear a few people apologize to the colleagues they shouted at during the battle. Everyone is standing, smiling, relieved. Except for James. He sits at his desk, staring at the screen.

I walk over and read the message flashing in red letters.

<<NO VIRUSES DETECTED>>

"What's wrong?"

"Nothing," he mumbles, eyes still on the screen.

I settle into the chair beside him and try to make eye contact. "Are you sure?"

"I'm sure. It's nothing."

※

THAT NIGHT, everyone comes over to our habitat for dinner. Harry mans the grill, wearing a T-shirt with a logo for a fictitious restaurant called "Apocalypse Grill."

Grigory stands beside him, drinking a cocktail that I'm pretty sure is ten parts vodka, one part something else. He started the night speaking English. Now, as his blood alcohol rises, the Russian words are slowly creeping in every now and then. Lina stands next to him, drinking a Beck's. It's weird seeing a branded beer after the world economy has collapsed, but recovering items from the now thawed cities has become a big business. Salvage companies have been scouring the world for bottles of medicine, beer, and whiskey. Those are the biggest sellers—not diamonds and gold. The Long Winter has changed us in ways I never imagined. And I never imagined Grigory and Lina getting together. It's always the quiet ones that surprise you.

Min and Izumi sit at a wooden picnic table near the grill, talking quietly. Their budding romance is the worst-kept secret in Camp Seven, and it's going at a glacial pace, like a chess game where each player takes months to consider their next move.

James and his brother Alex are laughing about something, but I can see in my husband's tired eyes that his mind is elsewhere. I had thought I would tell him about the pregnancy tonight, but I sense that this still isn't the time. I'll wait until tomorrow.

Beyond the house, the kids are running in the open expanse of hard-packed desert, playing soccer, Oscar serving as referee. At the height of the Long Winter, I wondered if I would ever see kids playing soccer again. But here, against the backdrop of the setting sun, the world looks normal again.

But it's not normal for us—not for James and his team. They've told everyone outside the group that tonight's celebration is for the completion of a new drone design. This is what endless war looks like: lies to the people around you and danger they never see.

Inside, the younger kids are playing with a robotic dog James made a few years ago. My sister, Madison, and Alex's wife, Abby, are whispering in the kitchen as I approach them.

"This looks like gossip."

"Maybe it is," Madison replies, a coy smile on her face.

"That means it's definitely gossip."

"It's gossip," Abby admits. "Rumor is that Izumi and Min are moving in together."

"Her place just listed on AtlanticNet as available in forty-five days," Madison says.

"She could be moving out of the camp," I reply, mostly to make conversation.

"Doubtful," Madison says. "That group from the *Pax* is inseparable." She takes a sip of wine. "But we're thinking about it."

A bolt of fear runs through me. "You and David?"

"He wants to move to Atlanta. He's heard that they're going to start a lottery for farmland—like the old days when the West was settled. He wants to be there, says the entire economy is starting from scratch again and we need to get in now or we'll miss the boat. It's like colonial times again."

"Alex thinks the same thing. Wants to move to London, says the schools will be better there." Abby finishes the last of her wine. "But I keep thinking, it's already freezing there, what if the Winter returns? We'd be evacuating again."

"It's a bad idea," I say absently.

"Yeah," Abby replies. "I think we'll end up in Atlanta. London is just a flight of fancy for him."

"No, I mean it's a bad idea to leave Camp Seven at all." They both look at me, waiting for a reason. But I can't tell them what I know. So I tell them what they already know. "Look,

Camp Seven is still the safest place to be. NASA is here. We've got a bunker, hardened greenhouses, water supply. It's better to wait for now."

"Do *you* have gossip?" Madison asks. When I don't reply, she presses me. "Is the grid back?"

I bite my lip. "I just think you should wait, okay? Can you trust me?"

Madison stares at me, silently prompting me, but I don't say a word.

Abby sets her glass on the counter. "I'm going to check on the kids. It's too quiet out there."

Madison pours herself another glass of wine and then holds the bottle up. "Wine?"

"No, I'm good."

She narrows her eyes, boring into me as if she can drill down to the secret I'm hiding. Her expression changes, as if her drill has found pay dirt. It's almost creepy how easily she does that.

I lead her to the master bedroom and close the door, hoping no one can hear the secret I'm about to share. This feels like middle school all over again.

"I'm pregnant."

She throws her arms around me, splashing a little wine on my back.

"Is James excited?"

I hesitate. "He will be."

"You haven't told him?"

I cock my head to the side. "Not exactly."

"Why not... *exactly*?"

"I'm waiting for the right time."

She stares at me, the drill out again, probing for an answer, but she seems to get nowhere this time.

"He's had a lot on his mind recently," I explain.

"Such as reasons we shouldn't leave Camp Seven."

"Such as you're correct."

"Okay. Well, I'll talk to David about staying." She smiles at me. "I'm so happy for you."

❄

WHEN EVERYONE'S GONE, we put Allie down in her crib. Sometimes when she's had company over, she puts up a fight. But she's worn out tonight and is fast asleep within minutes.

James and I sit in the living room, watching the news on the TV. When a segment about Richard Chandler starts playing, James rolls his eyes and trudges toward the bedroom. Chandler is apparently touring the Atlantic Union, rallying people to move back to their homelands, insisting that the three remaining governments are dictatorships. That guy loves being on TV.

James is tucked under the covers, eyes closed, when I come to bed.

I still get the impression something is bothering him. I wish I knew what it was; I wish I could help.

He opens his eyes when I climb into the creaking bed. "Hey."

"Hey."

"Thanks for having everyone over. I know it was short notice."

"Thanks for blowing up those huge asteroids."

That elicits a sharp chuckle from him. "There's no asteroid I wouldn't blow up for you."

"And would you do one more thing for me?"

"Anything."

"Tell me what's bothering you."

"Nothing."

"And if it was something, what would it be?"

James closes his eyes for a long moment. Then, his voice flat, he says, "If it was something, it would be the fact that it was too easy." He stares at the ceiling. "The grid is smarter than that. Hurling asteroids at us is just... too simple for them."

"What are you going to do?"

"I'm going to get some sleep for the first time in two years, and when I wake up in the morning, I'm going to figure out what I can't get my head around right now."

He closes his eyes again, and I scoot close to him and turn out my light.

I'll tell him tomorrow.

❄

I AWAKE to the sound of the bedroom door flying open. I hear footsteps and see a silhouette of a figure moving toward the bed, reaching out, grabbing James forcefully, and shaking him.

For a brief moment, I'm paralyzed with fear.

It's still dark out. The lights in the living room cast a soft glow into the bedroom, too dim to make out the intruder's identity. The figure shakes James harder and then lifts him up, the strength displayed incredible. James finally startles, grabs the hands holding him, and wrestles against the grip like a fish on a line.

A wave of nausea rushes over me. I fight not to throw up.

A voice, clear and calm, rings out in the bedroom.

"Sir, please. You have to go."

Oscar.

James's own voice comes out scratchy and soft. "What?"

"Asteroids. They're going to make landfall."

Keep Reading *The Solar War*!
Get your copy now at:

AGRiddle.com/Solar-War

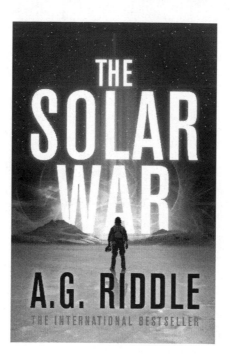

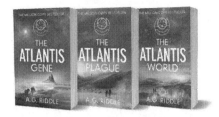
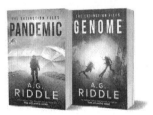

AUTHOR'S NOTE

Dear Reader,

Thank you for reading *Winter World*. This is my seventh novel, and it was the hardest to write, mostly because of the events occurring in my life.

Novels reflect their creators. They're a window into our beliefs, our fears, and our fascinations. And they sometimes evoke our state of mind at the time they were written. I wrote *Winter World* during the winter of my own life, a time when my mother was dying. She had just been diagnosed with a rare lung condition (two, actually: PVOD and PAH). She was sixty-four. We learned that there was no cure for her condition, and no treatment.

The only option for survival was a double lung transplant. So, even in her weakened state, with slim chances of survival, she came to live with Anna, Emerson, and me, and began pre-transplant rehabilitation in Durham several times each week. It was a long road to get her body in shape for the transplant. And once she accomplished that, getting listed on the transplant registry was another challenge. Perhaps the greatest hurdle was being selected for transplant. Rightly so, they select the patients in greatest need and with the best chance of survival. We waited weeks, then months, always on alert, ready for the call at any hour. She was hospitalized twice, and recovered both times. We all knew time was running out. The doctors at Duke were doing everything they could to keep her alive, but her body wasn't cooperating. It felt like the light was going out on the person who had given me life, the center of our family, and the gravity around which we all rotated, the body that held our family together. Our world was slowly freezing and dying.

Then, unexpectedly, the call came at 2 am. By ten the next morning the transplant was complete. The hope we felt was indescribable, as if we had been pulled back from the edge of a cliff. She walked two days after her transplant. Things looked promising. Then fate intervened again. She experienced a rare post-transplant complication (hyperammonemia). And then another (thrombocytosis). Both times, the doctors took extraordinary measures that saved her life. But there was only so much they could do. Five weeks after the transplant, she passed away. Like the characters in *Winter World*, I felt as though the sun had gone out. The weeks after were the darkest of my entire life. I stopped working on the book, or doing anything else.

I felt my life would never be the same. Perhaps it won't be. But eventually, I started writing again. I finished the novel and edited it and started going into the office again and out to lunch and doing the things I had done before. There were times when life was going right along and I would forget that she was gone; moments when I would take a picture of our two-year-old daughter playing and raise my phone to text it to her and only remember in that moment that I couldn't send it to her, that the number that popped up would never be answered again.

Loss leaves land mines. They're unavoidable. And they hurt,

but you have to keep marching past them, knowing you'll hit a few, but the person you lost would want you to.

Like the characters in *Winter World*, the sun is shining again in my life, but my world will never be the same. If you've experienced loss, I know what you've been through. If you haven't, you will. And I hope you'll remember this letter. The sun dims and sometimes it goes out completely. But the sun always rises again. Time heals all wounds, but enduring those times is what defines us. We have to take care of ourselves during the winters of our lives. I hope you will.

- Gerry
    RALEIGH, NORTH CAROLINA
    22 OCTOBER 2018
    WRITING AS A.G. RIDDLE

ACKNOWLEDGMENTS

I couldn't have completed *Winter World* without the extraordinary team around me.

My thanks first go to my wife, Anna, for her support during the incredibly trying period when I wrote this novel. The last few years have been difficult, far more taxing than most marriages could have survived, but I believe there are better times ahead.

I also want to thank my literary team, including Danny and Heather Baror, Gray Tan, and Brian Lipson. Writing is a solitary exercise, but being a successful author is a team effort. You all have brought my work to readers around the world and put it in front of film and tv studios. I'll forever be grateful for your efforts.

David Gatewood edited this novel and made fantastic corrections and suggestions. Four other early readers made significant contributions that greatly improved the work: Lisa Weinberg, Judy Angsten, Fran Mason, and Carole Duebbert. A number of beta readers caught typos and issues we all missed, and I'm incredibly grateful to them as well. They include Katie

Regan, Kim Myers, Kristen Miller, Michael Gullion, Justin Irick, Teodora Retegan, Paula Thomas, Lee Ames, Julie Greenawalt PhD, Norma Jean Fritz, Cindy Prendergast, Michelle Duff, Kay Forbes, Sylvie Delézay, Sue Davis, Kris Kelly, Blake Rosier, Dave Renison, Aimee Hess, Karin Kostyzak, John Schmiedt, Gareth Thurston, Heather Leighton, and Skip Folden. Thank you so much for all of your time and work on my novels over the years.

And to you, my readers, without whom this show simply wouldn't go on. Thank you for following my work.

- Gerry

ABOUT THE AUTHOR

A.G. Riddle spent ten years starting internet companies before retiring to pursue his true passion: writing fiction.

His debut novel, The Atlantis Gene, is the first book in a trilogy (The Origin Mystery) that has sold over three million copies worldwide, has been translated into 20 languages, and is in development to be a major motion picture.

His fourth novel, Departure, follows the survivors of a flight that takes off in 2015 and crash-lands in a changed world. HarperCollins published the novel in hardcover in the fall of 2015, and 20th Century Fox is developing it for a feature film.

Released in 2017, his fifth novel, Pandemic, focuses on a team of researchers investigating an outbreak that could alter the human race. The sequel, Genome, concludes the two-book series.

His most recent novel, Winter World, depicts a group of scientists racing to stop a global ice age.

Riddle grew up in Boiling Springs, North Carolina and graduated from UNC-Chapel Hill. During his sophomore year in college, he started his first company with a childhood friend. He currently lives in Raleigh, North Carolina with his wife, who endures his various idiosyncrasies in return for being the first to read his new novels.

No matter where he is, or what's going on, he tries his best to set aside time every day to answer emails and messages from readers. You can reach him at: ag@agriddle.com

** For a sneak peek at new novels, free stories, and more, join the email list at:

agriddle.com/email

Made in the USA
Middletown, DE
20 February 2020